Praise for Denzil Meyrick and the
D.C.I. Daley Thriller series:

'Touches of dark humour, multi-layered and compelling'
Daily Record

'The right amount of authenticity . . . gritty writing . . .
most memorable'
The Herald

'Meyrick has the ability to give even the least important
person in the plot character and the skill to tell a good tale'
Scots Magazine

'Following in the tradition of great Scottish crime writers,
Denzil Meyrick has turned out a cracking, tenacious
thriller of a read. If you favour the authentic and credible,
you are in safe hands'
Lovereading

'Difficult to put down – it's definitely Scottish crime fiction
at its best'
Scottish Home and Country

'Soon to be mentioned in the same breath as authors such as
Alex Gray, Denise Mina and Stuart MacBride . . . very
impressive'
Ian Baillie, *Lennox Herald*

A note on the author

Denzil Meyrick was born in Glasgow and brought up in Campbeltown. After studying politics, he pursued a varied career including time spent as a police officer, freelance journalist, and director of several companies in the leisure, engineering and marketing sectors. He lives on Loch Lomond side with his wife Fiona.

DARK SUITS AND SAD SONGS

A D.C.I. Daley Thriller

Denzil Meyrick

First published in Great Britain in 2015 by Polygon, an imprint of Birlinn Ltd.

Birlinn Ltd
West Newington House
10 Newington Road
Edinburgh
EH9 1QS

www.polygonbooks.co.uk

Copyright © Denzil Meyrick 2015

The right of Denzil Meyrick to be identified as the author of this work has been asserted in accordance with the Copyright, Designs and Patents Act 1988.

ISBN 978 1 84697 315 4
eBook ISBN 978 0 85790 850 6

9 8 7 6 5 4 3

British Library Cataloguing-in-Publication Data
A catalogue record for this book is available on request from the British Library.

The publishers acknowledge investment from Creative Scotland towards the publication of this volume.

Typeset by Hewer Text (UK) Ltd, Edinburgh
Printed and bound in Great Britain by Clays Ltd, St Ives plc

For my granny, Margaret Pinkney, *née* MacMillan,
who read to me endlessly and told me her stories.
Though she passed away over forty years ago,
I miss her still.

'Sinners, whose love can ne'er forget the wormwood
and the gall'
Edward Perronet

Prologue

Solemnly, the pontoon bell tolled, roused by the breeze that blew across Kinloch from the Atlantic beyond, carrying the promise of a milk-warm beginning to another glorious midsummer day. The first sepia light of the sun embraced the sleeping town in its glow.

As though roused by this, the wheelhouse door of *The Alba* swung open. The sun reflected softly off the varnished oak door, flashing more keenly from the polished brass of the porthole, as Walter Cudihey strode out onto the narrow deck, his face a mask, eyes dark. In his left hand he carried a petrol can, his right, bunched into a fist, grasped something small and out of sight.

With a fluidity of motion that belied his age and physique, he loped over the side of the vessel and onto the pontoon decking. He cast his gaze across the oily blue waters of the loch, over the steep side of the harbour wall and on to the road and beyond, where stood a solid granite structure, silhouetted in the first light of morning. Atop this monument to the war dead of Kinloch was a simple cross, black against the glow of the rising sun. Cudihey turned his back on the memorial and, facing east, sat neatly cross-legged on the wooden planking, his pupils pinpricks in the morning light.

He sat for a few moments and then, neither changing his expression, nor removing his gaze from the horizon, lifted the can and poured its contents over himself. The clear liquid splashed over his bald head, soaking the small fringe that was the remnant of his hair and drenching his white T-shirt, Bermuda shorts and the wooden decking as it began to glug deeply from the emptying Gerry can.

Cudihey, eyes now closed against the stinging fuel, blindly laid the can down, flicked the cap off a brass petrol lighter, hesitated for a heartbeat, then with a quick downward flick of his thumb ignited a flame which quickly spread up his arm and consumed his whole body, first in red, then green, fire. The fire crackled deeply as Cudihey's body surrendered to the flames, rendering down like a Sunday roast.

Seabirds cried and distantly a dog barked as a dark pall of putrid smoke spread from the harbour and across Kinloch, souring the early morning air. As the flames spread to the decking, globules of burning fat found their way to the loch and hissed in the still waters. A woman screamed as the whole length of the pontoon began to blaze.

A black mass, momentarily visible through a veil of fire, slowly toppled backwards as the ruined decking collapsed into the water, sending a wave of steam into the fetid air.

1

Jim Daley woke with a start. Squinting at his watch, he noted the time was 5:28. Propping himself up on one elbow, he tried to collect his thoughts, as well as take in his surroundings. His mouth was dry, his head throbbed and he felt slightly squeamish; an undeniable product of the overindulgence of the night before. Like far too many nights recently, he thought.

As the early morning rays poured through the flimsy curtain, he was dismayed to find that he was taking up far too much of a small double bed, which, while it wasn't his own, wasn't exactly unfamiliar. The walls were adorned with modern prints and arty black-and-white pictures; above his head, a straw hat trailing a bright red ribbon was pinned to the wall.

Beside him, the long auburn hair of the woman he had spent the night with cascaded across the white pillow and framed her round face. Her breathing was heavy and her long lashes flickered as she slept and dreamed. He took in her pale beauty for only a moment before darker thoughts began to crowd his mind and the sickness at the pit of his stomach returned, as cloying and insistent as ever.

With as little commotion as his large frame would allow, he levered his legs over the side of the bed, looking at the messy floor for any sign of his own clothes. Alongside a lacy bra, discarded black tights and a pair of knickers – so slight they barely merited the name – lay his shirt; light blue and huge amidst the other garments. On top of it lay a silver foil packet, torn open to reveal a used condom, knotted then tucked neatly back into its former home. He sighed as he rubbed at the stubble on his chin.

As he pulled on his shirt he noted in the wardrobe mirror that his face, despite gaining lines and shadows hitherto absent, was noticeably thinner. Unfortunately, as he breathed in to fasten his trousers, the extent of his persistent gut banished any fleeting joy. He removed his jacket from the back of the room's only chair and winced as coins fell from the inside pocket, jangling noisily in the quiet room; though not enough to wake his sleeping companion, who merely turned her head, rearranging the display of her hair on the white linen. Despite himself, despite the difficult situation he had engineered, despite the habitual deep pangs of Catholic guilt, he smiled. She was so beautiful. He donned his jacket then stepped over the rest of the mess towards the door.

Once in the narrow hallway, he did his best to collect his thoughts. He had always been an early riser, though this was, even for him, a smaller hour than normal to be awake and fully functioning; especially after drinking wine the previous evening, which he could still smell on his breath. As he reached the lounge his mobile phone burst into life, demanding his attention. He picked it up from the coffee table, noted the missed calls, and read the new message, a frown exaggerating the lines on his forehead. He was about to start looking for the house phone when a sound from behind prompted him to turn round.

'Morning, sir . . . Jim,' she said with a smile, raising her eyebrows at her initial mistake. Daley looked into her ice-blue eyes, down to her small, upturned nose and red lips, the lower of which had a slight pout. Even under the folds of her dressing gown her long, graceful limbs were obvious, as was the cleft between her breasts that sent a shaft of desire through him. Not for the first time, he was reminded of a young Liz.

'Morning,' he smiled. 'How are you?'

'Fine. Tired, I guess. Trouble?' She looked at the phone in his large hand.

'If Brian was here, he would say, "a policeman's life is not a happy one". I have to get in ASAP. I was going to give them a quick call – do you know where the phone is?' He looked at her pleadingly, a comic grimace on his face. 'The bloody signal here is a pain in the arse – thanks,' he said as she handed him the phone, retrieved from under a magazine on the couch.

'Coffee?' She yawned.

'Eh, yes,' he replied, looking about for somewhere to sit. 'Just a quick one, then I'll need to get going. You know how it is.'

She smiled at him weakly; she knew all too well exactly *how* it was. He was her boss, more than twenty years her senior and they had been lovers for almost seven months.

'If they ask for DC Dunn, tell them you don't remember exactly who I am.' She looked over her shoulder with a grin as she made her way to the small kitchen.

He watched her pad away. In all honesty, it was difficult, very difficult. In order to keep their relationship secret, he had encouraged her to move from her flat in the town centre to a pretty little rented cottage on the outskirts of the village

5

of Machrie, five miles outside Kinloch, off the road and down a farm track, where even the most determined gossips of the town would find it difficult to uncover their secret – or so they had thought. Within days of her move though, and less than twenty-four hours after his first visit, he was stopped in the street by a local acquaintance, who felt it was 'only right tae let him know jeest whoot everybody was sayin'.' After a period of coolness, during which he felt lonelier than ever before in his life, he had returned. Since then, though trying to remain as discreet as possible, they'd carried on their illicit affair, and soon, if anyone had really cared in the first place, the nods and winks stopped – in the main, anyway – and life returned to some sort of normality.

He began by promising himself that he couldn't love her, that it was all part of life's rich experience. Then, when she wasn't there, he felt an emptiness that gnawed at him; unable to sit down, stand up, sleep, or perform any of the other mundane activities of which most of life comprised. He loved to be around her. She was kind, with a quiet determination and dry sense of humour. They made sense together; they had similar tastes, they laughed at each other's jokes, and both understood the demands of a career in the police force.

As he overheard her moving around the kitchen, he could hear she was singing a song to herself. Like him, she loved music but was tone deaf, making it impossible to discern the tune she was murdering. He looked at the ceiling, rubbed his eyes and sighed. He knew he shouldn't have carried on with this relationship. They had kissed on the day he had saved her life, the day he showed Liz the pictures of her in the arms of Mark Henderson – the day his life had changed. He had tried to reason with himself, but to no avail. Liz's absence had left a gaping hole in his life, one that only his young subordinate appeared able to fill.

He was careful to dial 141 before entering the number for Kinloch Police Office; even though gossip, rumour and speculation had died down, he didn't need to rekindle the fire.

'Daley here,' he said, almost yawning. 'What's up?' He listened for a few moments, then began to rub his forehead, muttered a hasty goodbye and clicked the phone off.

'Not good, I take it?' Mary Dunn's face was serious as she passed Daley the steaming mug of coffee.

'No. Not good at all. In fact, I would get dressed if I was you.' He gave her a weak smile, as he tentatively sipped the strong coffee.

She watched him walk to his car and drive away. Certainly, he was not the young, groomed, tanned and moisturised specimen of manhood held up as the ideal to women of the twenty-first century; he was almost twice her age, but it didn't seem to matter. She thought he was fine; confident without being arrogant, brave but also thoughtful. He made her feel special, he made her heart leap.

Dunn brewed another cup of coffee. Soon she would have to put on her mask, pretend that the man in the glass box wasn't the man she loved, but what he had been from the beginning – her boss. She pushed the hurt from her mind, telling herself that this was just the way it had to be right now. She didn't want to analyse it all too closely. She didn't want reality to come up short.

The telephone rang. Someone in Kinloch Police Office was about to tell her something she already knew.

2

As Daley drove down Main Street, he could see that despite the hour a large crowd had gathered near the pontoons. A small number of uniformed officers were struggling to maintain order; it looked as though they were fighting a losing battle. He parked his car as close to the loch as the throng would allow and made his way towards the scene. Black smoke was still visible in the clear air and an acrid smell, carried on the warm breeze, assaulted his senses.

'Excuse me,' Daley shouted as he tried to shoulder his way through the gathered locals.

'Aye, let the officer past,' a member of the crowd called.

'C'mon, let the main man through!' someone else insisted. 'Can you no' see how tired-lookin' he is?' This spread a frisson of mirth amongst the early morning onlookers.

'Nae wonder. I'd be stayin' in my bed a' day wae that wee cracker.' At this, many of the locals – despite the visceral scene before them and the bitter smell – burst into gales of laughter.

Though he was used to the banter, the early hour and something about the locus made him angry; the crowd of people so anxious to see the remains of a fellow human being made him feel suddenly sick. He turned on his heel. 'Right, that's enough! Someone has lost their life here and all you can think to do is laugh and joke. I am treating this as a crime scene until I know otherwise, so I want you all to move back and let us get on with our work, otherwise I will be instructing my officers to make arrests. Constables, if you would.' He beckoned to the uniformed officers, who began to push the now much more pliant gathering away from the pontoons.

Daley ducked under the yellow police tape and felt his trousers strain at the behind. Thankful that they remained intact, a small mercy, he walked to the edge of what was left of one of the buoyant decking piers that made up the yacht moorings. Members of the fire brigade were aboard a small wooden vessel, the front of which was badly burned. It was secured next to what could best be described as a gaping black hole which had turned the far end of the decking into an island. He stepped towards the uniformed sergeant and two suited figures who had their backs to him, all peering into the shallow waters of the loch.

'Good morning, gentlemen. An update please, DS Rainsford.'

A tall young man in a sharply tailored suit walked towards him. His long thin face and angular features lent him a haughty look; he wore his hair short and parted to one side. He was slightly taller than Daley who, faced with such sartorial elegance in his junior, felt the subconscious need to adjust his hastily knotted tie.

'Good morning, sir. As you can see, I thought it best that we try to remove the body from the water as soon as possible.' He gestured towards three men who were waist deep in water, two of whom Daley recognised as members of the local RNLI, the other a fire and rescue officer. The lifeboat men wore orange wetsuits, while the fireman had to make do with a pair of yellow waders, over which water was already lapping. 'The tide's on its way in, sir. I trust you appreciate the need for action – even before SOCO get here.' Rainsford's accent sounded neither Scottish nor English – neutral, Daley always thought.

'What about corruption of the scene?' he asked, anxious that no evidence be lost in the attempt to retrieve the body from the loch.

'If we don't get the body out of there it'll start to degrade rapidly, I'm afraid, Jim.' Daley turned towards the short, fat figure of Dr Richard Spence, one of the local doctors, all of whom, given Kinloch's remoteness, dealt with police matters as and when necessary. Daley liked the man, unlike some of the less police-friendly members of the practice, and respected his opinion.

'That's the trouble with this type of thing,' Spence continued. 'Fry 'em then immerse them in cold water. It's a bit like doing it with a side of beef, bits will start coming off – especially in salt water. Best we get him – or her – out of there as soon as we can, Jim.'

Daley thanked the doctor, then turned back to the DS. 'So what else do we know?'

'I spoke to the pontoon manager on the phone a few minutes ago, sir. The boat's called *The Alba*, she docked here yesterday lunchtime. A man named Walter Cudihey booked the vessel in and paid his berthing fees by credit card; the manager's going to email me the details as soon as he gets into the office. I'm also checking with the RYA to see if he's registered with them.' He smiled confidently. 'Apart from fire and rescue personnel dealing with the fire on board the vessel, nobody has touched it.' Rainsford raised his brows and looked down his nose. 'Thought it best we wait for you before commencing a search, sir.'

Daley nodded curtly. 'Yes, you did the right thing, DS Rainsford.' The young detective sergeant had been in place for nearly four months; he was efficient, knowledgeable and bright, though something about his manner irritated Daley. Perhaps it was his honours degree in sociology, his trim physique, or his somewhat patronising manner – maybe a mixture of all three. He supposed he reminded him vaguely of his hated brother-in-law, Mark Henderson. In any event there was something about Marcus Rainsford that Jim Daley didn't like. And he couldn't ignore the obvious: simply, DS Rainsford, despite his undoubted intelligence and grasp of the minutiae of police procedure, lacked one thing – he wasn't Brian Scott.

It took over an hour for the body, by way of an impromptu hoist, to be removed from the loch, during which time SOCO officers arrived to carry out a forensic assessment of the craft and what was left of the pontoon. The body was being prepared to be taken to Glasgow by helicopter so that a detailed post mortem could take place. Locals lined the street as Daley drove up the hill and in through the gates of Kinloch Police Office.

'Excuse me, sir.' DC Dunn was already at her desk, her open laptop displaying some hazy black-and-white images. 'I thought you might want to see this,' she said, gesturing towards the screen.

Daley leaned over her, placing his hand on the back of her chair to prop himself up as he squinted at the laptop. Her hair smelled of strawberries and he watched, absently fascinated, as she used the keyboard scrolling function with one long thin finger to rewind the on-screen footage.

'Here, sir.' The image froze, bringing to a halt a long array of numbers at the top of the screen which meant little to him; in the bottom right-hand corner, the time was displayed as 04:17:23. 'This is footage from the CCTV camera at the head of the pier, sir. It covers the area quite well, though – well, you'll see for yourself.' She clicked an arrow on the screen and the image began to move.

Though the picture was monochrome it was well defined. There was a flash as the cabin door of *The Alba* swung open, revealing a short, fat bald man, wearing a T-shirt and shorts, carrying a large square container in one hand. Daley watched as he jumped easily onto the pontoon and out of shot.

'What now?' he asked, for some reason looking at the top of Dunn's head.

'Just a second – keep watching, sir.'

There was a flash which momentarily turned the laptop screen white. As the glare faded, the flames that now engulfed the yacht could be seen flickering on the extreme left of the picture.

'There we have it,' said Daley, standing up with a long sigh.

'No, wait a minute, sir, that's not all.' Dunn set the image swirling backwards at high speed as she rewound the footage. Daley, leaning back over her again, looked on as the time on the bottom right of the screen scrolled backwards. 'Once I isolated the actual event, I thought I'd do a quick recap to see what happened in the time prior to the fire.' She looked up at Daley and smiled at him. 'Watch.' She stopped the footage at 02:07:48.

Again the cabin door swung open, though this time no sunlight flashed against the porthole. Two men stepped onto the narrow deck of the vessel, one of whom looked very unsteady on his feet. Daley watched as this man was helped over the deck and towards the pontoon by the man with the bald head and Bermuda shorts. Dunn stopped the image, just as the unsteady figure stood up straight and looked in the general direction of the camera. There was no mistake – even at this distance, Hamish's face was unmistakeable.

'Oh no,' Daley groaned.

3

She had never taken to Kirkintilloch; part of her still yearned for Glasgow's East End. Her friends, her family – or what was left of them – just about everyone she cared for, lived somewhere in that much-maligned side of the city. The move to Kirky, as the town was known by most of its populace, had been a compromise.

She supposed that while her children had lived at home she had been too busy to worry about her surroundings, but now that they had both spread their wings, she had much more time on her hands – well, much more time in the house, after all that had happened.

A photograph on the mantelpiece caught her eye. The man stood straight; his arms pinned to his side, his hands, balled into fists with thumbs pointing to the ground, were adorned with white gloves. She smiled as she studied his chiselled features, only just visible under the black-and-white checked cap with the high brim and black polished peak. Even from here, she could make out the sharp crease in the uniform trousers and sleeves of the tunic. She smiled at the serious young face; an expression so at odds with what she knew of the man. The picture had been taken many years before; just after they had married, in fact. Her chest had filled with pride as she watched her man, Brian Scott, at his passing out parade from the police college. A tear meandered down her cheek.

Her fond reminiscences were disturbed by a sharp knock on the door. Through the glass panelling she could make out the uniformed figure; the gold braid on the cap indicated that not just any officer had come to call.

'Willie!' She invited the immaculately dressed figure into her hallway. 'I canna remember the last time I saw you. How's Sheila and the weans?'

'Aye, fine, fine. A' grown up noo, same as yours. What aboot yoursel', Ella, how are you coping?' The man was tall and thickset; with one meaty hand, he pushed the cap to the back of his head and embraced her in a bear hug.

'Put me doon, you big bugger,' she squealed. 'Come on in, take the weight off them huge feet o' yours – an for fuck's sake take that bunnet off, you look like the Duke o' Edinburgh.'

'Aye, these uniforms get mair fancy by the day. Did you ever?' he said, pointing at the high-necked jumper that had replaced the tunic she'd just been looking at in her husband's photo. 'By fuck, they'll have us wearing baseball caps next – especially since this Police Scotland palaver.'

'But what's a' that jazz on your shoulder mean? I've been aboot the polis for a long number of years noo, an' I've never seen anything like it.' Ella stood back, admiring her old friend as she pointed him to the big leather recliner.

'Ach, I'm Deputy Assistant Chief Constable, would you believe. What a bloody mouthful, tae. Chief Superintendent did me just fine. An' I've got tae traipse a' the way oot tae Kincardine every bloody day noo. I never liked Tulliallan when me an' your Brian were probationers, an' I've seen nothing in the last few weeks tae change my mind. All a piece o' nonsense tae – every bugger knows fine that this new force will end up being headquartered in Glasgow, or not far away; it's the only thing that makes sense. Mind you,' he said, 'we'll get the usual bollocks fae the Edinburgh mob.'

'I'm afraid I've lost touch with what's goin' on since – well, you know,' she said, with a deep sigh. 'Things have changed. I'll no' lie tae you, Willie, there's been times when I just feel like stayin' in my bed an' pulling the covers over my heid.' She sat down on the sofa opposite him.

'Och, we all feel like that some days, Ella. We lost oor wee pal Jinky last week. Bugger me, I cried fit tae burst. Aye, a great pal he was, tae.'

'No' quite the same, Willie,' Ella said, looking doubtful, as tears welled up in her eyes.

'What dae you mean?'

'Well, don't get me wrong, I know fine how fond of him you were an' that . . .'

'Aye, you can say that again.' Wullie rubbed at his forehead. 'Oor Sheila couldna bring hersel' tae clean his bedding. We were oot for a meal the other night an' she found wan o' his hairs on her skirt. We had tae go hame – beside hersel', she was.'

'Poor Sheila,' Ella sympathised.

'Of course, she wants another one, but have you seen the price o' poodles noo. Bugger me, they're wantin' nearly a grand for the bloody thing! Proper poodles, mind you, none o' these effeminate toy jobs. There was nothing effeminate aboot oor Jinky!' he said, his face growing red at the thought of such an outrage. 'I'm sorry, Ella, that was thoughtless of me. I shouldn't be comparing oor Jinky tae what happened tae your Brian.'

She looked at the black-and-white photograph again. The bright young face stared down at her from under the peaked cap. If only she could turn the clock back. 'Don't worry, Willie. Och, it's been hard, you know . . .' She burst into tears, prompting the big policeman to struggle out of his chair and embrace her clumsily.

'There, there, Ella. Things will get better, they always dae. Just you give it time. I've got an idea . . .'

Suddenly, from the upper floor of the house, movement could be heard, accompanied by the sound of a choleric, throaty cough. Rapid footsteps rumbled down the stairs and in a heartbeat the lounge door was flung open to reveal a dishevelled man in dark blue pyjamas, sporting a large orange stain on the right lapel, his hairstyle that of the recently risen, its salt and pepper clumps matching his beard.

'Just you get your hands off my woman, you big bastard.' The man's expression matched his language. 'I might have known, the minute I try tae get a wee bit o' extra shut-eye, the polis are right in here, trying tae get the knickers off my missus!' Slowly, his frown turned into a broad smile. 'How're you daein', Willie,' he said, holding out his arms to the other man. 'I thought that was your moanin' voice I could hear fae up the stair. Come here.' He enveloped the big man in an embrace, slapping his back.

'You rogue. No' had time for a wash an' a shave in the last couple o' days, I see. Aye, an' you've had John Barleycorn for company up there, by the smell o' things.' The large police-man recoiled slightly at the odour of stale drink. 'Aye, but it's good to see you. How are you, Brian?'

'Me? I'm just grand, Willie. No' quite as grand as you, mind you. Fuck me, you look like Lord Nelson.' Brian Scott, unkempt and stinking of alcohol, smiled at his oldest friend.

'Now, Hamish, you're going to have to tell me exactly what happened, from the time you met this man, to the time you left the boat,' Daley said firmly. He was sitting in a low chair in the cramped lounge of the fisherman's cottage. The room was dark, a haze of pipe smoke obscuring the old man who sat in the wooden rocking chair. A yellowing canvas depicting a fishing boat struggling through heavy seas hung over an old-fashioned iron fireplace. Adding to the sense of antiquity, two large oil storm lanterns hung either side of the painting on large protruding hooks. Neither polished nor prettified, they looked as though they had been used recently; which, Daley reasoned, they probably had. A fluorescent buoy stood next to an ancient radio, a plaster bust of Winston Churchill sat on a table constructed from old orange boxes, and a wooden fishing rod with a large brass reel stood propped against what looked like a coffin lid. The pervading odour was a mix of musty damp, the salt tang of the sea and the creatures that dwelt within it, overlaid by the woody scent of tobacco. In the gloom it was difficult to determine what was underfoot, but it reminded Daley of the beaten earth floors he had read about in novels of old Scotland. Between two frayed curtains, the sea was visible through a dirty window. Hamish's isolated cottage was about a mile and a half outside Kinloch, on the shore opposite the island that loomed over the loch, an almost perfect haven in all weathers.

On Hamish's lap lay the most enormous feline Daley had ever set eyes upon. It was emitting a deep, resonant purr, casually observing the visitor through yellow eyes, half closed, yet alert.

'What's his name?' asked Daley nodding towards the animal.

'Aye, his name, aye,' said Hamish hesitating. 'Hamish,' he replied eventually, with a small nod. 'Aye, an' before you say it, jeest don't bother. I know fine that it's a wee bit indulgent tae call your ain pet after yoursel', but jeest think aboot this; how many folk dae you know who name their children after themselves? Aye, a fair whack o' them. There's a family here called Robertson, an' bugger me, hardly wan o' them's no called Davie. As you would say in the legal parlance, "my case rests, your honour".' That said, Hamish took a long draw of his pipe and blew out more pungent blue smoke. Daley swore that the cat looked at him with a distinct look of disapproval.

'He's some size.'

'Aye, well spotted, Mr Daley. He's the son o' a wildcat, that's how. I had this lovely wee cat called Sheena. Aye, fair bonnie she was tae. Anyhow, she went oot this day, an' came back in a right distressed condition, a' bites, and big lumps o' fur pulled oot. Poor wee thing. At first I thought a dog or a pine marten had got a hold o' her, but then every night I wiz woken up by this cry, like a wean in distress, it was, screaming fit tae wake the deid.'

'What was it?' asked Daley, interested despite himself.

'The wild fella. On the third night I sneaked oot wae ma lantern, an there he was, slap-bang in the back green, as bold as brass; big, like a wee tiger – a Scottish wildcat. Well, I can tell you, it's nae wonder oor Sheena took fright, a big bruiser he was. One o' the most aggressive mating rituals o' the animal kingdom; they pin their paramour doon an' sink a tooth intae their neck tae pacify them until the deed is done. Anyhow, that's what happened, an' a few months later, Sheena produced this big bugger. Aye, an' she never went back oot that door again, no' once, despite me trying tae coax her.'

The cat turned its head towards Daley and stared at him with its piercing yellow eyes. 'He's a beauty, that's for sure.'

'Aye, I can see you've twigged the coffin lid, tae, Mr Daley.' Hamish sucked on his pipe. 'I've been meaning tae make mysel' a new table for a while, an' auld Kennedy the undertaker gied me that lid a few years ago. Thon table o'er there is only a temporary job. That said, I think I made it in nineteen fifty-nine, so it's done the job, would you not say?' The old man smiled, his sallow skin creasing around his slanted eyes. Daley, though, detected something different about the man's pallor: a grey tinge unusual for an individual who spent so much time outdoors, especially now, in midsummer.

'Are you feeling OK?'

'Ach, jeest too much o' the water o' life, Mr Daley. Everything in moderation they say, aye, but when the giving hand keeps giving, well, it's hard tae refuse.' He shrugged, as if to say he had resigned himself to the inevitable.

'Right, let's go back to the start, Hamish.' Daley was anxious to continue, despite his friend's hangover. 'You met him on the quay yesterday, is that correct?'

'Aye, you have the gist o' it there, right enough.' Hamish took another long draw of his pipe, sending blue clouds of smoke into the stuffy room. 'He asked if there was a ship chandler in the toon, so I directed him o'er tae Sean Hall's place, jeest across the road fae the pontoons. When he came back wae his stores, me an' him got talkin' – as you do, Mr Daley.' The old man smiled again. 'I was repairing my nets, an' he seemed maist interested in the whole process. No' somethin' you see much o' noo; the buggers jeest throw their broken nets o'er the side an' go an' buy new yins.' He shook his head. 'I blame their mothers.'

'What did you talk about?'

'You know yoursel', Mr Daley, once you get a dram or two doon your neck the banter always gets better.' The old man closed his eyes for a second, as a broad smile spread across his face. Just as Daley thought he must have fallen asleep, he spoke again. 'Aye, guid company he was. An' forbye, he kept a guid bottle tae. Nane o' your blended poison. An expensive malt, Mr Daley, you'd have enjoyed it yoursel', I don't doubt.'

'That's great, Hamish,' Daley said, wanting to move the old man off the topic of malt whisky. His expression was enough to spur Hamish on to more pertinent recollections.

'Quite stout, tae, Mr Daley,' said Hamish. 'Looked a lot aulder than he actually was – only fifty-something, if I recall. Mind you, he worked for the Scottish government, I daresay that's enough tae age any man.'

'Yes, we found that out earlier. Did he seem in any way depressed, or down, Hamish?'

'No, not at a'. The very opposite, in fact. Good man wae a story.' Hamish suddenly flung his head back and laughed. 'Did you ever hear the one aboot the fisherwife and the kipper?' he asked Daley, who frowned. 'However, there was somethin'.' Hamish leaned forward, as though about to share a great secret, a look of extreme concentration on his face.

'Yes. What?' Daley bent towards him conspiratorially, hopeful that the old man had remembered something of relevance.

Just at the point Daley thought he was about to speak, Hamish suddenly sat back and reached for the battered blue mug on the small table beside his rocking chair, then looked most disappointed to discover it contained no more of the tea that had been assuaging his whisky-induced drooth.

'Here,' Daley said, holding his hand out, 'I'll get you another mug of tea. You have a good think about what happened last night. This is really important, Hamish.'

He left the old man puzzling as he made his way to the room next door that served as the kitchen. Though the surroundings looked much as they must have done fifty years before, Daley was relieved to see that everything was clean and tidy. A row of newly washed, if somewhat chipped, dishes stood in a grey plastic rack, the only modern implement in the room. He found a squat electric kettle, tarnished silver, similar to the one his mother had used when he had been a boy, filled it with water from a brass tap, then set the kettle to boil by plugging it into a socket that had no on/off switch. Hamish the cat, who had followed him, sat next to the kettle with the same still self-possession of his owner. He only moved when the detective lifted his hand to give him a pat, displaying a most magnificent set of fangs, and emitting a menacing hiss.

As the water began to gurgle, Daley let his mind wander. There were many reasons a person might want to take their own life: debt, indiscretion, crime, a failed love affair – he knew all about that – or any number of other reasons. Why though, would anyone choose to end their life in such a prolonged and painful manner? He shuddered as he

22

imagined the agony that Walter Cudihey must have endured as his life ended in a blaze of excruciating fire.

As he walked back into the dim sitting room with two steaming mugs of tea – much to his chagrin, there was no coffee in the house – he was pleased to see Hamish sitting forward in his chair, a look of triumph on his face.

'Aye, Mr Daley,' he declared, taking the mug in his unsteady hand, 'there is something, right enough.'

'Good, carry on, Hamish.'

'Well,' the old man closed one eye, leaned towards Daley and spoke in low tones. 'At one point he did get a wee bit melancholy – the drink can dae that tae any man. Anyhow, we had been laughin' an' jokin' – rememberin' the fishin' an' how things had gone doon hill, an' how the world was goin' tae hell in a handcart – bright stuff, you know,' Hamish related, still with one eye closed.

Daley wondered how cheery a conversation about the demise of the fishing industry could be, but said nothing.

'Jeest a' o' a sudden, he got an attack o' the glums – we were at the end o' the bottle, right enough, an' I must admit my ain mood went intae a bit o' a decline.' Hamish reached for his pipe and took a long puff, adding more blue fug to the room. 'Aye, he got fair doon, as I remember. Telt me how he was thinking this would be his last trip doon the water, how things had gone astray, he'd done the wrang thing.' Hamish stopped, eyeing Daley mysteriously.

'Yes, good, Hamish. What had he done wrong?'

After a short pause, Hamish flung himself back in the chair, sending it into a rapid rocking motion.

'If you're asking me for an opinion, I'll tell you: the man was scared, aye, scared witless. Kept banging on about mistakes and the evil he'd brought on the world.' Hamish took another puff. 'Och, I've heard a fair amount o' shite over the years fae folk who canna handle their drink, get the glums and start talking oot their ain rear end, but something aboot Mr Cudihey was different. I remember saying there was only one way he could cleanse his soul – efter whoot he'd done, of course.'

'Which was?'

Hamish suddenly sat up straight in his chair. 'Well now, you see, that's jeest the thing. For the life o' me, I canna remember.'

4

The man struggled. His hands were tied behind his back with the same dirty rope that had been used to bind his feet. His legs and backside had gone numb with cold, semi-submerged as they were in the fetid bilge water that sloshed about the hold of the trawler. In the half darkness he could make out a heaving mass of grey-blue prawns, wriggling inside plastic boxes packed with ice, making a rustling noise he associated more with their land-bound insect cousins.

He let out a silent sob, and tried again to free himself from his bonds. A large drip of water landed on his head; this had happened so often, and the water was so cold, that each drop felt like a hammer blow. The motion of the boat made him heave again; vomit stung the back of his throat and nostrils and dribbled down his chin.

Suddenly, a metallic squeal rent the air and a shaft of bright golden light streamed into the hold as two figures descended the iron steps. The men, both shod in rubber sea boots, splashed thorough the water to where the trussed man lay.

'You will be pleased to know that your journey is almost at an end.' The tallest of the two men, silhouetted against the bright light, spoke in a distinct Eastern European accent. His companion let out a quiet snigger by his side.

'For fuck's sake, let me go,' he managed to say, in what was meant to be a shout, but in reality emerged as a hoarse whisper, so ruined was his throat with vomit, saltwater and fear.

'You will be free, soon enough. Though, I suspect not the kind of freedom you desire.' The tall man spoke again, slowly and with the precision of someone speaking carefully in a foreign language. Again, his shorter companion guffawed.

'Pavel, fetch him,' the taller man commanded.

The bound man yelled in pain as, with remarkable strength, Pavel reached out and, with one arm, grabbed him by the bonds that fettered his hands and pulled him to his feet. His head swam as he was flung over broad shoulders and carried towards the light. His head bounced off the hull of the vessel as he was lifted onto the sunlit deck.

Unceremoniously, he was thrust up against the fishing boat's side, and again his head took a battering, leaving him weak; only Pavel's iron grip on the collar of his filthy sea jacket prevented him from sinking to his knees.

'You have been a messenger for us for a long time, no?' the tall man said, staring straight into the face of his captive.

'Yes,' he managed to say. 'I only made one mistake. I was under pressure.' Though his voice was cracked, he spoke with an accent straight out of the English public school system. 'You must understand how difficult it . . .' He didn't get a chance to finish his sentence, as a blow thumped him in the solar plexus, expelling the breath from his lungs.

'Not as difficult as things are about to become,' said his captor. 'You are about to send your most important message.'

With that, blows began to rain down on the defenceless man, as he struggled for breath and consciousness. Soon, broken and bloodied, he lost his battle and descended into darkness. Untying his hands and feet, they went to work.

Kirsteen Lang frowned as she opened the door to her small office. The window was closed and, though it was not yet midday, it was stiflingly hot. As she wrestled with the catch on the window, she cursed the lack of air conditioning in the admin department. Now she was an albeit temporary and very junior member of the First Minister's retinue, she could look forward to a change of office, or even a desk in one of the more open-plan and exclusive areas of the building, for the time being, at least.

She breathed in deeply as fresh air poured in through the window. From below she could hear a guide describe the building and its original design by the Spanish architect Enric Miralles, who died before its completion, to yet another group of tourists. She suspected that the many nagging flaws still contained within its walls were down to the fact that Miralles' wife, who had taken over the project on her husband's death, had not possessed the same eye for detail and design enjoyed by her late husband. She had overheard an MSP mention this briefly in the new, bright and open Festival café bar, only to be hushed by his colleague who, in a stage whisper, warned as to the dangers of straying from the tight bonds of political correctness. In fairness, though, this Scottish summer was proving unusually hot.

Though she was a civil servant, she was drawn to what she perceived to be the glamorous world of politics and its habitués. In her mind's eye, she saw herself taking deft control of First Minister's Questions with a well-timed witticism or two; or causing a buzz in the halls and corridors of the

27

building as she swept through, her own retinue in tow. After all, she reasoned, she was clever and well educated, unlike some of the ill-mannered, badly turned-out politicians, with halitosis, glottal stops and fifty-quid suits from Asda. In her opinion, to lack ambition in one's mid twenties was to invite torpor and subsequent atrophy in middle age. A lack of ambition was something Kirsteen Lang could never be accused of.

As she booted up her computer, she was startled by a loud knock on the door. 'Come in,' she called, expecting the spotty youth who delivered the interal mail. She was surprised to see a tall man in a dark suit squeeze his way into the room between the door and the filing cabinet.

'Kirsteen Lang?' The man asked, fishing into the inside pocket of his jacket.

'Yes.'

'I'm DC Gillies, from Police Scotland,' the young detective said, flourishing his warrant card. 'I'm here to follow up on an inquiry from our colleagues down in Kintyre. Can I sit down?'

'Yes, of course.'

The policeman sat down, then retrieved a notebook from his trouser pocket. His size made her office look even smaller; he looked out of place, like an adult sitting in a child's chair during a visit to a primary school.

Kirsteen smiled sweetly at the handsome detective and ran her hand through her long blonde hair. 'How can I help you?' she enquired.

'I believe you have a colleague called Walter Cudihey?' the policeman asked, looking straight at her. Despite his sharp suit, manicured fingernails and perfectly groomed hair, with commensurate designer stubble, Kirsteen identified a working-class Edinburgh accent, which reminded her of some of the MSPs she dealt with on a daily basis. She sat back in her chair, drawing her jacket over her chest, less keen now to impress.

'Yes, he's my boss,' she replied, with a cool smile. 'Though, actually, I'm on secondment to the First Minister's office at the moment,' she added.

'I see.' The young detective looked down at his notebook, seemingly unmoved by the eminence of Kirsteen's temporary appointment. 'I'm afraid to say, I have some bad news for you.'

'Sorry?' Kirsteen felt a twinge in her stomach.

'Mr Cudihey died this morning. Our inquiry is at an early stage at the moment, though I think it's safe to tell you that he appears to have taken his own life.' The detective removed a pen from the inside jacket of his pocket. 'Can I ask you a few questions about your colleague?'

'Yes . . . Yes, of course.' Kirsteen tried to compose herself, despite feeling the discomfort of another bead of sweat making its way between her breasts.

He was face down in powdery white sand and the sun was warm on his bare back, the sea lapping at his feet. He tried to move, but the effects of the beating sent sharp pains through his whole body, and his head ached. He waited for another blow, dreading the return of his tormentors. As he listened, only daring to take shallow breaths, all he could hear was the gentle swish of the surf and the cries of seabirds wheeling overhead.

What seemed like an eternity passed. The tang of the ocean mixed with the smell of his vomit and blood. With hope rising in his chest and despite the pain in his arms and back, he tentatively raised his head, using his right hand as a prop. His low perspective offered him a restricted view of an expanse of white sand, which glowed in the bright sun like snow. A low rocky hill beyond formed part of the rough machair.

Feeling safer by the moment, gingerly he tried to force himself up from the sand. Carefully, he let himself fall onto his side, so that he could inspect his surroundings. Relief flooded his soul as he realised he was alone on a deserted stretch of beach. He had survived; the thought thrilled him.

Then he retched violently, coughing up blood and phlegm onto the sand. Pain flared through his body and he struggled to breathe. He looked down at his bloodied body and saw that he was completely naked. Bruises showed on what little of his skin wasn't covered in congealed blood; his blood. He could see that the sand around him was darkening. He needed to find help, or he would bleed to death right here, with only the gulls to witness it.

But he couldn't move. He managed to shuffle around to face the sea and was heartened to see no vessel on the water, save a distant oil tanker, miles out in the blue haze.

I've survived! It was a punishment, but I've survived!

He felt the need to pass wind, but something was wrong. There was a pain; something was lodged between his buttocks. He was suddenly uncomfortable on the soft sand. In agony again, he reached down and managed to run the tip of his fingers along the crack of his backside. There it was: a hard, immovable plug, rough like a rock, protruding from his anus. He scraped and pulled to no effect, other than sending pulses of pain through his body.

He suddenly felt sick, the pain in his stomach made him cry out. Not only had he been beaten, but they'd poisoned him. He needed to shit – but he couldn't. He felt a sickening rumble through his stomach and intestines. If his bowels started to move, they would rupture, killing him slowly and painfully. Unless all the blood drained from him first.

Another flash of agony made him scream.

His sob of realisation sent seabirds squawking over the little island and high into the blue sky. He was going to die here.

5

On the way back from Hamish's, Daley stopped at the pontoons to see how the search of Cudihey's yacht was progressing. The boat had been moved to a pier unaffected by the fire, so Daley was able to walk to the side of the vessel. It was now almost lunchtime and the hot sun was high in a flawless blue sky. Though the crowd of onlookers had dispersed, a few individuals still lingered on the esplanade that overlooked the loch, anxious to glean any information they could about the events of earlier that day. Feeling too warm, he took off his suit jacket and slung it over one shoulder.

One of the SOCO team, red-faced inside his hooded overall, greeted him.

'Hot work, Sergeant McCaig?' Daley asked with a smile, noting the officer's nametag. 'Turned up anything of significance?'

'To be honest, not a lot,' McCaig replied, pulling back his hood to reveal a thick head of close-cropped, curly hair. 'The usual kit you'd expect: clothes, navigation equipment, a few books, some stores, probably more empty whisky bottles than is healthy. Apart from that, not much. Oh, apart from these items.' He delved into his pocket and pulled out a small flash drive and a piece of paper that looked as though it had been torn from a book. 'He obviously has a bloody good camera, so I took the liberty of downloading the images from the flash drive for you to have a look at,' McCaig continued. 'Mainly landscapes, from what I can see – one beach in particular, by the looks of things. Only one image of an actual person, a young woman, a pretty one, at that. That's all that was on there, no sign of the camera itself. I've emailed the images to the office.' He handed Daley the small device.

'Thanks,' he said, pocketing the flash drive. 'No notes, logbooks, personal papers, things like that?'

'Not unless they're well hidden. We're in the process of stripping things down to the bulkheads, so if anything turns up, I'll let you know. All we've found is this.' He handed Daley the piece of torn paper inside a polythene evidence bag. It turned out to be a page from a road atlas, showing much of the west coast of Scotland. A line drawn in red ink from the edge of the page, ending at a point in the north of the Kintyre peninsula, was the only point of interest.

'Any idea what this depicts?'

'No. I've made a copy and sent it to you, too. We'll analyse it and see if we can find anything from the paper itself. Long shot, though.'

Daley made his way back to his car, which was parked at the head of the pier. It was truly a beautiful day. He gazed out across the loch to the island at its head, as gulls shrieked and soared. He wondered if the weather was fine where Liz was and how she – they – were getting on. He banished the thought from his mind.

*

33

'Sir.' DS Rainsford put his head inside the door of Daley's glass box. 'We had ACC Manion on the phone when we were out. He asks if you can give him a call ASAP.' He handed Daley a yellow Post-it note. 'Any joy with the old boy?'

'No, nothing. The problem is he's sure Cudihey mentioned something, but he can't remember because he was so pissed. Hopefully his mind will clear, though I'm not counting on it.'

Daley thought for a few moments after Rainsford left. What did Willie Manion want with him? He hoped he was not about to be asked more intrusive questions about his private life. He picked up the phone and dialled the number that Rainsford had given him. After being put briefly on hold by a brisk secretary, ACC Manion spoke.

'Jim, how are you?'

'Fine, sir. Just fine. Congratulations on your promotion.'

'Yes, cheers, Jim. And to you, too, after the happy, well, you know . . .' His voice tailed off, as though he had just realised that he'd said something wrong. 'All happening doon there in Kinloch, I hear,' Manion continued, more brightly, anxious to move the subject on.

'Yes, sir, a suicide. A spectacular one at that.'

'That's one of the reasons I was calling, Jim. A lot of interest from the press already, would you believe. Anything that involves politics attracts them like flies.'

'Yes, and don't tell me – it got leaked to the papers.'

'Exactly that, Jim. You know fine what they're like in yon parliament. Mair holes than Swiss cheese. I suppose I shouldn't be sayin' things like that – not wae my new job an' a.''

'Yes,' replied Daley. 'How are things with Police Scotland? I haven't even got my new warrant card yet.'

'Aye, I think it's fair tae say that we've encountered a few difficulties. No' least that carry-on wae the new logo. That's what happens when you get a load o' policemen pretending they're businessmen, eh, Jim? Anyhow, we'll have tae move carefully with this suicide. I know the guy wasn't a big player in government, but anything with a whiff o' distaste aroon politicians an' they get jumpy. I've already had the First Minister's office on the phone. So be careful, Jim, if you don't mind. I'll be dealing wae this, so just gie me a shout tae let me know how things are getting on.'

'Will do, sir,' Daley replied. 'You said you had a couple of things to discuss?'

'Aye, that's right, Jim.' Manion hesitated, and Daley feared more questions about his private life. 'I was oot seeing your wee pal earlier.'

'Brian?' Daley asked, knowing the two were good friends. Having joined up together they had maintained their friendship, despite very different career trajectories.

'Aye, he was in good form.' Manion sounded doubtful. 'No' quite himsel', you understand. But no' too bad neither.'

'I'm glad to hear it. I haven't spoken to him for a couple of weeks.'

'Well, you'll get a chance tae, soon enough. I've managed tae persuade him tae come back tae work. Light duties, you understand. Mainly office-based work – tae start off wae, anyhow.'

Daley was surprised that Scott had decided to come back. Nearly every time he'd spoken to his friend recently, he'd been drunk, swearing he was going to take the compensation package on offer and quit the force all together. 'How is he? I mean, getting shot is as traumatic as it gets, sir.'

'Och, you know oor Brian, restless as usual. Aye, an' when he's time on his hands, you know fine what he gets up tae. He's driving Ella mad; pissed a' day. He needs tae get back tae work, or else he'll be needing a new liver.' Manion's chuckle was mirthless.

'So, some light duties at HQ, sir?'

'No, not quite. He's needing a change o' scene mair than anything else. You'll have your hands full o'er the next few days, wae a' that's going on. Who better than your old buddy tae help you?'

'Yes,' replied Daley, surprised by this news. 'But what about the investigation?' Since his recovery from gunshot wounds, Scott had been questioned by officials anxious to know how he had been overpowered by a man in protective custody, allowing him to escape. 'And what about Superintendent Donald?'

'You leave John Donald tae me, Jim,' Manion replied confidently. 'An' remember, he's *Chief* Superintendent, noo that he's king o' his ain castle.'

'I'll give Brian a call,' Daley said, relieved that Manion was in charge of Scott's rehabilitation. Underneath his rough and ready persona lurked a keen mind and determined personality; he was more than a match for Daley's superior, John Donald, despite Donald's eminence in the new Police Scotland set-up. 'When can I expect him?'

'Tomorrow, Jim. No time like the present, as my old granny used tae say. Mind, you reel him in, though. He can coordinate things at the office. This Cudihey thing is perfect fodder for him just noo. It'll free you up tae get on wae the investigation on the ground, knowing Brain will have the admin covered.'

'Really?' asked Daley, only partially in jest. 'Admin is not exactly his strong suit, sir.'

'Och, he'll be fine. Any problems, just gie me a wee shout,' Manion said, brightly. 'We owe him, Jim. Did I tell you,' he continued, his voice less cheerful, 'we lost oor wee poodle?'

After a lengthy conversation as to the devastation wrought by the death of the much-loved family pet, Daley heard Manion hesitate.

'I shouldn't be telling you this, but I've been given quite a task, Jim,' said Manion in more hushed tones. 'Aye, by the new Chief Constable himself, would you believe?'

'Task?'

'Let's say that you're not the only one tae notice that things are not how they should be around oor friend John Donald. My job – aye, quietly, so tae speak – is tae get tae the bottom of it. I know I can count on you and Brian – well, hopefully Brian, if he can pull himself together and stay off the bottle. You'll be hearing much mair about it shortly.'

The call ended, and Daley took time to absorb what he'd just been told. He was pleased that DS Scott was returning to work, though on the last few occasions he had seen his old friend, Scott had most definitely not been himself. He supposed, if nothing else, he could use Scott as a sounding board, much in the way he had always done. As far as paperwork was concerned, he'd leave that to someone else.

The fact that Manion was heading a high-level, albeit clandestine, investigation into Chief Superintendent Donald was surprising, but welcome, news. He and Daley had got to know each other through their mutual friendship with Brian Scott. Manion was a down-to-earth, no-nonsense cop of the old school. What he lacked in finesse, he more than made up for with experience and gut instinct. Even better, at last Daley had someone at a senior level that he could trust.

In the few hours since the young detective had departed, Kirsteen Lang had been through nearly all of her social media archives: photos, conversations, posts, records of places she'd been – her whole life over the last year or so. She had carefully edited the part of her affairs that, however remote the possibility, she didn't want anyone poking their nose into.

She sat back in her chair; the job was done.

A ping from her PC alerted her to a new email. She swapped screens, to find a message from the First Minister's office. She was to report there as soon as was convenient to speak to a communications officer.

Her heart sank.

She pulled her large, expensive leather bag from the floor, plunging her hand inside in search of her make-up bag. She looked at herself in a hand mirror; apart from looking slightly pale, she was happy with what she saw. Her lips were red and full, and her eyes sparkled, framed by mascara and some subtle eye shadow. A quick touch up here and there and she was ready.

Kirsteen walked out from behind her desk and opened the door of her office, hesitating for a moment to take a deep breath, before making her way down the corridor. Whatever happened, she was determined that nothing would spoil her chances. Not the police, not Walter Cudihey – not anyone.

6

The Taylor family sailed up the west coast of Scotland every year. Most years were wet, cold and – in the main – miserable. Grey sea and greyer sky, punctuated by moments of sheer beauty on the rare occasions the sun decided to bestow its warmth.

This year was different. This year blue skies were the norm. As family patriarch Stephen Taylor, like his father before him, had always maintained, there was nowhere in the world more beautiful on a sunny day than the western seaboard of Scotland. As the sun beat down from the blue sky, with just enough of a breeze to drive the small yacht on, for once, the rest of the Taylor family agreed.

Alice Taylor was perched on the bow of the vessel, her head raised high, soaking up the warmth of the sun. Occasionally, the sea sent refreshing flecks of water over her tanned skin and short dark hair. This was to be her rest, her calm before the storm of exams she would face over the next few years. At fifteen, she was half aware that this was the last summer of her childhood, though she would never have admitted this out loud to her sophisticated peers at the smart private school she attended in Edinburgh.

Her attention was caught by a welter of gulls hovering, diving and squawking over the water about a hundred yards in front of their boat. She strained her eyes to see what was causing the commotion and could just make out something floating between the waves.

'Dad!' she called. 'Come and have a look at this!'

Stephen had also spotted the gulls and was almost at her side when she shouted. He stood tall at the bow, supporting his spare frame with a mast stay. 'Steer to port, Andrew,' he called to his son, now at the tiller. 'I want to try and circle round whatever that is in the water.' His son shouted back, and the deck took on a slant as the boat arced towards the gulls, which were unperturbed by the proximity of the vessel.

As they edged nearer, the frenzy of seabirds was almost deafening. 'Looks like something's dead up there, Alice. Probably a seal or something. Maybe it's best that you go to the wheelhouse and help your brother; might not be a pretty sight.' As he spoke, a putrid stench enveloped the boat.

'Oh, that's horrible!' exclaimed Alice, wrinkling her nose in disgust.

Stephen Taylor said nothing. From his vantage point, as the boat began to circle the patch of discoloured water, it was obvious why the gulls were so animated.

'Get into the wheelhouse now!' He glared at Alice, the tone of his voice enough to ensure she complied instantly with his request. 'Tell your mum to bring me the radio, quickly!'

As the Taylors' yacht slowly circled, the body of a naked man was now unmistakeable, floating in a patch of ruddy brown seawater.

*

'Kirsteen, come in.' Despite his slight frame and diminutive stature, Gary Wilson had become a force to be reckoned with in Scottish parliamentary circles. He was the press troubleshooter; the go-to man should anything untoward threaten the government, or worse still, the First Minister. Although he was not in charge of the communications department, it was rumoured that he had turned down the post on many occasions, preferring a role in the shadows, where practitioners of the dark arts of press and political manipulation flourished. His job description was 'Special Advisor – Media', nebulous enough to allow him an almost unlimited remit. A hard-bitten, fifty-something, ex-tabloid journalist from Glasgow, he had seen it all, done it all and scooped it all. Now his job was to hush it all up. It was a job he excelled at. He relished the power, the cachet and the fact that he didn't have to rely on an increasingly precarious newspaper industry for his daily bread. His nickname, Stalin, spoke volumes. He knew where all the bodies were buried, and made it his business to reward a large number of casual informants for any information that further added to his burgeoning black book, in which misdemeanours, indiscretions and dark secrets waited until the time they could be deployed against politicians, members of the press, government mandarins, or anyone who stood in his or, more pertinently, his boss's way.

Kirsteen trembled slightly as Wilson showed her to a chair. He seated himself in front of her, behind his large and imposing desk. She knew that her seat being closer to the ground than his was a deliberate ploy to undermine her confidence, and maybe even to compensate for his lack of

height. However, as Kirsteen licked her dry lips, she acknowledged that it was working.

'Now, Kirsteen.' Wilson's voice was low and barely audi-
ble. 'Tell me about Walter Cudihey.' He steepled his fingers
in front of his lips and stared down at her.

'Oh, it's so sad. I only heard this morning.'

'How, may I ask?' Wilson's expression didn't change.

'From a detective,' Kirsteen hesitated. 'He came to see me
earlier. I . . .'

Without taking his eyes from hers, Wilson reached across
his desk and picked up his phone. 'I want Dunsmore in my
office in fifteen minutes,' he said, with no little malice. 'I left
clear instructions this morning that if the police appeared
asking questions about the Cudihey situation, I was to be
informed. Everything through me!' He slammed down the
phone.

'Sorry, did I do the wrong thing?' Kirsteen asked, her
heart thumping in her chest.

'That all depends on what you said.' He sat back in his
large chair, passing his hand over his close-cropped scalp.
'Please, do tell all.'

Despite herself, Kirsteen gulped. She took a deep breath,
knowing that her whole career – her future – was in the
balance.

Daley listened quietly. Richard Spence, the duty force
doctor was speaking from Kinloch's lifeboat, on the way
back from picking up a body found in the sea by a passing
yachtsman.

'Not happy about this at all, Jim,' he said in quiet tones.
'When will you be leaving the office?'

'It's nearly seven already,' Daley replied. 'I'm only here because of what happened earlier. Best not to say too much on the boat. Walls have ears, if you know what I mean.'

'And so do portholes,' Spence replied, alluding to the notorious thirst for gossip amongst Kinloch's populace, seven of whom were the crew sailing the boat he was now on. 'Suffice it to say, you're going to have to get SOCO down again.'

'Really? Well, that won't be a problem. They haven't left yet.'

Daley ended the call and sat back in his swivel chair. It was feast and famine working here. Weeks went by doing little apart from making sure due process was being followed – his duty as acting sub-divisional commander – and investigating minor thefts and assaults and flushing out petty criminals. Routine police work; nothing different to the problems that any detective, anywhere in the country, expected to deal with on a regular basis. He had managed to bring many of the town's petty dealers to book, as directed by Donald, but that had been easy. Then this: two bodies in one day.

The phone on his desk buzzed.

'Yes. What now?' he asked, irritably.

'A personal call for you, sir.' The desk sergeant's voice was strangely hesitant. 'Your wife, sir.'

Daley froze.

'Sir?'

'Put her through,' he ordered. As the phone clicked, he heard Liz's voice, and the cries in the background made him shudder. The baby.

7

'So you looked at his warrant card, and then?' Wilson was leaning on his desk with both arms straight, staring down at Vincent Dunsmore, head of the parliament's security detail, who was visibly squirming in his chair.

'He showed me his warrant card and told me that he was investigating a minor theft from one of the committee rooms – a member's handbag.She had reported it an hour or so before,' Dunsmore said, his jowly face crimson with stress and discomfort.

'Don't such matters normally get referred to you, rather that the police?'

'Well, yes. However, it's not uncommon for members – especially new ones – to automatically call the police if they feel they have been the victim of crime. It's not something that happens very often, to be honest.'

'Don't fucking smile at me, you twat!' Wilson bellowed. 'I asked you personally to take charge today. I told you that we had a potential problem and that the fucking police and press were likely to be swarming about. You let a cop into the building to question one of our staff about a very delicate matter before I'd even had the chance to brief her.'

'Ah,' Dunsmore's face reddened further, 'more bad news, I'm afraid.'

'What? For fuck's sake, what other fuck-up could you possibly have made in the last few hours?'

'I've been checking with the local CID. They didn't send anyone to interview Kirsteen Lang,' said Dunsmore quickly, as though anxious to confess.

'Oh, brilliant.' Wilson put his hands on his hips. 'So if this guy wasn't a fucking detective, who the fuck was he?'

'We . . . we can only assume that he was a journalist.'

Wilson put his hands in his pockets and looked at the floor. 'Get out,' he said in a low voice.

'Sorry?'

'Get fucking out!' roared Wilson, a look of sheer fury on his face. He walked around his desk and caught Dunsmore, who seemed momentarily paralysed, by the collar of his jacket and hauled him out of his chair, ushering him to the door. 'Don't go home until I tell you, you stupid bastard.' Wilson opened his office door and propelled Vincent Dunsmore into the corridor.

'So how have you been?' asked Daley. The words sounded as though they were being spoken by someone else; his face felt prickly and there was an ache in the pit of his stomach.

'Oh, you know.' Liz's voice was strained. In the background, he heard another voice hushing the baby.

'Who's with you?'

'Mum's come over for a while. You know, just to help out. This is a full-time job,' she said, in a weak attempt at humour.

'Brian's coming back to work.'

'Oh, really? Tell him I wish him well.'

There was silence; not unusual during their recent conversations. Daley looked at the calendar on his wall, casting about for something to say that didn't sound lame or uninteresting.

'I decided to agree to the test.' Her voice was flat, matter of fact.

'Really, what changed your mind?' Daley was surprised. Liz had exploded when he suggested that they subject her baby to a DNA test. In his own mind, the detective was convinced that the child was the product of a relationship between his wife and her brother-in-law, Mark Henderson.

There was a pause. 'I can't stand this, Jim. I'm sad, lonely – I'm bloody devastated. My whole world's collapsed and you know it. I love you, for fuck's sake. We have a child, something you always wanted and you won't see me, you won't talk to me. You won't even hold our baby.' She started to sob.

'I'm sorry, Liz. You know how I feel. You hurt me, you fucking destroyed me. Those pictures . . .' He felt his throat tighten.

'So he bought me a car. So I kissed him. So what! I didn't have an affair with him, what more can I say?'

'You and him have been flirting for years. It's always made me feel sick, sick to my stomach. Do you know what it's like to be in a room with you both?' It was Daley's turn to shout. 'It's as though nothing else in the world matters. You only have time for each other. The touching, the laughter, the banter, the gazing into each other's eyes, the smiles you can't keep off your faces. Me – or your sister, for that matter – might as well not exist. It's all about Liz and Mark. You just fit. You look right together, in a way you and I never have, never will. Even if you can't see that, everyone else fucking can!'

'I know about you and her.'

'What?'

'I know about you and your *new friend*. You're not the only one who made friends in Kinloch, you know.'

'Oh, so you listen to the tittle-tattle from here now?' Daley was off his stride. This was something he'd dreaded, but with Liz back in Renfrewshire he'd put it to the back of his mind; distance had made his marital indiscretion seem almost acceptable. Besides, she had been the one who had rejected him first.

'I'll give you time to think about it. Not long though. You need to provide a sample of your DNA. If you don't do this, Jim, that's it. We're finished. You can take up with that young girl properly, stop sneaking about. I'll wait to hear your decision, but I won't wait long.' Liz ended the call.

He held the receiver in mid air for a moment or two. Was he more taken aback by the fact that Liz had agreed to the DNA test, or that she knew about his affair? Though he supposed that when it came to expertise in marital indiscretion, she was a master, so probably the former.

Tired, drained and desperate to leave the office, Daley headed out to meet the lifeboat in which Dr Spence was bringing back the body found in the sea not far from a deserted stretch of the Kintyre coastline. Despite his fatigue, his policeman's intuition, a warning bell that something was not right was ringing in his head.

As luck would have it, when he pulled his car up by the pier, he spotted the distinctive orange-and-blue vessel

47

re-entering the loch. The light and warmth of the midsummer evening was soothing as he waited. In his head the endless merry-go-round of Liz, the baby, Mary Dunn and Brian Scott turned, each presenting their own problems as they passed. To add to this parade, the charred figure of Walter Cudihey and the stench his burning corpse had left hanging over the town for most of the day, imprinted itself on his brain. And now, here he was awaiting the delivery of yet another problem.

As arranged, the SOCO van drew up beside him just as the lifeboat was being secured alongside the pier. As usual, its arrival had attracted a small knot of curious locals, anxious to discover the reason behind the vessel's call-out.

'How you daein, Mr Daley? Whoot's happenin'?' asked an old man. 'Jeest doon tae see whoot's aboard? Or mebbe you know that already,' he said, eyeing the SOCO personnel as they donned their white overalls at the side of their van.

'Nothing for you to worry about, Wattie,' Daley replied. He was in no mood to play pass-the-parcel in the endless round of local gossip; gossip that he was now an integral part of.

'Aye, jeest as you say. Though it's no' much that worries me these days.' The fisherman winked. 'Naethin tae dae, and a' day tae dae it. Mebbes a few too many drams, noo and again. A wee bit like your man, eh?'

'What man?'

'Och, your friend Hamish. Taking another go at it this afternoon; came oot the Douglas Arms like a steam train at full tilt. Aye, taking both sides o' the road, would have taken three, no doot, if the option had been available tae him. Steamin' drunk, aye, fair mortal.'

'Well, each to his own, Wattie.'

'Aye, I daresay you have the right o' it there, Mr Daley.' He rubbed at the grey stubble on his chin. 'His faither died o' the booze, you'll be mair than aware, I don't doubt. Two of his uncles, tae. Aye, the whole family are fair steeped in the drink, an' that's a fact.'

'Well, thanks for the information. Now, if you don't mind, I have things to do.' He smiled at Wattie, who winked back at him again. He tried not to listen to any of the gossip that passed his way, though, as a policeman, sometimes there was a kernel of truth to be sifted from the detritus. In any event, he was surprised to hear that Hamish was drinking heavily for a second day; strangely disconcerted, in fact. As he waved down to Dr Spence on the prow of the lifeboat, he put this to the back of his mind.

Along with the SOCO team, Daley climbed gingerly aboard the rescue vessel, anxious not to tear the backside of yet another pair of trousers. In his head, he could hear Brian Scott making some ribald comment about his physique. He had actually managed to lose some weight over the last few months, but this had been prompted by stress and the absence of his wife, rather than a diet or fitness regime. These days, when he looked in the mirror he saw a man who seemed to have aged five years in as many months. Despite everything, he was looking forward to seeing Scott again; the man who had been his touchstone for so much of his career. Someone to help bear the burden.

'Down here, Jim.' Spence led Daley down steep metal steps into the body of the boat. The cabin had been converted into an emergency room, ready to help save the lives of those who had been pulled from the sea.

A body lay underneath a green rubberised sheet on a metal gurney bolted to the floor.

'I must say, Jim, I've read about this kind of thing. Never thought I'd be unlucky enough to come across a case of it though.' Spence stood over the corpse. 'I know you are, well, not the strongest stomached police officer I've ever come across. You might want to take a deep breath.' He removed the green sheet.

Daley saw the body of a man, unusually placed face down on the gurney. Ordinarily, the many cuts and bruises across his legs and back would indicate a beating of some sort, though Daley was aware that all kinds of trauma could be inflicted on a cadaver at sea.

'You'll note this,' Spence continued, pointing to the exposed backside of the corpse. Badly discoloured by the ongoing process of putrification, as well as exposure to salt-water, many contusions adorned the backside. Without warning, Spence leaned over the body and parted the cheeks of the dead man's buttocks.

Daley could see something pale in colour, covered in blood and gore, but still discernible as foreign to the body.

'What is that, Richard?' Daley could already feel the bile in his throat.

'I'm not sure yet, but my guess would be some kind of fast-acting, strong adhesive – super glue, if you like, probably augmented with some rubber adhesive material inside the rectum.'

'What?'

'Yes, no wonder you look surprised, Jim. A favoured method of execution employed by drug cartels of Mexico, Colombia and Russia, I believe. Very nasty. They usually feed their victim up and insert the plug, often giving the victim something to induce diarrhoea. Of course, the bowels can't void in the normal way, so they burst. Dreadful way to go. The cuts and abrasions to the backside have been caused by his desperate attempts to remove the obstruction, I suspect. Though it might not be what actually killed him. His internal injuries are so severe, he couldn't have survived long – glue or no glue.' Spence relayed this information in the detached way Daley was used to hearing from the many clinicians he had come into contact with over the years.

'Yes, I've read about this, too. It's often a punishment for senior gang members who stray, or informers, I believe.' Daley gulped, doing his best to stave off nausea.

'Apparently they often jump on the victim's stomach in order to cause greater pain, though it's impossible to tell if that's what's happened in this case. Jim.'

Daley was kneeling now, looking at the dead man's face, lying side on. 'I know this man. It's Rory Newell.'

Daley hurried back up the steep metal steps and into the glorious evening sunshine, and spewed copiously over the side of the lifeboat, much to the interest of the small group of Kinloch residents who were looking on.

As he tried to compose himself, Daley remembered the desperate search for Rory Newell. He had stolen his uncle's RIB and disappeared during Daley's first investigation in Kinloch. Daley had suspected that his links with drug dealers had been responsible for his disappearance then, and now he knew.

The thought of the punishment dished out to Rory Newell made him retch again.

'Aye, canna say I've seen that before,' said Wattie, shaking his head. As he watched the stricken police officer retch again, others in the crowd added to the general murmur of agreement.

8

He pulled the car over in a lay-by about three miles outside Kinloch. His breath was heavy and he could feel beads of sweat making their way down his forehead. His mouth was dry, but with none of the bitter taste of stale alcohol that he had become so used to over the last few months. He inhaled deeply, desperately trying to stave off the panic he felt in his stomach, a feeling that had been steadily growing since the previous evening when his wife had told him that there was no way he was getting a drink; certainly not before the long drive he had in front of him early the next morning.

He tried to compose himself by winding down the car window and taking in the warmth and scents of summer in Kintyre. He reasoned that there were much worse places in the world to start back at work. He took one last gasp of fresh air, wound up the window, turned up the air conditioning, then gunned the accelerator.

Scott sighed as Bob Marley's classic blared from the car stereo. 'You got it wrang there, son. It was the deputy that took the bullet, no' the sheriff,' he whispered to himself.

For Brian Scott, reality beckoned.

*

Gary Wilson's lip curled in distaste as he took in the modern art that covered the walls in the office of the Minister for Rural Affairs, Food and the Environment. Forced to have some of the available catalogue of paintings on the wall of his own domain, he had opted for a photographic silhouette of the New York skyline, rather than this ridiculous tumble of swirls, geometric images, clashing colour and confusion.

He wondered why someone like Elise Fordham would tolerate such rubbish. In his opinion, she was one of the party's rising stars; politically aware, intelligent, tough and unflappable. She was not afraid to stand on toes, politically or literally, a quality no politician could possibly do without if they wanted to scale the ladder to success. To him, she most closely matched the First Minister in terms of political sure-footedness and the ability to crush opponents with incisive wit and withering put-downs, or to use that same quality to deflect criticism when the nonsense came from her own side.

'Morning, Gary.' Fordham swept in, a nervous political advisor in tow. 'Make yourself useful and get me and Gary a drink. Coffee?' She looked at Wilson with a smile, acknowledging his nod. 'The usual for me, and no fuckin' sugar this time!' The thin young man in the cheap, ill-fitting suit almost bowed his way out of her presence as she closed the door behind him.

Fordham spoke in much the same way she always had. She was from a tough, former mining village in the heart of Lanarkshire, and it showed: no airs, no graces, straight to the point. Despite this formidable exterior, in her mid thirties, with short dark hair, dark eyes and soft features, she was able to use her femininity to great advantage, should she want to. Only an eye as jaundiced as Wilson's detected the hint of a double chin on her smooth round face, put there by hard work, long days and a poor, eat-on-the-run diet. Like Wilson, she was a former journalist; from his own paper, in fact. Unlike him, she was a graduate in the politically ubiquitous PPE: politics, philosophy and economics. Despite this, he still liked her and thanked the heavens that this growing crisis came within the remit of her ministry.

'Right, Gary, down to business. This bastard Cudihey is going to be an embarrassment, right?'

'Slightly more than that, it would appear,' he replied, looking up at the ceiling. 'There has already been an intervention from a third party purporting to be the local plod, but on examination nothing to do with them.'

'What then, the press? If it's anything to do with Paddy Sinclair at the Daily Shag, I'll string the bastard up.'

'That's just it, Elise. It would appear not to be our friends from the fourth estate, either. I'm still investigating, but unless it's a deep-cover job from the BBC or Channel 4, or some freelance nut-job, I'm sad to say that we have something else to worry about. I'll have a more definitive answer for you by close of play today. There's something about all this I don't like, though.'

Fordham stared at him blankly. He knew that, behind those dark eyes, she was already calculating the possible political consequences of the situation.

'So, now the obvious question: who the fuck is it?'

He told her about the impromptu interview of Kirsteen Lang, as well as an update regarding the spectacular suicide of Walter Cudihey, all of which she took in without demur, sitting quietly behind her desk.

'Oh fuck!' she said loudly when he had finished.

'I see you have reached the same conclusion as me.'

'Spooks?'

'If my enquiries with the TV people come up with nowt, then I think we have to view that as an extremely likely possibility.'

'Is that the same as a potentially verified outcome?'

'No, but getting there,' he replied, smiling at her contempt for political double-speak.

'OK. If so, who? Not MI5, I hope?'

'Too early to say. I'm going to have to drop everything until we get to the bottom of this. I'll need full access to Cudihey's personnel file, as well as Kirsteen Lang's. Oh, and anything from the Whip's book of the dark arts, too, regardless of how closely guarded it might be. I'm sure you can arrange that.'

'If I can't, I'm sure the First Minister can.'

'Bit early to get them involved, don't you think?'

'Aye, maybe, Gary. But if you don't come up with anything concrete in the next few hours, I'll need to flag it up. You know how things are just now. We're all on our toes in case the dirty-tricks brigade from Westminster show their faces and try and ruin the project.'

'Project Thistle, by any chance?'

'I wish you wouldn't call it that, Gary.' She smiled.

'Freedom, by any other name. Anyhow, I'll leave all the funny handshakes and secret codes to you lot. Give me a couple of hours; at least we'll know by then who we're not dealing with.'

'Aye, good man,' she sighed. 'And do me a favour – find out exactly what we have on the ground down in Kinloch. Politically and otherwise, if you know what I mean.'

The door burst open to reveal a skinny young man in a bad suit holding three Styrofoam cups of coffee in two hands.

'Sorry,' he stammered. 'I couldn't knock because of these,' he continued, holding up the beverages as evidence.

'Arsehole,' Wilson said, as he pushed past him and through the door. 'And who said you could have a fuckin' coffee?'

Elise Fordham watched her young aide deposit the drinks onto her desk, then dismissed him. From the inside pocket of her tailored suit jacket, she removed a tiny key, then used it to unlock a small drawer in her desk. She retrieved a black diary from within, then reached into her handbag and, after some fumbling, produced a cheap mobile phone. She typed four capital letters, then sent the message to a number she had retrieved from the diary. The message read: *M O F Z.* She waited for it to send, then placed the diary and phone back into the drawer, which she locked.

As she lifted the coffee to her lips, she was perturbed to note that her hand was trembling.

9

At nineteen, his mind should have been occupied by thoughts of girls, sex, study, work, friends, family, a drink down the pub, football, holidays, music, clothes; any manner of things. Instead, all that mattered for Malky Miller was his next fix, a new opportunity to stick a needle into one of his diminishing number of useable veins, and feel the chemically induced orgasm overtake his senses. Well, that, and money, the commodity that facilitated his habit.

He'd had his first joint when he was in primary school; his father had been a user and his mother an alcoholic. He had grown up in Glasgow's East End, in one of the city's worst schemes; one blighted by violence, drugs and deprivation. Did citizens in the bohemian West End care that their fellow Glaswegians were dying of overdose, malnutrition, alcohol abuse, beatings, stabbings? Many of the middle class did their best to ignore these issues.

In an effort to rid the city of some of these 'problem' families, a plan was hatched. Why subject these people to the high-rise horror of badly maintained multi-storey misery, with zero amenities and even less hope, when they could be miserable elsewhere? The answer was simple: relocation.

Small towns on the edge of Scotland's economy, where fishing, crofting, distilling, small-scale mining or ship building had once provided a good living, could be allowed to thrive again, this time as support networks for stricken fellow Scots. Hence, working on the principle that exposure to sea air and sound rural values, combined with a change of scene and distance from malevolent influences, could only be of benefit, many of the most troubled individuals Glasgow had to offer found themselves breathing in the tang of the ocean and taking in the views of green fields, dark hills and big skies.

Sadly, instead of integrating their new inhabitants into the community, these towns and villages found themselves increasingly blighted by the same problems that had prompted this urban exodus in the first place. Doors once left unlocked were firmly bolted; the friendly faces in the street turned into those of people the locals neither recognised nor liked the look of. The smart tenement flats that lined the main streets, where well-to-do merchants once brought up their families became dens where crime and depravity flourished, and from which only grasping landlords profited.

Malky Miller was a fine example of this. He had been placed in 'community care' by social services when he was seventeen, then moved to Kinloch, where he could be more closely monitored by social workers and hopefully given a fresh start away from the influence of his troubled family. In his second week there, a friend of his had caught the bus from Glasgow and brought Malky his first haul of drugs to sell. Now, two years on, with many customers and much less danger than in the city, Malky had become one of Kinloch's most affluent dealers.

Today, he was going up a level; such was his success that he was being rewarded with a visit from the boss, or someone so close to the boss that it made no difference. He had tidied up his flat in anticipation. Consisting only of a living room with a curtained-off galley kitchen, a tiny toilet and shower room, and a bedroom just big enough to contain the double bed, this housekeeping hadn't taken long. Sweaty, and a bit shaky after his exertions, he sat on his large recliner and stared at the huge flatscreen TV that dominated the room and was, apart from the Audi A3 parked down the street, one of the few trappings of his financial gain. Had the children of Glasgow's deprived families been properly educated and mentored, some of them would undoubtedly have become captains of industry, such was their acumen for business. The ruthlessness and greed that drove Malky differed little from his peers working in financial services all over the world, though it was just possible that Malky was a more likeable person, a trait that made him good at selling.

Fighting the desperate desire to shoot up – he wanted to be straight for his visitor – he sprang up from the recliner and walked across the room. In front of an old fireplace sat a three-bar electric fire which Malky reached behind to produce a black cloth bag. He looked into it and smiled. The heft of notes, drugs and requisite paraphernalia felt good in his hand; though not his only stash, this was his biggest. He checked them all, many times, every day, just to make sure they were there. He replaced the bag behind the fire, stood up, felt dizzy, then returned to the recliner as quickly as he could. He hoped they would come soon. He needed a fix.

*

'Welcome back, Brian.' Annie held her arms out wide as Scott walked into the County Hotel's vestibule. 'How're you daein'?' She was genuinely pleased to see the detective.

'I'll be doin' a lot better when I get a dram or two doon my neck. That bloody road doesnae get any better.'

'Here, gie me your cases, I'll get Bobby the cellar man tae take them up tae your room. C'mon in an' get a bite tae eat, an' a refreshment, tae. After a', it's nearly twelve, an' you've had a long journey.' Annie ushered him into the wood-panelled bar. 'Whoot time is Mr Daley expecting you?'

'Och, dinnae worry aboot oor Jimmy. He knows the score. I'm on light duties for the next few months, so I'll just ease myself in tae things gradually.'

'Here's the menu,' Annie said, sitting Scott at a table near the bar. 'Noo, whoot can I get you tae drink. On the hoose, mind.'

'Good stuff, Annie, I don't mind if I do. A dram, please, better make it a double, since you're offering.' DS Scott smiled and sat back in his seat. The drive to Kinloch had been longer than he remembered. The road was a long and winding one, the scenery glorious and, since he hadn't driven much in the last few months, he had decided to stop at regular intervals, get out of the car and have a smoke, as much to enjoy the view as to calm his trembling limbs.

'There you go.' Annie placed the small glass containing the large whisky in front of the policeman. 'Noo, whoot are you wantin' tae eat?'

'Och, I'll have a couple o' drams first. An aperitif, Annie, eh?' he laughed.

'Whootever you say, Brian, whootever you say.' She smiled broadly at her customer as he drained the glass and held it out to her.

'I'll have another one o' them, my dear.'

Despite the heat of the day, Malky was shivering when a sharp knock on the door momentarily banished his yearning for heroin. His visitor had arrived.

His line of work meant Malky was security conscious; he had to unlock two heavy bolts, a mortice and a Yale latch, leaving the heavy chain in place, just in case. Through the crack of the door he saw two men, the taller of whom smiled.

'Malky? I have the correct address, yes? Darren sent me.' This was the pre-agreed code name, so Malky undid the chain and let them into his flat.

'Right, guys, can I get you a beer or something? Or would you prefer something mair interesting?' He smiled knowingly at the new arrivals.

'Yes, I think the last option,' said the tall man. Malky couldn't place his accent, but reckoned he might be a Pole; some of the new Polish community in Kinloch were his customers. The other man, shorter and with muscles almost showing through his black leather jacket, was silent, though he had a grin plastered across his face.

'Aye, nae bother, man.' Malky hesitated for a heartbeat, then, deciding that these men were more likely to reward him than steal from him, reached behind the fire for the black cloth bag. 'This is good stuff, man.' His fingertips had just touched the bag when he felt a sharp pain in his neck. He tried to stand up straight, but already his balance had gone. He collapsed backwards, conscious but unable to move. He tried to scream, to shout out, but nothing but a breathy hiss issued from his mouth.

'You have been injected with a muscle relaxant. There is no point trying to move.'

In the background Malky heard a chuckle, deep and menacing. He felt his bowels empty.

'You should have played our game, not yours. Too many of you scum think you can take us for fools and use our money as your own. Lessons have to be learned. Pavel.'

The squat man bent over and something flashed before Malky's eyes – the gleam of a serrated hunting knife. He tried to scream again, but nothing came; he struggled to move, but the only part of his body obeying his commands were his eyes, as he looked up in horror at the man with the knife.

He felt the searing pain as the knife cut into his throat just above his Adam's apple. Despite the powerful drug, his limbs began to twitch, the rest of his body weighed down by his attacker. The last sounds he heard were the desperate gurgle of air as his windpipe was cut and the laughter of his murderer, who, once he had slit the teenager's throat, inserted his thick fingers into the livid wound.

10

Daley became aware of a commotion somewhere down the corridor from his office. As he walked towards the reception desk, the sounds of agitated voices, lots of them, grew louder.

The small reception area that greeted visitors to Kinloch Police Office was packed with people. Behind his high counter, Sergeant Shaw was doing his best to be heard, to no avail. When Daley walked into the room behind him, the racket grew louder.

'Aye, wae my ain eyes, I tell you. As plain as the nose on your face!' one man shouted.

'I couldna believe it neither, Norrie,' a woman agreed. 'I've never seen anything like it, an' I don't want tae again . . .'

The rest was lost in the clamour of voices; Daley could see more people trying to get in through the door. Fearing a stampede, he stood beside Shaw and held his arms out. At six feet three, he more or less dominated the room, apart from a couple of gangly youths, who looked impossibly tall.

'Right!' Daley shouted. 'What's this all about? Norrie, you first.'

'Aye, well, it's like this, Mr Daley,' said Norrie, a balding middle-aged fisherman. 'You know fine I'm no' prone tae any kind o' histrionics. I'm a straightforward, honest man.'

At that, there was some sniggering. 'That incident wae the quotas was nothing tae dae wae me. I was asleep below deck when the fishery officer came aboard.'

'Please, ladies and gentleman,' Daley called, 'can we just hear what Norrie has to say.'

'Thank you, Mr Daley. Tae cut a long story short, we had a bit o' engine trouble last night, and by the time we'd fixed the bloody thing it was well efter midnight. Me an' the boy were jeest passing Paterson's Point on the way hame, aboot three this morning, when we saw it.'

'Saw what?'

'They lights in the sky, Mr Daley. They were in the distance, at first, flashing lights o'er Arran. Is that no' right, Kenny?'

'Aye, you're on the right track there, Norrie,' agreed one of the tall young men.

'In whoot only could've been seconds, this ball o' colour, whootever it was, jeest shot intae the air an' came right at us. Came clear o'er the top o' us, maybe two or three hundred feet above the boat. Aye, no' a whisper, nothing, quiet as a moose.'

'Have yous been on that Navy Rum again?' someone called from the crowd.

'I'll jeest ignore that,' Norrie said, with a glower in the general direction of the insult.

'There was a hoor o' a racket no' long after, Norrie,' said Kenny.

'Aye, you're right, son. A kinda rushing noise, like the wind, Mr Daley. An' then, jeest a wee while later, this massive explosion.'

There was silence for a heartbeat, then, as though on cue, the voices raised into a rabble once more.

'OK!' Daley shouted, raising his arms. 'I take it you're all here to report similar experiences?' This was greeted with shouts of agreement. 'Right, in that case, I want each one of you to make a written statement. Sergeant Shaw here will take you one by one into an interview room. We have to do this in an ordered way, so please try to be patient. Norrie, you first.'

'Aye, thanks, Mr Daley. I wisna sure whoot the polis would think o' this. I'm glad it wisna jeest us that saw the bloody thing.'

'No,' Daley said, searching the worried faces. 'I can tell you've all seen something, whatever it was.'

'Aye, you have the right o' it, Mr Daley,' said Norrie, as he was being shown into an interview room by Shaw. 'You'll be wantin' tae see Kenny's video, tae, I've nae doubt.'

'Video?'

'Aye, he filmed maist o' it on his phone, did you no', Kenny?'

'Aye, Mr Daley. I've got it a' here.' Kenny held his smartphone up for Daley to see.

'Dae you no' think you should be giein' Mr Daley a call?' Annie asked, looking at Scott with concern. He had polished off nearly a bottle of whisky and she noted that most of the plate of food she had placed in front of him had been left untouched.

'Ach, it'll be fine, Annie. You're a dreadful woman for worrying,' Scott slurred. 'When you've known big Jimmy for a' the years I have, well, you have a mutual respect, regardless o' what pips are on whose shoulder, if you know what I mean. And if you don't mind me sayin', Annie, my dear, I've always thought you were a fine-lookin' woman.'

'Ach, away wae you, you auld charmer. I'll get you a cup o' black coffee, an' we'll phone the police office, how's that?'

'Black coffee, fuck all. I'll have another quick dram; one for the ditch, you understand. Noo, where the fuck are they fuckin' keys?' Scott stood unsteadily, searching his pockets.

'You'll likely have lost them,' Annie replied, patting the pocket of her jeans to make sure Scott's car keys were still there. 'I'll need tae get another bottle. Jeest you wait there till I get back, I'll no' be long.' She pushed through the door behind the bar and into the small office behind the reception desk. On the wall hung a list of names and numbers which Annie ran her finger down until she found the number for Kinloch Police Office.

Brian Scott didn't notice his old friend and colleague when he entered the bar, engaged as he was in a heated debate with another customer about football.

'It wouldnae matter what team it was, it's still a disaster for the whole country.'

Daley noticed that his speech was slurred and his eyes were half shut in his red face. 'Brian, can I have a word?'

'What?' Scott turned around so quickly on the high bar stool that he nearly took a tumble. His annoyed expression was soon replaced by a wide grin as he recognised Daley. 'Big man, it's yoursel', come on in an' I'll get you a dram.'

'It's OK. Come with me.'

'Aye, whit is it, big fella? No' another pair o' trousers away, I hope.' Scott laughed uproariously at the thought.

'Come on.' Daley heaved his DS off the barstool by the scruff of the neck and marched him towards the hotel's vestibule which was mercifully quiet.

'Is there a fuckin' fire or whit?'

'Right, Brian, listen to me.' Daley's expression was dark. 'I know you've been through the mill in the last few months; nobody needs to tell me that. But I haven't seen you sober in, well, since I can't remember when. Every time I come to your house, no matter what the time of day, you've been on the piss. In your own time, that's up to you, though after what your body's been through, I'd have thought you would want to give it time to recover. Anyway,' Daley talked over Scott's protests. '*Anyway*, that's none of my business. What is my business is when one of my officers, no matter who they are, turns up for duty in the state you're in. What the fuck's wrong with you?'

'Ach, it's being back – comin' doon that road. You know yoursel', a bloody nightmare. An' me feeling like this,' he rubbed at his stomach, 'well, it's enough tae send anybody ontae the bevy, is it no'?'

'Right. This is where it starts and ends, Brian, have you got me? At least Annie had the good sense to give me a call and tell me what state you were in. When would you have stopped? When you fell over?'

'Nah, nah, Jim, come on, man. A few drams tae take the edge off. It's no' easy for me being back doon here again, no' after what happened. Even you must realise that.'

'I know what it's like, trust me. But you have to get back into it, OK?' Daley's tone was less harsh now. 'Get back in the saddle, you got it?'

'Aye.' Scott shuffled from foot to foot, both hands in his pocket, looking at the floor like a naughty child. 'C'mon, then. Gie me a lift up tae the office and we'll get intae it, big man.'

'Office? Bugger off! If I let you anywhere near a police office now, I'd get my jotters, quicker than you'd get yours, and rightly so. Get yourself up the stairs and into your bed. Watch TV, read a book, listen to the radio, anything, just don't come back down here. I'll see you up at the station at nine tomorrow morning. Sober. Got it?' Daley grabbed Scott by the lapels and looked straight into his face. He could see Annie lurking behind the reception desk, pretending not to hear. 'Will you make sure this bloody reprobate has nothing more to drink, Annie?'

'Aye, yes, nae bother, Mr Daley. I'm . . . I apologise for lettin' him get intae such a state. Och, it was so nice tae see him back in one piece. I should have thought aboot it mair.'

'Don't blame yourself, Annie. This here,' he nodded to Scott, 'is big enough and ugly enough to know better. Send him some dinner up to his room, please, and as much coffee as he can drink.'

'Judas,' Scott muttered under his breath, squinting at the hotel's proprietor.

'Enough! Get up those stairs!' Daley shouted. He waited until he had seen Scott, somewhat unsteadily, ascend the staircase and head off to his room, accompanied by the sounds of the Eagles' 'Hotel California' spilling from the bar's jukebox.

In the inside pocket of his jacket, he felt his phone vibrate.

'Daley.' He listened intently for a few moments. 'I'll be there in two minutes. Watch him, please,' he nodded to Annie, who smiled back, sheepishly.

11

Gary Wilson watched the CCTV footage again, this time with Superintendent McClusky, from the Edinburgh division. Having spent more than thirty years working in the city, there weren't many cops he didn't recognise, especially since, up until the formation of Police Scotland, he'd been in charge of recruitment for the old Lothian and Borders force.

'Well, do you know him, Donnie?' Wilson asked testily.

'No. I've never seen him in my life. He's definitely not one of ours, that's for sure. What about the press? An undercover job, perhaps?'

'No. Nobody will hold their hands up to it, and trust me, I've exerted all the pressure I can. Legally, that is. You've got contacts with our friends in dark places, though; can you do me a favour?'

'Spooks? No way. Since the Edinburgh Agreement, everything's closed down. The London-based intelligence agencies are, no matter what they say, in de facto hush mode. All friendly contact has disappeared.'

'But it could be one of them, yes?'

'Oh aye. When it comes to them, anything could be anything. But why?'

'Cudihey.' Wilson almost spat the name out. 'There's something about him I've missed. He wasn't just some slap-headed yes man, counting down the days before he could retire to Skye, or some other shithole. There was more to him.'

'There is another possibility, of course,' McClusky said thoughtfully.

'Which is?'

'This Cudihey torched himself in Kintyre, am I right?'

'Yes.'

'Well, as you can imagine, Gary, the amalgamation of our separate little bands hasn't gone quite as smoothly as our well-spun PR would have you believe. Glasgow still consider themselves to be the centre of the universe, the arrogant bastards. I wouldn't put it past them to have stuck one of their own men on the job, despite the new protocols.'

'Well, check it out for me, will you? I need to know who and what I'm dealing with here. This is starting to make even the First Minister's Office a bit jumpy. They haven't told her in person yet, but they'll have to soon. It's a sensitive time for us all.'

'I'll do what I can, Gary.'

'I would be most grateful. Some nice security consultancy contracts in the offing,' Wilson smiled, 'ideal for a newly retired senior officer.'

'Message received and understood.' McClusky nodded and stood up, replacing his braided cap on his head.

Once he'd gone, Wilson took a battered diary from his desk, thumbed through the pages, then picked up his phone.

After a pause, he said, 'Well, how the devil are you, John? Or should I say Chief Superintendent Donald.'

*

71

As Daley entered the hallway of the flat, his first thought was how different the dwelling's interior was compared to the dingy, rundown close and staircase that he had just walked through. Though lacking any personal touches, such as paintings or photographs, the flat was well decorated; the carpets thick and clean, the walls freshly painted.

He was still angry at DS Scott, though he was intrigued by the call from DS Rainsford who'd been vague. Daley wondered why.

As he walked into the lounge, the answer was obvious. There, amidst a small knot of police officers, lay the body of a young man. He was covered in blood, his eyes frozen wide in horror. It took Daley a few heartbeats to realise what was different about this murder victim, what was making the bile in his throat rise even more than normal. The victim's tongue was protruding, not from his mouth, but from a livid slash in his neck, through which it had been pulled.

'An Italian necktie, sir.' Rainsford's voice sounded loud in the quiet horror of the flat. 'Florentine mafia, or Colombian, modus operandi, I believe. This isn't just a murder, it's a punishment. And a warning, sir.'

Not for the first time in his career, Daley had to remove himself from the scene. Standing on the filthy landing, he took deep breaths and added another grim image to the nightmare gallery of violent death he had accumulated over the years.

'Fucking Kinloch.' Chief Superintendent John Donald swore under his breath as he looked out from his top-floor office in his new domain, the headquarters of the Argyll and West Dunbartonshire Division of Police Scotland. He took in the busy road that ran in front of the large building, and the rooftops of the town of Dumbarton beyond. This was his own fiefdom now; in effect, he was more like the autonomous chief constable of a small force, rather than a divisional commander, under the old regime. This was all he had ever wanted, all he had worked for over the last twenty-eight years. But he had never been so miserable. Everything, he realised, came at a price; he had the job, the power, the kudos, and now it was time for that price to be paid.

He looked again at the piece of paper in his hands. The spectacular suicide of a civil servant, and what could only be termed as the executions of two others, all in and around Kinloch. His nightmares were now manifesting themselves in cold-blooded reality. To make matters worse, the murky beasts of politics had their noses in the trough, and none other than Gary Wilson – surely the darkest purveyor of the dark arts – was leading their line. There were few individuals who genuinely frightened John Donald; Gary Wilson was very near the head of the queue, alongside one or two people Donald didn't want to think about, especially not now.

There was a quiet tap at the door. 'Come in,' he shouted.

'Sorry to bother you, sir.' A tall, thin man in the uniform of an inspector entered the room. His grey hair matched his face, which was lined and careworn; he looked like a man in his mid-sixties, rather than the forty-something-year-old he was.

'Yes, what now, Layton? World War Three broken out on Kinloch's seafront, no doubt.'

'No, sir. I have a request for information, sir.'

'From who?'

'Narcotics and Organised Crime, at the Met, sir.'

73

'Oh fuck. Give me it.'

'Here, sir.' Layton handed Donald a red file.

Donald read the document, Layton standing at his side and looking straight ahead. 'Book me on the early flight to Kinloch in the morning, Layton. Also, make sure one of these bastards picks me up at the airport and books accommodation. Make the arrangements with Daley directly, he knows my preferences.' Donald dismissed his underling, who left as quietly as he had entered.

He sat behind his desk, put his head in his hands, and let out a long sigh. 'Fucking Kinloch.'

12

He had always considered boats the best way to move about; so anonymous, not observed by CCTV cameras, or nosey cops, or even many members of the public. The boat was nice, not ostentatious, but just big enough for him and his companion to be relatively comfortable as they went about their business. They would change boats in a while, as they had their previous craft.

He looked up at the thickset frame of his friend, Pavel, standing behind the wheel. Layers of solid flesh bulged where the back of his neck should have been. He was wearing a thick jumper against the chill of a misty morning, under which the broad knots of his arms were still obvious. His frame was squat, almost square. Two years in an FSB cell in Moscow had robbed him of both his empathy and his voice; the only sound he made now was laughter, the volume of which indicated his mood.

They had been together since the Balkan Wars in the nineties. He supposed that the things he'd done – they'd done – had robbed him of pity, too. Captives first of the West, then mistrusted and ill-treated in equal measure by their new masters in Moscow, he'd made up his mind that he and Pavel would never again have to bow, scrape, or toe anyone else's line. They would be their own paymasters; the captains of their own destiny. Governments, crime gangs, global conglomerates, even individuals, from all over the world, paid and paid well for them to do their job. Their efficacy and ruthlessness were now legend throughout the criminal underworld. The growth in their reputation matched that of their Swiss and Cayman Island bank accounts. Soon they would be able to retire; soon, but not yet. So they continued their work. They had already been busy; so busy, in fact, that tonight they had decided to relax. They had sailed away, for the time being, from their most recent job, and were taking it easy. It was their privilege.

He looked at his glass; another one empty. His head was already starting to swim, but he wasn't ready to sleep yet. He had been uneasy taking this, their most recent commission. It was for the man who had set them up, made them what they were, but still, he was unsettled by it. They would have to operate within a small community where they couldn't fail to stand out, but the huge amount of money on offer was enough to consign these concerns to the back of his mind. Someone very rich and very powerful was seeking revenge, and he and Pavel were his instruments of persuasion, destruction and everything that came in between.

'The mist is still bad, yes?' he shouted to Pavel.

His companion nodded as he descended the stairs, then his face burst out into a large smile.

'Another half an hour, and when it is fully light, we will find an anchorage, sleep off this shit,' he said, holding his glass up for Pavel to fill. Before the large man could complete his task, though, he was flung off his feet. There was a loud bang, then a jarring scraping noise, and the boat's progress halted.

'Quick, Pavel, get up,' he said to the man on the floor at his side, as he, himself, struggled to get out of the low chair, the effects of the vodka impeding his movement. 'We've hit something!'

Alice Taylor ran from her berth, up the narrow steps and onto the deck of the family yacht. She had been jolted from her sleep by an ear-splitting bang, a collision which had flung her against the side of her bunk. On deck, her father was in the cockpit. He had a gash over his left eye, which was pouring with blood.

'Dad! Are you OK? What happened?'

In the mist she could see the outline of a vessel at right angles to their own boat.

'Stephen, Stephen!' Alice heard her mother call. 'Quickly, there's water everywhere. We're sinking!'

As her father got unsteadily to his feet, he grabbed her arm. 'Get onto the radio and broadcast a mayday to the coastguard. Our position's on the sat nav.' He struggled down below deck to help his wife and son.

Alice was well acquainted with emergency procedure. She pulled up the handheld radio from its holder next to the wheel, pressed the green button, then hailed the coastguard.

She had just managed to give a brief summary of their predicament and location when she heard the throaty roar of a powerful diesel engine. There was a tearing noise as the other vessel pulled free of the temporary embrace caused by the collision and began to move away from their boat.

'Come back, we need help!' Alice shouted as the cabin cruiser sailed clear of the yacht. She felt their boat list sharply;

77

no doubt more damage had been caused when the other vessel had struggled free.

The mist had cleared somewhat; enough for her to make out the name of the *Corinthian* as it pulled away. In the cockpit of the vessel she could see the figure of a broad-shouldered man with a shaved head, laughing as his boat sped away.

'Alice, quickly!' her father shouted as he reached the top of the steps, her mother and brother behind him. 'Get into the tender, we're sinking fast!' He was already making his way to the stern of the boat where a small dinghy was secured. Normally used to access shallow harbours that they couldn't get to in the larger yacht, today it was their lifeboat.

Still carrying the radio, Alice followed; the image of the laughing man on the other boat seared onto her memory.

Daley had decided to spend the night in his bungalow, where officially he now lived alone, though he had spent hardly any time there in the last few months. He had been put off his stride by the call from Liz, not to mention the day's death and horror.

Dunn had looked crestfallen when he had told her he thought it best they cool things off for a while. Considering the seriousness of the crimes they had to investigate, and the likely appearance of Chief Superintendent Donald, it seemed the sensible thing to do. Mercifully, Donald had left Daley to his own devices so far and hadn't been in Kinloch for some time. His exalted position in the new national force had kept him occupied elsewhere. That wouldn't last forever; he knew the man too well.

Dunn had asked if his decision was due to Liz's phone call. The question had caught him by surprise, but he should have realised that tongues in the station would wag. It was a small office, and Daley felt as though he was under scrutiny a lot of the time.

He stood on the wooden decking, watching the early morning sun burn its way through the mist. To his left most of Kinloch was on display, lights twinkling under the foggy blanket, while on his right the large island loomed over the entrance to the loch, protecting the town from the Kilbrannan Sound, a sept of the restless Atlantic beyond. It was at times like this – alone, troubled and deep in contemplation – that he most missed his old smoking habit.

Thoughts of tobacco turned his mind to Brian Scott. His colleague and friend had always enjoyed a fag and a drink; most of their peers in the job did. Somehow though, since winning his fight for life, a fight that at one point had looked to be lost, he had crossed the line. Daley recalled one of his recent visits to Scott's home, where he had watched his DS dispose of most of a bottle of whisky before moving onto beer; all that was left in the house. There was a profound sadness, and a lack of confidence, in his usually ebullient companion. Struggling with demons was something with which Daley had sympathy – he fought his own, continuously – but deep down, Daley feared that his right-hand man's time as a police officer might be over.

He felt sorry for Mary Dunn, too. But he had repeatedly cheated on his wife. That was how he felt about it – cheating – even though he and Liz had been apart for months. It somehow seemed wrong, now that Liz had been in touch. Did he owe his wife the chance to prove she was right, that his fears about Mark Henderson were unfounded? He had been pulled from the depths of despair by Mary as his marriage crumbled and his best friend hovered between life and death. He was warmed by her affection and touched by her devotion to him, but every time they made love, there would be a moment – just an instant – when he thought of Liz. Only the other night, as he'd passed his hand over her smooth skin and caressed her soft breasts, as she'd moved astride him with her head bent down and her long auburn hair covering her face, he'd almost gasped at her resemblance to his wife. He was part of Mary's world, but not of it. In twenty years she would still be younger than he was now, and where would he be? If he followed in his father's and grand-father's footsteps, the answer was simple: dead.

Death: there it was again. Did the workings of his mind always have to end in the same way?

Suddenly, the sun burst from behind the island, trans-forming the scene. Grey water turned blue and the grass a deeper, more vivid shade of green. Above the loch, seabirds flocked, united in a renewed frenzy.

Kinloch faced another day.

Daley walked back into the bungalow and picked the blue-and-white paper bag from the dining-room table. He carefully tore the packaging apart, read the instructions briefly, then set about the inside of his cheek with a small spatula. He placed the results into the plastic jar provided and sealed it tight, before heading for the bathroom. He had to give a sample of fresh morning urine, which, after some difficulty, he managed to provide, then sealed the test tube up as instructed and placed both it and the other small jar in the large padded envelope.

He wondered if the people who would open that bag would realise how much they could make or break his life.

The baby was his, or it wasn't. No need to complicate matters.

He promised himself not to think about it for the rest of the day.

To take his mind off domestic affairs he decided to study the photocopy of the map found on Cudihey's boat. His investigation had so far uncovered the solitary fact that the line drawn on the map terminated on a nondescript stretch of beach to the north of Kinloch. Despite staring at the map intently, nothing more would come.

Scott sat on the end of the single bed in his room in the County Hotel. Sweat was pouring from his forehead, and he was finding it difficult to swallow. He reached down for the bottle of water on the floor which, with trembling hands, he made three attempts to open, before propelling it against the wardrobe with such force that it left a dent in the door panel.

When he rose to his feet he felt the world spin and almost fell backwards again. He took a moment to steady himself, then walked through to the tiny bathroom where he turned on the tap above the sink and poured himself a cold glass of water. He emptied it in three gulps, his tremor so bad that the tumbler rattled off his teeth. After a further two refills, he splashed water over his face and wetted his hair. This done, he looked at his reflection. He had always hated hotel shaving mirrors; they were illuminated with such ice-white intensity that every wrinkle and blemish in his face was made glaringly obvious. The dishevelled figure that returned his gaze bore no resemblance to the image of himself he carried in his head. The man before him looked old and tired; bleary eyes stared from a lined face, and he could make out individual pores on his nose and bulging eye bags.

He passed his hand over his chin; his fingers rasped over salt-and-pepper stubble. He tried to remember what had happened the previous evening, but found it hard to piece together the run of events. He remembered Daley, Annie, the bar, but little else. He had a gnawing feeling at the pit of his stomach, a notion that he wasn't flavour of the month – again.

Without warning, he felt his bile rise, so he quickly bent over the toilet bowl and retched. He stared down at the contents of the pan, which were black and reeked unhealthily. Flecks of dark vomit now covered the front of the shirt he had slept in. It was almost eight thirty. He needed to brush his teeth and banish the awful taste that filled his mouth; he needed to shower and change quickly; he needed to pull himself together.

Instead, Brian Scott leant against the sink and wept.

13

They were cold as they drifted, waiting for help. The oars, normally contained within the tiny vessel, had been dislodged in their rush to save themselves from the sinking yacht, the stern of which still poked out above the petrol-blue water as they wallowed in the small tender nearby.

Thankfully, much of the mist had lifted and they had a reasonably clear view in the direction from which they expected help to arrive. They shivered from shock, the open sea and their damp clothes.

Alice could not force the image of the laughing man from her mind, no matter how hard she tried. They had been in peril for their lives and he had sailed away, caring nothing for their plight, despite it being his fault. They'd been at anchor off the sea-lanes, displaying the correct lights; he had hit them and then callously left them to their fate. The thought made her sick.

Her mother was sobbing quietly, her head buried in Stephen's chest as he stared into the distance for the lifeboat. Her brother was slumped forward; despite their situation, he'd managed to drift back off to sleep. Typical, Alice thought.

Though only a mile or so from the coast, they were stranded, alone and vulnerable, with only a few millimetres of vulcanised rubber between them and the cold, vast empty ocean. The sky looked huge and the waves, despite the bright sunshine, were cold and forbidding.

Alice sat tight, and prayed that help would come soon.

He hadn't felt panic for a long time. His world was so ordered, so well planned and structured, that the feeling was all the more unsettling because of its unfamiliarity. To be in control was to be at ease; he no longer controlled this situation.

'So you saw someone on deck, then what, Pavel?'

He watched as the other man wrote furiously on a notepad that he retained for such communication. He snatched the paper and read: *It was a girl. She was standing on the deck. She saw me. She called for help as we left.*

She had seen them; she could describe the boat – or even identify it by name. They now had presence where they'd sought earnestly to have none. They were suddenly tangible; they could be pointed out in a crowd, or pulled from a database somewhere. People knew they existed, that they were there. They could be pursued; caught and questioned. This whole house of carefully placed cards was about to topple.

'Quickly, Pavel,' he said, getting to his feet. At least the adrenaline had cleared his head. 'They are at least two hours from rescue; it will take that time for help to come from Kinloch.' He bent over a sea chart. 'We are, at the most, only half an hour away. We will put an end to this problem. Now.'

Pavel started to giggle as he ascended the steps into the cockpit of the cabin cruiser, while his companion removed an elongated leather case that had been battened down onto a shelf. He unfastened the clasps to reveal a long barrelled rifle with a sight attached to its upper casing. He took a magazine clip from the case, checked it, and forced it into the corresponding slot on the rifle. He made his way onto the deck above then looked about. The sea mist had almost lifted. The rifle was so powerful, its range so long, that his victims wouldn't know where death had come from. He smiled; the resolution to his problem was at hand.

Scott made his way through the crowded CID suite; whiteboards, strange faces and a general buzz were clear indications that a full-blown murder inquiry, or in this case, inquiries, were underway. He noted how drawn Daley looked, then remembered his own face in the mirror earlier, and the fact that he was late. He was managing to keep his panic under control – just.

'How are you, Jim?' Scott did his best to sound happy. His bleary eyes, though, spoke of something different.

'Rough night, Brian?' Daley asked.

'Aye, you could say that. More like a rough mornin', tae be exact.'

'Well, it's a new day, Brian. It's great to have you back at work, mate.'

Scott hadn't expected a warm greeting. As he'd gone through the agonies of getting ready for work, more of what had happened the day before had come back to mind. He had been supposed to report for duty. In fact, he had begun work the moment he stepped into the car at home, so, technically, he had been drinking on duty. It was unlikely that anyone other than his friend, Daley, would have been as understanding.

'Are you looking forward to getting back into it?' Daley asked.

'Aye, sure, Jim. I cannae wait to get stuck in.' As the words came out of his mouth, he doubted their veracity. Did he want to be back at work? Was he looking forward to getting 'stuck in'? His dry mouth and trembling hands indicated a resounding 'no!'

Daley sat Scott down and briefed him on what had happened in the last few days. A spectacular suicide and two gruesome murders were a lot, even for a detective of Scott's experience, to take in.

'And to make matters worse,' Daley got to his feet, 'our highly esteemed leader should be here at any minute.'

'Oh, you're fucking kidding me on,' Scott said, his pallor becoming a shade greyer. 'I thought it would be great getting back intae the swing o' things doon here, kinda oot o' the way. I'll tell you, Jim, I don't think I can cope wae him just noo, honestly.' There was a pleading look in his eyes.

'Tell me about it,' said Daley, massaging his temple with his thumb and forefinger. 'Even worse now that the bastard's the divisional commander. Listen, you know where I am with this. I'm sure he made you spring MacDougall for a reason; I'm sure he's up to something. We just have to find out what. As you know, I've been digging about since you've been, well, incapacitated. Something's not right. I just can't put my finger on it.'

'Aye, good stuff, Jim. Mind you, I wish I was still incapacitated. I don't know aboot you, but I feel as though I've landed on a different planet. Nothin' seems the same. I'm no' even working for the same police force any more. And noo I've got the prospect o' the dark lord grabbing me by the bollocks.'

'Listen, put him out of your mind. He'll have other things to worry about. And I suppose we'll get used to our new employers, Brian. At the end of the day we're still chasing after the same lowlife bastards. That'll never change.'

'Aye, it doesnae help when one o' the lowlife bastards happens tae be your boss.' Scott's resigned look made Daley smile.

'I've been told it's light duties for you only, my old son. I've got a wee list here of folk I'd like you to talk to today. It'll get you out of the office while your man's here. After that, I want you to finish early and go back to the hotel and get a sleep. Tonight, you're going for a wee sail.'

'Eh?'

'Lights in the sky, Brian. Lights in the sky.'

He reckoned it would take less than thirty minutes to sail back to where the collision had taken place. This meant that he should have sight of the yacht and its occupants soon. He kept sighting with the scope on the high-powered rifle. The mist had completely lifted now, and the sun was hot on the back of his neck. Pavel, too, was squinting into the distance across the sea, the ripples of which sparkled in their path. To the right of their boat a porpoise arched out of the water, returning to it with hardly a sound. The sea smelled sweet and salty, and left a tang at the back of the throat.

'They can't be far away now, Pavel.' He cradled the sleek rifle against his cheek. His weapon of choice was the McMillan TAC-338, favoured by the American military. It was the most deadly sniper's rifle of all time. His had been tuned to utter perfection by a Russian gunsmith to suit his own exact specifications. He'd had a custom-built cheek piece fitted, a mould made from the fingers of his left hand was replicated on the barrel grip, and the trigger had been lightened to just under three pounds of pressure. The weapon felt like an extension of his own body; it had ended many lives while at the same time enriching his own. If he could get within a kilometre of his target he was confident that he could eradicate the problem. The sea was calm, and despite the alcohol he had consumed, he didn't doubt his abilities for one second. Only memories stood in his way. He took his eyes from the sight and shook the thought from his head.

Alice was beginning to warm up, as the sun beat down on the tiny vessel and its wretched occupants. A few moments ago, the handheld radio had burst into life; the Kinloch lifeboat would be with them in just over an hour. The voice of the lifeboat's coxswain had boomed confidently out of the device and, for the first time since the accident, she had seen the tension ease from her father's face. All they had to do was to sit and wait.

Alice angled her head into the sun. She figured that she might as well work on her tan as they awaited rescue. After all, as her father always maintained, every cloud has a silver lining.

'I see them!' he shouted, spotting the stern of the yacht poking up, proud of the waves, through the powerful scope. Beside it bobbed a dinghy, in which he could see four figures. 'Slow down, Pavel. Stop when I tell you.' He leaned forward and looked through the sight. 'We need to get a bit closer, but not too much.' Taking into account the slight undulation of the ocean, he was still too distant to be certain of a hundred per cent kill. He needed a hundred per cent kill rate.

*

Something made Alice turn around. At first she wasn't sure what, then she realised that she could hear something in the distance. Having spent a lot of her short life at sea, she knew that sound travelled across the water with much greater ease than over land. She could make out a speck on the horizon.

'Dad, there's a boat out there! Look, over there!'

Her father turned his head, shading his gaze from the glare of the sun with his hand. 'Oh yes, I can just about make it out. Bugger, my good binoculars are still on the boat. Maybe we won't have to wait for the lifeboat after all.' With that, they both started to wave their arms, soon joined by Alice's mother and brother, who, newly awoken, looked confused.

After a few minutes of waving, it was obvious that the vessel, whatever it was, was getting no nearer.

'They can't have seen us,' Stephen said with a tut.

For some reason she couldn't explain, despite the warm sun and the promise of rescue, Alice felt a sudden chill, as she looked out at the small, unmoving shape.

They were close enough now. All he had to do was measure the rise and fall of both boats in his mind, and calculate how to execute an effective shot. He decided to shoot on the rise; though the swell seemed insignificant, it was exaggerated by distance and magnification. This target would be difficult, but he'd experienced worse.

He cradled the butt of the rifle in his arm; everything felt right. Even the slight haze didn't present a real problem. He narrowed his eye in the sight. Through the crosshairs, he could make out faces; he picked out the tanned face of the dark-haired girl. Behind him, anticipating the kill, Pavel started to giggle. Normally, this would not have worried him, but now he felt so irritated by it that he stood up and swung around to face the squat man, holding the weapon at his waist, finger still on the trigger.

'If another sound comes from your fat pig's head, Pavel, I will kill you,' he snarled. He leaned back on the gunwale and, once again, took aim. There she was: dark eyes, brown skin, bright and young. He was going to end her life, rob her of her future. He hesitated; suddenly he was no longer in the present. The years dropped away. He froze.

He sees her, the old woman, as she hunches across the street. The basket at her side swings to and fro as she slouches along. Her only protection is the black scarf that almost covers her head and face. If they can't see you they can't kill you.

He tried to steady the rifle and stop his hands from shaking.

'Baka!'

A call from long ago echoed in his head as he tried again to focus on the girl.

Concentrate. He pulled the butt of the rifle close into his neck, holding it close like a lover.

'Pazi Snajper!'

He pulled out of the shot, looking at Pavel now, standing on the deck of the boat, not the dusty street in Sarajevo.

He leaned back into the rifle. The girl's face was framed in the sight, and he followed the movement of the boat up and down, waiting for the moment the little craft would linger on the apex of the swell. He curled his finger around the trigger.

A shot whined through the air – not his, but another.

She falls in slow motion, the old woman on the bright dusty street. Her basket is tumbling through the air, spilling its meagre contents as he watches. A fish falls from a white paper bag, arcing through the air in slow motion.

He blinked the vision away, waiting for the boat to rise.

'*Baka!*'

He heard it again, the tiny voice bringing more perspiration on his brow.

He is with her now, kneeling at her side. 'Be a good boy. Run. Run from the dragons,' she says, her voice a fading whisper.

He desperately tried to shake the old woman from his mind's eye.

The little boy stands over his grandmother as she rattles her final breath. His small hand reaches for hers. She stares at him with sad brown eyes as her life ends. For a moment her lips move in a silent goodbye.

'*Baka!*' *The boy calls out in pain. He stands in the middle of the dusty, deserted road; a tiny boy in the middle of a big war. He wills the dragons to take him to his grandmother, but they do not roar. Their fire doesn't touch him in the street in Sarajevo, long, long ago.*

They must roar again now.

He clenched his teeth and shook his head. The memories that tortured him were getting worse.

14

He hated that vision; that memory. It haunted him still; what had happened to that little boy?

He pulled away from the gun sight and closed his eyes. He breathed in the warm air. He had a job to do; he had a smaller war to win.

He squinted back into the sight; he could still see them in their dinghy. He focused again on the girl. There was something strange about the way she was staring, motionless, straight ahead. Though he knew it was impossible, he could have sworn she could see him and knew that she was going to die. His right forefinger curled around the cold trigger. He took a deep breath and waited again for the rise of the swell.

Alice stared at the boat, transfixed, oblivious to all that was going on around her.

She was jolted into reality by her father, who had leapt to his feet.

'Over here! Yes! God bless the Royal Navy!'

Aware now, Alice heard a low noise. She looked up to see the growing outline of a warship, sounding its claxon in the distance to let them know that help was on the way. She, too, raised her hands to wave.

As he squeezed the trigger, a noise made him flinch. The butt of the rifle forced itself into his shoulder a moment after the barrel flashed. He swore to himself and got to his feet.

'Quick, Pavel, we have company. Wherever they are, steer in the opposite direction. Full speed!' He dashed below, carrying the weapon with him, low and out of sight, protected from view by the gunwale. He hadn't had time to check the outcome of his interrupted assassination attempt, nor the nature of the new vessel they had for company; he just knew that they had to get away. The shot was not perfect, the blast on the horn had made him flinch, but he was confident that he had done the job, killed the girl. Their task now was to disappear.

There was a rush, then a pop akin to a balloon being burst, though deeper and less crisp. A piece of rubber hit her in the face, and her father fell backwards. Something was wrong; she was sinking into the bottom of the dingy.

'Fuck,' her father swore, as his son levered him up and back to his feet. 'The bloody boat's burst. We're sinking.'

Alice felt a chill at her feet, rising up her leg. Seawater was streaming into the tiny vessel as its shape and structure began to collapse. Her mother screamed, but her father – as so often was the case – urged them all to be calm.

'We all have our lifejackets on. We're going to get wet, but that destroyer will be with us in a matter of minutes. Hold on to each other!' he shouted, as he grabbed his wife's fluorescent jacket. 'Let the lifebelt take the strain. We'll float until they get here.'

Their little dinghy was nearly submerged now; the cold water at her waist was making Alice gasp. As though in recognition of their plight, the warship gave three long blasts. Alice looked up. The vessel was much larger now; she could make out the frothing white wake as the Royal Navy steamed to their rescue.

The lifebelt rose around her neck as it bore her weight in the water. Alice looked for the smaller boat that had been motionless for so long, but there was no sign of it.

Alice gasped again as the cold seawater lapped at her chin.

'This bloody place! Just what the fuck is going on?' John Donald cursed, as he banged his fist on the desk. 'This is grotesque,' he said, flinging down the crime scene photograph of the young man, his tongue sticking out from the slash in his bloody neck. 'What progress have you made?'

'He spoke to someone earlier in the day at the shop downstairs where he was buying air freshener. Whoever killed him did so brazenly, in broad daylight, in his own home. There's no sign of a struggle at the door, the locks weren't forced, so it would appear they were invited in,' said Daley.

'Air freshener? Not the first purchase I would have expected a lowlife like this to make.'

'No, sir. Clearly he was expecting company; somebody he wanted to impress.'

'Impress?'

'Don't you give your house a quick spray before your guests arrive?'

'Indeed not. I leave all domestic matters to my good lady. In any case, our home is not a fucking crack den like this stupid bugger's. I daresay you have to attend to that type of thing yourself now, eh, Jim?' Donald smirked, breaking off his tirade, unable to resist the opportunity.

Daley said nothing, making sure his expression remained the same, despite his boiling blood. 'This was an execution, sir, plain and simple. As was that of Rory Newell. We were right about him all along; somebody is sending out a message, a very strong message, sir. I've informed the Serious Organised Crime Agency, of course, and they're studying the crime scene evidence.'

'Did you know Rainsford spent a spell on secondment with the Carabiniere in Florence? This looks like bloody mafia shit to me, or something similar. Get him in here.' Donald waved his hand at Daley and turned his gaze to a document on his desk.

As Daley strode towards the door, desperately trying to hold his temper, Donald spoke again. 'While we're at it, send DS Scott in to see me. I expect to see a change in his attitude if his return to duty is to be a permanent one.'

'Afraid I can't, sir. He's working a split shift today; on obs tonight, so he's not on duty at the moment.'

'Obs duty?' mocked Donald. 'That decision should have been left to me. Get someone else to do that, and get Scott back here now. Fuck knows, he's probably got his face in a bloody glass, already.'

Daley turned in the doorway. 'Direct order from the ACC, sir,' he lied, then smiled as Donald waved him away with a dismissive flourish of his hand. Despite the gesture, Daley knew he had won.

15

Daley was looking at a grab taken from Kinloch's CCTV footage during the window of time around Malky Miller's murder. Though he had no reason for his suspicions, he didn't like the look of the man walking down Kinloch's Main Street with his head bowed. He stood out, was different somehow; certainly he wasn't a local man, though Daley knew he could be an innocent tourist or businessman. The clip was only a moment longer than three seconds, and Daley had watched it over and over again. There was something about the way this man walked, his gaze permanently fixed to the ground. He wore a dark jacket and a cap underneath which Daley was sure he was bald; no hair was visible on the side of his head, though, from this angle, it was hard to tell. His build was striking; he reminded Daley of a wrestler, or a rugby forward. Somehow, to the detective's eye, he didn't fit.

'I want some stills blown up from this. And take a look around the time it was taken and see if we can find this character anywhere else on CCTV,' said Daley to a young DC. He leaned back in his chair, deep in thought, as the detective left his glass box. These were vicious, pitiless crimes that left him sick to the stomach. He had seen the full spectrum of man's inhumanity in the course of his career, but this was at the extreme end.

And what about Cudihey? Was his horrific suicide a final gesture of defiance, a desperate attempt to cleanse the soul with fire, or a two-fingered salute at an uncaring world? Or was it something else entirely?

A knock rattled his door and Rainsford entered. 'I thought I would let you know, sir, that a member of the Scottish Government is paying a visit to Kinloch.'

'Really, when?'

'Tomorrow, sir. Apparently it's some kind of fact-finding mission.'

'Oh, brilliant. Does his majesty know yet?'

Rainsford gave Daley a puzzled look, then realised who he meant. 'I thought it best that you inform the Chief Superintendent, sir.' He smiled. 'Apparently she is bringing her own security detail, so it will cause minimum disruption to us, at least. The whole visit is to be low-key, I'm told.'

'Just what we need. Get me the details, please, and I'll tell the boss. Who is this official?'

Rainsford looked at the document he was holding for a few moments. 'Elise Fordham, sir. She's the Minister for Rural Affairs, Food and the Environment. Their party will consist of her and two others; an assistant and someone from the communications office. Plus protection officers, I assume.'

'Who from the communications office?'

Rainsford turned a page over. 'Gary Wilson, sir. That's all the information I have.'

'That's all the information I need. Gary fucking Wilson.'

'You know him, sir?'

'Oh yes, I know him. If you worked in the eighties in the Glasgow Police, you knew Gary Wilson, let me assure you. A bastard, a complete bastard. The fun never ends.'

The sheer size of the warship that had rescued them prevented it from entering Kinloch's harbour proper, so the Taylor family were being transported to the pontoons aboard a tender, piloted by a petty officer and a young rating. The Navy had managed to winch the family's dinghy aboard and were going to attempt to salvage their yacht which, thanks to modern buoyancy aids, was still partly afloat, stern up in the water.

'As the lieutenant said, sir, the local harbour master will want to speak with you at some point, and the coastguard. The police, too, I've no doubt. A dreadful set of circumstances,' the petty officer said to Stephen as they neared Kinloch. 'I'm pleased that we were in the vicinity. That's our good deed done for the day.'

Alice looked out of the small cabin window. She was wrapped in a silver thermal blanket, as were the rest of the family. The sailors had been kind and efficient; they had been checked over by the ship's doctor, offered a shower and a change of clothes, and before they left the warship, given a hot meal. Though she didn't think that the dark uniform trousers and jumper she had been kitted out with were very flattering, she had been glad to get out of her wet clothes and warm up. The Captain had even radioed ahead to book hotel rooms for them, to give them a chance to talk to the relevant authorities and sort out transport back to Edinburgh. She looked up to see the rating, who didn't look much older than herself, staring at her. She smiled, making him blush and look away.

Her thoughts turned to what they had just experienced. Though she couldn't be certain, she felt sure that the vessel that had lurked for so long on the horizon was the same one that had sunk their boat. She knew it was insane, but remembering the whoosh prior to their dinghy sinking, she could have sworn that they had been hit by something. When she had told her father this, he dismissed her theory with no little scorn. As far as he was concerned, the little boat had been damaged in the collision and the whooshing noise was merely the sound of it bursting.

As the young crewman jumped adroitly onto the pontoons and began securing the tender, she pictured the laughing man aboard the boat that had sunk them. She shivered.

'Elise who?' Donald asked, from behind the desk in his temporary office.

'Fordham, sir,' said Daley. 'Minister for Rural Affairs, Food and the Environment.'

'Oh, bollocks, don't they realise we're up to our necks in shit here?'

'Interesting to note that she is from the same department as our suicide case, sir.'

'Does that surprise you, Jim? Have you ever met a politician who could keep their nose out of anything?'

'One more thing, sir. Miss Fordham will be accompanied by Gary Wilson from the communications department. I'm sure I don't need to remind you about him.'

'Ah, no, indeed. Well, we'll just have to make the best of it. Let's hope they stick to their word and this visit is as low-key as they suggest,' Donald said, lifting the receiver of his phone. 'If you'll excuse me, Jim, I have an urgent phonecall to make.'

As Daley left the room he had the uneasy feeling that the imminent arrival of Gary Wilson was no surprise to his boss.

Here we go again, he thought.

As he walked down the corridor towards the CID Suite, Rainsford hurried towards him. 'Sir, you remember the family who discovered our body in the sea?'

'Yes. Taylor, isn't it? The guy's big in some business in Edinburgh.'

'Yes, sir. As you know, they were on their way here to be interviewed by ourselves. Apparently, they were hit and sunk by another boat early this morning. Rescued by a naval destroyer a few hours ago.'

'Where are they now?'

'County Hotel, sir.'

'Right, you and I will take a wander down there. For one thing, I need a drink; secondly, as my old gaffer used to say, everything happens for a reason, so let's go and try to find out what that reason is.'

Daley walked into his office to pick up his jacket. The large room was a hive of activity; there were whiteboards displaying crime scene images, timelines and maps with locations numbered and marked in red; detectives were poring over documents, making phone calls or staring at computer screens.

For the first time in months, despite the death, destruction and all of their attendant problems, he realised that he felt at home.

16

'Well, well,' Daley said, as he walked into the bar at the County Hotel. Brian Scott was sitting at a table with a plate of sandwiches and a large cup of coffee in front of him.

'Aye, you can smile all you want. I couldnae get a proper drink here if I tried,' he said, nodding in the direction of Annie, who was cleaning a pint glass with a white tea towel.

'No, an' you'll no' get wan neither, no' until you get back the night,' she said.

'I very much doubt our man will be back here before closing time, Annie,' Daley said with a smile. 'Most sensitive operation he's involved with. Could change the world, in fact.'

'Aye, you know what you can do with your "sensitive operation",' Scott said, glaring from under knitted brows. 'Two o' the things I hate most in the world – wild goose chases, and boats.'

Daley noticed that despite using both hands to hold his mug, Scott's trembling had sloshed some of the coffee onto the white tablecloth.

'The fresh air will do you the world of good, Brian, trust me.'

'It's no' the air that I'm worried aboot. Every time I come doon here I find myself oot on a boat. You know fine I hate the bloody water.'

'You've been all at sea since I've known you, Brian,' said Daley. He walked to the bar and spoke quietly to Annie. 'Are the Taylors here? I need to have a chat with them. Somewhere quiet, if you could arrange that.'

'Aye, no bother, Mr Daley. You can use the dining room, there's nobody in there. Dae you want me tae give them a buzz an' tell them you're here?'

'Yes, that would be great, Annie,' said Daley. He turned back to Scott. 'What time are you heading off, Mulder?'

'Och, in just over an hour. Aye, an' you can stick that Mulder piss up your arse, tae.' Despite his fragile condition, he managed a smile. 'Luckily, my dear wife had the good sense tae pack a warm jumper, an' a waterproof jacket. Fucking flippers I'll be needing next. If I'd wanted tae join the Underwater Branch, I'd have spent mair time at the baths in Maryhill when I was a boy.'

Daley watched the Taylor family as they walked into the County's large dining room. Underneath healthy tans, they looked pale. They were dressed in ill-fitting clothes that clearly weren't their own. Mrs Taylor's eyes were red-rimmed, and despite his outward calm, Daley could tell that her husband was stressed too, biting his finger nails as he ushered his family to the table where Daley and Rainsford were waiting.

'Please take a seat,' Daley said. 'There are plenty chairs. Well, you've certainly been through the mill, from what I've been hearing. I'm DCI Jim Daley, by the way, and this is DS Rainsford.'

'Stephen Taylor.' He shook Daley's hand. 'This is my wife, Andrea, and our children, Ian and Alice.'

'We'll take it from the top then,' Daley said. 'You found a body in the water.'

Scott made his way to the pier down Kinloch's Main Street, quiet in the early evening. He was to meet a fisherman called Norrie Deans at his boat the *Grey Gull*. The few people he passed smiled at him, or said a brief hello. Though it was still warm, he had a thick jumper and a bulky waterproof over his arm. It always seemed to be cold at sea, no matter how mild the weather on land.

As he reached the head of the pier, he spotted a familiar figure standing within a haze of pipe smoke.

'Well, now, how are you doing?' said Hamish. He was dressed in a fisherman's waterproof bib and brace set, over a thick dark jumper and sea boots. 'You'll be ready for oor wee adventure?'

'Naebody telt me you were coming, Hamish,' replied Scott, wondering just how hot the old man must be, clothed as he was.

'Ach, but I'm sure your pal has the dementia, or something similar.' Hamish looked at him, taking the pipe from his mouth and spitting noisily onto the ground. 'We had a conversation aboot it a' jeest this morning. I offered tae be your guide, so tae speak. Aye, he thought the idea was jeest inspired.'

'Aye, well, whatever. I take it you know what we're after, here?'

'Well, now, in my time at sea, I've been lucky enough tae witness maist things, so you needna worry that I'll be shocked, or faint away like a wee lassie. I'll gie you a take on my unique knowledge o' the coast. Aye, unsurpassed hereabouts, let me tell you.'

'Och, I better give the gaffer a phone,' Scott said, searching in his trouser pocket for his mobile.

'Oh aye,' said Hamish, flourishing a plastic carrier bag he had been holding. 'I brought this – tae serve against the chill, you understand.' With that he revealed a bottle of whisky. His eyes creased in a slant as a broad grin spread across his tanned face.

'Er, yes, well, I daresay that would dae the trick nicely.' Scott put the phone back in his pocket. 'Now, where's this boat?'

'The *Grey Gull*, there she is there.' Hamish pointed to a fishing boat at the end of the pier; of medium size in Scott's admittedly limited experience, but looking sturdy enough for him to be able to approach this latest naval adventure with more confidence than he would have thought possible an hour before. The fact that Hamish had produced a bottle of whisky had done a lot to soothe his nerves as well.

'Lead on, Hamish. This is a piece o' nonsense, but we might as well enjoy it as best we can.' Scott put his arm around the old man's shoulder as they walked to the fishing boat. 'Maybe I'll enjoy this light duty malarkey more than I thought.'

'So you saw someone on deck, Alice?' said Daley. 'Can you describe him?

'Yes,' Alice answered confidently. 'He was kind of big. Ugly. He was bald or with a shaven head – one of the two. I saw him quite clearly.'

'Do you think you'd recognise him if you saw him again?'

'Yes,' Alice answered quickly. 'I'll never forget his face. He was laughing at us as his boat sailed away. We could have drowned, and all he could do was laugh. I hate him.'

'Alice!' her mother chastised.

'It's OK, Mrs Taylor. I understand your daughter's sentiment. In fact, this could be most helpful. Would you mind coming up to the office, Alice? There's a picture I'd like you to take a look at.'

Have I found my man in the street? Daley wondered.

17

Scott swore as he clambered onto the fishing boat. Hamish, already aboard, held his hand out to support the detective as he manoeuvred himself off the pier and over the gunwale of the vessel. The tide was full, and the boat sat high in the water.

'Where's this Norrie character, then?' said Scott, looking about the deck for any sign of life.

'No, he'll no' be up here, he'll be doon there,' Hamish replied, gesturing over the far side of the boat as he tried to relight his pipe in puffs of pungent smoke.

'Eh?' said Scott, as he struggled over the nets, fish boxes and coils of rope scattered across the deck.

'That's Norrie's boat doon there.' Hamish puffed on his pipe, scattering a cloud of midges that had been bothering them since they came aboard. To exaggerate this effect, Hamish removed the pipe from his mouth and puffed out yet more tobacco smoke into the still air. 'Aye, Mr Scott, the curse o' Scotland, these wee bastards. Did I tell you the tale o' why they came tae plague oor fine nation?'

'Never mind that,' exclaimed Scott, looking over the side of the fishing boat. 'What the hell is that?'

'That's the *Grey Gull*. A fine wee craft she is tae.'

'"Wee" being the operative word. You pointed this boat oot when we were at the head of the quay.'

'No, no, indeed I did not. This is the *Winter Star*. It belongs tae the MacDonald boys. For whoot reason would I tell you this was Norrie's boat?'

'You distinctly pointed tae this boat wae your bloody pipe, just a few moments ago,' said Scott, looking askance at the small wooden vessel that bobbed alongside the larger fishing boat.

'Weel, jeest how was I tae point tae this boat when she was doon here oot o' sight? I pointed in the general direction o' the boat we were efter. It's no' my fault you grasped ontae the wrong end o' the stick wae such gusto.' He smiled, a look of satisfaction writ large over his face.

'And while we're at it,' said Scott, 'just how dae you intend tae get aboard that . . . that tub.'

'Ach, noo that's the easy bit. Norrie! Would you fling me up the rope ladder.' At this, a hatch popped open on the deck of the *Grey Gull,* and a plump-cheeked man sporting a greasy Breton cap stuck his head out and squinted into the golden sunlight of the summer evening.

'I might have known, nae show without Punch, Hamish,' said Norrie. 'We're having a wee bit o' engine trouble. Nothing terminal, you understand. I'll be finished in ten minutes or so. Jeest yous two enjoy the sunshine. Me an' Kenny will be oot in a minute.' With that, the hatch closed again.

'Brilliant,' said Scott, 'just brilliant. Here I am aboot tae surrender mysel' tae the ocean blue again, this time aboard the pride o' the Toy Toon fleet, and tae make matters worse, the engine doesnae work, plus I'll have tae perform fuck knows what acrobatics, just for the privilege of getting aboard.'

Alice walked the short distance from the County Hotel to Kinloch Police Office with Daley and Rainsford. They had asked her many questions about what had happened in the early hours of the morning, and seemed most keen to hear as much as she could tell them about the 'laughing man', as they now referred to him. She was troubled, though. Before the police had arrived, her father had warned her not to mention her theories about the sinking of their boat, for fear of making a fool of herself, or sending the police out on a fool's errand. But she was sure what had happened was down to more than reckless irrresponsiblity and she just couldn't dislodge him from her mind. The face, the laugh; all of it made her shudder.

Daley sat behind his desk, Alice beside him in another chair. Rainsford had been despatched to get coffee, a task Daley knew the detective felt was well beneath his pay grade.

'Now,' said Daley, booting up the laptop on his desk. 'I would like to show you something.' In a few moments, the machine burst into life and he found the file which contained the grainy CCTV footage.

Alice sat forward on her seat to get a better look. Suddenly, into frame, walked a man clad in black. Daley saw the girl's eyes widen.

'Hang on, Alice. I'll rewind this and stop it at the point where we have the best glimpse of his face under that hat.' Daley pressed a couple of buttons and the short clip rewound and paused, this time stopping just over two seconds in. The stocky man had raised his gaze in order to cross the street; it was a side-on view, but the best they had.

'That's him, that's definitely him!' The teenager stood in her excitement. 'There's no way I'll forget that face – ever.'

'You're absolutely sure?' asked Daley. But the look on Alice's face was enough to persuade Daley she was genuinely convinced that this was the same man who'd left the family for dead as their yacht sank.

'There's something else I want to tell you,' Alice said, her voice tailing off, as though she'd said something out of turn.

'Yes, by all means.'

As she was about to speak Rainsford pushed the door open; the look on Daley's face was enough to make him grimace and back out.

'Don't worry, Alice. If you know something else, no matter how stupid or trivial you think it is, just tell me. Nobody's going to make a fool of you or tell you off. I promise.' He smiled at the girl, trying to put her at ease.

'Just before the Navy found us, I saw another boat,' said Alice nervously.

'Yes.'

'Well, it was as though they just floated there, for ages, doing nothing.'

'What was the boat like?'

'That's just the thing, it was too far away to make out, but, well, you know.' She shrugged her shoulders.

'Know what?'

'Well, I just kind of felt that it was the same people who'd hit us, and they were just out there watching.'

'What made you think that?'

'Oh, I don't know. Just, like, a feeling. Do you know what I mean?'

'Oh yes,' answered Daley, who had solved many crimes over the years based on just that *feeling*.

'I told my dad, but he says it's ridiculous.'

'What, about the boat?'

'No. Well, not just that,' she said, sounding suddenly unsure. 'Before we sank – the second time, in our little dinghy – there was a noise, and a piece of rubber hit me in the face.'

'Why do you think that was?'

'Oh, my dad just thinks that the dinghy got damaged in the collision and sort of burst, like a balloon. There was a whooshing noise, then a kind of pop.'

'And after that the piece of rubber from the dinghy hit you in the face. Is that correct, Alice?'

'Yes.'

'And you think, what, that someone did this deliberately?'

'I think someone shot the boat and sunk it. I'm sorry,' she said, blushing, 'this sounds like the kind of thing you would expect a stupid wee girl to say.'

'Tell me, Alice. I know you saw this man, on board his boat. Did he see you?'

'Yes.'

'How can you be so sure?'

'He looked right at me. I called to him for help, and then he started to laugh.'

'Good,' said Daley, smiling at the girl again. 'You've been a great help, Alice. Thank you.'

The girl smiled back at him and tucked a strand of hair

behind her ear. She was bright, clever and pretty; she was lucky to be alive. Daley's blood ran cold.

Scott was grim as the small craft chugged out of Kinloch harbour, billows of dirty blue smoke issuing from its diesel engine into the still air. At least the sea looked calm; Scott rubbed his chin, reflecting with a shiver on some of his recent nautical experiences.

'Aye, a fine night for a wee sail, Mr Scott, is it no'?' said Hamish.

'I'm no' part fish, like you lot seem tae be,' answered Scott. 'Where I come fae, the closest we like tae get tae the water is putting it in oor whisky. Aye, an' stop calling me Mr Scott, it's Brian. Fuck me, Hamish, you've known me long enough now.'

'Just so, Brian. Talking of whisky, you'll be wantin' a wee dram, just tae keep the cold oot, you understand. I take it you have drinking vessels aboard, Norrie?'

'Indeed I do,' replied Norrie. 'In fact, you could say this is a drinking vessel, itsel'.'

'Very good,' said Scott. 'All the fun o' the fair here, I can see.'

'Noo, I'm no' wanting you tae think that all we do at sea is booze, Brian,' said Norrie wistfully. 'Under normal circumstances, I would be sober as a judge, fair scanning the horizon for hazards, weather and the like. But since Mr Daley was so kind as tae commandeer the boat for your research purposes, I'm happy tae partake in a sensation or two.'

'You'll no' want tae breach any o' the rules wae an' officer o' the law on board, Norrie,' observed Hamish, looking suddenly less sanguine. 'Aye, an' forbye, I've only got the one bottle, so your sensation might no' be a' you were hopin' for.'

'Not at all, Hamish, not at all,' said Norrie. 'Young Kenny here spent half the winter up in Glasgow at the nautical college. Though you might no' believe it, he's even got letters after his name noo. He'll be in charge o' the boat the very second the first drop o' whisky passes my lips.'

'Oh aye,' said Hamish. 'Well, wae the meagre store we've got on board, I'm thinking you'll manage fine tae navigate yoursel'.'

'Noo, Hamish, never let it be said that I'm backwards in coming forwards when it comes tae refreshment.' He reached under the bench he was sitting on and produced a well-worn canvas satchel. 'I brought two o' my best friends with me,' he said, holding up two bottles.

'Things are looking up,' Scott said with a smile.

At this, Kenny, the other member of the crew, a thin youth with bad acne and an anxious expression, tapped his captain on the shoulder. 'You'll remember I failed they exams, Norrie.'

'Ach, but you're some boy for the jokes, right enough,' answered Norrie. Then, in an aside to the young man, 'Kenny, son, there's mair tae life than exams. Jeest you keep your hand on your ha'penny. Aye, an' if you canna think o' something intelligent tae say, jeest don't say anything.'

They sailed past the island at the head of the loch, then out into the sound, Kenny staring out to sea, reflecting upon the fact that the only letters he had after his name were 'Navigation and Seamanship – FAIL'.

18

As he watched the yacht sink, he had cursed himself for being so stupid. He was angry with Pavel too, but what would that achieve? His companion had never been the same after the horrors he'd been put through. He'd been chained for months on end, naked in a freezing cell. Beaten and starved every day until, in the end, his captors had resorted to extreme torture. A hessian sack filled with pepper had been tied onto his head for hours at a time, which made his eyes and nose stream and hampered his breathing so much that he had passed out repeatedly, only to be brought back to consciousness with kicks and punches or a deluge of icy water. He'd been burned with cigarette ends, electrocuted and half drowned.

Then, bored, and certain they had extracted as much useful information as they were going to get, they'd strapped him to a table and cut out his tongue. He had been abandoned in the street, trussed hand and foot.

The villagers had brought Pavel to him. Slowly, so slowly, he had brought the broken man back to life. But scars remained; lacking a tongue, he would never speak again, and his mind had been irreparably altered. Gone was the strong, decisive man he had once known, the man to whom he owed his life. Could he blame this broken man for allowing himself to be seen as they sailed away from the sinking yacht? No, he could only blame himself. Had he solved this problem? Was the girl dead? He had to find out.

He sighed as they left the inlet in the old fishing boat. They had so many things to do.

Norrie checked the lobster creels, marked by fluorescent pink and orange buoys, cursing his luck as one by one they came up empty. They were sailing just off the tip of Arran now, not far from where the strange lights in the sky had first been sighted.

Though the sea had grown restless, Scott discovered that whisky was the cure to his seasickness. Though he had spent the day dreading this trip, now he was feeling mellow – happy, even – as they bobbed from creel to creel. The night was warm and the view stunning; a purple hue hung over Arran and the distant mound of Ailsa Craig. As the short summer night approached, even the gulls had ceased their cries. The sea lapped at the side of the vessel as Norrie found yet another empty creel and cursed.

'It's jeest as well the polis are paying for this wee jaunt,' he mused. 'It's clear we're having nae bloody luck the night.'

'Och, as you say, you've been commandeered. Sit on your arse an' have another swift one,' said Scott. 'This is a fool's errand, anyhow. Aye, an' I'm the fool.'

'Don't be so rash, Brian,' said Norrie. 'If you'd been here the other night you wouldna be treating this as lightly. I've been at sea a' my life an' I've never seen anything like it. Jeest weird it was. Is that no' right, Kenny?'

'Aye, sure is,' said Kenny. 'Like somethin' oot o' the movies, honest tae fuck.'

'Well, whatever.' Scott remained unconvinced. 'It's got me oot o' the road an' away fae my gaffer, so power tae it.' He poured the dregs from the first bottle they'd opened into Norrie's tin mug and raised his own in a toast. 'Here's tae lights in the sky, boys. Cheers!'

'There's nae end tae the strange things that happen at sea, Brian,' said Hamish, as he savoured his whisky. 'As a boy, I was oot wae my faither, not far from here, as it happens, when I saw it.'

'Saw what?' Scott asked.

'Och, hard tae explain, noo.' Hamish lit his pipe. 'It was jeest at the darkening; we were on oor way hame after fishing jeest off Ballycastle. My faither had intended tae be back intae port before dark, but we'd hit such a proud shoal of mackerel that he stayed with it until they disappeared. Aye, fair loaded we were, right enough.'

'Loaded wae this, by the sound o' it,' observed Norrie, holding up his tin mug.

Ignoring this, Hamish continued. 'I was sitting on the bow, jeest keeping a look oot since the light was so poor. We didna have a' the modern gadgetry they do the day. Nae such thing as sat nav, or even radar. You relied on your senses. Och, it was a better world a' the gither.'

'Will you get on wae the story before I sober up,' said Scott.

'All of a sudden, there in the gloaming, I saw it. A long boat, like nothing I'd ever seen before: sleek an' dark, wae a huge square sail an' a horse's heid prow.' The old man closed his eyes. 'Rows of oars, a' hitting the water at the wan time, apart fae that, not a sound.'

'What did you do?' asked Scott, enthralled despite himself.

'Och, I hurried aft, tae get my faither, but he'd seen it fae the wheelhoose, an' he was already oot on the deck.'

'What happened then?' Kenny looked on, wide-eyed.

'Dae you know whoot this place used tae be called? Well, I'll tell you,' said Hamish, not waiting for a response. 'The land o' the horsemen, aye, jeest that, land o' the horsemen. Noo, yous can scoff if you like, but I think whoot I saw that night wiz a glimpse o' the past. An' these horsemen weren't the yins that ride aboot on some cuddy, the horse was the one on the prow o' their boat. Aye, an' us in Kinloch are their descendants.' He crossed his arms, his tale over.

'So, what did your father have tae say aboot a' this?' asked Scott.

Hamish took a long puff on his pipe. 'He telt me tae say nothing, so that's what I did. The first time I spoke aboot it was nearly forty years later, an' my faither was long deid, an' – och well – I thought, whoot's the odds?'

'Was this tae that professor, Hamish? Caused quite a stir, a few years ago, did it no'?'

'Aye, Norrie, indeed it did. Professor George Welby, o' Cambridge University, no less. He used tae come tae Kinloch in the summer wae his boat. Well, tae cut a long story short, he invited me aboard for a dram or two, an' we got speakin'.'

'Aye, I bet you didna say much until the bottle was near the end, and you were after another,' said Norrie.

'No, not true. He was a professor of ancient history. He was tellin' me a' aboot his theories on a people called the Phoenicians. Apparently they were fine sailors, fae thousands o' years ago. Knowing I was a mariner mysel' he brought oot this book, aye, an' there it was, plain as day.'

'What was?' asked Scott.

'The very boat I'd seen a' these years before, horse's heid, prow, the lot.' Hamish sat back, looking into the darkening sky. 'He reckoned that they came a lot further north than whoot maist o' his colleagues thought. He was convinced that they were the horse people that gave Kintyre its name. Aye, there you are.'

'That's one for oor Jim,' said Scott. 'He's never got his heid oot o' a book.'

'Maybe, no' so much time on his hands the noo, whoot wae his wee friend tae entertain,' said Norrie, smiling.

'Eh?' replied Scott, confused.

Suddenly Hamish jumped to his feet, sending a shower of pipe tobacco from his pouch onto the deck. 'I've remembered!'

'Remembered what?' asked Scott, brushing tobacco from his trousers.

'Windmills,' said Hamish. 'That's whoot Mr Cudihey was moaning aboot. Windmills. I've been trying tae remember since the poor bugger killed himself. Aye, he was a modern-day Don Coyote, right enough; tilting at windmills, he was.'

'Oh,' said Scott, bemused. 'I'm afraid I'm no' right up tae speed with that investigation. Dae you think oor Jim will want tae know?'

'Oh, aye, fair demanded I tell him everything I could remember aboot my conversation wae Mr Cudihey, so he did.'

'Who the fuck is this Don Coyote?' asked Norrie. 'I thought a coyote was an American dug.'

'Ach, I mind fae years ago, back when I was at the school,' Hamish said, puffing his pipe again. 'This fella Coyote used tae charge at the windmills a' day wae his horse an' a lance. In

117

the days o' chivalry, you understand. I canna think where the dug would come intae it, mind.'

They sat in silence for a while, gazing out over the sound. The purple hue had darkened to midnight blue. A tinge of green showed faintly over Arran, as the stars began to shine bright in the velvet sky, reflecting their pinpricks of light on the dark sea.

'Is the man you're after no' called Quixote,' said Scott, pronouncing the name phonetically.

'I wouldna think so,' said Hamish. 'That's a wile stupid name.'

He looked at the mobile phone, and was pleased to see that he had a strong signal. He'd had a few conversations with the man he was about to phone over the last few months; all had been brief and he had always been the one to end the call. He always detected fear in the voice at the other end; this, in his experience, was not unusual. Most people panicked when he talked to them.

He dialled the number, making sure that his information would not appear at the other end. He always used pre-paid phones, bought on the black market, changed frequently, and utterly untraceable.

The nervous voice he had become so used to answered.

'I need information, and I need it tonight,' he said, before the man on the other end could interrupt.

'What? Did you not get my message? I can't do this any more. I demand . . .'

'You are in no position to demand anything. I know you will be aware how badly things have gone for certain individuals recently. Make sure that you do not join their number. A yacht was sunk off the north coast of Kintyre earlier today. A naval vessel rescued those aboard. I want you to tell me what happened. Did any members of the crew survive?'

He listened to the brief reply, then ended the call. He stroked his chin and closed his eyes. Gripped by rage, he threw the phone hard against the side of the vessel, smashing it. Why had he been so stupid? The risk now was too great. He had two options: abandon this mission and admit failure; or continue, and finish what he had begun. In his world, reputation meant everything. He had no real choice. He had to remove the problem to be able to finish his mission. The job would be difficult, with the risk of detection high, and so he would have to do it himself.

'Pavel, steer for our mooring point,' he called. 'We have to go back to Kinloch; this time, by road.'

He remembered the dark, intelligent eyes he'd seen through the gun sight, and his mind turned to dark thoughts.

Scott was chillier now, but with his jumper on and whisky in his belly he didn't mind. Norrie had produced cold bacon rolls which they tucked into heartily, their hunger fuelled by alcohol. As seemed to be the way of these things, the second bottle was going down faster than the first, with only one more round left in it. It helped that young Kenny had been ordered to abstain, as he was now in charge of the vessel. The unsuccessful quest for lobsters now over, they had sailed to the exact point where the lights had been seen, and as DCI Daley had requested, moored and waited.

'I could get used tae this sailing carry-on,' said Scott. 'I've never seen a night sky like this in my life.' Away from the glare of light pollution, everything was clear; the vast sweep of the Milky Way slathered across the sky as billions of distant suns shed their ancient light on the small boat and its four occupants.

'Ach, we could sit here until next Christmas and nothing would happen,' Norrie said, looking about. 'I knew fine this would be a waste o' time.'

'No' tae worry, eh?' said Scott. 'It'll still be the most lucrative trip you've been on for many a long year, by the looks o' them empty creels. Jim telt me whit compensation you were getting for this wee jaunt.'

'I suppose you have the right o' it there. Even so, we'll wait oot for another half an hour or so, then make for hame. Fuck me, we'll have damn near run oot o' whisky by the time we get back,' replied Norrie, cracking open the last of their ration.

'Dae you mind that good auld song Andy Stewart used tae sing?' asked Hamish, a slur obvious in his voice. '"Oh, Campbeltown Loch, I wish you were whisky, Oh, Campbeltown Loch, och aye . . ."'

Without even thinking about it, Scott could remember the words to this Scottish classic, so he and Norrie joined in, the youthful Kenny looking on and shaking his head.

'C'mon, son,' said Norrie, breaking off his singing. 'Join in, you fuckin' misery.'

'How can I? I've never heard that song in my life.'

'Jeest shows you,' shouted Hamish, 'education's fair gone doonhill, right enough. No' a clue about Don Coyote an' his windmills, noo he doesna know the words tae "Campbeltown Loch". Fine folk, the Campbeltown folk. I'm off the McMillans fae there, myself, you know.'

'Shut up!' shouted Kenny, staring over Hamish's head. 'There's they lights again!'

Scott looked to his left at a whirling ball of light that seemed to be hovering over the sea, just off the Isle of Arran.

'Fuck me!' shouted Norrie. 'We're gonna dae it by the book, this time. Gie me o'er that radio, Kenny. I'm going tae inform the coastguard.'

Scott watched the lights. He had seen nothing like them before; flashing white, occasionally punctuated by sparks of colour, and perhaps the most eerie aspect was the fact that not a sound seemed to come from the object.

'Noo, wait a minute,' said Scott, trying but failing to get to his feet. 'I've got a camera here, that Jim gave me. We'll need tae get this on film.'

'I'm on it,' shouted Kenny, who already had his smart-phone held out in front of his face. 'I'm going tae put this up on YouTube. They're brighter than they were the last time, would you no' say so, Norrie?'

Norrie, busy trying to send his report to the coastguard, nodded, an uneasy look on his face. 'I canna raise them, jeest static on the line.'

'Just don't you bother wae view tube, or whatever it's called. Whitever you get on that camera is police property, son,' warned Scott.

Hamish was motionless, staring at the lights with unblinking intensity, his pipe left to go out in his hand. 'Well, now,' he said, 'do you no' learn something new every day?'

In a split second, flashing white changed to pulsing red, and the strange light soared into the sky at unbelievable speed. Kenny struggled to keep the lights on his screen, but, as they stopped again, he managed to locate them.

After hovering for only a few seconds, the ball of light suddenly grew.

'Look out,' shouted Norrie, 'it's coming right at us!'

As he ducked, Scott heard a rushing noise, followed a heartbeat later by a massive bang that made his ears ring. As quickly as they had appeared, the lights were gone.

The four men looked at each other in silence.

'Fuck me,' said Scott eventually. 'Where did you get that whisky, lads?'

19

Elise Fordham looked out over the sea as the plane soared into the blue sky. Gary Wilson was sitting beside her; two junior aides, including the hapless youth in yet another cheap suit, were behind them. Across the aisle sat a couple of protection officers, who were – rather incongruously, considering they were in the aircraft and out of the sun – both wearing sunglasses.

'Would you look at Starsky and Hutch, there,' Wilson whispered to Fordham. 'Can you ask them to try and look less sinister, Elise?'

'You guys,' Fordham said, leaning across Wilson. 'Lose the shades, eh.' Looking unmoved by this instruction, the pair complied silently.

'Arseholes,' muttered Wilson, under his breath. 'I take it the local cops know we're coming?'

'Oh aye,' Fordham confirmed. 'Not that we'll be in need of any support. It's not as though we'll be doing much politically, though no doubt we'll have to make small talk with some local dignitaries, or the like; lunch with the Chief Superintendent. You know the score, Gary.'

'Oh, I know the score,' He shook his head. 'I dread to think what passes for a dignitary way out here. The village oaf, I shouldn't wonder.'

'Now, now, all valued members of the electorate, and citizens of this fine country of ours.'

'The former being of greatest concern to you, I would hazard.'

'You're very cynical, Gary. Has anyone ever told you that?'

'Many times. Though mainly those who confuse cynicism with the exigencies of realpolitik.'

A head poked in between the headrests in front of them. 'Are you no' that woman fae Edinburgh?' asked a middle-aged man. 'I know your face fae that programme on TV with thon baldy guy. Och, whoot's its name?'

'*Question Time*?' asked Fordham brightly, displaying her winning political smile.

'Nah, let me think.' The man's face was now wedged between the seats, forcing in his cheeks and puckering his mouth. 'Was it no' *MasterChef*, or maybe, *Saturday Kitchen*. Aye, one o' the two.'

'Er, no, I'm sorry. I've never appeared on either of these programmes,' said Fordham, doing her best to end the conversation by purposefully looking away from the man and out of the window.

'Is that a fact? And who might you be?' the man asked, swivelling his eyes towards Wilson, whose abrupt answer was thankfully drowned out by the plane's overly loud intercom.

'Ladies and gentlemen, you may be interested to know that we are flying over the south of the Isle of Arran where apparently, over the last few nights, lights in the sky have been spotted by a number of local fishermen. So keep your eyes peeled for little green men,' said the captain, his tinny voice oozing sarcasm. 'Back on this planet, we'll be landing at Kinloch in just over twelve minutes. The weather there is as glorious as it was in Glasgow. Thank you for flying Scotia Airways.'

'Did I really just hear that?' said Wilson wearily. 'I wonder what you've got us into, coming down here.'

'We have to make the right noises about Cudihey; be seen to pay our respects. The guy worked in my department, and who knows why he decided to do what he did. It would appear heartless not to show face.' She was whispering, anxious in case the man in front of them could overhear, even though he appeared to have lost interest and was sitting forward in his seat. 'Hopefully, this will draw a line under it all.'

'I wish I shared your confidence. In my experience it's best to let sleeping – or indeed in this case, dead – dogs lie.'

'There we are, back with the cynicism.' Elise Fordham looked back to the blue sea. She remembered Walter Cudihey sitting in her office only days before he died. As hard as she tried to banish the memory, a dark shadow crossed her mind.

Daley passed an image of the man in the CCTV footage to his colleagues in Interpol. They, no doubt, would try to match it up with thousands of similar images from all over Europe and beyond.

He was anxious about the Taylor family; so anxious, in fact, that he'd placed a uniformed officer in the County Hotel to make sure nothing untoward happened to them. He was waiting for analysis of the family's dinghy to confirm, or not, that Alice was correct, and the small inflatable boat had indeed been sunk by a gunshot.

In his heart though, he felt he knew the answer already. He was sure the initial collision between the two boats had been an accident. The only explanation as to why this man, or those men, had returned, was to effect the elimination of somebody who could possibly identify one of them. If Alice's theory was correct, they had come very close to succeeding.

He had three bodies: one suicide, two brutal murders. Were these incidents connected? Had Walter Cudihey killed himself knowing that he was about to be murdered like the others? What, if anything, was the connection?

There was a knock at his door and it swung open. John Donald stood in the doorway, grey and worn. Unusually, he was wearing a sweatshirt over a pair of jeans, he was unshaven and dark shadows circled his eyes.

'Jim, sorry to interrupt,' said Donald, sounding uncharacteristically hesitant. 'Need you to do me a favour, actually.'

'Yes, sir.' Daley tried to work out the last time he had seen Donald without either his uniform or a suit on. 'What can I help you with?'

'You know we have the Minister for Rural Affairs arriving this morning. Well, I'm supposed to lunch with her but, as you can see, I'm in no state to do so. Must have picked up a bug or some damn thing, I feel awful.'

'Oh, I see. I'm not sure how this involves me.'

'I'd like you to attend the luncheon in my stead. It's only for an hour or so. Headquarters are keen that someone of a senior rank is there; they can't spare anyone else to come down at this late stage.' Donald coughed, then held his stomach as though he felt sick.

'OK. Though I'm reasonably stretched here myself. But tell me what the score is and I'll do it.' The resentment wasn't lost on Donald.

'Now, Jim, I've bolstered your investigation team

considerably, plus you have resources from outwith our area to call on, should you need them. What's an hour of your time?' Clearly Donald had regained some of his composure. 'The only place I could think of was the County. Oh, and Gary Wilson will be there. I'm sure you'll enjoy seeing him again.'

'Nothing would give me more joy, sir.'

'You know the kind of thing, bit of chit-chat. Be sure to make reassuring noises about how well the new force is shaping up.'

'Is it?'

'What?'

'Is it shaping up, sir?'

'Of course it is. High time we rid ourselves of all that ridiculous Glasgow–Edinburgh rivalry. Best thing that's ever happened.'

'If you say so, sir,' replied Daley, remembering Donald's previously scathing views on the standard of any policing east of Motherwell. 'What time will this lunch kick off?'

'One o'clock. Inspector Layton, my aide, will accompany you. Please leave any matters pertaining to divisional, or Police Scotland, business to him.'

'What can I talk about? The weather?'

'Try not to be smart, Jim. It doesn't suit you.' Donald grimaced. 'I'm afraid I have to get back to my hotel room.'

'Yes, sir. I'll let you know how I get on.'

'Yes, whatever,' said Donald, clutching at his stomach again as he opened the door. He hesitated. 'Wear a uniform, please.' With that the door slammed.

'Fuck,' Daley swore to himself. 'I don't even know if my bloody uniform fits.'

*

As he was about to leave the office his phone rang. A rather hoity-toity official from the MOD was put through to Daley.

'I'm Neil Samuel,' the man said flatly. 'I need to discuss an item that has come into my possession and of which you have a copy.'

'Sorry? I'm not sure what you mean.'

'I want you to destroy the copy of the map discovered on Walter Cudihey's boat. It is of no consequence to your investigation, but it is of interest to us. I'd be obliged if you could accede to this immediately, Chief Inspector.'

Daley was never at his best when demands were made of him so peremptorily. 'Why has the MOD taken possession of evidence pertinent to the suicide of a member of the public? Walter Cudihey was not a member of the military, so everything discovered on his yacht is part of my investigation.'

'DCI Daley, I had hoped that you would be reasonable about this. You will be hearing from your superiors about this. Good day to you.'

With that, the line went dead, leaving an exasperated Daley still holding on to the phone. He could see the map in his mind's eye. Now there was no doubt: it did mean something and, far from destroying it, he was determined to find out what it meant. It would have to wait though – lunch called.

Kirsteen Lang decided to walk the mile and a half to work in order to clear her head. Thankful that she had so far managed to avoid the taint of Walter Cudihey's suicide, she had treated herself to a bottle of Chardonnay the previous evening. She was trying to walk off the empty calories as she strode through the crowd of early morning shoppers and tourists already thronging the busy Edinburgh thorough-fare. The sun was warm, and the smell of exhaust fumes and fast food overlaid the malty tang of brewing beer and a hint of the sea, all of which combined to produce the odour so redolent of the city.

Her meeting with Gary Wilson had unnerved her, espe-cially when it turned out that she had given a full, though less than frank, statement to a man who wasn't the police officer she had been led to believe. She reasoned that she could hardly be blamed for this, a point of view shared even by Wilson, who had seemed much more perturbed by this than by Cudihey's death.

As she looked into a shop window in which expensive handbags were artfully arranged, her mind drifted to the previous evening. She had spent hours searching through her laptop, iPad and smartphone, making sure all traces of her dealings with Cudihey were erased. She'd even taken clan-destine advice from a tech-savvy friend who instructed her as to how to erase these files so that their retrieval would be impossible, even for a forensic specialist.

Kirsteen walked past a shop window displaying mobile phones of varying size and design. She paused; she had been considering upgrading her current model. It was then she felt her heart sink. Prior to having a contract phone, she had used a pay-as-you-go device, now consigned to the back of her bedside table drawer. Though it hadn't been used for a long time, she knew some of the information held in its memory could prove damaging. She had to make a decision: if she ran back home she could remove the phone from the drawer, hide it on her person, then wipe its memory later. But to take this possibly incriminating device to her place of work, given the current circumstances, could potentially prove even more risky.

She sighed, deciding that the possibility of her flat being searched was now a remote one. It was only extreme caution and a touch of paranoia that had pushed her to excise her old boss from her digital life. Thinking about it, she was sure that Wilson was more preoccupied with the bogus police officer, rather than bothering about a phone she hadn't used in almost a year.

Feeling brighter, she stepped out into the road to continue her walk to work, just as a white van rounded the corner sharply and at speed. The collision sent her body high into the air. Her bag slipped from her grasp, disgorging its contents over the road, as her body landed with a heavy thud on the bonnet of a parked car. Blood streamed from her nose and mouth onto the metallic silver paint. As the red stain began to taint the cascade of her blonde hair, a woman screamed and ran to help, but it was too late.

In the distance, brakes screeched as a white van sped through the early morning traffic.

20

'Sir,' shouted Rainsford, running across the car park. 'Just received this email from Interpol, sir. I thought you would want to see it before you left.'

The printout was three pages long and contained a number of images of varying quality. Daley quickly read the email.

We have provisionally identified the image you sent us as that of Pavel Abdic, originally from Serbia. Via the Bosnian army, he became a mercenary, serving widely in European and Middle Eastern conflict zones. He was recorded as fighting on the Chechen side of their conflict with Russia, where he was captured by the Russian Armed Forces. In the second Chechen conflict he appeared to switch sides and worked in clandestine ops, with a number of associates, for the Russians.

Since then, we have information that he and a number of others have been involved in the assassination of government officials, senior organised crime members, industrial leaders and members of the public in various parts of the world, including Israel, the USA, Russia, Japan, Australia, Hong Kong. The full list is long.

Needless to say, this man is wanted in a number of countries, and is extremely dangerous.

The identification level at the moment is at 68%.
We are working to improve this figure and a list of main
associates will follow.

Daley looked at images of the man Interpol reckoned had
been in Kinloch the day before. Some of the pictures were
old, but he could definitely see the resemblance to the CCTV
footage. But what would a man like that be doing in Kinloch?
Why would anyone pay for a professional assassin to come
here and kill drug dealers who, despite the police's best efforts,
were ten a penny? More questions he had no answer to.

'Get a hold of Alice Taylor,' he said to Rainsford. 'But do
it quietly. I don't want to alarm her parents. See what she
thinks of these. If there's any more from Interpol, give me a
bell, OK?'

As Daley drove out of the car park, he had the uneasy feeling that no matter how challenging his problems over the last
few days had been, they were only the tip of the iceberg.

The stolen car with the altered number plate stopped in a
lay-by, fringed with trees, beyond which the Atlantic broke
lazily on a rocky beach. The man reached for his phone and
made a call. He spoke briefly, his accent Eastern European.
'Everything has been done as I ordered. I don't care what you
think, it is unimportant. You have done as you were asked. Be
ready in case I need more help.' He hung up.

Daley was relieved, but only slightly. He had managed to
fasten the button of his uniform trousers, but only just. He
marvelled at the fact that though his face was noticeably
thinner, his gut continued to grow. The new tunic, displaying

a Chief Inspector's insignia on his epaulettes, felt entirely foreign. He stood in front of the mirror and placed the hat with its braided visor on his head. The man that looked back at him bore very little resemblance to the young cop who had first put on a uniform more than a quarter of a century before. The clothes had changed almost as much as his body; he longed for the days of the old tunic jacket, which would have covered some of the bulges now on display through the tight T-shirt that now passed for the top half of his uniform.

He looked at his watch and sighed; he had twenty minutes to get to the County and meet the Minister. He was surprised by a knock at the door.

'Good afternoon, sir,' said Layton. He was tall, thin and looked unnaturally grey. 'I know we have a luncheon to attend, but I need to speak with you, and this would appear to be the perfect opportunity.'

'Come in,' replied Daley, inviting the Inspector into his home. 'If this is the speech about what I can and can't say in front of Elise Fordham, don't worry. I've already had it.'

'No. It's something much more important.' Layton sat down on the sofa opposite Daley. 'What I am about to tell to you is top secret, with all of the usual restrictions and consequences that normally apply.'

'Yes, of course.'

'I know that you have your misgivings about Chief Superintendent Donald. These have been noted and acted upon. I have been seconded from Special Branch to shadow Mr Donald in order to try and ascertain just what, if anything, is going on.'

'Really? I mean, yes,' responded Daley, put off his stride by Layton's directness. 'I'm sure my superior is involved with things he shouldn't be. I assumed it was just political manoeu-vring but I get the feeling now that it's something more.'

'I can't divulge any of our suspicions, or indeed findings, at the moment, DCI Daley. Suffice it to say, our investigations are ongoing.'

Daley remained silent for a few moments, desperately trying to take in what he'd just been told; an internal police investigation was one thing, Special Branch was another beast altogether. 'So why the promotion? He's in charge of a whole district of this new force now; damn near an old-fash-ioned county Chief Constable.'

'I must remind you, officially, that John Donald – at the moment – continues to have the total support of senior officers within the new force. He is a talented executive officer. Unofficially, I don't need to tell you about the art of entrapment, DCI Daley, and of the inherent dangers involved in such an operation. Without going into too much detail, it was felt that, unencumbered by superiors, Donald would be freer to operate in the way he so chose. If his subsequent activity turns out to be felonious, and our suspicions are confirmed, so much the better.' He paused, looking meaningfully at Daley. 'If not, we shut up shop and leave the Chief Super to his stellar career. I know this will be a surprise to you, DCI Daley, but perhaps not a shock. In any event, I know you are aware that ACC Manion is involved in an internal investigation. He is also working alongside us, and so I advise that if you have any questions, they be addressed directly to him.'

Layton was right; he was surprised that this was happen-ing, but not shocked that something was at last being done.

'So what now? Who knows about this operation?'

'Need-to-know basis and very senior executive officers only.'

'Why me? I'm his subordinate, but I'm hardly at the cutting edge of his empire down here in the sticks.'

'It was deemed that you needed to know.'

'Why?'

'I'm afraid this is the last of your questions I'm able to answer. However, I can reveal that we have reason to believe that our suspect's activities are centred in some way on Kinloch. Again, questions that must be asked of ACC Manion.'

Daley was lost for words. He didn't know what shocked him more; the fact that the Chief Superintendent could be up to something criminal in this remote part of Scotland, or hearing him coolly described as a suspect.

'What now? I mean, how do we proceed?'

'As normal. I'll inform you of any changes to the landscape if and when they occur.'

'And how do I know you are who you say you are, and I'm not part of some elaborate entrapment operation?' Years in the police force had taught Daley a healthy scepticism.

'On that point, DCI Daley, you are going to have to trust me. Now, I think it would be prudent to leave. Lunch awaits.'

As Daley raised himself out of his easy chair, he felt even more uncomfortable in his police uniform.

There was a queue at reception when Daley and Layton arrived at the County Hotel. Annie was busy trying to explain the complexities of their stay to a group of bemused Japanese tourists.

'You'll – need – tae – come – wae – me,' she shouted, one word at a time, in the hope that someone would follow her upstairs. Daley waved and smiled at her before being ushered into the dining room by a harassed-looking waitress.

A large table, set to seat twelve at the far end of the long dining room, was empty save for Charlie Murray, a local councillor and former Provost of Kinloch, when such a title existed. He was a large bald man, squeezed into a suit that looked at least two sizes too small. His shirt collar looked likely to decapitate him at any moment. Daley had met him on a number of occasions and quietly admired his direct, no-nonsense approach to local politics.

'How you, Mr Daley,' he said, greeting the policemen. He spoke in a slow Kinloch accent; Daley reckoned that nothing much hurried Charlie Murray.

Daley introduced Layton then settled down to look at the menu. For once in his life, his appetite felt diminished. The shock of Layton's revelations was still reverberating through his mind. He'd suspected something wasn't right for a long time – after Scott's shooting, and the note he'd left Daley outlining Donald's clandestine order to free MacDougall, he had made his fears known to certain individuals within the force who would, he reasoned, be capable of doing something about the problem. This had been more in hope than expectation; he had no direct evidence apart from his own gut instinct, certainly not enough to initiate a disciplinary action against a senior officer. When Donald had been promoted to commander of the new force district, he'd feared his warnings had fallen on deaf ears. Now that he knew Donald to be under official investigation he felt a strange disconnection.

What if he had been wrong? What if Donald was a perfectly honest cop who, apart from his appalling manner and venal attitude towards his subordinates, was about to be brought low by nothing other than idle speculation and personal prejudice? He tried not to think about it, and settled down to focus on the lunch instead.

'Jeest like this crowd to be late,' Murray observed. 'Government? They canna spell the word.' It was clear that Elise Fordham and Charlie Murray were on opposite sides of the political debate. 'There's things happening in this toon that no right-thinking person should tolerate. We're a dumping ground for a' the shit o' the day. Aye, jeest send them doon tae Kinloch, oot the road – that's the attitude, without a doubt.'

'You'll understand that I can't make political comments, Charlie,' said Daley, sipping at the soda water and lime he had just been handed. 'Off the record though, you have my sympathies.'

'Ach, I know fine whoot position you're in, Mr Daley. Awkward, right enough. The whole toon admires how you've stuck tae your task since you came here. You'll know whoot they're callin' you, no doubt?'

'What?' asked Daley, not sure if he really wanted to know.

'Wyatt Earp,' Murray answered with a smile. 'Fuck me, you would need tae be, whoot wae a' that's been going on here. Folk butchered in their ain hooses, an' settin' themselves on fire. D'you know, that kind o' thing would have been unimaginable jeest a few years ago. I didna start locking my ain front door until 1994, an' that's a fact.'

'Again, as you know, Charlie, I can't say anything about these incidents, apart from that investigations are ongoing.'

'Aye, jeest so, Mr Daley, an' you're the very man tae get tae the bottom o' it all.' He paused to take a large gulp of beer. 'Better get this doon me before that nippy sweetie arrives. No doubt we'll have tae suffer some shitty wine along with her patter. No' weather for wine, this. As soon as I take wan swallow o' the stuff the sweat will pure lash off me.'

At that, a couple of other guests arrived – one of the local ministers, and the owner of a construction company. 'Hello, Reverend McMichael, how are you doin'?' shouted Murray, in his booming voice. 'If you've got your beer goggles on the day, you'll be disappointed – nothing but empty rhetoric for lunch. Aye, I needna ask if you've got the beer goggles on, eh, William,' he said to the thickset businessman, who gave him an embarrassed smile. 'You're like your grandfaither. I mind him oot wae the horse and cart, aye, an' a fine swally he had, tae.'

There was a flurry of activity at the dining-room door as Elise Fordham and her party made their way into the room.

'Gentlemen,' Fordham said, smiling at them all. 'Please take a seat. No need for formalities around me. How are you all?'

'Aye, jeest fine,' replied Murray, who pointedly hadn't stood to greet Fordham. 'I'm fair starving, tae. It's high time I got something back fae a' that money I've handed oot in taxes o'er the last fifty years.'

As Fordham shook hands and introduced herself to everyone, Gary Wilson smiled at Daley. 'Well, well, James Daley, formerly of Glasgow's finest. How are you? Are they only making uniforms in the one size now?' he said, smiling at Daley, who automatically pulled in his stomach.

'Nice to see you again,' Daley lied. 'It's always great to see someone doing better for themselves after such a difficult start in life. From the gutter press to the corridors of power, no less.'

'*Touché*, Chief Inspector.'

'I hear you're staying with us the night,' Murray said to Fordham. 'Probably jeest as well.'

'Why's that?'

'A' this hysteria, folk deid in the street, not tae mention the UFOs. Ach, I'm sure a woman wae her ear tae the groon like you has it a' taped, digested, an' ready wae a' the answers.' Murray smiled wickedly.

'Well, yes, of course, yes,' said Fordham, looking less than confident. She was about to embark on her default speech about Kinloch, when Murray interrupted.

'Aye, good stuff. When I organised the public meeting for tonight, I couldna foresee that someone as senior as yoursel' would be able tae attend. The folk o' Kinloch will be fair chuffed. Lots o' things, including the fate o' the nation, tae discuss. A rare privilege for us oot here in the sticks, right enough. Votes galore in it, I shouldna wonder.'

'Oh well, I'm sure I can say a few words,' replied Fordham. She was long enough in the tooth to know when an unavoid-able political trap had been sprung. 'It'll be my pleasure to meet the good folk of Kinloch.'

'Excellent,' replied Murray. 'Noo, whoot's for dinner?'

'Don't you mean lunch?' said Wilson, glaring at the councillor.

'No, I mean dinner. When you're in Kinloch, dae whoot the Kinloch folk dae. At this time o' day, we have oor dinner.'

Daley smiled to himself, as Gary Wilson and Elise Fordham exchanged a brief, anxious glance.

'Noo, have yous a' seen the menu?' asked Annie, ready her

with her pad and pen. 'Jeest tae let you know, the lasagne's off, an' the roast beef is roast pork the day, doon tae the fact that wee Alistair at the butcher had some fine cuts goin' at a great price. If any o' you are vegetarian, it'll be the macaroni cheese, or salad wae a boiled onion.'

After sitting in his tight trousers for well over an hour, Daley was relieved when the meal ended and he was able to get up from the table. On the whole, it had been a reasonably light affair; four other local bigwigs had arrived, including a stick-thin woman from the Chamber of Commerce who proceeded to eat more quickly than Daley thought humanly possible, and consume wine at such a rate that she was well into her second bottle when the Minister stood to take her leave. The caustic Murray commented that she probably only got fed and watered at official functions, hence her physique. 'Aye, she only gets oot once a year. Her man's the maist stingy bugger you're ever likely tae meet. Poor lassie's starved, by the looks o' things.'

Daley and Layton made their excuses to those still around the table and left. As he was passing, Daley stopped to speak to Annie, less frazzled now the Japanese tourists had departed.

'You've your hands full today, Annie.'

'Aye. Mind you, great tae see the place buzzin'. It's a' this nice weather. No' a toon as pretty as Kinloch when the sun's oot, Mr Daley.'

'Absolutely. Anyway, I better get back to the grind.'

'Oh, before you go. Who will I make the Taylors' bill oot tae?'

'Oh, just to me care of Kinloch Police Office, Annie. That should be fine. I'll get it processed and the money to you as soon as possible.' Daley smiled. 'How are they getting on, anyway?' He hadn't seen any sign of the uniformed cop who'd been assigned to the hotel for their protection, so assumed that he was upstairs in the corridor outside the Taylors' room.

'They left this morning,' replied Annie. 'Jeest as well, whoot wae all these Japanese appearing all o' a sudden.'

Daley stopped in his tracks. 'Have they gone home?'

'No, I don't think so. Mr Taylor said something aboot taking advantage o' the kind offer an' making the best o' whoot o' their holiday was left tae them. They've gone tae a wee cottage doon on the Weirside Road. I thought you would have known aboot it. I'm sure Mr Taylor said that it was the polis who'd organised it.'

'Where is this cottage, Annie?' asked Daley. He turned to look at Layton, concern etched across his face.

21

'That was a nightmare,' said Fordham, sinking back into her seat in the large hired car. 'Bloody public meeting. Bastard!' She shook her head as they drove the short distance to view where Walter Cudihey had set himself on fire. 'Fucking UFOs. I mean, come on. Looks like you were dead right about this bloody place, Gary. Gary?' Caught up in her own thoughts, she hadn't noticed that Wilson, sitting in the passenger seat in front of her, was on his phone.

'I see. Yes. Keep me informed,' he said, then ended the call. 'Fuck.'

'What's wrong now?'

'Not good, not good at all. Kirsteen Lang's been killed in a road accident.'

'Really? I mean, well, I don't know what to say. Poor girl.'

'Yes, poor girl, indeed.' Wilson's eyes were blazing. 'I'm an old hand at this game, Elise. I've seen a lot – enough shit and dirty tricks to last me a lifetime, and the only way I've survived is by listening to that little voice in my head telling me that something is very wrong and to get my arse out the door as quickly as fucking possible, before all the shit or whatever it is lands on my front step.' He looked angry and exhausted at the same time.

'And don't tell me, you're hearing that voice now?'

'Hearing it? It's bloody deafening. What the fuck's going on, Elise?'

'I wish I knew,' she replied. 'I really do. Couldn't it just be an accident?'

'Aye, and natural coincidences are as rare as altruistic politicians,' said Wilson.

'We can talk about this later, OK?' Fordham nodded towards the back of their driver's head.

'Whatever you say, Minister.' He shook his head and turned his weary gaze to the loch where Walter Cudihey had killed himself.

Daley burst into the CID room at Kinloch Police Office. He had tried to raise Donald on his mobile on the way up from the hotel, but the call had gone straight to voicemail.

'DC Maxwell, I want you to find out anything you can about who booked the cottage for the Taylor family yesterday. You, you and you,' he said, pointing to three detectives, 'draw firearms. Now!'

In a few minutes, thanks to Sergeant Shaw's willingness as duty officer to overlook much of the procedure when handing out weapons, the four policemen bundled into a car and headed for the cottage on Weirside Road. Although he couldn't picture the property, Annie had told him how to get there and that, since it was the only dwelling at the end of a stretch of rocky beach, he would be unlikely to miss it.

They sped out of the yard and down Main Street, lights flashing and sirens wailing. Though the cottage was less than three miles out of Kinloch, Daley still worried that he would be too late. Soon, the buildings thinned out, and they sped along a narrow road with the sea sparkling to their left under a clear blue sky. On passing Hamish's home, which faced the island at the head of the loch, the road turned sharply right. Looking into the distance, Daley could see a small cottage on the shore under a looming hill.

'That's it over there,' he shouted to the driver, who nodded. It was so close to the town, yet utterly secluded. Daley could see figures outside the dwelling as the police car sped along the single track road, then onto a dirt path. Mr and Mrs Taylor were standing by two deck chairs, looking surprised by the dramatic arrival of the police car.

'Alice – where is she?' shouted Daley, not bothering with formalities.

'Oh,' answered Stephen Taylor, holding a mug. 'She's about somewhere, beachcombing, I shouldn't wonder. Is there a problem?'

'Which way did she go?'

'Down there, behind the cottage,' Taylor answered. He and his wife were beginning to look alarmed. 'She took a rucksack with water and some sandwiches. Just what is going on?'

'Quick, come with me.' Daley grabbed Stephen Taylor by the arm, forcing him to drop the mug, spilling tea across the coarse machair grass. 'Show me where she went.'

They stumbled along the rocky beach. Boulders of varying size and shape made haste impossible. To their left, the sea hissed as waves broke on the rough shore. The glare on the water was bright and Daley squinted along the stretch of beach as he picked his way between the rocks as quickly as possible.

'I'm really worried now,' said Taylor. 'You arrive with

sirens blaring and all of these questions. Please, tell me, what's going on?'

About three hundred yards down the beach, Daley spotted a car parked at the end of a rough track. 'Quick, see if anyone's about who might have seen her!' he shouted to his men.

As they approached, it became obvious that the vehicle, an old Ford Mondeo, was empty. Daley climbed up from the shore and onto the track. He tried the door, surprised when it opened. Inside, the car seemed devoid of any signs of use. The ashtray was empty, as were all of the little compartments on the door and between the front seats. As a detective checked under the back seats, Daley pulled open the glove box to find it empty as well. He ran his eyes over the dashboard, and noted a boot release sign by the steering column, which he pulled. Walking to the back of the car, he popped the lid; only a spare tyre and a heavy wrench were visible. He pulled aside the plastic matting that lined the boot, which revealed nothing more.

As he slammed the lid shut, a call made him look up. Further down the beach, DC Maxwell was holding something up.

'Oh,' said Taylor, a look of panic on his face. 'That's Alice's rucksack.'

As Daley stumbled back onto the beach he saw Maxwell pull a plastic box from the bag. When Taylor reached the young detective, he grabbed the bag and looked inside.

'Her sandwiches and water.' The policemen looked on as he unzipped a small compartment on the front of the rucksack. 'Her phone. Alice would never leave her phone. I only bought it for her yesterday to replace the one she lost when the boat sank.' Taylor looked at Daley in panic.

Daley thought for a moment. The car was completely empty, not even a discarded sweet paper or empty plastic bottle to be seen. The only sign that anyone had been in the vehicle was a patch of muddy sand in the footwell under the steering wheel, and a strong smell, reminiscent of fish. Daley looked out to sea; in the distance a small boat was rounding the point.

Daley picked up his phone. 'Sergeant Shaw, get me the coastguard. Tell them to call me on this number, now!'

'Why are we here?' asked Wilson. He and Elise Fordham were walking along a stretch of deserted beach a few miles from Kinloch. The Minister had instructed her security detail to follow them at a discreet distance, well out of earshot. They'd paid their respects to Walter Cudihey by laying flowers near the fire-ravaged section of the pontoons. To Fordham's surprise, a journalist from the local paper had been there; this visit was supposed to be of the kind that people heard about after the event – a personal tribute rather than another photo opportunity. However, she had done her best to look grief-stricken as she laid flowers by the charred decking.

'You're going to have to trust me on this,' said Elise. 'We had some problems with Walter Cudihey – that's all I can say at the moment.'

'What kind of problems?'

'I can't give you details, but let's just say he wasn't happy with certain environmental policies we were pursuing.'

'Right,' replied Wilson. 'So, I'm to believe that because this clown felt so strongly about when the bins get emptied, or what he should or shouldn't recycle, he decides to turn himself into the Olympic torch and his trusty assistant gets half a ton of van on her head?'

'I don't know. It wasn't about bins, anyway, and we don't know if what happened to Kirsteen Lang this morning was anything other than an accident. Tragic, but an accident all the same. Cudihey and I had a full and frank discussion about something a few days before he . . . well, he did what he did.'

'OK. So what was the subject of this discussion?' Wilson indicated quotation marks with both hands.

'I can't tell you. It's a very . . . Come on, Gary, you know the score here.'

'Don't give me that political bollocks! One dead civil servant is regrettable, two – from the same department, in a matter of days – could become political dynamite, and you know it.'

'Right, Gary. I hear you. All I can say is that I want you to give me a couple of days on this, then – if things get shitty with the press – we'll talk again. You must understand, I'd have to get clearance from the top to be able to tell you anything.'

'What do you mean, if things get shitty with the press? They already fucking are! The tabloid boys were onto this little accident within an hour of it happening. Because Kirsteen Lang was on secondment, they haven't made the connection between her and Cudihey yet. But they will, have no doubt about it.'

'I'll have to think,' said Fordham, biting her lip. 'Fuck. This is the last thing we need at this sensitive time.'

'Aye, I'm sure. Well, trust me, it's about to get a damn sight more sensitive. And I'm in the firing line here. I'm the one who'll have to answer all the bloody questions and I don't know the first thing about it!'

'I know you, Gary. You can spin this until we decide what to do.' She nudged him in the ribs, forcing a smile.

'Enough of the doe-eyed shit!' he shouted, his face turning a shade of crimson. 'That might work with some sweaty old MSP with bad breath and a libido that won't lie down, but it won't work with me. This is serious – we still don't know who interviewed Lang about Cudihey. Do we? Oh, fuck off!' Wilson turned on his heel and stormed off down the beach.

Daley took the call from the coastguard on his mobile, giving details of the location and a quick explanation of the circumstances. The efficient woman on the other end said she would call him back when they'd taken action. It was a long shot, but he wanted the fishing boat he had just seen stopped.

'You think my daughter has been abducted!' Taylor shouted. 'Why? We're not even from this bloody place. Why do you suspect this? Surely we've been through enough.'

'I'll be straight with you, Mr Taylor,' answered Daley. 'Your daughter identified a man on the boat that hit you. My early investigations point to the fact that this man is highly dangerous.'

'You mean . . . Oh God.' Taylor's eyes widened in sudden realisation.

Daley's phone rang. 'Yes, I understand,' he replied in answer to the person on the other end. 'Thank you. Please keep me informed.'

'What was that? What action are you taking to save my daughter, Mr Daley?'

'The coastguard have directed a naval vessel in the area to intercept the fishing boat we saw.'

'You think my daughter has been taken onto a fishing boat?'

Just as Daley was about to answer, one of his detectives called over. 'Look, sir. Over there, by the trees.'

Daley followed his colleague's line of sight. Sure enough, emerging from the copse of trees on the hill beyond the beach, a figure could be seen walking towards them.

'Alice. It's Alice!' shouted Taylor, stumbling over the boulders towards his daughter. Daley and the other police officers followed.

'What's happening?' Alice managed to ask, just before her father enveloped her in a tight embrace, tears of relief flooding down his face. 'I thought I saw a hoopoe. I followed it into the trees, but I lost it,' she said, her voice muffled by her father's hug.

High on the hill above, the man looked down through the sight of his rifle. He could take a shot, but the distance and elevation made it difficult, and there were too many bodies in the way. He shifted his sight from one face to another; through it, he could make out the individuals quite easily. The girl was entwined in her father's arms, surrounded by a group of men. He stopped at the man in the ill-fitting police uniform. He was tall, with dark hair. Unlike the rest, he was looking about, taking in the scene. The man's finger curled round the rifle's trigger.

22

Brian Scott was sitting in Daley's glass box, nursing the mother of all hangovers. They had made it back into port just before six in the morning. Having consumed a great deal of whisky on the boat trip he had absolutely no idea how – or when – he had made it back to the County Hotel. Fortunately, he'd had the presence of mind to set his alarm before they left, so at two o'clock he'd been jolted from a restless sleep, with a dry mouth, an aching head and a momentary sense of dislocation that left him wondering just exactly where he was.

He was shaking so badly he had to hold his coffee to his lips with both hands. He remembered being in a pub in Glasgow's East End with his father. He must have been fifteen or so; the pub had been filled with football supporters getting ready to go to an Old Firm game. Amidst the singing, scarves and high spirits sat a man who looked impossibly old, the wrinkled skin on his face providing the backdrop for two rheumy yellow eyes, bloodshot and sad, which stared out at the world above a bulbous nose, itself a spectacular shade of purple. The young Scott had watched as the man, with visibly trembling hands, tied his blue-and-white scarf to his right wrist, then looped it around the back of his neck. He gripped his pint glass, brimful of beer, and pulled on the scarf with his other hand, to slowly winch the glass to his mouth without – much – spillage. The ragged cheer from the men elicited a mirthless smile from the old man, as he reversed the process and gently laid his glass back onto the bar. Scott had looked on, mesmerised, as the man's hand, now at his side, shook as though he had just lifted a heavy weight, or been shocked in some way.

'I see you watching auld Jockie,' his father had said, wiping pint froth from his lips with the back of his hand. 'What age dae you think he is?'

Scott shrugged his shoulders. 'I don't know – a hundred?'

'Nah,' his father replied, cuffing his ear playfully. 'Your man there is a year younger than me – he's forty-eight.'

Though the complex nature of the aging process and its subtleties of perspective were unknown to the teenager, the man in front of him looked at least twice that age. He had looked at his father in disbelief.

'I'm telling you, son, it's the truth. The bevy can be a good friend tae you, but by fuck, it doesnae half make for a bad gaffer.'

All these years later, as Scott looked at his reflection in the glass of Daley's office, he saw that man again. He was forty-nine; right now he looked a decade older. These days, he spent all his time waiting for the moment he could place a glass to his lips and feel the warm embrace of alcohol set him free from his gnawing anxiety. His nose wasn't purple – yet – but at the memory of his father sitting beside him, all those years ago, a tear slid down his cheek.

He was jolted back to some kind of reality when the phone in front of him burst into life.

'Cornton Vale on the line for you,' said Shaw. 'They have a message from a Miss MacDougall, currently residing there. It's for the boss, but I thought you might want to take it since he's not here.'

'Aye, put them on.' He hadn't forgotten the promise he'd made to Frank MacDougall, as his old neighbour's life had drained away into the sand. He felt a pang of sorrow as he thought about Frank's daughter, that bright young girl, consigned to Scotland's only women's prison for the next few years. He took the call.

He caressed the trigger, waiting for the moment he could gently squeeze and release it. The large man in the police uniform was talking on his mobile phone now. He ranged the sight to his left; there she was, the girl, her father holding her at arm's length, saying something to her. He inched his shoulder forward in readiness for the recoil that the powerful weapon would impart. He aimed at her head, just above her right ear; wounding wouldn't do, he had to be sure of a kill.

He squeezed the trigger to just before its firing point, the moment between life and death. He took a deep breath, which he wouldn't exhale until the job was done, a bullet lodged in the girl's shattered skull. He shuddered, as the phone in his trouser pocket vibrated, easing his finger from the trigger and forcing his eye from the sight.

'What?' he spat into the device, then listened for a few moments. 'You have failed me again. This failure will be your last, unless you make sure that this problem goes away. If I have to abandon my mission, your life will be worth nothing.' He ended the call and stared down at the distant group of people, this time without magnification. They were making their way along the beach, back towards the cottage.

Daley entered the office like a hurricane. 'Where's Superintendent Donald?' he roared, as he thundered down the corridor towards the CID Suite.

Scott jumped out of his seat as Daley strode into his glass box, sending papers and a small silver quaich flying from the top of a filing cabinet as he slammed the door open against it. 'Jim, what's happening?'

'Bad stuff, Brian. Very bad stuff,' replied Daley. He picked up the phone from his desk and pressed two buttons. He hesitated for a moment or two then flung the receiver onto his desk when his call remained unanswered. 'Get me Inspector Layton, someone,' he shouted into the office, the tone of his voice sending a couple of detectives hurrying to do his bidding.

'Sit doon, man,' Scott implored. 'You'll gie yourself a heart attack.' Daley's face was beetroot red and a thick vein bulged on his temple. For a moment, Scott feared that Daley's anger was targeted at him, but realised this wasn't the case as Daley let loose a volley of expletives directed at John Donald.

Briefly, Daley told Scott his suspicions about their boss's behaviour, many of which Scott shared, but he was careful to leave out Layton's revelations as to the clandestine investigation into Donald's suspected activities, as well as Manion's place in it all.

'So you think he's at it,' said Scott. 'What aboot the car you found on the beach?'

'Registered to a guy in Motherwell who died three months ago, Brian. Clean enough not to attract any suspicion, initially anyway. I've got the forensics boys onto it, though I doubt they'll find anything.'

'Why not? Have some faith, Jim. Fuck knows, half the time that's a' we've got tae hold ontae.'

'No, Brian, that kind of faith's not enough here. These murders . . . they're professional. I bet any money that car's as clean as a whistle.' Daley sat back in his chair and raised his eyes to the heavens. He knew that, yet again, Alice Taylor had been lucky to escape with her life. The real question was, why had she been placed in such danger? Donald couldn't have known of his suspicions about the men that had sunk the Taylors' yacht, that one of them might be one of Europe's most dangerous criminals; nor could he have known that it was almost certain their dinghy had been sunk by a sniper's bullet. Or could he?

'Why did that bastard move the Taylors, Brian? He looked like death earlier. Why go to all the trouble of finding a cottage for them?'

'That's a hard one, Jim. What does this Taylor guy do? He's big time, isn't he? Pound tae a penny, the gaffer will have done his best tae put oot the red carpet. It might not be what you think.'

'No,' replied Daley, staring into space, deep in thought. 'He owns some kind of engineering company, I think.'

'There you are then. QED. Donald gets one whiff that this guy Taylor's worth a few bob, an' reckons he'll add tae his long list o' impressed acquaintances by puttin' him an' his family up in a nice wee cottage at the taxpayers' expense, while he kicks his heels waiting for us an' the marine accident boys tae dae our stuff. You must admit, that's no' exactly oot o' character.'

'You're right. Even if there is something in this, all he has to say is that his concern was for the wellbeing of the family after their ordeal. Fuck!'

'You know yoursel', big man, you need tae be up damn early in the morning tae catch that bastard.'

After a sharp knock at the door, Layton appeared. 'DCI Daley, you wanted me?'

'Yes. I need to talk to you, urgently. Brian, could you give us a few moments?'

'Would it be in order to talk with you in Superintendent Donald's office?' Layton asked. 'I too have something I'd like to draw your attention to. Much easier in there.'

'Yes, of course, I'll be with you in a few minutes. No sign of Superintendent Donald, I take it?'

'No, still in his sickbed, I suspect,' said Layton, closing the door carefully behind him as he left Daley's office.

'I'm missing something here, Jim. What's happening?' asked Scott.

'Listen, Brian, I can't tell you everything – well, not now, at least. You'll have to trust me on this for the time being.'

'Whatever you say, big man.' Scott stared blankly at the desk in front of him.

Daley knew that his friend's nose was now out of joint. In normal circumstances the pair had no secrets, personally or professionally; it was the way they had always done things. But Scott had been absent for a long time, and Daley knew how fragile he still was. Not to mention his drinking which, looking at his colleague's bloodshot eyes across the desk, was still a problem.

'Oh, aye, another thing tae add tae your woes,' said Scott, attempting a conversational tone without much success. 'I had Cornton Vale on the blower a wee while ago. Sarah MacDougall wants tae see you, in person. That's all they would say.'

'Really? Wonder what that's about.'

'No' for a wee catch-up, I wouldnae think.'

'Brian.' Daley leaned across his desk. 'Listen, I need you back, but I need you straight. You know what I mean.' He looked the detective sergeant directly in the eye. 'The drink, you're going to have to knock it on the head.'

'I know. I know fine, Jim,' said Scott. 'It's been hard, you know. I mean, being shot, it just kinda knocks the stuffing out o' you. Aye, literally.' He managed a weak smile.

'Give me a while. Honestly, I'll tell you everything,' said Daley, getting up from his chair. 'If I have to go and see Sarah MacDougall tomorrow, it'll take up most of the bloody day. I'll need you to cover for me. Properly, you understand?'

'I will, Jim. You know I won't let you down, big man.'

'Good. I'm afraid that your light duties are about to become heavy ones.'

'Fuck, have they ever been any other way? Oh, see when you come back fae Layton, I need tae talk tae you.'

'What about, Brian?'

'Lights in the sky, Jim. Lights in the sky.'

23

Superintendent Donnie McClusky flung the car door open and rushed up the spiral staircase to the third floor, followed by three colleagues. They were in luck; the door to the flat was still intact. He looked on as the well-built constable used the steel ram to batter down the door, then burst through, into a neat hallway with a red carpet and plain white walls, adorned here and there by trendy posters and small prints. McClusky was relieved; it looked as though nothing had been disturbed. They were the first on the scene.

The flat was comprised of one bedroom, a small kitchenette with a round table, shower room with toilet and sink, and a lounge. One large sofa and an easy chair sat at right angles to each other facing a large television. Everything was neat and tidy, there was no clutter and the whole apartment smelled fresh, the scent emanating from plug-in air fresheners in the hall and bedroom.

'Right, I'll take the bedroom, Constable Stewart, the lounge. I want one of you on the door while the other checks the kitchen, cupboards and bathroom. Anything that resembles an electronic device with a memory has to be removed. And any documents, photographs, scribbles, any bloody thing. Time is of the essence, so get going!'

McClusky had searched many properties in his thirty years in the police force; he'd looked for people, stolen goods, firearms, drugs – just about any conceivable thing. This case was different, though. Wilson's call had been unspecific. All he knew was that they were looking for evidence either written or stored electronically. His job was to remove it.

At first glance, there didn't appear to be anything in the tidy bedroom. A small double bed was covered with a brightly patterned quilt and pillow set. On one side of the brass headboard hung a trilby hat with a feather in it; on the wall above hung a framed photograph of a pretty young woman with long blonde hair, standing on a beach in front of a stunningly blue sea. She was wearing a yellow bikini, which highlighted her tanned skin. The woman was Kirsteen Lang. He felt a pang of regret that such a young, vibrant and beautiful woman had lost her life. He forced this thought to the back of his mind, where it took up residence with the ghosts of so many others. He looked behind the picture, then dismantled the frame, which contained nothing apart from the photograph itself.

Next, he walked over to the wardrobe. The rail bowed in the middle with the weight of the clothes that hung there. Dresses, coats, jackets, jumpers and shirts were crammed in, dangling from hangers of various descriptions. He decided to leave the job of searching pockets and collars to one of his junior colleagues. In any case, he reckoned that a search of Miss Lang's clothing would elicit little of interest. He rifled through a chest of drawers, finding underwear, T-shirts, jumpers, socks, hankies – nothing out of the ordinary. The drawers were lined with paper which he lifted, but there was nothing to be found underneath.

All that was left in the room was a bedside cabinet, short and square, with a cupboard and one narrow drawer. In the cupboard he found a box of photos, an old diary and a jewellery box, which contained an array of bangles, rings, necklaces and earrings in gold and silver. He was just about to open the drawer when his foot caught on something on the floor. Underneath the bed, just poking out, was the edge of a laptop. He smiled. Not a very inspired hiding place, if hidden it was. He threw it on the bed, and turned his attention to the drawer of the bedside cabinet.

Inside was an assortment of things: a watch, the time stuck at five past ten, some pens, an erotic paperback novel, a tube of lubrication jelly and a vibrator. He took everything out and felt around the inside of the drawer but, finding nothing, replaced the items. When he tried to shut the drawer, it jammed, so he rearranged everything and tried again, but the drawer refused to close properly. He removed it again. Then two things happened at once: his eye alighted on a dark object that had been hidden right at the back of the drawer, and he became aware of raised voices outside the room and the sounds of a scuffle. Instinctively, he lifted the black smartphone from its hiding place and slid it into his trouser pocket just as the door opened and three men in dark suits forced their way into the small bedroom.

'Put everything back where you left it, please, sir,' ordered a middle-aged man with swept-back grey hair, a goatee beard and an English accent.

'Indeed I will not,' replied the superintendent. 'I'm here on parliamentary, as well as Police Scotland, business. Just who the fuck do you think you are?'

'I'm from MI5, the other officers here are from SIS. We

have taken possession of this locus, as is our right on the basis of national security. I want your men to replace everything they have moved in the property and leave, as quickly as possible.' McClusky was about to reply decisively in the negative when a familiar head popped around the bedroom door.

'Please comply with these gentlemen, Donnie. Whatever's been moved or bagged, put it back where it was.' As quickly as he had appeared, the new Chief Constable of Police Scotland disappeared out of the door. McClusky, not taking his eyes from the dark-suited man with the goatee, straightened up and dropped the drawer on the bedroom floor.

'Oops. I'm afraid I haven't got any time for spooks,' he said.

'I don't give a fuck, mate,' replied the MI5 officer. 'I'm not going to be picking it up.'

As McClusky left the flat with his police colleagues, he put his hand in his pocket and felt the smartphone. He had something to show Wilson; he just hoped it would be of some use.

'Well, what happened?' Wilson demanded, when McClusky called him later.

'Not good, Gary. About ten minutes after we got there our friends from the south arrived with Lamont. My hands were tied. They took the lot.' He paused, waiting for Wilson to answer, but nothing came. 'I have got one piece of good news, though.'

'Good news? What the fuck's that.' Wilson had been trying desperately to work out what was going on. The original interview of Kirsteen Lang by the bogus detective bore all the hallmarks of secret service involvement, but what were they after?

'I managed to smuggle a smartphone out of the room. One of our IT guys had a look at it.'

'And? For fuck's sake, Donnie, this is not the midnight fucking movie, tell me what the fuck is going on!'

'Och, the usual stuff, selfies, emails, social media, all of which we're going through. One thing stood out, though. An email from Cudihey.'

'Yes, and what?'

'I'm sending it to your phone, have a look for yourself.' A second later, Wilson's phone chirruped to tell him he'd received an email.

From: Walter Cudihey
To: K G Lang
Subject: NKV Dynamics 6628232373

Wilson read the message three times. He recognised the name, but the number was a mystery.

'So what do you think, Donnie?'

'The name belongs to a company registered in Luxembourg who manufacture wave energy appliances. As for the number, well, it could be an invoice, or an international phone number. We're still digging.'

'Good work. At least we have something to connect this to. Could just be work-related, though. You'll need to dig further with this. I've been delayed in this fucking tip overnight,' said Wilson ruefully.

'Why so?'

'Don't fucking ask. I'll give you one piece of advice – never get involved with parliament, or worse still, politicians.'

'Don't worry,' said McClusky. 'We'll have to be quick, though. Whatever we have, likely the spooks have it too. They've got her laptop and tablet, as well as all her personal papers. It won't take them long to sift through everything.'

'I don't care what you have to do, or how you have to do it, work this problem for me, Donnie, and I'll make sure you'll get your reward.' Wilson knew where he'd heard about NKV Dynamics recently; it had been at a party fundraiser in a posh Glasgow hotel. The speaker had been impressive, well-briefed, entertaining and moved amongst the corporate hosts with a confidence that he greatly admired. That speaker's name was Elise Fordham.

Daley was in Scott's room at the County Hotel. Despite being clean and tidy – obviously attended to by the hotel staff – the place stank of stale booze. He was staring at the television while Scott busied himself in the bathroom, from which issued a tuneless whistle punctuated by splashing and expletives.

Everything was impenetrable; nothing seemed to tie up. If the man on the boat that had sunk the Taylor family was who Interpol thought him to be, there could be no doubt that he faced one of the greatest challenges of his career. Certainly, the level of sadistic violence displayed in the two murders he was investigating was absolutely consistent with the kind of horror this man was famous for, but why here, why Kinloch? What on earth would bring one of Europe's most wanted men to this little town?

The warm breeze through the open window made the

stained net curtains billow into the room. He could hear the patter of smokers, customers from Annie's bar, standing at the hotel's front entrance, momentarily expelled from the enjoyment of one habit in pursuit of another.

Tomorrow he would make the long drive out of Kinloch to visit Sarah MacDougall in prison. He wondered how the young woman was coping with life behind bars. Ironically, she had found herself incarcerated only a few miles from the upmarket private school where she had been educated. She had lost her brothers and father in tragic circumstances, while her mother was now being cared for in a nursing home, her mind ruined by vascular dementia. Only the most resolute of individuals would be able to cope with such hardship. He hoped Sarah was one of them.

His thoughts turned to Liz and their child. Ever since he had submitted the DNA test, he had found himself thinking of the baby as his. He resolved to pay Liz a visit in their Howwood home, before he returned to Kinloch. Tomorrow promised to be an interesting, if arduous, day.

'Did I tell you that Rainsford thinks he knows what the line on Cudihey's map is?

'No, what?' shouted Scott.

'Some kind of undersea communications cable. He's looking into it now, though trying to get anywhere without crossing our friends at the MOD seems a difficult task.' Daley rubbed at his chin, trying to figure out how everything fitted together. Now that the MOD and Special Branch were hovering on the periphery of the investigation, anything was possible.

'Noo there we are,' said Scott, bounding from the bathroom, replete in white shirt, dark suit and polished shoes. 'I don't want tae be oot o' place at this meeting. It's no' often the likes o' me get tae rub shoulders wae government ministers.'

Daley smiled. For some reason, his DS seemed inordinately impressed that he was about to meet Fordham at the public meeting in the town's large George Hall. After tales of his experience with UFOs the previous evening, Daley felt it important that he relate them to Fordham in person. While Daley was no believer in the supernatural, it was undeniable that Scott and his companions, plus many other sincere Kinloch citizens, had seen something in the sky. The question was: what? The old airbase, now decommissioned, had been used to test military aircraft in the past, but since the RAF and USAF had abandoned it, he had been assured that it was only used for civilian purposes, including the local air service to and from Glasgow.

'She's a wee cracker, tae,' said Scott, knotting his red tie in the wardrobe mirror, anticipating his meeting with Fordham. 'I wouldnae mind a close encounter wae her, any night o' the week.'

'You've got the wrong colour tie on if you're trying to impress her.'

'Eh?'

'Should have worn a yellow one, or tartan, maybe.' Daley realised Scott's interest in politics only extended to wondering how much booze and fags would go up in the budget. He was pleased that his friend appeared to have taken his advice and stayed clear of alcohol tonight. Scott was as bright and breezy as Daley had seen him in a long time.

'Right, that's the tie on. Just give me two seconds, and I'll splash on some aftershave.' Scott went into the small bathroom and closed the door behind him.

Daley got up off the bed with a groan. 'Come on, Brian, get a shift on. We're going to be late.'

'Hold your horses, big man.' Scott opened the blue toilet bag on the counter beside the sink. Beside the aftershave, deodorant and toothpaste, an unopened half bottle of vodka called out to him. He closed his eyes and sighed. As he tried to get the top off, he was dismayed to note that his hands were shaking. 'I'll need tae get a scarf o' my ain,' he whispered to himself. He took a deep breath and cracked open the vodka, being sure to disguise the noise with a well-timed cough. He put the bottle to his lips and glugged down a couple of mouthfuls, screwing up his eyes as the spirit burned his throat. Almost gagging as he felt its warmth travel down to his stomach, he quietly screwed the lid back on and replaced the bottle at the back of his toilet bag, from which he removed another bottle containing a jade green liquid. He gargled with the mouthwash, then spat it out and wiped his face with a flannel. Already, the vodka had begun to enliven his senses; the anxious feeling at the pit of his stomach was fading as the quick fix of alcohol did its job.

'Come on, Brian!' Daley shouted.

24

'OK, Elise, tell me again about NKV Dynamics,' said Wilson. His voice was barely above a whisper but it still held a menace that made Fordham squirm. They were sitting in the lounge of their hotel, hastily booked, next door to the George Hall, where the impromptu public meeting, called by locals worried by strange lights in the sky, was about to be held.

'What's to tell, Gary? I take it you've Googled them, so what more do you want me to add?' Fordham replied, smiling at a woman who was staring at her from across the room.

'I know all the public shit, that's easy. What are they all about? What is it the public aren't told? Do you really think I've been involved with politics this long without realising there's always more to it than that? Give me the full story, Elise, not the fucking waffle you feed this lot,' he said, at the same time smiling across the room at the staring woman, who was now whispering into the ear of the man beside her, without taking her eyes off Fordham.

'They're a renewables company, you know that, Gary. They manufacture wind and wave power technology. One of the top players in Europe. We're in partnership with them to exploit our brilliant natural resources. They are also bidding for more contracts around the coast. We're going to turn

Scotland into the greenest, most energy-efficient country on the planet. Did you know that this country could produce all of its electricity from green sources in twenty years if this works out the way we want?'

'I suppose these undersea contraptions are preferable to the monstrous windmills you're throwing up everywhere, but don't fob me off, Elise. When we get back tomorrow, I'm going through this with a fine-tooth comb. I want to know everything there is to know about NKV Dynamics.'

Elise Fordham removed her gaze from the woman across the room, who was now pointing them out to a bemused young waiter. She looked at Wilson levelly.

'What?' he asked.

'I don't know if we're going home tomorrow, Gary. Please don't make a scene,' she said, smiling sweetly.

'I hope you're fucking kidding,' he whispered, finding it more difficult to plaster a grin across his face.

'No, I had a word with the First Minister's Private Secretary. He's considering whether or not we should stay here a bit longer – to take the flak over this UFO stuff. Apparently the press are sending journalists in their droves down here. There's to be news crews from Japan, the States and Bolivia here tonight, apparently.'

'Eh? I'm supposed to brief you on what the press is doing, not the reverse. If you ask me, this is a publicity disaster waiting to happen. We should get as far away from here as we possibly can. I'm going to phone the FM's office.'

'Listen, Gary. I don't need to tell you how unfortunate Cudihey's suicide and Kirsteen Lang's death are for us. This UFO thing is heaven sent. Everybody wants to talk about little green men, and the more they want to do that, the happier I'll be. Now, come on, we need to get into the hall before the hordes descend.' She stood up, smoothed down the front of her skirt and walked across the room, smiling benignly at everyone as she went. Wilson, left sitting on his own, felt more unsettled than at any other time he could remember. He just couldn't work out why.

As Daley and Scott walked through the vestibule and into the large hall, they were impressed to see how busy the place was. Over half of the seats were filled with locals whose murmurings created an excited buzz in the large space.

'I'm thinking this Minister better be up tae speed wae what's going on, or this mob'll eat her for breakfast,' said Scott, waving a greeting to two uniformed constables standing in front of the stage. 'I wonder if she read my report?'

'It was passed to her,' replied Daley. 'Though in my experience of politics, be prepared for their version of events bearing little resemblance to what happened to you on the boat, Brian.'

'How you, Mr Daley,' said a familiar voice from behind the detective.

'Hamish, how are you?'

'When this business is over, I'll be needing a wee word with you, as nae doubt your able assistant here has telt you.'

'Oh fuck,' said Scott. 'Sorry, Jim, I forgot a' aboot it. Your man here's remembered what he forgot. I meant tae tell you earlier.'

'You mean your conversation with Cudihey, Hamish?' asked Daley

'Aye, jeest that. It came tae me in a fit o' inspiration when I was oot on the boat. I'm thinking that they lights in the sky

168

had something tae dae with it, right enough.' He removed the pipe from his pocket, and sucked at it, unlit, as he stared around the room.

'Well, that's something at least,' observed Daley. 'I'll take a statement off you later, as soon as we get out of here.'

'An' how's your heid?' asked Hamish, pointing his pipe at Scott. 'I had a right drooth when I woke up this afternoon. Mind you, nothing like a few drams and an evening sail tae let you know you're alive, an' nae mistake.'

'Aye, well, you did have a few, Hamish,' Scott said, clearing his throat. 'I hope we'll get some kind of explanation fae the politicians tonight,' he added, quickly changing the subject.

'You never know,' said Daley, looking at his DS knowingly. '*Three Men in a Boat*, eh?'

'Four men, Mr Daley. Well, three men an' a boy, right enough.' Hamish smiled.

'Here, we better get a seat before there's none left,' said Scott, walking over to the nearest row of seats.

'Aye, lead on, Mr Scott, lead on.' Hamish followed the detective, leaving Daley stroking his chin. Scott should have told him that Hamish had remembered his conversation with the wretched Cudihey, whether it turned out to be of significance or not. He had hoped that, once back in the swing of things, following the usual routines and procedures, Scott would have toned down his drinking. It was increasingly obvious that this was not the case. Despite the application of mouthwash, Daley had noted the fresh taint of alcohol on his colleague's breath before they left his hotel room. He remembered an old sergeant's words: 'When you start planking the bevy around the house, you know fine you've got a problem.'

It was clear that Brian Scott was keeping booze in his bathroom. Daley let out a sigh and took a seat.

Elise Fordham looked out from a chink in the curtains; the room beyond seemed much more cavernous than it had looked from the outside. Row upon row of seats were filled; it was obvious that the citizens of Kinloch were most anxious to hear what she had to say about the UFO sightings. She was no stranger to public speaking, but even she was surprised by the attendance. She spotted four camera crews setting up their equipment, while beyond, on a balcony at the end of the hall, a spotlight was being focused. Soon its light would fall on her.

A table and four chairs had been arranged on the stage. At least the short notice meant none of her political foes had made it to Kinloch. The stage party was to consist of her, Wilson, Charlie Murray, who would chair, and a man with a ginger moustache, Ian McIntyre, chairman of her party in Kinloch. At least she would have someone local guaranteed to support her; though he seemed nervous, agitatedly fiddling with a row of pens sticking from the breast pocket of his jacket, while pacing up and down the stage.

Murray stalked across the stage towards her. Despite his bulk, he walked easily and looked utterly at home, about to face the large audience. On seeing him approach Fordham, Wilson quickly finished his telephone conversation and hurried to the Minister's side.

'Poor Ian gets himsel' in a wild state before these kind o' events,' observed Murray, looking over to the younger man, who, eyes closed and head raised, appeared to be either trying to memorise something he wanted to say, or offering up a silent prayer. 'I'll dae the introductions, an' outline jeest whoot's been happening in the sky. Then you can say whoot you want.'

'What about Mr McIntyre?' asked Fordham.

'Och, nae doubt he'll have something tae offer, though I canna be sure if it'll be any use or no'. Aye, he's fair excitable, but I thought it was only fair tae have some kind o' political balance on the platform. Especially since you an' me come fae opposite sides o' the debate, so tae speak.' He grinned. 'Ian, come over, son. It's time we got this show on the road. An' if you're needing tae go tae the lavatory, noo's the time. I'll no' need tae remind you o' that embarrassment up in Firdale during the last election campaign. Fuck me, you near shat yoursel'.'

McIntyre visibly jumped, before making his way towards the rest of the group.

'Brilliant,' whispered Wilson into Fordham's ear. 'Our man's a gibbering oaf with loose bowels. Ever felt as though you were being set up?'

'Shut up, Gary,' Fordham hissed. 'I'm sure he'll be fine.'

'Tell that fat bastard I'll handle the Q&A.' Wilson gestured to Murray, who had taken his chair behind the desk and was adjusting a microphone. 'I've been standing in the hall. Lot of bloody press out there, more than you would credit. TV crews, too. Let's see if we can turn this into something positive. Fuck knows, we need to.'

'If this was a straightforward public meeting, one man and his dog would be here. One mention of little green men, and the whole bloody place turns out.'

'Let's be honest, Elise, the thought of visitors from space is a fucking lot more interesting than the dross you lot peddle. Who can blame them?'

'You're a real ray of sunshine, Gary.'

But Wilson had stopped listening, looking at his phone instead. 'My good friend in Police Scotland has just tipped me the wink as to what those numbers mean on the email found on Kirsteen Lang's phone.' He watched Fordham, gauging her response.

'Really, what is it then?'

'They're map coordinates, Ordnance Survey. A point on the coast, not far from here, as it turns out.'

'Oh,' Fordham replied, her expression inscrutable. 'Fancy that.'

Wilson followed her to her seat. Nobody else would have spotted it, but he had. Elise Fordham was frightened.

'Someone always takes the fall. It is the way things are. If you don't want to fall, you stay away from the edge. In this matter, it is quite simple.' The voice on the phone was foreign, yet it was familiar.

'I don't know what you mean. For fuck's sake stop speaking in riddles!' shouted Donald. He was sitting on an old bench looking out over a rocky bay and towards the Atlantic. The sun shone a rich gold onto the slick, dark waves, seeming to transform them into molten metal.

'We placed Daley in Kinloch for a reason. You said he said would clear out those who stood in our way. A proper policeman.' He snorted his derision.

'Yes, and he's done a good job. He's made significant arrests within the illegal narcotics chain; I've reported them to you. He removed the Machie threat, which could have caused you real problems. He's the best detective I've worked with – tenacious, intuitive, smart. You must admit I chose him well.'

'He has done well, apart from one or two exceptions, which we have been forced to clear up ourselves.' The voice was slow and menacing, the Eastern European accent enhancing the sinister qualities.

'Yes, and to do so in such a way as to place us all under scrutiny. We have to work within the confines of the law. Of course we know who is responsible for dealing drugs, but we have to have proof. It was stupid, really fucking stupid, to butcher that boy in the way you did. The shit is landing on my head; we'll have half the force here soon,' replied Donald, his voice cracking with stress.

'Please don't tell me my business. Messages have to be sent to those clever enough to read what they say.' The voice was silent for a few heartbeats. 'What was done, has to be undone.'

'Fucking riddles again!' Donald stood up, the golden sunlight flashing on the face of his expensive watch. 'Tell me what you want me to do, then I'll tell you if it's possible.'

'The road for us is now relatively clear. We can put the next part of our plan into place. We believe Daley has information that is detrimental to our project, and to you personally.'

'What do you mean, detrimental?'

'He has, or may soon have, information that will make life much more difficult. Quite simply, he is no longer an asset, he is a liability. We need to know how much he knows. We are working on that now.' The man's voice was cold. 'The very man who has cleared the way for business to proceed will be the same man who will hinder it. Remember, he is not like you; he does his job well, then he goes home. He doesn't check his foreign bank account, because he doesn't have one.'

'I can have him transferred – suspended, even. He's been sleeping with a young colleague. He doesn't think I know, but of course I've made it my business to know,' said Donald, more confidently. 'And in any case, what about the girl? I thought eliminating her was our priority.'

'Circumstances change, so priorities shift to suit them. Daley's knowledge is now our priority. It turns out that the girl is more interesting than we could have imagined.'

'What do you mean?'

'Fate has intervened. She has connections that could be beneficial to us.'

'What? Oh, never mind the bloody girl, do what you want with her. I'll suspend Daley. I'll throw so much at him, his career will be over. I can link him in some way with his brother-in-law, who is under investigation, as well as the young DC he's been fucking.'

'And you think honest policemen with ruined careers don't talk, or pass on their information to the press or colleagues? To anyone who will listen? We will find out what information Daley is in possession of, then we will make decisions based on that. You will help us in all of this. Find out what he knows!'

Donald's phone went dead. The Chief Superintendent sat down with a thud and held his head in his hands as the sun sparkled on the ripples of the calm ocean.

25

'As we all know, there are many strange things that we don't understand. We need only take one look at the government in Westminster to confirm that creatures from another planet are already with us,' said Fordham confidently, her voice booming from speakers placed around the large hall. She paused, slightly disappointed by the ragged snigger her joke had elicited. 'More seriously though, today I have been in contact with the RAF and our much-esteemed Astronomer Royal, Professor Black. He tells me that at this time of year, there are many extraterrestrial phenomena, with perfectly plausible explanations. For instance . . .'

Elise was stopped mid flow as Norrie got to his feet in the middle of the hall. 'I'm no' bothered whoot some arsehole wae a fancy title has tae say,' he said. Cameras flashed, and, out of the corner of her eye, Elise Fordham caught the Japanese cameraman shift his focus from her to the rotund middle-aged man in the short-sleeved shirt and tie, knotted so badly that it was no more than a hand's length. 'I was commisioned by the polis themselves tae take a detective oot tae sea tae get the handle on whoot was goin' on,' shouted Norrie, his voice amplified by a boom microphone held over his head by a young man in jeans and a T-shirt. He looked pleased with this announcement, and eyed the hall with pride. 'It's the second time I've seen it, an' there's nothin' at a' natural aboot whoot's up there!'

'Ladies and gentlemen,' shouted Fordham, trying to be heard above the din of applause. 'Of course, I have by no means made up my mind as to what's been happening here over the last few nights.'

'I seen them tae,' a young woman with white-blonde hair and a thick fringe shouted. Again, one of the two boom operators rushed down the hall and held the microphone over her head. 'Me an' Alistair were jeest oot for a wee stroll up at the plantin', an' there it was – huge. I nearly sh—I mean, I got a hoor o' a fright.'

'Aye, but whoot aboot the lights in the sky?' shouted a stocky man with dark hair, sitting at the front of the audience wearing a replica Scotland football shirt, much to the delight of the Kinloch audience, who roared with laughter.

'Jeest you shut it, Arnie,' the girl replied. 'I'm telling you, Mrs, these lights were weird!'

'OK, as I say, I want to hear from you all in the fullness of time . . .' Again Fordham was stopped in her tracks as a middle-aged woman stood, her hair pulled tightly back into a ponytail. 'I was talkin' tae Norrie the day, an' I'm telling you, my tumble dryer stopped at jeest the same moment he was looking at they lights. Aye, an' it'll no' go back on again. Whoot dae you intend tae dae tae compensate me for that?'

'Aye, good try, Jean,' shouted Arnie. 'My car broke doon tae, an' a wee green man ran intae oor hoose and stole ten grand oot o' the kitchen press. Can I get some o' this compensation?' Arnie's fellow townsfolk laughed again, as Fordham shuffled uncomfortably from foot to foot on the stage.

'All right,' she said with a smile, holding her arms out in an attempt to quieten the hall. 'I know it might sound ridiculous to some of us, but it's clear that many of you have had an unusual experience in the last few nights. I can assure you that I'm taking this very seriously indeed. Over the next few days, my colleagues and I will be looking into what's been happening,' she continued, pleased at the general murmur of consensus in the hall, 'and members of my department will hold regular surgeries in the town hall so that folk can come and tell us what they've seen, or ask any questions they like.' At last, she was getting her point across, which was a great relief.

'I've got a question.' Suddenly a familiar voice sounded behind her, as Charlie Murray spoke. 'You say you've been having a wee chat wae the Astronomer Royal. Is that man in London, or in Edinburgh? So, depending which of them you spoke tae, who funds a' this regal stargazing? And can we expect it tae continue under this government, or will it a' continue tae be an exclusively *royal* pastime?' His political point made, Murray sat back from the microphone to hear the response.

Fordham gave her trademark crooked smile as she started to answer the question, a smile that said, 'I'm going to answer your ridiculous question, but it's hardly worthwhile.'

Wilson – who'd watched this tactic a hundred times – looked on, trying to stop his lip from curling in distaste at the scene unfolding before him. Fordham was doing her best to try and maintain some kind of order. Murray, large and immovable behind the table, was adroitly turning the political point scoring in his favour. Despite his many years in politics, Wilson had never witnessed such familiarity within such a large crowd; nearly three hundred people were behaving as though they were sitting in their front rooms having a casual chat, not in the presence of one of Scotland's political masters – not to mention the world's media. He nudged Ian McIntyre, who was sitting beside him, nervously fiddling with a pen.

'Come on, man, speak up, attract the Chair's eye,' he whispered from behind his hand. 'You need to give the Minister some help here.'

'Oh, yes, of course,' replied McIntyre, dropping the pen and putting his microphone to his mouth. 'Mr Chairman, I would like to make a point,' he said, pulling at his moustache nervously.

'Aye, go ahead, Ian,' Murray replied, looking on with raised eyebrows. 'I'm sure Miss Fordham will be happy tae gie her throat a rest.'

'An' gie us peace,' shouted Arnie. 'On yoursel', Ian, boy. Gie it the full bhuna!'

'Well, the way I see it,' said Ian, squirming in his seat, 'the way I see it is that . . .' Suddenly he sat bolt upright. 'You'll need tae excuse me, Mr Chairman, I'm no' feeling very well.' He rushed out of his chair in a flurry of scattered pens and paper, sending the microphone to the stage with a hollow thud and whine of feedback.

'The toilet's jeest doon the stair an' tae your left,' announced Murray through his microphone, as McIntyre disappeared through the curtains at the back of the stage. 'I hope there's plenty bog paper in there, tae. You'll need to get something done wae they bowels o' yours, son.' The hall exploded in laughter.

Wilson took in the scene with a resigned look on his face.

Just below him, at the side of the hall, he watched a Japanese reporter talk to his cameraman, directing him to take a sweeping shot of the whole audience. A fucking laughing stock, he thought to himself, as Fordham looked over and shrugged her shoulders. She was a talented orator but Kinloch would have tested the rhetorical talents of Martin Luther King, Jr. He felt his phone buzz in his pocket.

Vodka stopped the memories during the day, but they invaded his dreams as he slept.

He is herded onto the lorry with the rest of the men. He had been punched in the face by a Serbian soldier and his jaw no longer works properly. He looks on in despair as an old man is battered to the ground, beaten and kicked until his pitiful attempt to defend himself ceases.

A toddler is swung through the air, her chubby ankles held by a laughing soldier. Her screams are silenced as he lets go and her tiny skull shatters against a wall.

Everyone looks old, even the young men. He knows them all, but they look different, bones where once was flesh, their familiar faces aged almost beyond recognition. Only the soldiers are tanned, fat and smiling.

He is pushed onto a truck behind a boy two years older than him. He knows him from school. He smells the stench and sees the dark stain of shit on the boy's jeans.

'We're going to die,' the boy cries.

Screams rend the air as the trucks pull away. Women – old, young, mothers, wives, daughters – reach out, desperate to save their menfolk. He watches as a woman is hit with the butt of a rifle. She spits blood and teeth onto the road.

They are on the road now, threading between burned-out

cars, debris from ruined houses, more soldiers and rotting
corpses, around which flies buzz and swarm in the summer
heat. A pretty girl is on her knees, two soldiers standing over
her, one holding her head. The soldiers on the lorry cheer as they
drive past.

He jolted awake with a start. He was lying on a bunk in the
fishing boat; his throat was dry and he had a familiar sadness
in his heart, a sadness that had been with him for so long that
he couldn't remember life without it.

He saw his phone flash on the Formica table in the centre
of the cabin. He looked at the device. His instructions had
changed. He remembered the overweight man in the police
uniform as he looked at the picture on the screen. Everything
changed; it was the way of things. He was pragmatic.

'An' as I've said before, tae the council, aye, an' even the polis,
there's no way I can run my business for much longer until
these roads get sorted,' shouted a tall man. 'Aye, folk are still
wantin' taxis, but I canna afford tae keep up wae the repair
bills. These aren't jeest potholes, I saw wee Erchie the accor-
dionist oot swimmin' in one the other day.' More laughter
rippled through the hall.

Fordham looked around at Charlie Murray, who merely
sat back in his chair, allowing the meeting to chair itself.
She knew he was revelling in her discomfort. She had
already been harangued about the cost of bus travel,
complaints about health care, a perceived lack of tourism,
the colour of the newly refurbished town hall, and a question from one woman about whether the local supermarket
would be stocking her preferred soap powder soon, as there
hadn't been any for weeks. Through all of this, Murray had

remained silent, making no attempt to discourage such off-topic questioning.

Fordham caught sight of Wilson's exasperated expression, and knew it was time to end the meeting. As adroitly as she could, she thanked the audience for coming and assured them that she was taking matters very seriously.

'As I have already stated, I will make sure that these phenomena are investigated over the next few days, and if any of you have further disturbing experiences, do not hesitate to report them to the police, or to bring the matter up at the regular consultations that I will initiate over the next few days.' She paused for effect, hoping at least to end the meeting in a controlled and professional way. 'Never forget that, no matter what, our government is busy making sure your rights, safety and prosperity are always at the very top of our agenda.' She stepped back from the microphone to indicate the meeting was over.

Just as desultory applause was beginning to spread through the hall, Fordham was dismayed to see a tall man in a smart suit, his hair cut distinctively short, stand up, his hand raised. A boom microphone was quickly propelled above his head.

'Could I ask one question, please?' he asked in a measured and instantly recognisable American accent.

'Yes,' she smiled from the stage, 'though could you make it brief? I have a number of other pressing matters to attend to, I'm sure you understand.'

'Absolutely, of course. I would just like to know if the community here in Kinloch will profit from the massive wave and wind energy initiative currently being researched ahead of development on the coast a few miles north of here?'

Amidst the subsequent hubbub, Murray leaned forward in his seat and spoke loudly into his microphone. 'Everybody will need tae be quiet an' let the Minister answer the gentleman's question.'

He hadn't reckoned with her political talents though. Fordham leaned toward the microphone and simply said, 'I'm not quite sure to what exactly the gentleman refers, however if it is a question about the government's continued efforts to create for this country a sustainable and ecologically moral power network, then I must tell him that currently everything is under discussion and all possibilities are being examined. The coast of Kintyre is no different to the rest of our coastline here in Scotland. We know that such research will lead to us becoming self-sufficient in green energy by the second half of the twenty-first century.' Then, without taking a breath, she thanked the audience again, turned on her heel and made her way back through the curtains at the back of the stage, quickly followed by Wilson, who glared at Murray as he passed.

'An' that, as they say, is that,' said Murray, as less than enthusiastic applause echoed briefly around the George Hall.

'I sincerely hope you've got some fags on you, Gary,' said Fordham as she made for the door.

'Here,' he replied, ushering her into the dressing room. 'Our friends from Kinloch will try to pigeonhole you at the back door. We'll stay in here for half an hour or so, until they get fed up. I'll tell the minders to wait in the corridor and keep the locals at bay.' With that, he slid a silver bolt in place, locking them in the narrow room. 'Catch,' he said, throwing a cigarette to Fordham.

'What about the smoking ban, Gary?'

'After the shambles you've just presided over, smoking behind the bike shed will be the least of your worries,' said Wilson in a harsh whisper, as he spun a white lighter across the small space between the Minister and himself. 'Everything was bad enough before Uncle Sam chipped in.'

'Yeah, strange one. How he knows about our renewables project up there, I've no idea. Maybe spotted research vessels in the sound or something?'

'Don't be so fucking stupid. Didn't you see his haircut? Fucking military. CIA, even – stands out a mile. This is getting hot, Elise. Too hot for me.' He looked at her through bloodshot eyes. 'I just got a message from my friendly copper. The spooks have found something on Kirsteen Lang's hard drive.'

'Mr Daley, you're the local chief of police around here, am I right?' asked the tall American, holding out his hand to shake Daley's. Scott was squinting across the loch as he drew heavily on a cigarette, Daley waiting patiently at his side.

'Well, yes. Not exactly how we would term it, but as close as we get to that kind of thing in this country,' replied Daley, taking the man's hand. 'You are?'

'Michael Callaghan. Please just call me Mike, everyone else does.' He shook Daley's hand vigorously. 'Kinda lovely here, yeah?' he observed, looking across the loch, burnished silver in the evening light. A family of swans, in search of bread crusts, swam towards the crowds spilling out of the hall. The noise of people talking and laughing carried across the water. One man, Arnie, was singing and dancing past the pier, much to the amusement of his friends.

'Yes, it is,' Daley replied. 'Interesting point you raised in there. You seem very well informed.'

'Oh, just a concerned tourist, you know. I love it here; everything is so unspoiled and fresh. Sort of the way things are meant to be.'

'Are you stayin' for long? I'm Brian Scott, by the way.' The detective also held out his hand for the taller man to shake. 'I'm the deputy.' He grinned.

'Oh, I don't know. I've been looking around for some business opportunities. I'm in the golf game. This place is like golf heaven. Do you know, I drove my first shot right across the Atlantic Ocean onto the green this morning? I know a lot of folk back home would love to do likewise.'

'And you wouldn't be in favour of wind turbines spoiling your view?'

'Got it in one, Mr Daley. Got it in one. I won't keep you guys from your business, it's been great meeting you,' he said. 'I'm sure you cops have your work cut out down here. Such a tragedy with the guy who set himself on fire. What a way to end your life.' He looked at Daley levelly. 'You'd have to be real desperate to want to do that.' He smiled, then walked away.

'Aye, cheerio,' said Scott, under his breath. 'If he's a businessman, I'm in the Salvation Army.'

'You know the Americans, Bri. But I agree, he does have a kind of military bearing.'

'Military bearing? He looks like General MacArthur.' Scott stubbed his cigarette out on top of a bin. A few yards down the street, Mike Callaghan ducked into a large black SUV and sped away.

26

Sarah MacDougall's day began like all the others had over the past few months, and like they would continue to, she supposed, for a very long time. A harsh buzzer roused her from a fitful sleep and she eased herself over the side of the bed. In her mind, she went through her daily mantra, counting down the days until she was eligible for parole.

She had been sentenced to six years for conspiracy to supply controlled drugs as well as a host of smaller charges. She knew that she was clever, much cleverer than the majority of her fellow inmates in Cornton Vale; many of whom were pitiful victims of society, rather than a danger to it. Yet here she was.

Her love of reading had landed her a plum job as an assistant in the library. There, amongst the shelves, life seemed normal; she could almost be back at her expensive private school. The librarian was a civilian, and their chats about literature and life had brightened the dark world into which she had been thrust. She was studying philosophy now, a pursuit that unlocked the doors of her restricted world to infinite ideas and possibilities. It was an escape from her regimented routine, lived amongst people she, in the main, despised. Though she reminded herself that, such had been her father's upbringing and subsequent career in crime, she was merely one step away from these people – removed by a single generation and a fortune in feloniously obtained money. What did she have to be so proud of?

Well, she had her brain, her intelligence.

Today could change things for her, get her out of this place. She had worked to set her mind free; now it was time for the rest of her body to follow. Her father had told her secrets during their brief bid for freedom, before he had died in the sand; she had wrestled with this knowledge during her trial and incarceration. What she knew – the secrets she had been told – she was certain others would want to know. The question had always been when best to make this private knowledge public. At what point could it be used to her best advantage? What forces would be released by opening this Pandora's box?

Her knowledge had the power to change things – to set her free. But her possession of this information could also destroy her. As she pinned back her hair – dull now, with no expensive highlights or slick cut – she thought about the slim volume on the shelf in the library: her last will and testament. She wrote something on a scrap of paper, folded it, then tucked it into her pillow case. There it would remain until the evening. She did this every day, just in case. In the evening things would be different. Knowledge was power, and power would set her free. For the first time in a very long time, she felt her spirit soar.

The radio programme he was listening to was retro and, for him, nostalgic. Songs from the eighties played as he drove along the beautiful winding road, away from Kinloch.

Sunlight glinted on the waters of Loch Fyne, flashing through the trees, just like the strobing effects in the night club all those years ago when he had first set eyes on Liz. 'We met at midnight in Paris,' she used to say. It sounded sublime; many of her friends remarked upon its romance. What she omitted to tell them was that Paris was a club in the back streets of Paisley.

It all seemed like a very, very long time ago.

Could he rekindle his relationship with Liz? Would the spark of the love he felt for her, would always feel for her, be enough to set fire to their relationship again? And what about Mary? She had called him when he arrived home after the public meeting. She sounded sad, alone and confused; her voice was small when he declined the invitation to spend the night at hers. When he'd told her that he was to visit Liz the next day, she'd put the phone down.

He turned the radio off. Nostalgia was all very well, but it was an indulgent emotion; what was tear-jerking poignancy for one brought a cold shiver of embarrassment to another. No matter what he decided to do, somebody was going to get hurt: Liz, Mary, himself, their baby – her baby. Frustrated at the circles in which he seemed to be turning, he tried to drag his thoughts back to work, and what Sarah MacDougall would say.

There was something he was missing, he was sure of it. He had come to rely on his inner voice, the nagging doubt that told him all was not well, despite appearances. What had happened over the last few days had been bad, but he had the feeling that it was only part of a greater, much more sinister, whole. Cudihey's death, the appearance of a known assassin on the streets of Kinloch, and the horrific executions of

Malky Miller and Rory Newell all jostled for his attention. John Donald's face kept flashing before his mind's eye. Yes, he was being investigated, but it was all very subtle. Daley had thought about it a lot since Layton's revelation; he reasoned that if senior management had thought Donald to be in some way compromised, they would never have let him loose as commander of a division in the new force. As always, wheels within wheels. He was sick of it, all of it; he could foresee the job to which he had given the best years of his life becoming more and more political, a setting for behind-the-scenes deals catered to the advancement of those who occupied executive positions, who were more worried about their pensions and reputations than their real purpose: to solve and prevent crime.

He thought of Sarah MacDougall. She had lost everything, including her freedom. He gunned the car along a straight section of road towards the white buildings of the village in the distance.

His phone rang, and Rainsford's voice spilled into the car, confident as always – another perk of private education.

'Sir, I've just been warned off from any further investigation into the map found on Cudihey's boat.'

'By whom?'

'ACC in charge of discipline. He was adamant, sir. Any information about it, or about the lights in the sky, is to be passed to him, then he will inform the relevant department.'

'The MOD, no doubt.'

'He didn't say,' said Rainsford. 'Oh, one thing, though. I discovered that this is the line of a cable, but not an old telegraph as we had thought.'

'What is it, then?'

'Apparently it was laid just after the end of the Second World War. That's where my enquiries have to end, I'm sad to say. There was a lot of military activity around Kinloch in those days. Something to do with that, sir?'

Daley thought for a moment. 'You have a smartphone, don't you? One of your own, I mean, not the one you've been issued with.'

'Yes, sir, but . . .'

'Keep plugging away on that. And use your mobile network, not the office wifi. To coin a phrase, "I don't think we're alone".'

Education and exercise, that's what existed now for Sarah MacDougall. They couldn't lock up her mind, and exercise helped her stay sharp. An enlightened approach to the imprisonment and rehabilitation of the prisoner in the twenty-first century meant that a well-equipped gym was available for those who didn't want to see their bellies fold over the top of a pair of baggy leggings.

Sarah put her head down as she pedalled hard, a constant need within her to better her performance on the exercise bike. She felt rivulets of sweat slither down her back as her breath shortened with the exertion. Soon, the natural high of an endorphin rush would help her cope with another day behind white walls, high fences and razor wire. She closed her eyes against the pain, shutting out the light in the bright room.

She didn't expect the blow which sent her face smashing into the bike's console, though the pain it engendered changed her life in a split second. She opened her eyes just in time to see a glimpse of her own blood as it slid down the screen displaying her time, speed and distance. Her world slipped beneath her, as though she was suddenly travelling at immense speed. She felt nothing of the second blow that turned her world, once full of hope and potential, dark forever.

Daley circled the looming edifice of Stirling Castle, following the road through a couple of roundabouts and over a bridge, then turned left, away from Scotland's old capital and towards one of its biggest prisons. He was on a straight stretch of road now, though numerous mini roundabouts, traffic lights and slow buses hindered his progress.

A flash of blue reflected in his rear-view mirror caught his attention. He took his foot off the accelerator and edged his car into the side of the road to let the ambulance rush past, the wail from its siren changing pitch as it drew level with him. He watched it thread its way through the traffic ahead in a flurry of lights and sound, and something cold gripped Jim Daley's heart. He pressed his foot firmly back on the accelerator and the car lurched forward.

Daley stopped at the front gate of HMP Cornton Vale just in time to see the ambulance disappear into the complex of white buildings. A security guard in a peaked cap and a white shirt with epaulettes walked towards the car. An identity tag swayed across his paunch as he neared the vehicle.

'DCI Jim Daley,' he said, through the open window, passing his warrant card towards the guard for examination. 'I have an appointment to interview an inmate.'

'Picked a bad time, DCI Daley,' replied the security guard. 'We're in lockdown. There's been an assault on one of the prisoners. Doesn't sound good, but don't quote me on that, will you, mate. Just pull your vehicle into the side over there, and we'll be with you as soon as possible.'

The churning feeling at the pit of Daley's stomach told him that something was very wrong. He pulled his phone from his pocket and scrolled down his contacts list. His call was answered by a harassed secretary.

'DCI Daley here. I think we spoke yesterday.'

'Eh, yes. Yes, of course. You arranged a visit at the request of a prisoner, I believe.'

Daley could hear voices in the background, but decided to press on. 'I've been told to wait at the front gate – some kind of problem within the prison. Would it be possible to come in?'

'Can you hold for a few seconds?'

Despite the secretary having placed her hand over the phone, Daley could make out muffled voices. He reasoned that emergencies were by no means uncommon in Her Majesty's Prisons, so why did he feel so uneasy?

'DCI Daley, I've just received clearance from the deputy governor. Please approach security at the gate. I'll issue them with new instructions.' The phone went dead.

Daley was ushered into the visitors' car park by two prison officers, and then escorted on foot into the building. He noted an air of quiet urgency amongst the staff, though the young man who was his guide remained uncommunicative.

'Chief Inspector, please come in,' said Deputy Governor Malcolm, from behind his large desk. He looked about fifty but, Daley reckoned, was at least ten years younger. 'I'm afraid to say that your trip would appear to be in vain,' he continued, gesturing to Daley to take a seat.

'Meaning?' Daley asked, his heart sinking.

'Sarah MacDougall was attacked just before you arrived, in the leisure block. I'm sad to tell you that as a result of the injuries she sustained she has passed away. Our staff did their best, but . . . We have two inmates in custody, and your colleagues from Stirling are on their way.'

Daley sat quietly for a few moments. He remembered the bright young woman he had first met in the remote farmhouse that had been her father's bolthole. Another life wasted. All three of Frank MacDougall's children were now dead, not one of them having reached the age of twenty-five. Only MacDougall's wretched wife survived, living out her days in a nursing home as the disease that had put her there ate away at her mind. Considering the tragedy that had befallen her family, it was perhaps for the best.

'I need to see her possessions,' he said to Malcolm. 'She asked to see me today, she had important information, so I would like to see anything that could point to what she intended to say.'

Had Sarah MacDougall been killed to stop her from speaking out? To be killed on the very day that she had requested to see him was surely no coincidence.

'Who knew that I was coming to see her today?'

'Oh, me, my secretary, a couple of other officers and other staff. I'd have to check. The librarian, too. Sarah was studying in the library – she was a trustee in there, as well. Would you like to see the crime scene?'

'Not really. I'll leave that to our colleagues in Stirling. I'd like to see her cell, though, then perhaps I can have a chat with the librarian.'

'Yes, I'll arrange it. I'd better have a quick chat with the governor. Will you excuse me? He would pick today to be on leave. I'm sure it will be fine, though.'

'Thanks,' said Daley, as Malcolm walked out of the room. He leaned back and rubbed his eyes, wondering what he could have done differently to save Sarah MacDougall's life.

27

Scott was sitting in Daley's office when DS Rainsford flung the door open. 'I've just had headquarters on the phone. They're looking for Chief Superintendent Donald. Do you know where he is?'

'Nope, I've no' set eyes on him,' said Scott, putting down his mug of coffee with shaky hands. 'Where's his assistant, that Layton guy?'

'Inspector Layton is looking for him too. Not a sign of him at the hotel. The manager tells me she hasn't seen him since yesterday afternoon when he went back to his room, feeling unwell. She just assumed he was still holed up in there.'

'What aboot his motor?' asked Scott.

'Still in the hotel car park,' Rainsford shrugged.

'I'll have a scout around. He's likely oot for a run or somethin'. Trust me, you'll no' get shot o' that bastard so easy. We can always hope he's been abducted by aliens. I mean, that's quite possible doon here. Especially after what I saw the other night.'

'Not very helpful, DS Scott. Please let me know if you find him,' said Rainsford, looking pointedly at Scott as he lifted the mug to his lips again, with a trembling hand.

'Aye, you try getting shot, you posh bastard,' he said, under his breath, as Rainsford left the room. 'Maybe your hands would shake, tae.'

Scott thought for a moment. He wondered where Donald was; whatever he was doing, he didn't want to be involved. These thoughts were dismissed when the phone on Daley's desk rang.

'Aye, DS Scott.'

'It's ACC Manion. He asked for DCI Daley, but when I said he wasn't in, and you were, he asked for you, Sergeant,' the PC on reception duty informed him.

'Oh, right, put him through,' said Scott. 'How you, Willie, what can I do you for?'

'Hello, Brian. Listen, I need tae talk tae you. I hear Jim's off somewhere today, am I right?'

'Aye, he'll be back the night or tomorrow morning. What's the problem? Want his mobile number?'

'No. You'll do,' Manion replied. 'The forensic boys have come up with a few things fae this Kirsteen Lang's computer. It would appear she and Mr Cudihey were mair friendly than we thought. She was away sailing with him, at any rate. We found a lot o' pictures on her hard drive she'd no' managed tae erase.'

'This is the lassie that was killed in the RTA yesterday?'

'Aye, Brian, that's her.'

'Why would she erase a' the stuff from her computer?'

'Now, if I knew that, I'd be as clever as you. I'm emailing some stuff doon. Some o' these pictures look as though they've been taken on the coast round Kintyre, or so I'm reliably informed by the expert in topography, or whatever it's called. I want you tae have a look an' see if you can pinpoint where, Brian.'

'Aye, nae bother, Willie. I'll take a look an' get back tae you. There's an old guy here, a retired fisherman, sounds right up his street. All very mysterious. I know Jim's no' happy wae this case.'

'Who would be, Brian? I could dae without this myself. In my experience, mention the word politics an' all the shit o' the day appears. See what you can do for me, eh?'

'No problem, sir.'

'Oh, did I tell you, Brian, we're off tae get another poodle at the weekend. He'll no' replace wee Jinky, mind. But och, the hoose was just empty, you know what I mean?' He went on to describe the pain of life without the aforementioned Jinky bounding about.

'Right enough, Willie. Aye, great stuff, just what you need. It'll be great tae see the new addition tae the family, so tae speak. I'll get back to you as soon as I have something.' Scott grimaced as he finished the call with his old friend. 'I hope this new poodle doesnae stink and lick my face the way the last fuckin' one did,' he muttered under his breath as he went in search of Manion's email.

Daley looked around the cell. It was neat, tidy and bright. Had it not been for the peephole in the door and the bars on the windows, he could have been in a downmarket hotel room. A single bed sat against the wall under the window. A wardrobe stood in the opposite corner, beside which was a desk and chair, with a mirror on the wall behind. Under the desk was a set of drawers which Daley opened to begin his search. The first two contained underwear, socks, prison issue T-shirts and jumpers; nothing of significance. On the top of the desk was a cheap writing pad, beside a framed picture of a teenage boy wearing a muddy football kit. Despite never having met him, Daley recognised Cisco, Sarah's older brother, who a few years after that picture was taken would be butchered in the stairwell of a Glasgow high rise. Daley looked at the young face with the broad smile. Not for the first time in his life, he thought about destiny. What was the destiny of the small child who had changed his life? What was his, come to that? He tried to focus on the job in hand and take his mind from the distraction of Liz.

The contents of the second pair of drawers were more interesting. Letters and photographs were neatly stacked next to a pile of books. Daley skimmed through the letters – many from friends, and a couple from Sarah's mother, written in a child's hand – then looked through the books. Novels by Jane Austen, Proust and Thomas Hardy sat beside books on philosophy, politics and economics. Daley sighed again; what a waste of a life. He held each book by the spine and flicked through the pages in case anything had been placed between them; on initial investigation, at least, nothing was apparent.

On the small cabinet beside her bed, Sarah MacDougall had placed two framed photographs and a small radio. The first photo showed a group of girls in school uniform; he spotted a young Sarah in the middle. The second was of her parents; Frank and Betty MacDougall stared out in monochrome, both smiling. Despite her expression Daley thought he could see unhappiness in the woman's eyes.

A further two slim drawers in the cabinet contained very little. Apart from another couple of books and three magazines – two on current affairs and one on history – there was a notepad with some doodles and a packet of chewing gum. It looked as though his search would be futile.

'The Stirling boys will want to bag this lot up,' Daley said to the prison officer standing at the door.

'Yes, sir,' he replied. 'Are you finished?'

Daley looked about. 'Yes, just about, I think.' He looked at the bed; as unlikely as it was that something would be hidden in or around its frame, he thought he might as well be thorough. He bent down, gingerly, and looked under it; the space was empty. He stood, threw the duvet cover and pillows onto the floor, then lifted the mattress and searched underneath and around it; again, nothing. As he lifted the bedding to throw it back onto the bed, something fluttered from the pillowcase – a small scrap of paper. Daley quickly reached for it.

CVL:Phil/231-01

Daley thought for a moment, looking around the small cell. 'Right, lock this up until Stirling CID are ready to have a look,' he ordered. 'Now, if you don't mind, I want to go to the prison library.'

Scott was in the passenger seat alongside Rainsford, who was driving.

'So you reckon you know where this is?' he said, turning to the man in the back seat.

'Och aye,' said Hamish. He was still studying the image Scott had given him, in which a pretty girl with a tanned face and blonde hair smiled at the camera. Behind her, the sea and the coastline were easy to make out. 'That hill's Dundraven, an' that's Dundraven beach. If I had a penny for a' the times I sailed past there, I would be a rich man noo, and nae mistake.'

'Well spotted,' said Rainsford in his clipped tones. 'I must admit, I thought this was going to be a wild goose chase.'

'Have faith, son,' chided Scott. 'It's no' a' contained in books an' the internet, you know.'

'Indeed it's no',' said Hamish. 'I don't know whoot end is whoot when it comes tae computers, but I can navigate this coast wae my eyes closed, an' that's a fact.'

They drove on for a short while until Hamish pointed out a lay-by ahead, where they parked. At the far end of the lay-by, a small gate opened up onto a rough track, down which they set off. The sky was deep azure, the long grass a vibrant green, and the scents of honeysuckle and the sea heavy in the air. They followed the track to the top of a small hill, which revealed a breathtaking scene. A long stretch of white sand bordered the calm ocean. In the distance, islands could be picked out in the shimmering haze, one of them with a series of dramatic conical peaks.

'Aye, in front o' you are the Paps o' Jura,' said Hamish, pointing with the stem of his pipe. 'Beside it, the wonderful island o' Islay.'

'What's that landmass over there?' asked Rainsford, clearly impressed.

'The Emerald Isle.' Hamish's eyes creased into a smile. 'Aye, Ireland. Right bonnie, is it no'?'

'Who needs the Costa del Sol when you've got this on your doorstep, eh?' said Scott, filling his lungs with the heady scents of sea and shore.

'Who needs the Costa del Sol, period?' said Rainsford.

The three men made their way towards the shore, with the buzz of insects, the insistent call of seabirds, and the lazy swish of the tide as their soundtrack.

Daley immediately knew why Sarah had sought the library as her refuge. It could have been any library, almost anywhere in the world. Apart from the barred windows, and white utilitarian buildings beyond, it would be easy to forget that you were in the heart of a prison.

A woman with short dark hair, who looked to be in her early thirties, approached Daley, holding out her hand for him to shake.

'Elaine Wright. I'm the librarian here,' she said with a weak smile. Her eyes were puffy and she looked as though she'd been crying.

'Nice to meet you, Elaine. I'm DCI Daley. You knew Sarah MacDougall reasonably well, I believe?'

'Yes.' A tear made its way down her cheek. 'It's so terrible, what happened to her. I can't believe it.' She wiped the tear away with the back of her hand. 'She was such a lovely, clever girl.'

'Yes, she was,' said Daley. 'She would come here most days, I take it?'

'She was a trustee, Inspector Daley. So she was here nearly every day. As you can see, we're not exactly rushed off our feet, so she spent a lot of time reading. She had started a course on philosophy, too. I have the details here,' she said, bending down behind her desk.

'Can you make any sense of this?' Daley handed her the piece of paper, retrieved from Sarah MacDougall's pillowcase.

The librarian studied it for a second, then smiled. 'Yes, this is one of our library references, for a book on philosophy, as you might expect. If you follow me, I'll show you.'

Daley did as he was told and followed the librarian through the maze of shelves.

'Here we are,' she announced. She reached down to the bottom shelf and pulled out a book: a faded copy of Ludwig Wittgenstein's *On Certainty*. She handed it to Daley, looking suddenly uncertain.

Daley felt the heft of the book in his hands for a few heartbeats, before turning it upside down by its spine and leafing through the pages with his thumb. As he had expected, a tiny envelope – most probably homemade – fluttered to the ground. In neat, rounded handwriting it was addressed to DCI Daley.

'Oh,' the librarian said uncertainly. 'What can that be? I mean, addressed to you. It's very strange.'

'Yes. Did she mention anything to you? You know, fears or worries? It seems that you were the one person in here that she spent a lot of time with.'

'No. I mean, not really. We spoke about her course, and books we had both read, of course. Very little else. I have strict rules to follow when it comes to my relationships with the prisoners. I'm sure you appreciate that.'

Daley noticed a sudden change in her manner. 'Yes, absolutely. Since this is addressed to me, I hope you don't mind my removing it. After the sad events of earlier this morning, it's now evidence in a murder inquiry.'

He left the library and was taken to the office of the deputy governor, where he was seated in an anteroom. Malcolm was busy in a meeting, no doubt focused on the murder of Sarah

MacDougall. He welcomed the opportunity to open the envelope and read its contents.

Dear Mr Daley,

When my father and I were trying to make our escape, he told me something that he urged I should use if ever things became too much for me to bear, or if I felt threatened in any way; incidentally, I feel both emotions at present. He was also most insistent that I should pass this information to you, and only you, in person if possible. I have been warned off, told to keep quiet, but I don't intend to. If anything has happened to me, you need only search from where the words come to find the answer. I think it is part of the human condition to want to bare one's soul, but I think I am about to learn the hard way to be more careful to whom I unburden myself.

I know that you are a clever man, and I hope that this information may help you restore some balance to our small part of the world; though I fear that the ramifications of what I know go far beyond the shores of Kintyre. I am also aware that – and I know this sounds clichéd, please forgive me – if you are now reading this, then my worst fears have been realised.

My father made it clear to me that he knew of corruption at a very high level within the police force. Apparently you were sent to Kinloch to clean things up to make way for something else. He told me that powerful people had their tentacles spread throughout our society, to the highest possible levels.

He only had one name: John Donald. But there's also someone higher. Another police officer, more senior to Donald, was involved, but he didn't know the name. He

*believed that this corruption went far beyond the police force.
That is all I know.*

*I'm sorry that I didn't get the chance to tell you this in
person. It would appear that my attempt to enter the world
of crime, to emulate my father, was doomed from the outset.
I console myself with the fact that death is not a part of life,
that we do not live to experience it.*

Please help my mother, if you can.

Trust nobody.

Sarah

Malcolm's voice made Daley jump. He hurriedly folded
Sarah MacDougall's note, put it back into the envelope and
followed the deputy governor into his office.

'Stirling CID are interviewing the assailants now,
though I don't believe they're getting very far. Two lifers
with nothing much to lose. I must tell you that both the
investigating officers and the governor are most unhappy
that you appear to have taken it upon yourself to interview
members of our staff, and conduct searches outwith the
official investigation.'

'Shut up,' said Daley, who remained standing.

'I beg your pardon.' Malcolm made to rise from behind his
desk.

'Sit fucking down. I want you to take steps to detain Elaine
Wright. I'm just about to arrange for local police officers to
arrest her. How carefully do you vet your civilian staff, Mr
Malcolm?'

'Very carefully. In fact, my background is in HR, so I know
all there is to know about the processes we use to make sure
our staff are of the highest quality. We have strategies in

place to ensure absolute effectiveness; no doubt beyond the comprehension of a non-professional.'

'You little twat. How long has she been in place? Less time than Sarah MacDougall has been languishing here, I reckon. I'd bet anything that your incomprehensible strategies have led to Sarah MacDougall's death. Make the call.' Daley watched as Malcolm picked up the phone and instructed his security staff to detain the prison librarian.

'Now, I must insist that you leave.' Malcolm stood to his full, average height.

Daley looked down at him and smirked. 'Human resources, I might have known. We've got people like you, too.'

'Hard-working professionals, without whom no organisation could operate?' replied Malcolm sarcastically.

'No. Self-important arseholes, with no function other than to make work for themselves and for others who have proper jobs.' He turned to leave, then spotted a crash helmet sitting on a filing cabinet. 'Are you a biker, Mr Malcolm?'

'Yes, and why is that of any consequence?'

'You just don't look the type.' Daley smiled and left the man muttering under his breath.

28

'There you are. Of course, you would need tae be oot at sea tae get the full effect, but if that's no' the backgroon tae the pictures, then I'm a Quaker,' said Hamish, as the three men stood on the white sand looking up at the hill beyond the beach. The surf broke lazily on the shore while, high above, ravens twisted in the clear blue sky.

Scott wiped the perspiration from his forehead with a handkerchief. His jacket was slung over one shoulder, as was Rainsford's; even he looked uncomfortable in the heat, made fiercer as it reflected off the powdery white sand. Now and then, Scott could feel the hint of a breeze at his hot neck. He wondered where the nearest pub was, a pint of cold lager was just what he needed. Well, perhaps a couple.

'What's over there?' asked Rainsford, pointing to a small compound, contained within which was a steel hut, like a domestic garage; it looked out of place in these surroundings. Razor wire topped the fence, which looked new and well maintained.

'Whatever it is, naebody's supposed to get in, that's for sure,' said Scott.

They walked over to the fence, Hamish's tobacco mingling with the earthy scent of plants and the salty tang of the ocean. 'It'll be the electric folk,' he said. 'I mind they put a contraption like this at the end of oor street when I was jeest a boy. Electricity was brand new in Kinloch in those days, aye, an' naebody trusted it, I can tell you. Poor auld Mrs McSorley had a terrible death.' He shook his head at the memory.

'Was she electrocuted?' asked Rainsford.

'Aye, she was that, son. Cooked like a roasted hen, no' one bit o' her no' charred an' burnt. You could smell it doon the length o' the fields. I mind my mother puttin' the Sunday roast on the table, the week after. No' one o' us could take a bite, an' that's a fact.'

'How did it happen?' asked Scott, as they approached the high fence, looking for anything to identify the compound's purpose. 'Faulty wiring, nae doubt. I've had a couple o' close ones when the wife forced me tae dae some DIY. Fucking cut the whole street off for near ten hours. She never asked me tae dae anything like it again, mind you. Every cloud.' He winked at Rainsford.

'Och no, it was sheer stupidity on her part, the auld soul,' said Hamish. 'As I say, the mysteries o' electricity were as unknown tae us in they days as the dark side o' the moon. The poor bugger was in a tin bath in the front room. The water was getting' cauld – it was near Christmas, if I recall. She thought tae boil a kettle, you know, tae warm her bath up a wee bit. She wiz a canny auld bird though, she spotted the wee two-bar fire she had blazing away, an' reached oot and pulled it intae the bath wae her – tae heat up the water, you understand. The Monk heard a great calamity fae upstairs – he was in the flat below – so he went running up. Och, whoot a sight; her lying roasted, wearing only whoot God gied her tae. I don't know whoot he thought was worse.' Hamish grimaced.

'Fuck me,' said Scott, horrified by the mental picture Hamish had conjured up for him. 'What a tale. You said she was discovered by a monk?'

'No, no. *The* Monk; his nickname. No' many folk in the toon without some kinda nickname or other. They called him that cos o' the big bald spot on the back o' his heid; been there since he was a boy. Mind you, there was nothing monkish aboot his behaviour, if you know whoot I mean.' He winked.

'Meaning?' Scott asked.

'Well, now you see, it wiz lucky poor auld Mrs McSorley wisna breathing, that's a' I'll say aboot it.'

'I thought she was an auld woman,' said Scott, mystified.

'Aye, so she wiz, but that wiz nae barrier tae the Monk. Shag a barber's—'

'You two, shut up and come over here!' shouted Rainsford. Uninterested in Hamish's tale of tragedy, he had made his way further along the fence. When Hamish and Scott caught up with him, he pointed to a small white plaque, attached to a gate with double padlocks.

BY ORDER OF THE MINISTRY OF DEFENCE: KEEP OUT. TRESPASSERS WILL BE PROSECUTED.

'Not what we expected,' said Rainsford.

'No, certainly no,' Scott observed. 'What the fuck is it?'

'Strange that Lang would have her photo taken with this in the background,' said Rainsford, pointing to a blur in the photographs, visible just behind the girl in every shot.

'Ach, maybe just a coincidence. We'll need tae find oot

what this is all aboot though, just in case,' said Scott, peering through the fence at the metal building.

'Look up there.' Hamish pointed across the heather with his pipe to where an old-fashioned blue caravan sat under a knoll, about half a mile from where they were standing. 'How dae we no' jeest take a wander o'er there? You would think that whoever's in there will know aboot this place.'

'For a fisherman, Hamish, you make a fine policeman,' said Scott. 'Come on an' we'll gie this a look. It doesnae look tae me like that caravan's a tourer. In fact, how did it get here?'

They made their way across the heather, to the flurry of wings and anxious squawks of birds nesting nearby.

'I hope it's not boggy,' remarked Rainsford. 'These shoes cost me a bloody fortune.'

'You should buy them fae Asda, like me,' said Scott.

Daley had a heavy heart as he drove down the road, Stirling Castle behind him. Thoughts of John Donald reverberated in his head; at worst, his superior was involved with organised crime, taking backhanders in return for information, or maybe getting members of the underworld out of a tight spot with the police. Judging by Sarah MacDougall's note, the situation was more serious and widespread than he would have thought possible; corrupt senior policemen – perhaps even very senior policemen – and beyond. She had said that this cancer, whatever it was, reached the very highest level. Did this mean something bigger than the police?

Now, armed with this information, who could he trust to tell about it? Nobody knew the contents of Sarah's letter but him. He had left the prison before any of the investigating officers could ask any awkward questions. No doubt these questions would arise, but by then, he would have had time to think.

Daley had always deplored corruption. When he was a young cop it had been normal for some of the more senior men to overlook the flaunting of licensing laws by certain publicans, in return for free booze or fags, though that was the very tip of the iceberg. Vital pieces of evidence went missing; cases were found as 'not proven' in court, based on technicalities; suspicious mistakes were made by police officers who should, and did, know better.

He hated the feeling of isolation, of not knowing to whom he could turn. It made him feel angry and stressed, but much worse, it made him feel scared.

He looked at his watch. If he drove straight back to Kinloch, he could be there in around three hours, where he could make a start on deciding just how he was going to use the new information.

Then he thought of Liz.

He'd promised to visit her. They had a lot to discuss; so many things had gone wrong with their marriage that it would be hard to know where to start. He was angry about the affair he suspected she'd had with her brother-in-law. Though he'd had an affair, too – was still, maybe, and perhaps wouldn't stop having one. He was fond of Dunn, very fond, but did he love her with the heart-aching passion he had for his wife? Did that even exist any more? Yet he couldn't bear the idea of his marriage being over; the thought made his head spin.

He had to see her. He saw a sign for Glasgow, and his heart

started to pound. He was going to see Liz, and the baby. He was going home.

Scott peered through the dirty windows of the caravan, shading his eyes from the glare of the bright sun with both hands and trying to see inside. Filthy net curtains made this an impossible task, though with Rainsford banging on the door, it was pretty certain that nobody was at home.

'Try the door,' said Scott, having given up on looking through the windows.

'Should we? I mean we're on shaky ground, no warrant et cetera,' Rainsford replied.

'Fuck me, son, can you no' hear the cries for help?'

Hamish smiled at this example of pragmatic policing at work, as Scott tried the handle of the door, with no success.

'Have you got a penknife, Hamish?'

'Aye, noo hold on. I've got a wee selection o' tools here.' Hamish delved into the bib pocket of his dungarees. The first item he produced was a rusty-looking bodkin, which he handed to Scott.

'Is this for darning your socks? You must know somebody with fuckin' big feet.'

'You're not going to pick the lock, are you?' asked Rainsford.

'Nah. I'm going tae peel an apple.'

Hamish's rummage turned up a packet of fisherman's lozenges, a Jew's harp, pipe tobacco and a pair of ancient spectacles before he produced a Swiss Army knife, which looked remarkably well maintained.

'As my faither always said: look after your knife, an' your knife will look after you,' said the old fisherman as he handed the penknife to Scott.

'Aye, the very thing,' said Scott. 'This spike thing will dae the job.' He inserted the little tool into the lock, twisted it a couple of times, grimaced, stuck his tongue out, then after a small click, relaxed and handed the knife back to Hamish. 'Be my guest, DS Rainsford,' he said, swinging the door open. 'There's mair tae life than what you learn in the police college, son.'

Rainsford frowned and ducked through the low door of the caravan.

It was dark inside, so Scott pulled open the curtains to reveal the cramped interior. There was a bench seat under the window that extended along the walls on three sides. In the middle of the floor sat a small table with two chairs, to the left of which was a gas fire, built into a unit which provided cupboard space and shelving, on top of which was a framed photograph of a small yacht.

'That's that poor soul Cudihey's boat,' said Hamish. 'I'm certain o' it. Whoot a gentleman he was, tae. No' feart when it came tae doling oot the amber nectar.'

Despite the dank feel, Scott noted that little or no dust covered the surfaces, and a week-old copy of the *Herald* was folded on top of the bench. 'No' long since there was some-body here,' he said, picking up the paper.

Rainsford was making his way along the length of the caravan. There was a small galley kitchen with a two-ringed cooker nestled neatly between the cupboards, the surfaces of which provided worktop space. A white plastic kettle sat beside a tiny microwave oven and a jar of instant coffee. There was a tiny sink and a fridge, which was switched off. Rainsford opened the cupboards one by one, finding only a half-empty bottle of whisky, a few tins, a bottle of ketchup and three packets of instant mash.

Rainsford did a quick check of the toilet but, as in the rest of the caravan, found nothing of interest.

A final room sat at the end of the corridor. Rainsford opened its flimsy door. 'Eh, Sergeant Scott, I think you'd better take a look in here.'

29

Daley hadn't been prepared for how he would feel, not prepared at all. As if being back in Liz's company after so long wasn't enough, the tiny child he was holding elicited feelings within him he'd never known existed.

'Can't you feel it?' asked Liz. 'Don't you just know that you are holding your own son?'

Daley couldn't speak. His day was being bookended by death and birth. Unfortunately, he was much more accustomed to the former. Of one thing, there was no doubt: this child had its mother's eyes. He stared, mesmerised, at the tiny bundle in his arms.

'Oh, Liz,' was all he could say.

Covering the wall behind the caravan's bed, photographs of varying sizes were pinned. Mostly, they were of the stretch of beach outside. The others, apart from one, were of a ship – taken from many angles, distances, and, by the looks of the differing overhead conditions, over an extended period of time. In the very centre of the collage, one image – the largest – was framed by everything else. A young woman, with long blonde hair, smiled at the camera.

'That's Kirsteen Lang,' said Rainsford. 'I saw her picture

on an email from Edinburgh yesterday, after she was killed in an RTA. She worked with Cudihey.'

'I'm no' sure he just thought o' her as a work colleague,' said Scott. He had picked something up from the floor, in the narrow gap between the bed and the window, and held it up to show the other two men.

'Tae think,' said Hamish, a look of horror on his face, 'I spent a maist convivial evening aboard that Cudihey's boat, no' thinking for wan second that he was a sexual deviant.' He shook his head in disgust.

Scott examined the item with distaste; he was holding a flaccid inflatable rubber doll, artificial blonde hair sprouting from its head, and an enlarged photo pasted across its face, the mouth cut away to allow the pouting 'O' of the doll's lips to poke through. Again, Kirsteen Lang's features were unmistakable.

'You're a fair-weather friend, Hamish. He was a real gent wae a good pouring hand a couple o' minutes ago,' said Scott. 'I'm all for good working relationships, but this is taking things too far,' he continued, laying the sex toy on the bed.

'What's that stuff in its nose?' asked Hamish.

'I think we can safely it's not a summer cold,' replied Scott, grimacing.

Daley cradled the child; he didn't want to hand him back to Liz.

Her mother had been in the house when he arrived and, needless to say, his reception had been frosty. Liz's parents had never been keen for her to marry a policeman, whom they considered to be beneath their social status. The events of the last few months had done nothing to improve this relationship. On his arrival, Liz's mother had simply glared at him, picked up her handbag, and left without another word.

'How is Mary Dunn?' asked Liz.

'Do we really want to go there now?' replied Daley. 'It's not as though you haven't had *friends* during the course of our marriage, is it? Do you want me to enquire after their collective health?'

She looked at the floor. Daley had never seen her look so run down. Her hair was lank, and she was wearing leggings and a loose white T-shirt that bore a stain on the shoulder. He was used to the woman who looked as though she had sprung fully formed from the pages of a glossy magazine; this transformation was unexpected.

'I'm sorry. I don't want you to take pity on me, but this has been one of the hardest times of my life. I don't know what I would have done without my mother, I really don't.' Liz burst into tears.

'Listen, I know it's been hard. It's been hard for me, too.'

'Then why wouldn't you believe me? Why have we been miles apart, living separate lives, when this should have been the happiest time of our lives!'

'You know why, Liz,' said Daley, trying to calm the baby who was starting to object to the raised voices. 'Let's be honest, we hardly had the perfect marriage, did we?'

'I thought you were happy.'

'No, you thought that I would put up with anything because I loved you so much; you relied on it.' He rocked the baby in his arms.

'And do you? Love me, I mean?'

He paused, and was just about to answer when the little

bundle in his arms produced a sound he wouldn't have thought possible from one so small.

'Here, give him to me.' Liz gently took the baby and held him to her breast. Despite himself, Daley thought his heart would burst.

After a few moments he replied. 'Yes, of course. I'll always love you.'

'You don't even know his name.'

'No . . . I'm sorry.'

'Moonrise.'

'What? Moonrise? Really?'

She stared at him for a few heartbeats, then a smile lit up her face. 'You tit, did you honestly think I'd call him that?'

'Well, if I'm honest, I didn't know what to think. I never . . . Well, we never spoke about it.'

'I was waiting to talk to you about it. I have been calling him something, though.'

'What?'

'James.' As she said the name, James Daley stopped crying and buried his head into his mother's breast.

He looked at Abdic, asleep in the chair, his head lolling forward, and thought back to the first time he'd seen his face.

The large, squat man grabs him by the scruff of the neck. He is pulled from a line of bedraggled men; some crying, others praying, the rest silent. They are standing above the pit they have just dug. They are standing above their own graves.

His captor drags him over to a man with grey hair, smoking a cigar, his uniform adorned with medals and insignia. Words are exchanged; harsh words, in a language he doesn't understand. Without warning, he is flung to the ground.

He manages to pull himself up just as the man with the cigar barks the order, and the guns fire. The ragged men, with whom he had stood until only a few minutes ago, fall backwards, or drop to their knees.

One man, young, wearing a football top, is twitching on the ground, both hands held above his body, shaking uncontrollably, like someone left out in the cold. A soldier walks over to him, takes a pistol from his belt and calmly shoots the man through the head. He shivers no more.

It is then he realises that the huge man who had pulled him away, Pavel Abdic, has just saved his life.

He tried to force the memory from his mind. When he didn't concentrate, these memories always surfaced; they played in the background, on an endless loop in his head, just waiting for him to pay attention.

He hated chance. His instructions kept changing, which made him feel uneasy. So many parts of this job were out of his control, and he was powerless. He felt that he was hurtling towards a conclusion, a final outcome he could do little to alter.

He watched two girls as they walked along the leafy street, chatting to each other as they passed large houses, all with ample gardens and drives, sporting two, sometimes three cars. It was strange how careless some people were with what was most precious to them.

He waited until the girls walked past his car, as he pretended to do something on his phone. He turned to the backseat and said, 'Pavel, I will tell you when it is safe to leave the car. Until then, remain where you are.' He started the engine.

The girls wore shorts and T-shirts, their legs and faces

pink from the summer sun; both were carrying tennis racquets. Staying a safe distance behind, he followed them until they reached the tennis club at the edge of the village, where one of the girls stopped and waved her hands in the air. For a second, he thought that somehow he had been spotted, but the pair were merely fooling around.

When the girls were only a few strides from the entrance, he shouted to Pavel. 'Now! Go!' He could see two people on court, one of whom stopped and stared as the two men rushed from the car towards the teenage girls.

One of the girls screamed, but was silenced by a punch in the face from Pavel. The other girl, who had tried to run, was caught and pulled back as she attempted to duck out of reach. The couple on the tennis court were shouting and running towards them. He looked up to see Pavel pull a handgun from his pocket, and the girl nearly struggled from his grip. A cloth soaked in chloroform over her mouth and nose quickly made her limp in his arms.

Pavel grabbed the girl from him and pulled her into the back of the car, while he jumped in and started the engine. It had all taken less than thirty seconds. He looked in the mirror as he gunned the car along the road; the other girl lay on the pavement, being helped by one of the tennis players, while the other talked into his mobile phone.

He sped out of the village until he came to a lay-by, where a nondescript white van waited. They exited the car, Pavel with the unconscious girl in his arms.

Quickly, the van pulled away. In the back, Alice Taylor lay for a few minutes before she began to move, lazily, as though rousing from a deep sleep. As she opened her eyes, disorientated by the motion and the gloom, she peered at the huge man sitting opposite her. Her screams made him laugh.

Daley sat in the living room, feeling less at home than ever. Liz had taken the baby upstairs to his cot. He could hear her talking gently to the child through the white monitor on the table. He felt elated and terrified at the same time. He had promised himself not to give in to the emotion of being a parent until he was sure that he actually was one. Yet here he was sitting in this room, listening to his wife soothe the child that bore his name, the child that she swore was his, to sleep. Gradually, James Daley's cries became happy gurgles and then a soft snore; all the time, Liz was humming a quiet tune.

His phone vibrated in his pocket. He noted Brian Scott's name and answered.

'Jim, where are you?'

'At home, in Howwood. Listen, Brian, I've got some bad news. Sarah MacDougall was murdered at Cornton Vale this morning.'

'I know. I found out about an hour ago, poor lassie.'

'I'm sorry, mate. I've discovered a few things. Something's not right, not right at all. I don't want to say anything on the phone, just . . . don't trust anyone. I'll brief you when I get back.'

'Things are moving on here, as well.' Scott told Daley about Cudihey's caravan, conveniently near the map coordinates they had discovered, and about its unusual contents. 'Aye, but there's worse,' Scott continued, as he heard Daley express his surprise. 'Alice Taylor's been kidnapped.'

'What? How is that possible? I thought they were being guarded at their home.'

'Aye, so they were. Turns oot, Daddy thought it was all right for her to go and stay with a friend for a couple of days. Since nobody else would know where she would be, he didnae think it was a problem.'

'Fuck's sake. Where did this happen, Brian?'

'Aboot twenty miles fae where you are now. I've got the number here of the investigating DS.' Scott passed the number on to Daley, who wrote it down in his notebook.

'OK, I'll take a trip out and look at the scene and see what they've got, then I'll come back down the road. I should be back by, oh, eight, or so,' said Daley, looking at his watch.

'Nae bother, I'll see you then.'

'And Brian, keep all of this as quiet as you can, do you know what I mean? And watch your back. Don't trust anybody, I mean it.'

Liz walked into the room just as Daley was finishing the call.

'Don't tell me – you can't stay,' she said, sitting down heavily and holding her head in her hands.

'I've got to go, Liz. You know how it is,' he said, remembering the last time he'd said those words, only a few days before.

'I want to come to Kinloch. Not today, but soon. I want us to be a family, Jim.'

He looked at her. 'Yes. I want that, too.' He'd said the words before he could stop himself.

Alice Taylor whimpered as the van bumped over rough ground. She kept telling herself to stay calm, to take things in, to remember. Even though her hands had been tied, she could still see her watch; they had been travelling for just under three hours. Occasionally, she had been able to glimpse patches of sky, or trees and buildings, between the headrests and through the windscreen of the vehicle. Even so, she had no idea where they were, or even in which direction they were travelling. She found herself saying a prayer which she repeated over and over again until it became a mantra: please help me, please help me.

Across from her, the huge bulk of the bald man, straight from her nightmares, snored, as his head lolled from side to side with the motion of the vehicle. He had laughed maniacally until the driver called out to him in a language she didn't understand, though it sounded a bit like the Russian her father sometimes spoke when he was conducting business on the phone. This had calmed the monster, as she thought of him; in fact, he had been almost gentle when he'd tied her hands together.

Again her silent prayer echoed in her mind.

30

'I need a favour, Philip, and I need it now,' said Wilson, the mobile phone hot in his hand. In the last few hours he had been trying to make sense of what was happening, and what had happened in the last few days. The more he thought about it, the more worried became. 'NKV Dynamics and Elise Fordham, what have you got?' He listened, then thanked the man. 'Listen, before you go, I need to know all you can find on our old colleague at the paper. All there is to know about Elise Fordham's time there, OK? But, Philip, it's sensitive.'

He put the phone down and stared down to the street from his hotel window. There she was, surrounded by cameras, journalists, her aides, security and the public – exactly where every politician wanted to be. He should have been on the street with her, but he'd feigned a migraine in order to stay in his room and collect his thoughts – work the problem, as an old editor who'd taught him the darker side of his craft, had called it. He was trying to work this problem, but something kept clouding his mind, obstructing his thought processes. He jumped as his phone rang again.

'Yes, Philip, that was quick. I'm glad to see you haven't forgotten the many skills I had to batter into that thick skull of yours.' He listened intently, then said, 'Are you sure?' After a short pause, during which he could feel his own jaw drop as he heard what the editor of his old paper had to say, he clicked the phone off and looked back out the window. Elise Fordham was still working the crowd; he could tell by the look on the faces of some of the journalists that she was doing well.

And to think I thought I knew you, he mused.

Daley pulled into the car park at Kinloch Police Office just after eight o'clock. The drive back would have been long, winding and monotonous had it not been for the glorious views. As he'd stared across the Atlantic towards the Irish coast, green in the haze, he could have been driving on one of the Greek Islands, or even the Caribbean. Even the town itself had an almost Mediterranean feel as he navigated the roundabout at the bottom of Main Street, the loch, bathed in golden light to his left. Through his open window he could smell summer: the warm salt tang of the sea breeze, overlaid by the odours of barbecues, petrol fumes and hot tar. The good folk of Kinloch sat on benches, or strolled along the seafront in various states of undress; one or two waved at him as he drove by.

He found Scott and Rainsford standing beside a clearboard adorned with various pictures and information, Cudihey's face at the centre, like a fat spider at the heart of a complex web. In the background, the investigation team still toiled away, desperately trying to find a morsel of evidence that would help give meaning to their investigations.

'All right, Jim?' asked Scott. His face was flushed, his habitual bonhomie overlaid by a restlessness that was immediately apparent. The bar's open, Daley thought. 'Done oor best here tae try and put everything intae place, as far as we can understand it, anyhow.'

'OK. Any response from Interpol on the possible ID of the guy who kidnapped Alice Taylor, with Pavel Abdic?' Daley noticed Scott and Rainsford exchange a look.

'Yes, sir,' replied Rainsford. 'But you're not going to like it.' Without stopping to hear Daley's response, he bent over a computer, and a face flashed up on the large screen. 'This man is known only as the Dragon. As you can see, sir, he fits the description of the eye witnesses present at Alice Taylor's kidnapping, even down to the scar on his forehead.' The screen showed a dark-haired, handsome man, with a lined face, a vivid red scar running almost horizontally along his forehead. He had a long, thin nose, high cheekbones and – even from the evidence of this blurred photograph – piercing eyes.

'Are Interpol confident that Abdic is who we think he is?'

'Yes, sir. Pavel Abdic and this Dragon are known confederates, both from the former Yugoslavia. The first record of them fighting together was as mercenaries in the Chechen War with Russia. It would appear that Abdic was captured by the Russians and left to the mercy of the FSB. So, miraculously, we find them being used as assassins and muscle, unofficially, but certainly under the command of the Russians in the second Chechen conflict.'

'So they swap sides?'

'Indeed, but not just that. Interpol tell us that until his capture by the Russians, Abdic had been the senior of the two. He had been high up in the Serbian army, and fled when order was restored. By the time the pair get involved in the second

Chechen War he appears to have taken a subordinate role to the Dragon.' Rainsford paused, lifting a piece of paper from a desk. 'Interpol say, "We consider Pavel Abdic and the man known as the Dragon to be, if not agents of the Russian state, certainly to be in the pay of one of its most prominent individuals; namely, oligarch Arkady Visonovich. He cut his teeth in the KGB and got very near to the top of the FSB before things broke down. He then emerged from the post-Yeltsin era as a billionaire, one of Europe's richest men. He made his money from grabbing huge tracts of the country's mineral wealth during the power vacuum after the fall of communism. He has legitimate holdings in businesses throughout Europe and beyond – both openly and covertly – but is known to have associations with drug cartels in South and Central America, as well as in Europe, particularly in Northern Italy."' Rainsford looked up. 'It goes on, sir, but basically, I think we can be sure that Alice Taylor is in real trouble.'

'Yes, I think we can,' said Daley. 'Fuck! So why haven't Interpol done something about this Visonovich guy?'

'They can't. A European arrest warrant was issued for him way back in 2000. He was wanted for war crimes in Chechnya, as well as involvement in organised crime in Sweden, Germany, Belgium . . . and more, sir. However, he doesn't set foot outside the Russian Federation now, and they have ignored at least twenty attempts by various foreign governments to try and extradite him.'

Daley looked at the screen, now showing Visonovich's picture. He had a round face, olive skin and narrow, slanting eyes. His hair, or what was left of it, stuck up in salt-and-pepper tufts above his ears and around the side of his head. 'Why here? What is there for these people in this area?'

'Hard tae say, Jim,' replied Scott, who had remained uncharacteristically silent. 'But when you see the way this boy Miller copped it, an' oor friend Newell, well, it's no' the local thugs' way of goin' aboot things, is it?'

Daley swallowed. What he was hearing was almost unbelievable, but somehow it made sense. In light of what he knew about Donald, it made a lot of sense. 'And what about Cudihey and his windmills?'

'This Cudihey guy's a mystery. As we said, Jim, whether he just had a wee notion for the lassie Kirsteen Lang, or they had some kind o' relationship, who knows? Looking at him, and looking at her, you would say it was unlikely, but he was keen on her. That fuckin' rubber doll is a' the evidence you need of that.' Scott screwed up his face at the thought.

'But why there? Why all the photographs of that ship, the pictures taken at the beach? Why the caravan, come to that?'

'You would say it was a wee bit too much o' a coincidence. There's another strange thing – no' far fae the caravan we came across this wee compound. Here, take a look for yourself,' said Scott, handing Daley some photographs. 'The only thing we know is that it belongs tae the MOD.'

'We'll need to find out what it is,' said Daley as he looked at the pictures.

'The terminus of the cable we talked about, sir,' said Rainsford. 'I don't think we'll get much joy from the MOD, do you?'

'Oh, another thing, Jim,' said Scott. 'Edinburgh's preliminary investigations into Kirsteen Lang show something that might give us a lead.'

'What?'

'She was paying every month for a safety deposit box, an' a high security one at that. The Edinburgh Financial Investigations team are on it right now.' He was interrupted when the door to the CID room swung open and Inspector Layton entered.

'Sorry to interrupt, gents. Can I have a word with you in private, DCI Daley?'

'Yes, Inspector. Two seconds, please.' Daley stood. 'The girl has to be a priority. Even though she wasn't taken here, I think it's safe for us to assume that she is with the Dragon and Abdic. The questions is: are they back here?'

'I spoke to Mr Taylor about half an hour ago. So far he has had no contact from the kidnappers,' said Rainsford.

'Poor lassie,' Scott said, shaking his head. 'What I don't understand is, why would he be bothered aboot her noo, anyhow? He must realise that she's identified this Abdic character. What have they got tae gain by taking her?'

'Yes, that thought had crossed my mind, too. One other thing I want to know, doesn't this Dragon have a proper name?' Daley looked around for an answer.

'I asked Interpol that very question, sir,' said Rainsford. 'It would appear that his actual identity is unknown, though it's believed that he was orphaned during the war in the former Yugoslavia in the early nineties, when he was about ten, or so. The intelligence is that Abdic saved his life and brought him up as a kind of protégé.'

'Aye, an' noo he's the boss,' said Scott.

'Excuse me, gentlemen.' Daley turned to Layton. The pair walked into Daley's office; Layton closed the door firmly behind him as Daley took a seat and indicated that Layton do the same.

'I thought you should know, sir, that as of this afternoon, Chief Superintendent Donald has been suspended.'

'Why?'

'I'm afraid I can't tell you, sir. Orders from the Chief Constable.'

There's someone higher. Daley remembered Sarah MacDougall's note. He still had it in his pocket.

'So, where is he now?'

'Not sure, sir. Apparently he signed himself off sick this morning. He has to appear in front of a disciplinary panel next week; assuming, of course, that he is fit to do so.'

Daley thought for a moment, but decided to say nothing about the contents of Sarah MacDougall's letter. *Trust nobody.*

'Thank you, Inspector Layton. I take it you'll be heading back to HQ?'

'No, not immediately. I've been instructed to remain behind for a while, to carry out certain investigations. Oh, and to assist you in any way you see fit.'

'Investigate me, you mean?

'No,' replied Layton, his face betraying no emotion.

Stephen Taylor paced across the floor of his large office in the heart of Edinburgh, a small piece of paper in his hand. He read it again.

Go to the Auld Hundred Bar on Rose Street at opening time tomorrow morning, twelve o'clock. Sit at the downstairs bar and order a vodka and tonic. You will be handed a note. Finish your drink and take it out into the street to read. Follow the instructions carefully. If you bring anyone into the

premises with you, or fail to follow these instructions exactly,
your daughter will die.

The message was concise and to the point. He wondered why they had chosen the Auld Hundred. When they went shopping in the city his wife liked to have lunch in the restaurant upstairs; she loved the sticky toffee pudding.

He looked at the ceiling of his office in despair; why hadn't he been more careful? Why had he let her go to a friend's house? If she wasn't returned safely these questions would haunt him for the rest of his life. He had assumed that once they had left Kinloch and returned to Edinburgh they were out of danger. Even the police had been relaxed, though they had posted a car outside their Duddingston village home, just in case. Why had he listened to her? Why had he given in? They had been so careful that no one apart from both families knew where Alice was going.

What did they want from him? He looked at the phone on his desk. They hadn't told him not to inform the police, just to have no one with him in the bar. He pressed a button on the phone console. 'Gillian, get me the police, please.'

Daley watched Layton as he left the room. He wasn't naïve enough not to realise that if they suspected Donald of impropriety, they would investigate anyone close to him, especially the senior officers under his command. But he had nothing to hide. He was far more worried about Alice Taylor than any investigation into his probity.

Daley looked at his watch; it was almost nine p.m., though outside it was still daylight. He walked back into the CID suite. 'How long will it take us to get to that caravan and this compound you've discovered?'

'Aboot twenty minutes in the car, then a long traipse through the heather,' groaned Scott. 'Why?'

'Me and you are off for a wee wander then. Come on.' He picked up his jacket from the back of a chair and looked at Scott, who hadn't moved. 'What's the problem, Brian?'

'I'm dead on ma feet, here. Can we no' check it out tomorrow?'

'No time like the present. We shouldn't be much more than an hour if we get a move on. Hurry up.' Daley walked to the door. And the less time you have to drink yourself into oblivion, he thought, the better. 'Half of Police Scotland is out looking for Alice Taylor. I need to clear my head.'

Soon the pair were in the car and driving out of Kinloch, Scott looking out at the passing scenery, saying nothing. They drove for about twenty minutes, as Scott had predicted, before the DS broke his silence.

'In here, Jim.' Daley pulled the car into a lay-by, and then followed Scott, who was still quiet, down the grass track and onto a stretch of white sand. The sea had taken on a darker hue now and the distinctive Paps of Jura were shrouded in a purple cloak through which pinpricks of light were beginning to show, as the stars began to shimmer through the short hours of darkness.

'I know what you're doing,' said Scott, as they made their way across the rough grass towards the fenced-off compound.

'My job?'

'Trying tae keep me off the bevy. Dae you think I came doon in the last fuckin' shower, Jim?'

Daley stopped and looked at his friend. 'I need to tell you something, and I need you to be the person I've known for all these years, however bloody long it's been. I need the real Brian Scott back.'

'Aye, whatever. Just gie me a break wae this fuckin' drink shite. I know what I'm doin'. You try getting shot – I'll tell you, Jim, the stuff that I dreamed when I was unconscious, well, I cannae get it oot o' my heid. It was real, you know what I mean?'

Daley felt a flash of guilt. He had assumed that Brian Scott would recover quickly from his injuries and bounce back to being the effective police officer he had been for so many years. He hadn't considered the deep scars that his near-death experience had left; were bound to have left. Once it was clear that Scott's life was no longer in danger, Daley supposed he hadn't given the matter too much thought. As usual, he had been embroiled in the day-to-day business of running both the local CID, as well as the sub-division itself. Then there was Liz, the baby, and all the other attendant problems. He remembered his promise to Liz earlier in the day; he remembered Mary Dunn.

'Donald's been suspended.'

'What?'

'Donald's been suspended. Layton told me this afternoon.'

After a moment's quiet contemplation, Scott said, 'How dae I no' feel like pulling off all my clothes and running intae the surf for joy?'

'Read this.' Daley handed Sarah MacDougall's letter to his DS. Scott fiddled about in various pockets, found his reading glasses and squinted at the letter in the fading light.

'She should never have been in there, Jim.'

'That's not why I'm showing you this. I know it's a tragedy, Brian, but we have to grasp at anything we can get here.'

'How dae you know that it's right? She'd have said anything just tae get oot o' that place, dae you no' think?'

'No, I don't. I think that us being here, in Kinloch, is no coincidence. Right back to the start there's been something going on.'

'So is this why they've suspended his majesty?'

Daley shook his head. 'No, you're the only other person that's seen this, and that's the way it's going to stay, for the time being anyhow.'

'You're taking a risk there, Jim boy. That's material evidence in a murder inquiry, regardless o' whitever else it's saying. Anyway, who's these mysterious folk at the top?'

'I don't know, Brian. That's why I'm keeping this. The librarian at Cornton Vale saw me find it. She's bound to mention it to Stirling now she's in custody. But it's her word against mine and, let's face it, her word doesn't mean too much right now. When Stirling ask about it, I'll just play the daft laddie.'

'What's she in custody for?'

'Whoever had Sarah killed used the librarian to spy on her.'

'Bastards. But who wanted her killed?'

'That, Brian, is the sixty-four-thousand-dollar question. Old enemies of her father, or someone closer to home?'

'What, Donald? Come on, Jim, you cannae be serious aboot that, surely?'

Daley shrugged his shoulders. 'I can't be sure about anything. This new force doesn't help, either. At least we knew everybody before, now we don't have a clue who half the bosses are.'

'Gie me half an hour wae Donald. I'll just beat the truth oot the bastard.'

Suddenly, Daley flinched; a flash of light appeared over Scott's shoulder and illuminated the compound in a harsh white light.

'Get down, Brian!' shouted Daley, almost deafened by a rushing sound overhead that shook his very bones.

The two detectives lay prone on the machair as sand and muck flew over their heads. Daley thought his head would burst as the noise ramped up; the ground trembled with the sheer force of what was happening. Through his tightly closed eyes, Daley was still aware of the flashing light.

As quickly as it started, it stopped. Daley and Scott lay motionless for a moment, then the DCI lifted his head. 'What the fuck was that?'

'Lights in the sky, Jim. Lights in the sky. I don't care what you think o' me, I need a bloody drink!'

31

The bar at the County was unusually crowded. Annie waved at the detectives as they made their way through the throng towards the bar.

'How are yous the night, boys? I'll be getting a bonus if it keeps as busy as this. Mair power tae the wee green men, that's all I'll say. It's no' been this busy since the Americans were testing oot they invisible planes back in the eighties.'

'Eh? What do you mean?'

'Och, they thought it was a' hush hush, but we knew fine. It was the stealthy planes, or whootever they're called.'

'Stealth, do you mean?'

'Aye, that's it. Half the Americans were dating lassies fae the toon. No' many secrets between the sheets, boys.'

'There you are, Brian,' said Daley. 'Lights in the sky.'

'Aye, well, if what I saw the other night is anything tae go by that plane must be out of this world.' He handed a large malt whisky to Daley, who was scanning the bar for a free table.

'Shit. Don't look now, Brian. I've just found out why the bar's so busy.' Daley took a gulp of his drink and swilled it around in his mouth.

'Well, it's no' happy hour,' said Scott, looking at the paltry change he had just been handed by Annie. 'That bloody stuff costs an arm and a leg, gaffer.'

'Ronnie Wiley and his cronies are holding court at a table at the back.' Daley had to shout into Scott's ear to be heard above the din.

'What, *the* Ronnie Wiley?'

'Take a look for yourself.'

Scott stretched up and peered over the crowd. Three men were sitting at the back table, the one usually occupied by the policemen when they were in for a drink. Wiley spotted Scott and gave him a hearty wave. He said something to one of the men beside him, then got up from the table and started forcing his way through the crowd towards the detectives.

'Fuck,' said Daley. 'Here we go. We'd have been better off in the Douglas Arms.'

'Gentlemen, how nice to see you after so long,' said Wiley. He was about five eight, in his forties, with long hair pulled back into a ponytail. He was wearing a designer shirt and jeans, and gave the impression of somebody who was working hard to stave off the reality of his middle age, and failing badly. 'Can I get you hard-working men a drink?'

'No thanks,' said Daley. He noticed that the level of conversation in the bar had dropped dramatically.

'What brings you doon here?' asked Scott. 'Don't tell me they've run oot o' sleazy stories up the road?'

'Oh, come on, DS Scott. Do you think original sin is only alive and well in Glasgow? I can assure you that is most certainly not the case.' He eyed Daley with a smirk. 'Is that not right, Chief Inspector?'

Most of the drinkers around them had stopped their

conversations, and were now looking at the two policemen and the ponytailed journalist. Behind the bar, Annie looked suddenly worried, rubbing at a pint glass with a towel.

'As you know, Ronnie, a policeman's job is pretty universal. The same old problems crop up again and again – same old faces, too, come to that.' Daley smiled.

'I wonder, how are you getting on with the investigation of these dreadful murders – assassinations, more like? Now a girl connected with the investigation has been kidnapped, and is it not true that another woman who was helping the police with their inquiries was bludgeoned to death in the jail? And how is the investigation into the suicide of poor Mr Cudihey going, not to mention the UFOs that have been plaguing the area? I wouldn't have thought you men had time for a social life.' He grinned at Daley, showing a row of exceptionally white teeth.

'Noo, come on, please, sir,' said Annie, deciding it was time to intervene. 'The polis just want tae have a drink and relax after a hard day.'

'Certainly. I'm just chewing the fat with some old friends. Is that not right, gentlemen?'

'We're no friends of yours, Ronnie,' Scott said, his face like thunder. 'Jeest you dae your job, an' let us do oors, got it?'

'No problem,' Wiley replied with a shrug. He turned as though about to leave, then stopped. 'None of your other colleagues in tonight? DS Mary Dunn, for example?'

'She'll be back at hame turnin' doon the bed,' came a voice from the back of the room.

'Aye, wae the sussies on tae,' called another, raising a bawdy laugh from the bar.

'Rumours and gossip, Mr Daley, truly dreadful,' said Wiley. 'I'd better take a seat.'

'Aye, take the weight aff your feet,' said Scott.

'You're a loyal little dog, right enough, Brian.' He turned to Annie. 'A drink for everyone, and just put it on my tab,' he shouted, to a cheer from the assembled drinkers. As a surge of customers pressed against the bar, anxious to redeem their free drink while it was still on offer, Wiley was pushed against Daley. 'Be sure to give Mrs Daley my regards.' With that he forced his way through the crowd and back to his table.

'I'm ready for an early night,' said Daley, knocking back the rest of his drink. 'You should do the same.'

'Aye, Jimmy, aye. Just one more for the ditch for me.'

'Make sure it is just *one* more.' Daley put his glass on the bar, said goodnight to Annie and left. Fortunately, nobody seemed to notice that he'd gone.

'Gie me another, Annie,' shouted Scott. 'An' make it a large one.'

Daley jumped in his car. He'd just had the one whisky, so was fine to drive, but as he set off on the road towards Machrie, he wished he'd drunk much more.

Just before the village, he turned down a long, rutted drive that led towards a small white cottage. He parked his car beside the blue hatchback already there and walked towards the front door, gravel popping underfoot. To his left, the dying glow of the sun kept the darkness of the night at bay. The air smelled of cut grass, warm earth and the invigorating scent of the ocean, never far in Kinloch. He was pleased to see a light still on behind her bedroom curtains. As he was about to knock on the door, it swung open, Mary Dunn silhouetted in the bright light of the hall.

'Sir . . . Jim,' she said. 'I heard a car, I wasn't sure if it was you.' She smiled. It was a warm night and she was wearing a large men's T-shirt, her legs bare. 'Come in,' she said, brushing a loose strand of auburn hair from her brow.

Daley followed her into the cottage. She showed him into the small lounge, then walked into the kitchen, returning with a bottle of white wine and two glasses.

'Eh, not for me, thanks,' said Daley, with a nervous smile. 'I've got the car.'

'So you're not staying,' she said, her eyes downcast. 'You don't mind if I do, then?' She didn't wait for a reply, twisting the cork from the bottle and pouring wine into the large glass.

'You know I saw Liz.'

'Yes, of course. I take it that it went well.'

'Listen, Mary. It went the way it always goes. It never changes.'

'Oh, so you're in love with her again, is that it? Thanks very much, now fuck off, Mary.' She shifted her gaze from his, as tears brimmed in her eyes.

'It's not a case of being in love with her again. I've always tried to explain to you how I feel about her. It's just that I thought we could never be together again, you know.'

'Oh, great, and now you can. Happy families – you, her, and your brother-in-law's baby. I'm so happy for you!'

'I think the baby is mine, Mary.'

She sat back in her chair and drew her legs up under the T-shirt. He could see that she was making a mammoth effort not to cry. 'How do you know?' she said, through choked sobs. 'You can't have the results of the DNA test yet.'

'How did you know about that?'

'I'm a fucking detective, you know, not just your bit on the side. I found the instructions in your bin, if you must know. I've been waiting for something like this to happen for months. It doesn't make it any easier now it has.'

'You were never just my bit on the side. You must know that!'

'OK, then, fuck buddy, a shoulder to cry on. Whatever you want to call it to make yourself feel better.' She took a large swig of wine. 'What has she got that I don't? I'm young, and I would never hurt you in the way she has. You told me about all the things she's done to you, the affairs, all of the heartache. You've been in my bed for months, telling me how hard your life was with her, and now you've decided that it doesn't matter because you *love* her. Fuck you!' She leant forward and poured herself more wine, filling the glass to the brim.

'It's not like that. He's my son.'

'*If* he's your son, you mean.'

'I know he is, I can feel it here,' said Daley, placing his hand on his heart.

'So you're prepared to live a lie, just so that your son has a happy family. Well, I don't think it'll make anyone happy!' She sat back again, cradling her wine. 'My father left us when I was ten, you know.'

'You never said.'

'I don't speak about it much. He was a bastard. As soon as he left, our lives improved. My mother got a job back in the bank she had worked in before she'd had me, I went to school, everything was fine. Instead of me lying in my bed listening to them arguing, or my mother screaming, or my dad taunting her with his latest affair, we listened to music and watched the TV, we talked, we were a normal family. Them splitting up was the best thing that ever happened. What was left of my childhood was happy, just me and my mum, so don't think that trying to mould the perfect nuclear family will make everything OK.'

'I would never behave like that. I hope you don't think I would.'

'No? You might manage to be faithful, now you've sown your wild oats with me, but what about her? Do you really think she's changed overnight just because she's given birth? Don't be stupid, Jim.'

'I have to give it a go. I have to try.'

'Oh, just get out!' shouted Mary, throwing her glass against the fireplace, where it shattered spectacularly. 'Just leave me alone.'

Daley hesitated. 'I don't want to leave you upset like this.'

'Get out!' she shouted. 'Now!'

Daley got up from his chair and looked at Mary. She had buried her head in her knees, still drawn up to her chest, and was sobbing uncontrollably. He held his hand out to touch her auburn hair, but stopped himself. 'Will you be OK?'

'I'm fine, just leave.'

With great willpower, Brian Scott managed to drag himself from the bar after just three more drinks. In all honesty, he was fed up looking at Wiley's sneer every time he happened to glance in his direction.

'Yous both look wild and tired, Brian,' said Annie, as he made to leave the bar and go back to his room.

'Aye, force o' work, you know how it is. You've had a busy night yoursel', by the looks o' things.'

'Aye, I have that,' she said, then hesitated. 'It's my night off the morrow. There's a new Chinese restaurant jeest opened doon at the other end o' Long Road.'

'Oh aye,' said Scott, trying to locate his cigarettes.

'I jeest wondered if you fancied a wee meal, jeest as friends, you understand. You look as though you could dae with a good feed.'

'Eh, aye, I mean why not, eh? Be nice tae dae something for a change, rather than just sit aboot the pub and work. Better no' make it too early, mind. You know the hours I have tae keep.'

'What aboot half eight?'

'Aye, that should be OK. Unless we bump into a wee green man in the street, that is. I'll gie Jim the heads up tomorrow.'

'Great, it's no' a date then.'

'No, it's no'. We both know a date's just another word for a casual shag, these days,' said Scott with a grin. 'I'll get you in here, eh? I'm just heading for a quick smoke before I hit the sack. See you tomorrow.'

He left Annie behind the bar, and made his way to the smoking area at the back of the hotel. He jumped when somebody spoke from the shadows.

'Your boss doesn't like a slice of the truth, does he, DS Scott?' Despite the slurring, Wiley's voice was unmistakable.

'You bastard. If I was you, I'd get tae ma bed before they aliens get hold o' you an' take you to the Planet Arsehole, where you belong.'

Wiley moved to stand in front of the detective, close enough for Scott to make out his bloodshot eyes.

'You pricks are all the same. Just love the fact you've got a warrant card in your pocket and a wee bit of power. Aye, well, things are changing, Brian. Cops like you and Daley are dinosaurs, from another age. The new force is full of graduates, folk with brains, not backstreet bully boys like yourself that somebody was stupid enough to give a uniform to, back in the day.' He leaned in closer. 'I'm making it my business to expose bastards like you, make sure this new police force is a fresh start.'

'Very commendable, I'm sure, Ronnie,' said Scott, taking a long draw of his cigarette. 'Since my career's near up, I hope you'll indulge me one last time?'

'With what? The phone number for the bookies or the snooker halls where the rest of the down-and-out ex-cops hang out? No problem.'

'No, with this.' Before Wiley could move, Scott smashed his forehead into the other man's nose, sending him tumbling backwards with a sharp crack.

'You fuckin' bastard, it's broken,' screamed Wiley, his voice muffled by his hands on his nose and the blood in his throat.

'You need tae watch doon here, Ronnie. The polis are just no' daein' their jobs, know what I mean?' Scott kneeled over his victim. 'Might have been one o' they wee green men, eh.' He thrust his hand into Wiley's pocket and pulled out a small ball; dark and hard and covered with cling film. 'I'll just keep a hold o' your stash o' dope, Ronnie. Just in case you fancy a wee complaint against Her Majesty's Constabulary. Though I'm sure naebody saw nothing. That's the problem wae these attacks outside pubs, I've just stopped bothering wae them altogether. You have a good sleep now.' Scott got to his feet and walked back into the hotel, leaving Wiley whimpering on the ground.

32

Not for the first time, as he stared across the loch in the early hours of another golden dawn, Daley wished he hadn't stopped smoking. He was sitting on the decking outside his home, high on the hill overlooking the loch and the town beyond. To his left, the island that sheltered Kinloch from an angry sea's wrath loomed dark and immovable; he could see the white dots of sheep grazing near its loaf-shaped summit. Directly across the still waters, the dead of Kinloch lay under the burgeoning light of a sky that offered the hopes, fears and promises of another day for those who lived and breathed. For those in heavenly repose, the summer's warmth was but a long-forgotten whisper on the the wind.

He always looked at graveyards with the same melancholy. Was it here that his eternal resting place lay, soft and silent but surely waiting for him? Maybe, somewhere over there, his very own piece of earth, the soil to which he would return, was ready for him. Somewhere, the tree that would be his coffin was growing tall and strong, until the axe of his death brought it down.

He tried to force out these thoughts, only for Alice Taylor's pretty young face to parade before his mind's eye, followed by John Donald, the Dragon, Liz and Brian Scott. The grotesque corpse of Walter Cudihey; Malky Miller with his tongue pulled through the gore of his own neck; the look of agony on Rory Newell's face; the clever, beautiful, but misguided Sarah MacDougall, dead on a mortuary slab with her head caved in; and only a few miles away, Kirsteen Lang, a young woman he had only read about and seen, full of life, in photographs, now still and lifeless.

He thought of Mary, the smell, taste and touch of her, the warmth between them as she straddled him with her long legs and worked hard and slow to bring them both to climax, all the time arousing, mesmerising him. He could see her long auburn hair splayed across a white pillow as she lay sleeping after they made love. Why was it that, so often, when he thought of death, he remembered sex.

He still missed Liz, yearned for her, even, but how could he feel for someone else in this way? He knew of men who sought solace in the arms of other women to escape the mundane day-to-day treadmill of their marriages; the thrill was all in the search for new, yielding flesh. He was not like that. The mere act was without thrill unless he felt something more. And he had obviously felt something more for his young colleague. Many would have ended their illicit relationship without a second thought; he couldn't. He knew that in similar situations, Liz had disposed of lovers without a shred of regret.

Was the jump from death to sex his mind's way of telling him that his relationship with his wife was at an end – dead? Then he remembered the child who had stared at him so recently. He could see the world in that one tiny, crumpled face.

He looked up, just in time to see the flash of a shooting star arcing across the darker sky to his right, where night still had purchase.

Lights in the sky.

For Brian Scott the day began with an aching head, but not in the usual way. As he struggled up and sat on the side of his bed, he realised the pains in his forehead had more to do with its connection to a journalist's nose than to booze.

He was pleased that, though he had been drinking the previous evening, he could remember absolutely everything that had taken place: conversations, faces, places, even going to bed. Progress, indeed.

As his bare feet slapped across the cool tiles of the en suite, he heard a sharp knock on his door. Cursing, he padded back across his bedroom and opened it a crack. There, immaculately groomed and fresh-faced, stood DS Rainsford.

'Aye, son, how can I help you? I'd invite you in, but I'm in my scants,' said Scott, noting the uniformed officer standing behind Rainsford.

'This isn't a social call, DS Scott,' Rainsford replied. 'There's been a complaint about you, of assault. I need you to come with me.'

'What?' Despite his state of undress, Scott flung the door open and took a step towards the younger man, his bare toes almost touching the other man's tan brogues. 'If you're talking aboot that lowlife bastard Wiley, you can forget it.'

'This has nothing to do with Mr Wiley. A young woman has made a complaint that you sexually assaulted her in the early hours of this morning.'

'What? Aye, very good. And just where did this assault take place? In the bar doonstairs, wae half o' Kinloch watching? Wake up, son.'

'Step back inside, DS Scott. I need to search your room, as accusations of the use and possession of controlled substances have also been made.' Rainsford looked down his nose at Scott.

'Right, I get it. Listen, I found a wad o' cannabis resin in a journalist called Wiley's pocket last night, if that's what you mean.'

'Did you charge Mr Wiley, or lodge this evidence at the office?'

'It was the middle o' the night, so I just cautioned Wiley and let him on his way,' said Scott, already sensing the trap.

'That's not my information, DS Scott. A Miss Tracy Black has come forward to say that you invited her to your room last night on the pretext that you wanted to buy a class C controlled drug from her. Before the transaction was completed, you pinned her to your bed and sexually assaulted her. Now, please come with me, Brian. Or do I have to arrest you formally? Constable Latimer, please conduct a search of DS Scott's room.'

'You might have been tae university, son, but you are one stupid fuck,' shouted Scott as Latimer forced past him and began rummaging about in the hotel bedroom.

'I'm just following procedure,' said Rainsford. 'Something you seem incapable of.'

'Whoot's all this?' Annie was hurrying down the corridor. 'I heard voices.'

'It's a police matter, madam,' said Rainsford. 'I apologise

247

for any disturbance. DS Scott, please get some clothes on and come with me.'

Scott looked between the tall young man and Annie. 'Don't worry, my dear, just a misunderstanding. Dae you know a lassie called Tracy Black? Well, she's telt this fuckin' idiot here that I bought drugs fae her, and tried tae assault her. That's right, is it no'?' he asked Rainsford angrily, struggling into his trousers.

'Yet again, most unprofessional, DS Scott,' said Rainsford. He turned to Annie and said, 'Please ignore what you have just been told, madam.'

Annie was about to make her opinions known when a shout from inside Scott's room silenced the three on the landing.

'I found this, Sergeant.' PC Latimer handed Rainsford a small black ball, wrapped in cling film. 'Found it in DS Scott's trouser pocket,' he said, then looked at Scott and shrugged apologetically.

Rainsford rolled the ball around in his right hand, peeled off some of the plastic, and sniffed. 'DS Scott, I am arresting you on suspicion of the possession of a controlled substance under the terms of The Misuse of Drugs Act 2005. Please come with me.'

Just then, from behind Annie, a bright flash drew their attention. Standing down the hotel corridor with a photographer stood a slight man with a broad plaster over his nose.

'Have you got anything to say, Detective Sergeant Scott?' said Wiley.

The door to the room opposite Scott's cracked open, and the head of a bespectacled Japanese tourist poked through it. He looked astonished as he saw Scott being led away with a policeman's hand on his shoulder, a camera flashing as the photographer took shot after shot. Scott's loud objections filled the air with expletives that the bemused guest did not understand.

'It's a lovely day,' said Annie, with a forced smile. 'If you're on your way tae breakfast, I recommend the kippers, jeest in yesterday.' She cleared her throat, smiled again, then left the man scratching his head in the corridor.

33

Superintendent Donnie McClusky stared at a bank of large screens in the AV room of Edinburgh Police Office. The various camera feeds showed different sections of Rose Street, including the front of the Auld Hundred bar and restaurant. In the footage from inside the premises he watched a woman mopping the floor while a man placed bottles on a high shelf.

'When does the action start?' he asked.

'Taylor is en route now, sir,' answered a uniformed police sergeant behind a console, wearing a pair of headphones. 'We have him wired, but as he's driving at the moment all we can hear is Ken Bruce on Radio 2. I'll patch the audio through when he's parked.'

McClusky looked around the room. Call the new police force what they liked, this was a Lothian and Borders operation. Strathclyde had failed to save Alice Taylor, and now that the problem had landed in his lap, he intended to illustrate just how superior the men from the east were. He sat on a swivel chair and looked on idly as a pretty young woman walked down Rose Street.

Gary Wilson reasoned that he was much happier back behind his desk in the Scottish Parliament in Edinburgh, though happy perhaps wasn't the most appropriate word to describe his feelings.

He stared at the blurry photograph in front of him with a burgeoning sense of alarm. She was much younger and had blonde streaks through her long hair, but there was no mistaking Elise Fordham. She was shaking the hand of a swarthy man in khaki uniform as he smiled at her, surrounded by other men in uniform cradling firearms. In those days, few outside the Russian Federation had known Arkady Visonovich; he was merely a quick-witted former KGB enforcer, making himself useful to the right people. Wilson studied the photograph. Fordham's smile looked genuine, friendly even, and its warmth was returned by Visonovich.

He had used most of the resources at his disposal in order to make sense of what was happening. On the face of it, this was a picture of a young journalist, sent by a Scottish newspaper to cover the Second Chechen War, shaking hands with a junior Russian commander. Nothing unusual; journalists were encouraged to get as close as possible to those on whom they reported, especially in a war zone, where sound contacts might not just mean good stories, but rescue from difficult or potentially deadly situations.

Wilson picked up a document from his desk. It was a financial investigation into the board of a holding company, Axiom BV, registered in Rotterdam. About half way down the list was the name Arkady Visonovich, listed as a non-executive foreign associate director. On paper it didn't mean much; he was just another wealthy man with a dodgy past, and most probably present, involved in international business. It was as an old economics professor had told him: global trade was the last bastion of man's savagery. Wilson turned the page and scanned the companies listed under the Axion BV umbrella, and there it was, as plain as day: NKV Dynamics.

Wilson tucked the document and the picture of the young Elise Fordham neatly into the inside pocket of his jacket, left his office, and walked out of the Scottish Parliament and into the Edinburgh sunshine.

Stephen Taylor was breathing heavily as he left his car in the underground car park, only a couple of hundred yards from his destination, the Auld Hundred on Rose Street. He was nervous; he hadn't slept since Alice had been taken, and he was particularly aware that his every move was being monitored by unseen cameras, and that the sound of his very breath could be picked up by the small device taped onto the hollow of his chest.

As advised, he began to hum the opening bars of 'Message In A Bottle', the first song from his youth that came to mind. He was about to start the second line when a tiny bleep from his chest indicted that his wire was operational and that his protectors, observers – whatever they were – could hear him.

Why had he been so stupid? Why had he put his family at risk by following a hunch? Did it feel any better now that his suspicions had been confirmed, and his beautiful daughter was in the hands of ruthless psychopaths?

He turned a corner and there was the Auld Hundred, solid and familiar. Under normal circumstances he would be looking forward to taking the weight off his feet and enjoying a cup of good coffee, or perhaps a glass of wine, and something to eat. Now, he was being watched by half of

Edinburgh's police force, and trying desperately to save his daughter's life.

He looked at his watch. He had been told to enter the bar no earlier or later than midday. He was early, so he turned and affected to look into a shop window, dismayed that his right leg appeared to be shaking uncontrollably. For the next few minutes, he barely took his gaze from the timepiece on his wrist.

Princes Street Garden was busy, the sun tempting its worshippers out into the dazzling light. Wilson sat on a bench and opened the copy of the *Scotsman* newspaper he had just purchased. He scanned the front page; the main news was a prediction as to how long this beautiful, and rare, taste of summer would last. He took his phone from his pocket and pretended to answer it. Folded neatly behind the device were the documents he'd removed from his office. He ended his call, laid the phone down on his newspaper momentarily, then put it back into the inside pocket of his jacket, careful to leave the neatly folded document behind.

He sat for a few more moments, pretending to read the newspaper. Then he stretched, yawned, got to his feet and walked off.

He was less than fifty yards away when a young couple clad in flip-flops, shorts and colourful T-shirts took his place on the bench. They kissed and looked out across the gardens, the young man whispering into his lover's ear. They kissed again. After a few more minutes of public affection, they too got to their feet and walked away from the bench, a copy of the *Scotsman* tucked under the young man's arm.

*

As the second hand of his watch touched twelve, Stephen Taylor walked into the Auld Hundred. He sat at the bar and ordered a vodka and tonic, smiling weakly at the pretty, tanned woman who was serving. As she busied herself pouring his drink, someone tapped him on the shoulder.

'Excuse me, I know this sounds stupid, but are you called Stephen?'

'Yes,' said Taylor, leaning slightly away from the barman, not knowing quite what to expect.

'A man handed me this at the bus stop this morning, and told me to give it to the first guy who came through the door and ordered a vodka and tonic. He said to ask if you were Stephen. Is this some sort of prank or something?' He handed Taylor a large manila envelope. There was something small but bulky inside, and Taylor opened the package with shaking hands, terrified that it might explode. He pulled out a sheet of paper and began to read.

In a few moments he had finished, then, as instructed, he read the page again, making sure he understood what had been said. Still trembling, he gulped at his drink, placed it back on the bar and walked out of the Auld Hundred, taking the envelope with him. When he got to the middle of the pedestrian precinct, he reached into the envelope and removed a small silver object.

With one flick, the lighter ignited; and as he held its flame to the envelope, it did, too. Distantly, he heard the sound of police sirens. As the first cars rounded the corner in a flurry of flashing blue and blaring sound, the envelope gave the last of itself to the fire and rose from Taylor's hand as a floating sliver of ash in the golden light.

*

'What the fuck is he doing?' shouted McClusky, as he watched Stephen Taylor, who filled the large screen in front of him. 'I thought we had officers in the street – where are they?'

'Special Branch, sir. They won't want to be identified as police officers in case the perpetrators are watching,' said the sergeant sitting behind the control desk.

'So we just allow a valuable piece of evidence to go up in smoke? Brilliant!' McClusky watched as a police car skidded to a stop in front of Taylor, sending shoppers and tourists scurrying for refuge in shop doorways. One old man stood transfixed, slowly removing the old-fashioned cap from his head as his jaw dropped. For some reason, Taylor was standing with his hands raised in surrender, like a cornered murderer.

'I want to talk to Taylor, now!' McClusky ordered, as the controller replaced his headset and spoke urgently to the officers on the scene. Taylor was handed a mobile phone, and soon his voice sounded loud in the control room.

'What did you just do, Mr Taylor?'

'I was just doing as directed by the kidnappers. I was told to be at Haymarket station tomorrow at six p.m., and to burn the document and envelope with the lighter supplied. They made it clear that any deviation from their instructions would result in Alice being harmed. I wasn't going to take that risk.'

McClusky studied Taylor's face on the large high-definition screen, so sharp he could see beads of sweat on the man's forehead and the enlarged pores on his nose. He realised Taylor was under pressure, but his policeman's instinct told him there was more to what had happened; there was something furtive about his demeanour.

'And that was all the note said, Mr Taylor?'

'Yes, that was all it said.'

McClusky made a cutting motion across his neck to indicate to the controller that their conversation was over. Once the connection was broken, he said, 'I want Taylor brought here. Get men into the bar – I want it closed and everyone, especially the guy who handed the note to Taylor, brought in. Got it?'

Stephen Taylor was shaking as he was led towards a police car. Despite being a conservative, middle-class, law-abiding citizen, he was now sure of one thing: the police were his enemy.

As he walked past the old man in the cap he smiled.

'Aye, don't you worry, son,' the old man said, looked at him pityingly. 'Fuck me, but they smoking laws are getting right oot o' hand!'

34

The sea broke on the rocks of the tiny bay. Though he tried to stop the tide of memory from consuming him, he felt his thoughts drifting.

The rifle sits well on his shoulder, and is comfortable under his chin. He likes the cold feel of it, and its smooth, almost sensual, quality. He is ready for the recoil, which he reacts to like a boxer soaking up a punch, moving back with the motion to lessen the impact on flesh and bone. This weapon is an extension of himself: a sleek and deadly one.

Focus, he chides himself. Don't let these thoughts in.

A gust of warm wind rustles the tall pines and sends birds flitting from their branches, their indignant song punctuating the distant sound of gunfire from the ruined village far below.

He has assembled the rifle with love and affection. This, though, is a hard-won love: he had been beaten until he learned to show the weapon due reverence, be able to bring it to life only by touch and feel, blindfolded; burned by cigarette ends until, with trembling hands he got it right, over and over again. He has suffered for the right to be its master, this weapon that has filled his hopes and dreams for so long.

He watched a seal flop onto the shore, trying to stay in the here and now. There were beads of sweat on his brow.

He brushes away a fly as he squints into the sight. Two soldiers swagger across a yard, sending chickens flapping. The one with the braided epaulettes aims a kick at one of the unfortunate birds and laughs.

He takes a deep breath, the way he has been shown. Just before he exhales, he squeezes the trigger gently. His shoulder shoots back and he lets his breath out in a loud sigh as the weapon discharges its deadly force. He keeps his eye tight to the gun sight to see the explosion of red as the soldier who had only seconds before tormented the harmless bird falls backwards, his head gone.

Now he is the conductor of this symphony of death. Now he is the taker of lives, the captor of souls. Now he is the Dragon.

That was long ago, and many lives have been extinguished since. He breathed deeply, relieved, as he looked out of the cabin window at the restless sea.

Silent stares greeted Daley as he walked into Kinloch Police Office. Sergeant Shaw drew in his breath rather than say good morning. Distantly, he could hear raised voices; following them, he found himself outside the door of Interview Room One.

'And you're one arrogant big bastard! I was arresting folk when you were shitting in a dirty cloot, you fucking arsehole.' Scott's raised voice was unmistakable.

'What is going on?' asked Daley, bursting into the room. Scott was sitting opposite DS Rainsford and a visibly uncomfortable DC Dunn, who avoided Daley's gaze as he took in the scene. The red light on the recording console flashed to show that the interview was being taped.

'For the record, DCI Daley has entered the room at 08:55 hours,' stated Rainsford.

'Turn it off.'

With raised eyebrows and a frustrated sigh, Rainsford looked at his watch. 'Interview paused at 08:56 hours.' He leaned across the desk and switched off the tape. 'Sir, I really must insist, this is a gross breach of procedure. DS Scott is under arrest. I'm merely doing my job – I would appreciate it if you would let me do so unhindered.'

'DC Dunn, please leave the room,' said Daley, keeping his gaze fixed on Rainsford. Dunn stood, smoothed the front of her trousers, then departed.

'Thank fuck you're here, Jim,' said Scott.

'Shut up, Brian. May I remind you gentlemen that we have multiple murders, an apparent suicide and a missing girl to find, not to mention lights in the sky and all the rest that's going on. I cannot believe I've walked in here to see my two senior detectives in these circumstances. Speak, DS Rainsford, and make it fucking good.'

Rainsford sat down and crossed his arms in front of his chest. 'Sir, first let me say that I have been unhappy with certain aspects of the way you run the sub-division. I believe your casual approach has got us to where we are now.' He nodded across the table to Scott.

'What?' Veins were beginning to show on Daley's forehead.

'Too often, matters of procedure and professional etiquette are ignored.'

Scott rubbed his chin. 'I really wouldnae go there, if I was you, son. Trust me.'

'See, this is what I mean. Here is this man, under arrest and being questioned, and you burst in and stop the whole thing. I will have no choice other than to take this matter further, along with other matters pertaining to personnel in this office.'

'Meaning?' Daley asked, standing over Rainsford now, as Scott grimaced at the other side of the table.

'If I need to spit it out, I will.' Rainsford rose from behind the desk again and stared directly into Daley's face. 'Your conduct with DC Dunn is not only unprofessional, it is unacceptable. I have been wrestling with my conscience for some time over this; now is the time for action.'

Daley leaned on the table with both arms outstretched, his head bowed like a boxer on the ropes, struggling to regain his composure after being battered by his opponent.

'Get oot, son,' said Scott, looking up at the younger man. 'Honestly, get oot while you can!'

'Yes, I'll get out – with great pleasure, in fact. But I'm going to report this sorry mess to a senior officer at division,' said Rainsford, picking up his phone and notebook from the desk in front of him.

Daley lunged across the table at him, sending the recording equipment clattering to the floor. Rainsford, caught off guard, staggered backwards and thumped against the wall. Daley kicked away a chair and charged at the young detective, grabbing his neck and forcing him back as Scott tried desperately to get in between the two men.

Daley's eyes were bulging, his teeth bared in anger, white against his crimson face. He leaned into Rainsford, his hand around the detective's throat.

'Jim, for fuck's sake, calm doon!' Scott shouted, doing his best to force Daley away from his quarry. 'This'll no' sort anything oot.'

As Daley tightened his grip on Rainsford's throat, the

door swung open and Sergeant Shaw stuck his head into the room. 'I have Edinburgh CID on the phone, sir. They say it's urgent,' he said nonchalantly, as though walking into a room to find his sub-divisional commander throttling a junior colleague was the most normal thing in the world.

Daley released his grip, and Rainsford began choking and gasping for the air he had been deprived of. 'You two stay here!' he said, as he left the room, slamming the door behind him.

Scott picked up one of the upturned chairs and put it in front of Rainsford. 'Here, son, you better take a seat. You look as though you need it.'

'That guy is certifiable,' said Rainsford, still breathing heavily and rubbing the red weal on his throat.

'Aye, well, I did try tae warn you. What have I telt you? Polis work's no' a' done by the book, son. Aye, an' it doesnae a' come out of one neither. I'd nothing tae dae with that lassie, an' that dope came fae Wiley, the journalist who just happened tae be in the hall as you so kindly arrested me.'

'So? I acted on information and made an arrest based on the facts. I don't regret any of it, and I intend to pursue it. Don't think that DCI Daley will stop me.'

Scott picked up another chair and sat down. 'Aye, best o' luck, son. You saw what he was like there – just wait till he finds oot Wiley's ready tae splash this all over the papers.'

John Donald had been up since five in the morning. For the first time in a long time, he had eschewed alcohol the night before and was now feeling the benefits. He had driven from his home in the north of Glasgow to this forest park on the outskirts of Aberfoyle. His journey had taken just under an hour, during which time he had listened to Mozart's *Requiem* through the Audi's top-end sound system. He'd parked the car under the green boughs of fir trees and left the engine on to listen to the sublime final bars of the piece. As it soared, he stared across the car park, dappled by sunlight.

He then left the car and, with the aid of a long hiking pole, took a narrow path up through the trees and onto the hill. After nearly half an hour of brisk climbing, he reached a clearing that looked down over the town of Aberfoyle and the glorious landscape beyond. Despite the early hour, the sun was beating down, and he had tied the light sweater he was wearing around his waist.

As birds called from the trees and small animals rustled through the undergrowth, he remembered the days when, in pursuit of adventure, and not least to escape the privations of their poor part of the city, he and his friends had cycled the few miles to the Campsie Fells. With no gears, cobbled together from recycled parts of discarded machines, the long hill that led to where they could stow their bikes made for an arduous climb. But to smell the country, to get away from the smog and smoke of the city, was well worth the effort.

He remembered his first night under the canvas of the old army tent that his friend's father had provided. Though none of the five boys would admit to it, the silence scared them. As darkness descended and their campfire burned down to the embers, their gaze was drawn to the glow of the city's lights. Soon though, as they got used to their surroundings, the Campsie hills became their escape, their haven. While the children of wealthier parents took the well-trodden holiday routes to Ayr or Largs or, for the lucky few, as far as impossibly distant Blackpool, the lads from the poor end of the scheme made do with the hills above their city; to them so strange and exotic they might as well have been standing on the moon.

As Donald looked south, across the tree-covered slopes and beyond the town, he could see the Campsie hills now; the sight of them made his heart beat stronger as memories of happier, more carefree days sprang brightly to mind, unbleached by the relentless passage of time.

Would he ever be that free again?

He took his phone from his pocket and stared down at its screen. He knew that the signal would be strong and clear. When he had to speak to the man who now haunted his every waking, every sleeping, moment, he preferred to do so here, where the harsh realities of the urban world beyond always seemed lessened, diminished by man's primal need to return, especially in times of torment, to the hills and forests, to nature, where he had first been made flesh.

Within seconds of the designated time, the small device vibrated in his hand. He wavered, then accepted the call.

'You can speak, yes?' said the foreign voice on the other end, without the preamble of pleasantries.

'Yes, I can. Now look, I—'

'Be quiet. We all know how things are. We can help you, but first you have to help us.'

'Look where helping you has got me. I want guarantees, not empty promises. If you think you're going to sacrifice me, know that I will not go quietly, or alone. I have enough information to bring this whole fucking thing down.'

There was a brief silence, then the voice said, 'We have this planned. You will be free, you will be rich, and you will have a new identity, far from the cares of your current world. But first we need you to perform one more task.'

Donald stared across the miles to the Campsie hills. From nowhere, a single dark cloud loomed over the undulating skyline, incongruous in the azure light.

'What task?' He was too exhausted, too fearful, to fight any more.

'One of your colleagues is in possession of information that could damage us. Fortunately, he has chosen to keep this knowledge to himself. We must make sure that this continues to be the case.'

'And who is this person?'

'DCI Daley. He has to go.'

Donald took the phone from his ear for a moment and took long, deep breaths.

'I refuse, I utterly refuse.'

'You don't have a choice. Daley is always with someone, he is hard to remove. We want you to arrange this. You will receive a text message with the details of when and where.'

'And what if I won't do it?' Donald's raised voice sent a crow flapping from a tree. 'What if Daley doesn't want to meet me? Did you think about that?'

'You are persuasive, that is why we found you in the first place. But in this the choice is simple. One of you dies; I would prefer that it was Mr Daley. Fail me, and you will take his place.'

As the call clicked off, Donald sank to his knees, fallen pine needles pricking the skin through his trousers. Above, the sun shone, but in front of him, the dark cloud above the hills was spilling warm summer rain.

35

Daley was back in his glass box. He'd talked to Rainsford and Scott individually, and tried to pour oil on the troubled waters of Scott's arrest and his own subsequent behaviour. Though the young DS had agreed to hold back on bringing official charges against Scott, he demanded to be allowed to investigate the case further and reserve the right to take action if or when appropriate. Reluctantly, he had accepted Daley's apology, but made it plain that he would not take back his criticism of Daley's management, or his relationship with DC Dunn.

In short, it was a problem kicked into the long grass – or it would be once Daley had spoken to the venal Wiley. In normal circumstances, he'd have been able to consult his senior officer, but Donald, now suspended, was nowhere to be found. He realised how much better the slippery Chief Superintendent would have been able to deal with this situation.

His door swung open. 'The uniform boys have just picked up Wiley,' said Scott. Daley could see the look of relief on his face. 'Just gimme a few minutes wae him and I'll sort all this oot.'

'Shut the door,' said Daley. With a sigh, Scott did as he was told and sat himself in front of his boss.

'First, don't think for one minute that this is over, or that you can go in there and strong-arm Wiley into forgetting what he saw this morning.'

'He's no' filed the report, Jim. The hotel's broadband was doon, so he couldnae get it away. The boys were just telling me. We've won a watch here, big man.'

Daley shook his head. 'You don't get it, do you? Everything's changing, Brian. It's not how it was when we joined up. Look at the likes of Rainsford, or what Donald's become. That's the way the job's going. We're being left behind, and this new force has just underlined that.'

Scott shifted uncomfortably in his seat. 'So you're saying we're at the bitter end, eh, buddy?'

'I'm saying this isn't the way I want to spend the rest of my life. Look what it's done to you: you've been shot, battered, seen things nobody should have to. No wonder you want to get pissed all the time.' Daley stood up and rubbed his forehead with a sigh.

'You weren't exactly playing it by the book in there yoursel', big man. Aye, and no' wae what's been going on between you and that wee lassie. What's got intae you, Jim?'

The explosion Daley had expected to overtake him spluttered and went out like a damp firework. 'I don't know, Brian. I just don't know. We've both got problems, me and you. But for now we have to concentrate on finding Alice Taylor. Rainsford won't do anything for the time being. We can persuade Wiley to do a deal – probably.' He raised his voice for emphasis. 'Stephen Taylor has made the rendezvous and picked up a note from the kidnapper.'

'Good stuff, what did it say?'

'That's just it, only he knows. He burned it in the middle

of the street before anyone else could get a look at it. He said it was part of the instructions – they'd even provided a lighter. The Edinburgh boys smell a rat.'

'They do? Wae their powers o' deduction it's more likely to be the drains.'

Daley kicked at his desk in frustration. 'Listen, I need to go for a walk to clear my head. I'll be back in half an hour or so. I want you to get a meeting together – we need to see where we are. There's some progress on the vessel that this Abdic character arrived into Kinloch on, and some more details about his accomplice. I want you to chase up the MOD. I sent in an official request for information, but they've conveniently forgotten to reply.'

'No bother, Jim. Though you know as well as I do, if those bastards don't want tae tell you something, they'll stick tae it. And about this Dragon guy and his mate, I've got tae say, I don't like the sound o' either o' them. Fuck me, professional assassins – we've had enough bother wae the unprofessional ones. There's posters o' them been handed oot round Kintyre, but that's a long shot.'

'Clutching at straws, Brian. Who knows, hopefully that'll turn up something,' said Daley, picking up his jacket. 'Get the team together for midday, I won't be long. And please, try to stay sober and out of trouble.'

'Aye, I will. An' you try tae keep your hands off the hired help on your way oot.'

Daley hesitated before opening the door. 'Only you, Brian. Only you could get away with that.'

Elise Fordham had made up her mind. She had always made a concerted effort to stay as far away from professional controversy as she could, and trouble like this could extinguish even the brightest political flame.

Why had they been so stupid? She blamed Cudihey; he was an experienced civil servant who should have known better. Kirsteen Lang was bright and ambitious, but too grasping for her own good, determined to get to the top by any means.

Fordham took the small key from her purse and opened the little drawer in her desk. She took the phone from its hiding place then locked the office door, flipping over the no-entry sign. Closed. Meeting in progress. She smiled at the thought; the phrase had become a euphemism for sexual indiscretion within the parliament. 'I think they've had a meeting in progress' would be a charge levelled at MSPs suspected of becoming a little too close than their job descriptions required. Her smile faded when she realised that what she was about to do could be more damaging than a thousand affairs – to her, and even to her country.

Her thumb hovered above the phone's keypad; she wiped a bead of perspiration from her forehead. She pressed down, calling the only number on the contact list.

'We need to meet,' she said. 'Today, if possible.'

A few minutes later, in an office a few corridors away, these same words echoed in Gary Wilson's earpiece. He was pleased his instructions had been obeyed successfully; Elise Fordham's secret phone had been cloned. He sat back in his chair. Soon all of the pretence would be at an end.

Daley took a calming breath of the warm sea air as he walked along Kinloch's esplanade. The loch shimmered under the blue sky that had been a permanent fixture over the last few days. Locals and tourists sat on the green that bordered the seafront, eating an early lunch, sunbathing, reading papers or with their heads buried in phones or tablets. A group of boys were playing football, using their shirts as goalposts. Daley stood for a few moments and watched them. It took him back to his own boyhood, playing football in the park on a hot summer's day, the grass sun-bleached, the tar bubbling in the street. He remembered getting his hands covered with the glutinous black sludge and his mother painstakingly removing it with butter, then clipping him round the ear for her trouble.

A toddler in a white T-shirt and blue shorts was ambling across to him on bowed legs, an ice-cream cone clutched in one hand, much of it slathered down his rosy-red face. He smiled up at the detective, who bent down, leaning on one knee.

'Hello,' he said with a smile. 'Where's your mummy?' For a second, the expression on the little face changed to one of concern, but the child's grin soon returned as he heard his mother rushing towards him, fussing around the little boy and hoisting him into her arms.

'Noo, Kieran, how many times have I telt you no' tae be speaking tae the polis,' she said, with a wink at Daley. 'If you're like your faither, you'll see plenty o' them soon enough.' She raised her eyes to the heavens, then spirited the toddler back across the green to where her friend was sitting on a towel, licking an ice-lolly.

Daley crossed the green and climbed over the low wall onto the road beyond. Through the trees on the other side was a path, an old railway cutting, now used as a shortcut from the town's seafront to one of the schemes on its periphery. Eventually, this would take him on the road back to the police office.

As he followed the path, the sound of the townsfolk enjoying the sun faded, and he strolled on, the scent of honeysuckle and meadowsweet strong in the air. As he reached about halfway along the path, he was aware of footsteps behind him. Not until he felt a hard object being thrust into his back did he panic.

'Mr Daley, keep quiet and come with us. We have a gun pointed at your back.'

36

'DS Scott!' shouted Rainsford, slamming the door open, his face flushed.

'If you're about tae dae your Terminator thing again, fuck off,' declared Scott. 'You heard the gaffer: let's just get ready for this meeting. He'll be back shortly.'

'Abdic has been spotted at the pier shop in Firdale. The girl behind the counter just spoke to the cop who handed in the pictures yesterday. He's in a boat and it's still moored at the quay there.' Rainsford's face was pale and he spoke quickly, plainly nervous at the prospect of facing the notorious killer.

Scott was up like a shot. 'Right, come on. I'll get Jim on the blower. We can pick him up on the way. We better draw weapons. This guy's no' exactly your run-o'-the-mill criminal.'

Rainsford rushed off, and Scott dialled Daley's number – but the call went straight to voicemail. 'Jim, where are you? This Abdic guy's been positively ID'd at Firdale. We have tae be quick. Call me, now!'

Scott checked he had his cigarettes, then walked out of the office to find Sergeant Shaw handing out sidearms and bullet-proof vests. He stopped dead; suddenly his throat was dry and he felt his stomach protest. He tried to walk forward, but his feet were leaden weights. He closed his eyes and sent a silent prayer heavenward. *Dear God, keep me safe, please keep me safe.* He opened his eyes to see Rainsford looming over him with a vest.

'Quick, get this on. Where's the boss?'

'I cannae raise him. His phone just goes onto the message.'

'We'll try him again, but we can't wait. Sergeant Shaw, try DCI Daley's number, and keep trying until you get him.' Rainsford sounded imperious as he barked out the order. Shaw hurried to the phone but after a few moments shrugged his shoulders and shook his head, indicating he'd had no luck.

'Right, Brian, we'll have to go without him. He can follow us when he gets back in.'

'Aye, right, nae bother.' He knew as the senior officer – in service, though equal in rank – he should be taking charge. His legs were shaking as he walked outside into the bright sunshine. He wished Daley would appear. He wished he had a drink.

Daley had been thrust into a SUV then blindfolded. Despite his protestations, the men who had taken him – both of whom were armed – said nothing. His hands had been bound with parcel ties, and he jolted against the door of the car as they drove. He listened carefully, trying to glean something about his whereabouts from noises outside the vehicle, but he could make out little apart from the sound of passing cars, and the low rumble of the road below.

The vehicle slowed, and then came to a stop. In a few moments it pulled away again, only much more slowly, the way a driver would negotiate a long driveway, or a narrow road. In what Daley reckoned was just over five minutes, this slow journey came to an end. The man beside him opened his door and exited the vehicle. Daley frantically turned his head from side to side in a desperate attempt to orient himself. The door was tugged open and he nearly fell through it and onto the road.

'Get out.' A strong pair of hands grabbed him and pulled him from the car. Daley felt gravel beneath his feet. 'Stop!' one of his captors shouted.

Agonisingly, Daley stood still. He heard one of the men walking away; he didn't know where the other man was, though some sense told him that there was a gun pointed at his vulnerable flesh and bone.

All was silent, apart from the buzz of insects, the cry of gulls, and what Daley thought was the distant sound of waves breaking on a beach. He wondered whether or not he would hear the shot that killed him, or if everything would suddenly go black, his world disappearing in a last glimpse of the violence that had shaped his life. He breathed deeply.

After what seemed like an eternity, he heard a sudden movement from behind and, despite himself, recoiled in fear as he was pulled forward by his cuffed hands. The thick sole of his shoe caught the gravel and he tripped, managing to regain his stride after two or three staggered steps.

Soon he felt the ground change; it was solid now, smooth. Despite his blindfold, he realised that the light had diminished and the sun was no longer on his face. The sound of birds, insects and the sea was replaced by the echo of his and his captors' footsteps as they walked into some sort of cavernous space. A cold chill crept up his spine. A door creaked open, and he was pushed forward.

'Take that off,' said a familiar voice, and the blindfold was removed roughly from his eyes. There, in front of him, stood a lean man with short grey hair, shaved at the sides and sitting up in spikes on his head. He was dressed in a sports jacket, a light open-necked shirt and black trousers. He was lean and fit and had chiselled features.

'Mr Daley, I apologise for all this subterfuge. My reasons for it will become clear shortly. I hope you weren't too traumatised.'

'I can think of better ways to travel,' said Daley. 'Though you do realise that you've just kidnapped a police officer, don't you, Mr Callaghan?'

'I want all units to stop just outside Firdale. We'll pull up at the church. Is that received and understood?' Rainsford waited for replies from the other two vehicles then turned to Scott, sitting beside him in the passenger seat. 'Are you OK, DS Scott?'

'Aye, son, just dandy.'

'If you want to stay out of the operation, I understand. I realise that, after what happened to you recently, you probably don't want to get involved in a potential weapons scenario. I should have thought about it before we left the office. You are supposed to be on light duties, after all.'

'Just you keep driving, son. Aye, an' thank you for your consideration, but listen tae me, an' listen good. When we stop the motor, I'll be briefing the guys, got it?'

Rainsford bridled at Scott's suggestion. 'This is my case, and in the absence of DCI Daley, I'll retain operational control.'

'How many firearms ops have you taken charge o', son?'

'None – I mean, I only passed my firearms certification last year, so the opportunity has yet to arise.'

'Well, I've been authorised tae carry a weapon for twenty years, an' I've been on the wrang side o' them twice. This is nae time for point scoring, son. I'm senior in service, an' until Jim gets here, I'm in command. Just check that rulebook you've got in your heid, if you don't believe me.' Scott looked out of the window, while Rainsford gripped the steering wheel until his knuckles turned white.

'Fine,' he said eventually. 'It's your call. But I'll tell you something, DS Scott, if you fuck this up, I'll put you on paper before the day's out.'

'See after this is over, son, the last thing you'll be interested in is putting me on paper. You'll just be glad you're still alive, trust me.'

'So I'm guessing you're not a golf salesman then?' said Daley, now sitting in a leather swivel chair. Callaghan sat at the other side of a polished desk, neatly organised with just a laptop, pad of paper, jar of expensive-looking pens and a tiny stars-and-stripes flag standing proud. There were no windows, and the glass wall behind Daley was covered by closed blinds.

'You're a smart guy, Mr Daley. But hey, why the formality? I'm Mike, can I call you Jim?'

'Yes,' said Daley. 'Why have you brought me here?'

'Tell me what you know about Walter Cudihey.'

'That's impossible. I can't discuss police matters directly with you, I'm afraid.'

'Lighten up, Jim. I don't think there's much about the cases you're working on that I don't know about.'

'Meaning?'

'If I mention the Dragon, does that have resonance with you?'

Daley was taken aback. He'd only just found out about the Dragon himself. 'How long have you known about him?'

'Oh, he and I go back a long way. He was responsible for the murder of some prominent businessmen in the States, under contract. Of course, when I say businessmen, I use the term loosely. In the main, these guys were mobsters, or at least associates, but it put him on our radar. What we're interested in, Jim, is what he's doing in Kinloch.'

'You and me both.'

Callaghan fixed him with a hard stare. 'You're going to have to do better than that, Jim. Let's try again: what do you know about Walter Cudihey?'

'Cudihey worked for the Scottish Government,' said Daley. 'But you already know that.' He couldn't help but feel that Callaghan knew significantly more than he was letting on; perhaps he could be useful to Daley's own investigations in Kinloch.

'Why did he kill himself?' asked Callaghan.

'Honestly, I have no idea.'

'And what is the Dragon's role in this?'

'That's the part that doesn't make sense to me: an international assassin and his accomplice in Kinloch, of all places, murdering small-time dealers.'

'I know you've been pushing for information from your Ministry of Defence,' he said. 'You won't get anywhere with them.'

'I'll keep trying, as long as I believe that they have information pertinent to my investigation.'

'Yeah, and wait for months for the great wheels of British bureaucracy to turn? You don't have time for that, Jim, and neither do I. Take a look at this.' Callaghan pressed a button on the underside of his desk: the lights dimmed and a large projection screen rolled down the wall behind him. 'I think this may help you understand what's going on. I know you have some idea, but let's firm things up.' He smiled. 'Let me be clear, Jim, those in charge of our military would much rather you saw none of this.'

'Here, gie me the phone,' said Scott, grabbing the mobile from Rainsford's hand. They had called the girl who had served Abdic in the small shop on the pier in Firdale. The three police cars were in the grounds of the church, at the other end of the village and well away from sight of the harbour. 'Hi, darlin',' said Scott, as Rainsford raised an eyebrow at the greeting. 'Noo, just tell us what's happening. Is the guy still there?'

'Yes, he is – well, he's outside. He cleaned us out of vodka and cans of beer, bought some pizzas and tins of food. He's weird.'

'Weird, how?'

'Just the shape o' him. He's nearly as broad as he's long, and he doesn't talk, just points and laughs. He's standing on the pier now, smoking a cigar he bought. I don't think he's the full shillin'. Hey, is this guy dangerous, or somethin'?' She sounded scared.

'Naw. Just a wee bit simple,' said Scott, grimacing at the lie. 'Tell me, is there anyone else with him?'

'Oh no. He's on a tender, like a small day boat they would use for scallops or prawns. No' a big yacht or proper fishing boat or anything. When are yous guys coming tae speak tae him?'

'We're two minutes away. Just you stay where you are. The guy's mair frightened of you than you are of him, so keep out the way. We'll deal wae it.' Scott winced again as he ended the call.

'Do you think that was wise?' asked Rainsford. 'Wouldn't it have been better to ask her to leave quietly, get out of harm's way?'

'Oh aye – don't worry, darlin', there's nothing tae worry aboot, but get your arse oot o' there pronto before this big bastard superglues your butt cheeks the gither, or pulls your tongue oot through your neck. Great idea, son. They're no' stupid around here – she'll have heard all aboot what's been going on in Kinloch. If I'd said anything like that tae her, she'd have panicked.'

'So what do we do?'

'If we a' pile o'er the hill wae lights flashing, there's no sayin' what this bastard's capable of. The lassie's no' seen anyone else, but that's no' tae say there's nobody there.' Scott stroked the stubble on his chin. 'One o' us is going tae have tae get near enough to him without him twigging what's going on. Pull a weapon on the big bastard, then hope he sits nice until the rest o' us appear. The last thing we want is for him tae get a sniff that the polis are on the way.'

'I'll do it,' said Rainsford immediately.

'Aye, right, man in a sharp suit walking doon a wee pier in the middle o' nowhere. He'll smell a rat straight away. The rest are a' in uniform. There's only one of us that doesnae look like a policeman.'

'Who?'

278

'Me,' Scott said with a sigh. 'I'll take my jacket off and stick the shooter doon the back o' my strides. The bugger will never suspect a thing until I'm on him.'

'I'm not sure about this,' said Rainsford. 'In your current state – I mean, after your recent experiences – I don't think that it's wise you take this on.'

'Fuck that, the decision's made. Come on, we'll drive quietly tae just under the brow o' the hill, park the motors, then I'll go on foot. You lot keep an eye oot, an' as soon as I draw the pistol on him, pile doon ontae that quay as fast as you can.'

Rainsford looked doubtful. 'I want it said for the record that I'm not happy about this.' Scott didn't look at him as he drove the CID car out of the church car park and slowly down through the village.

'Your concerns are noted, DS Rainsford. Now, make yoursel' useful – call the office an' get them tae inform the coastguard. If this big bastard escapes, we'll need tae get someone on his tail quick smart. Fuck, why does everything have to revolve aroon the sea in this bloody place?'

In less than two minutes, the three cars came to a stop behind the prow of the hill that sloped down to the harbour. Scott jumped out of the vehicle, removed his flak jacket and thrust his pistol into the back of his trousers. He rolled up his sleeves, took off his tie and opened the neck of his shirt.

'See, could be a tourist oot for a wee stroll before lunch,' said Scott, grinning at Rainsford.

'Or the pub's first customer waiting for the door to open.'

'I'll ignore that, son.'

They edged up the hill. Keeping the rest of the men behind him, Scott walked to the top and, without turning around, said, 'Oor man's there, sitting on a bollard, taking in the air. Here I go.' Hands in pockets, DS Brian Scott made his way down towards the pier. He stopped, pretending to admire a well-tended garden, then carried on, looking out over the bay to the sea beyond.

'He might be a drunk, but he's a fucking brave one,' Rainsford whispered under his breath.

On the pier, the large man turned from the sea and looked up the hill, straight at Scott. Suddenly, the still air was filled with manic laughter.

37

Daley studied the map on the projector screen.

'You'll note these,' said Callaghan, pointing at a series of thin lines that snaked across the oceans. Most were depicted in white, some red, and a very small number black. 'Any ideas?'

'We found lines like this on a map belonging to Cudihey, as I'm sure you're aware.'

'Right on the money.' Callaghan smiled, his teeth gleaming even in the reduced light of the office. 'But do you know what they are?'

Daley shook his head.

'Anyone would think that, in today's modern world, information springs from the ether, out of a clear blue sky and straight into their computer or smartphone.'

'What's your point?'

'These little lines represent the conduits of something we use every day: the internet.'

'Surely global internet traffic is conducted via satellite?'

'Oh, sure, about five per cent of it is. The rest travels the world via this network of cables.'

Daley was surprised. 'Surely that's outdated technology now?'

'It's still the best, and the safest, way to do it. Satellites are all very well, but they can't process the huge amounts of information reliably or quickly enough. So the world is served by this – fibre-optic cables that ping information all over the planet faster than you can think.'

Daley studied the lines more closely, taking in their locations. He noted that one seemed to travel from the Washington area and terminate about halfway up the Kintyre peninsula, part of which was depicted on Cudihey's map. 'Why the different colours?'

'White lines are just your normal, run-of-the-mill stuff. You know, Facebook, Twitter, all that shit. Your searches – or most of them – come to you right through these.'

'To my *wireless* broadband.'

'Yeah, kinda ironic, isn't it? The only wireless bit is the few feet from your router to you.'

'So what about the red and black cables?'

'Red cables run more sensitive information: banking, some international diplomatic traffic, the stock markets and so on. It's probably more appropriate to consider this as the intranet rather than the internet.'

'Meaning?'

'Meaning that these connect points in a specific, rather than general, way. Access to the information that travels down these babies is limited. Nothing you raise on Google comes down these. It was down these cables that the world's economic systems nearly collapsed back in 2008.'

'And the black?'

'I can't tell you much about the black, Jim. But that's why you're here. Kinda frustrating, ain't it?'

Daley looked up at the map again. The line that travelled

between Washington DC and the Kintyre peninsula was black.

Scott tried to keep his eye on Abdic, still sitting on the bollard, without making it obvious that he was surveilling him. He was about forty yards away and, with each step he took, was finding it harder to hold his nerve.

Suddenly, Abdic stood. He started to walk towards Scott, his arms, knotted with thick cords of muscle, outstretched.

Scott, with only seconds to weigh up the situation, fumbled for his handgun. 'That's far enough, sir. Stop! I'm a police officer,' he shouted. He grabbed the butt of the pistol at his back just as Abdic broke into a run. Scott's hands were shaking and drenched with perspiration; he lost his purchase on the gun and it went clattering to the ground at his feet. He could hear the squeal of tyres as Abdic leaped towards him, driving a fist towards his solar plexus.

'Fuck!' Rainsford gunned his car down to the entrance to the small pier, sliding to a stop on the loose stones. He grabbed his sidearm from its holster and rolled out of the car, landing on the hard tarmac with a thud as the two police cars, lights flashing, pulled up behind him.

Though he'd had time to brace himself, Scott had never felt a blow like it. Abdic's balled fist caught him just under his ribs; light flickered and he thought he would faint. Though Scott was a full head taller than his attacker, he was less than half as broad. As Abdic enveloped him in an agonising, suffocating bear hug, then pulled him sideways, he was powerless to resist.

Rainsford rushed out from behind his car just in time to see Scott, his arms pinioned to his sides, disappear over the edge of the pier with Abdic, sending seabirds into squawking flight, and eliciting a muffled scream from the girl who was watching these events unfold from inside the shop.

'Jim, I cannot tell you what information runs along the black cables, but suffice it to say the Western world depends upon it to keep us safe from other nations, rogue states, the terrorist threat. They form the core network of NATO's security. You're going to have to take my word on this.'

Daley looked at the point on the Kintyre coast where the black cable found land. 'This cable comes in at Dundraven beach, am I right?'

'Yes,' said Callaghan, 'the fenced-off compound that you guys have asked the MOD about is where it comes ashore.'

'Why not run the cable directly into London?'

'In the event of any attack – let's say nuclear, or terrorist – London might be compromised. You'll know the old saying, "hiding in plain sight"?'

'Yes.'

'This is a perfect example: a nondescript little compound beside a little white beach, here on the lovely west coast of Scotland. What could be more innocent?'

'Don't tell me – someone's found it?'

'We don't know who, but we know it happened within the last eighteen months. The cable was compromised off the coast of Scotland, and we're trying our best to prevent it happening again. It was no coincidence that your Mr Cudihey had this on a map. The real question, the one we're all trying to solve, is where does he fit into all of this?'

'He worked for the Scottish Government. Surely they know about this cable?'

'Kinda out of his league, wouldn't you say? We know you found his caravan close to the cable's landing point.'

'And?'

'We need to know what was in that caravan. Who was he working with? What do you know?'

'Why should I tell you? You kidnapped and blindfolded me; how do I know I can trust you?'

Callaghan paused. 'I brought you here, Jim, to cut out the crap before this thing gets too big.'

'Well, let's cut the crap then,' said Daley. 'Tell me about the strange lights in the sky.'

'Jim, I think I can trust you. But you've got to give me something back.'

Daley sighed. 'Honestly, we don't know a lot. Seems like Cudihey was a bit of an oddball. We found sex toys and photographs of his colleague in the caravan. But there were photos of the compound as well, the undersea line. He obviously knew what it was, but I don't know who he was passing the information on to.'

'And what about the Dragon?'

'He and his accomplice murdered a local drug dealer and have now kidnapped a teenage girl called Alice Taylor.'

'You think there's any connection between these things?'

'Yes,' said Daley. 'I suspect there is. But I don't know what.'

Callaghan hesitated, and then got up from behind his desk. 'Come with me. I've got something to show you.'

Intrigued, Daley followed Callaghan out of the office into a dark, cold corridor. Their footsteps echoed on a smooth concrete floor as they turned a corner into a large hangar.

In the gloom, Daley could make out an indistinct shape,

lit only by a pale, barely perceptible white light that cast an ethereal glow over the object. It was about the length and height of a bus, but broader. Around its perimeter, soldiers with rifles stood to attention as Daley and Callaghan appeared.

'As you were, gentlemen,' ordered Callaghan as they neared the soldiers. 'Major Meyer, if you please.'

'Yes, sir,' replied a loud voice; there followed some more barked commands, then, slowly, the lighting levels were increased.

'I warn you, Mr Daley, once the genie is outta the bottle, he's hard to put back in.'

Daley's jaw dropped as the object was revealed. 'Tell me that's not what I think it is.'

'And what do you think it is?'

'A flying saucer, UFO, I . . . I don't know.'

'You wanna know something, Jim? You're just about right. Meet Aurora, the most advanced military aircraft the world has ever seen, and not many in the world have seen her.'

Rainsford rushed to the side of the pier, his pistol firmly grasped between both hands, two armed cops behind him. He looked cautiously over the side and was startled when he saw Scott lying on the deck of a small boat, his body still, his eyes closed.

'Brian,' Rainsford called out in a hoarse whisper, looking from one end of the boat to the other. 'Brian!' he called again. Scott didn't move.

Footsteps from behind them prompted all three police officers to turn, guns pointed at the girl from the shop who, at the sight of the weapons, let out a shriek.

'Get back behind the cars – now!' shouted Rainsford, as

the constable who had been left to guard the head of the pier beckoned to her to follow him.

There was a buzzing noise to his right, and squinting into the sun, Rainsford made out the sleek hull of a wooden pleasure boat hoving into view around the bottom of the pier. At the stern, an older man sat at an outboard motor, while on the prow, a blond boy stood staring at the boat tied up at the pier.

Rainsford waved frantically, and the man at the tiller got the message and began to turn his vessel in a wide arc into the bay, just as the craft below the police officers rocked sideways in its moorings. The sun glinted off Abdic's bald head as he hurled himself across the boat, darting behind the small cabin before the policemen could take action.

'We are armed police, give yourself up, Mr Abdic,' shouted Rainsford, cursing the situation in which he found himself. He had radioed for back-up, but that would be at least five minutes away. A lot could happen in that time.

The cackle of laughter began to echo across the water, coming from behind the cabin where Abdic crouched, his gun pointing at Scott, who lay pale and motionless on the wooden deck, only feet away.

38

Daley stared at the object before him. The aircraft was like nothing he had ever seen before. Where it began and ended was indistinct, the sharp lines of the wings tapering into invisibility. It drew in the light; none of the dim lamps in the massive hangar reflected on its surface. The cockpit was a slight swell in the smooth silhouette, picked out in a shade of black that shimmered like oil on water.

'Aurora,' said Callaghan, his voice low. 'We are all playing for big stakes here.'

'Aren't you worried that I'll rush off to the press with my story?'

'With all respect, do you really think anyone would believe an over-worked, overweight, forty-something small-town cop? The press would tear you apart, Jim.'

'Get real. Where do I fit in with all of this?' Daley gestured at the black aircraft, fading back into the shadows in the diminishing light.

'Follow me.'

The sound of Pavel Abdic's laughter was punctuated by two loud shots, the reports of which whined in the still air. The policemen ducked, and when Rainsford looked back up,

Abdic was standing over Scott's body, his gun pointed at the unconscious policeman's head. Sniggering to himself, with his gun trained on Scott and his eyes fixed on Rainsford, he kneeled down and began to untie the aft rope, one of two that secured the boat to the pier.

'I can take him out, Sergeant,' a young cop whispered to DS Rainsford.

'No. If you even twitch, he'll blow Sergeant Scott's head off. Do nothing.'

Abdic stopped what he was doing and thrust his gun nearer to Scott's head, making Rainsford jump back instinctively.

'No, no!' he shouted, holding his hand up, palm facing Abdic, to demonstrate that they weren't going to take action.

The huge man went back to his task, and the rope slipped from the rear of the craft and plopped into the still waters of the bay; the boat's stern began to drift from the pier. Abdic stood and pointed to the prow of the boat, where one remaining rope was all that secured the boat to the pier.

Rainsford nodded his head slowly, to show that he understood that Abdic intended to release that hawser too, then sail away, with Scott on board.

The young DS racked his brains as Abdic made his way over the recumbent figure of Scott and towards the front of the vessel. Just as he resigned himself to the fact that he was going to have to let Abdic escape, a sudden movement caught his eye. As the broad man stepped over Scott with his short legs, the policeman opened his eyes, then swung his foot up and viciously kicked Abdic between the legs. Abdic fell to the deck, clutching his crotch, his pistol spinning away from him. In one swift motion, Scott reached over, grabbed the weapon, and was on his feet, pointing it at Abdic, whose whole head had turned a deep crimson as he doubled over with pain.

'See what I mean aboot situations like this, DS Rainsford?' Scott shouted up. 'You never know what the fuck's gonnae happen. Get doon here and cuff this big bugger.' Scott smiled up at his colleague, who clambered down onto the vessel.

Scott rubbed his forehead and aimed a kick at the small of Abdic's back. 'Aye, an' that's for the wallop o'er the heid you gave me, you ugly bastard. I can always be sure o' a few things when I'm doon here: I'll drink too much whisky, an' some bastard will try tae hit me o'er the heid, shoot me, or get me on a fucking boat.'

Daley blinked as he walked out into the sunshine. The two men strolled across a long runway. Soon, they were on a grass verge atop a small rise; below them, a chain-link fence was topped with sharp metal stanchions and razor wire.

'Always amazes me that I'm so close to Ireland here, Jim.' Callaghan pointed into the distance, across fallow fields and towards the blue sea where in the haze a dark jut of land shimmered.

'My grandfather was from just across the water,' said Daley. 'County Antrim, to be exact. He came to Glasgow in the thirties, just after the Depression.'

'Well don't that just beat all. My granddaddy, too. Only when he left County Antrim, he turned the other way and landed in Boston. It's a small world, Jim.'

'And now here we are. You in the CIA, or whatever you're

in, and me a fat, small-town cop, with too much stress, and a complicated personal life.'

'We can help each other, Jim.'

'How?'

'In my country, we like stability. Here, well, things have changed.'

'Meaning what, the new police force?'

'That, but more generally too; politically and culturally. You guys on this island have worked hand-in-glove with us almost since we fought to leave you. Now I'm not sure how it's all going to pan out.'

'Everything changes, Mike, even countries.'

'Change for the better is great, but it depends on your perspective.'

'The breach in the undersea NATO intranet cable, it happened here, right?'

'Yes, somewhere offshore. We can't be sure, but we've got it pinned down to an area off the Kintyre coastline. That's why I'm here.'

'How much information did you lose?'

'That's where things get even more worrying. There's a lot of bad people would give their rotten hides to tap into that information.'

'And they haven't?'

'In the eighteen months or so since the breach took place, we have received no threats, no attempts at extortion, no breaches of security, no publicity. Not one damned thing.'

Daley thought for a moment. 'Maybe whoever managed to steal this information doesn't know how to use it, or even what it means? Maybe they didn't find anything of interest?'

'We have a rough idea what they got. It's sensitive stuff; makes Wikileaks look like the *National Enquirer*. That's what makes it all the more worrying. To possess the knowledge to not only breach the cable, but to do so in a way that it was almost undetectable, can have been done by only a handful of nation states, or their confederates.'

'You mean Russia, China?'

'Sure, those guys are in the frame.' Callaghan paused. It looked to Daley as though he was considering whether or not to reveal more. 'We all know that no organisation is clean, right, Jim?'

'Oh yes,' replied Daley instantly.

'So, suppose one of the countries you've mentioned, with all of the resources and expertise, go hunting and strike gold. Imagine that within their organisation is someone with so much ambition and drive they think they can benefit much more from what they've found than whoever is paying for them to be there; some power-mad, twisted bastard, willing to risk worldwide conflict to further their own aims. Get the picture?'

'Sure,' said Daley with a grimace, able to visualise just such ambition. 'But to gain what?'

'Money, power, influence, control – any of these things. At the end of the day, they're all subtle parts of a greater whole. Imagine what could be achieved by people so ruthless they could create a zombie state within the NATO alliance; control it from within. Politicians, security services, the military – everyone compromised.'

Daley looked out to sea. 'It would have to be a new state. Small, finding its feet, but with excellent credentials as to human rights, security and other issues.'

'You got it. We think your fireball knew something about this.'

'Cudihey?'

'Yeah, Walter Cudihey. We also know that a new crime organisation with tentacles in Eastern Europe, Asia, Central America and Italy has increased its activities exponentially in the last few months. All of the old cartels and gangs are being eradicated one by one, in Europe and beyond. Drugs are flooding the continent like never before.'

'And their merchandise has to come into its main market somewhere.' Daley was beginning to understand.

'And where better than here, the glorious west coast of Scotland. Such a vast coastline, full of little bays, empty coves, quiet channels – its a smuggler's paradise.'

'But first you have to get rid of the opposition.'

'Sure. Some overweight, over-worked, talented guy with a complicated personal life has to come in and clean up the town. We know that elements of your new police force – the old one, too – have been compromised.' He looked out to sea again. 'Jim, you know how politics works; you need money to succeed. But if it's not your money, you don't call the shots. The guys with the deep pockets do.'

'So it's all about money?'

'Yeah, sure, money, but not just hard cash. It's about being involved in the global marketplace, in cutting-edge industries, not just based in one country, but all over the world. You need that perfect storm of power and influence right across the board, and you gotta start somewhere, get a foot in the door.'

'Our government?'

'You tell me, Jim.'

'So what can you give me?

'NKV Dynamics. We've found their weak spot.'

'And we share information?'

'To a certain extent. Someone at the heart of everything is putting us all at risk. We have to find out who that is.' He patted the policeman on the shoulder. 'Let's get you back on the heat, DCI Daley. I think we can dispense with the blindfold this time.'

39

The intern knocked on Wilson's door, then waited until the barked invitation to enter sounded from behind it.

'You've got what I want?' asked Wilson, not taking his eyes from the document he was reading.

'Yes, Mr Wilson. The Minister is in a crisis meeting. I took my opportunity.'

'You've done well,' said Wilson, emerging from behind his desk. He walked over to the intern and snatched the file from his trembling hand. 'And remember, son, you've just breached the Official Secrets Act. If you breathe a word of this to anyone, you'll go down for longer than the Kray twins.'

The young man thought for a moment. 'Who are the Kray twins? Do they sit on the Labour benches?'

Wilson looked up, then grabbed the intern by his shirt collar and leaned in close. 'It means, you ugly little bastard, that if you ever mention this to anyone, you might as well go and do a Walter Cudihey, do you understand?'

'Yes, Gary – Mr Wilson. Sorry.'

'Good, now fuck off.'

The youth was about to leave when Wilson spoke again.

'Wait! This crisis meeting, what is it about?'

'Oh, to do with renewable energy. MBT are pulling out of all existing undersea wave power operations, and any similar projects in development.'

'And who the fuck are MBT when they're at home?'

'Miekle, Brown and Taylor. They've been working on our renewable energy strategy with another company from Holland.'

'NKV Dynamics.'

'Yes, them. Looks like they're the only players now, Gary.'

'Mr Wilson to you. Now, why haven't you fucked off?'

Wilson watched the intern leave, then opened the file he had just been given. Arkady Visonovich stared at him from the first page. 'Oh, very clever,' he muttered to himself. 'Very clever indeed.'

Daley found himself opposite one of the oddest-looking men he'd ever seen. Pavel Abdic was so wide he almost took up the entire length of the table. A local solicitor sat beside Abdic, looking nervous, while his client stared at DS Scott with a toothy grin.

'One last time, Mr Abdic, if you understand me, please tell me where Alice Taylor is,' said Daley for the fifth time, his impatience palpable. He knew from the notes sent to him by Interpol that Abdic spoke English, or had at one time. Now, however, he was either unwilling or unable.

'We're no' getting anywhere here, gaffer,' said Scott, who had a fresh white bandage around his head. 'You're no' for talking, are you?' he enquired of Abdic, leaning across the table and looking straight at him. Abdic grinned, then opened his mouth and pointed to the brown stump of what had once been his tongue.

The lawyer looked on in horror. 'This poor man's got no tongue!'

Scott sat back in his chair and looked at Daley. 'We're no' goin' tae get a whole lot oot o' this fella, Jim.'

'Interview terminated at 16:50 hours,' said Daley. They watched as Abdic was taken to a cell in handcuffs by three uniformed constables.

'He's the strangest cwient I've ever had,' said the lawyer, packing away his documents into a battered briefcase. 'I hope your colleagues up the woad have more success with him.' He nodded goodbye and left the room.

'We're no further forward finding Alice,' said Daley. 'You can bet this Dragon has her. I hope this exchange works out in Edinburgh later.'

'We'll find oot soon. It's the six o'clock train intae Haymarket, isn't it?'

'Supposedly. Apparently that was the only instruction left for Stephen Taylor in the note he burned. Though Edinburgh CID suspect that there was more to it than that. They have cops all along the route of the train, but observing only. Who knows what the bastard will do with the poor girl, but at least we have some kind of leverage now.' Daley looked at the chair on which Abdic had been sitting.

'I'll hang aboot and see what happens. I'll need tae be off by seven though, I've got a date.'

'With who?'

'Wae Annie. Well, it's no' a date as such, just a trip tae the Chinese. She says it'll gie me something else tae dae.'

'Apart from boozing, you mean?' said Daley, wishing he hadn't almost before the words had left his mouth. He was preoccupied by the thought that the arrest of Abdic, welcome as it was, would do nothing to advance the Alice's release.

'Listen, big man, I'm doing my best. Fuck me, I've only been back for five minutes, an' already the Michelin Man there's tried tae kill me. Gie me a break, Jim!'

'Sorry, Brian. You did well today. Your usual reckless self, but a good job, nonetheless.'

'Aye, just you pile on the praise, big fella. Wae adulation like that, my heid'll be the size o' a pin in no time. Aye, an' come tae that, where were you? You've been right mysterious aboot it.'

'Never mind that, Brian. You don't want to know, trust me. I'll tell you when I can.' He paused. 'We shouldn't lose sight of this morning's antics, either. We've got Wiley in on possession, but you know as well as me, with only your word against his, we can't pin anything on him. And you can imagine the stink he'll make when he's released.'

'We'll just get oor friendly solicitor there tae represent him. That'll do the trick. He'll likely go doon for at least a hundred years.'

Elise Fordham's ears were still ringing with the admonishment she'd received from the First Minister. That Scotland's pioneering wind and wave renewables company had mysteriously pulled out of any contracts in their own country was a political setback, but it was nothing she hadn't expected. In fact, in some ways, now that it was done, it was a relief. She was still holding on by her fingertips, and she knew it. But she had what she wanted; she just had to get through the last tricky operation and it was done, her mission complete.

She took a small mirror from her bag and attended to her

make-up, then pressed a button on the large phone in front of her.

'Erin, tell security I won't be needing them tonight. Affairs of the heart, if you know what I mean,' she added, with *faux* levity. The girl on the other end laughed knowingly and went about her business.

Fordham picked up the mirror and stared at herself again. The small wrinkles around her eyes, the lines across her forehead, deep-set when she frowned; were they the only price she would pay for betraying her country?

At exactly six p.m., the train from Glasgow arrived at Waverley Station. As commuters and tourists jostled to get on and off the train, Stephen Taylor stood on the platform, looking up and down the length of it, while in his heart he said a silent prayer.

The crowds cleared and nothing happened. Just as the doors closed and the whistle blew, a phalanx of policemen stepped out of their hiding places and descended on the carriages, much to the annoyance of those onboard.

'Every carriage, right now!' shouted McClusky.

Taylor sank to his knees and sobbed. He'd tried everything to save her, had probably lost the company he was in charge of. They had told him that if MBT pulled out of all Scottish wave power operations, Alice would be released, but he knew in his heart his lovely daughter was gone.

A fat woman in a stripy apron with a hot-dog logo emblazoned across it strode forward and shouted, 'Is any o' yous called McClusky?'

'I'm McClusky, what do you want?'

'There's nae need for the attitude,' the woman replied. 'There's a call for you in ma kiosk.'

McClusky followed her down the platform and into a stall which reeked of fried onions and sausages, overlaid by the aroma of bad coffee. A dirty white phone lay off the hook beside the till.

'Superintendent McClusky, who's there?'

There was silence for a moment, then a heavily accented voice spoke slowly. 'The situation has changed. Release Abdic and the girl will go free. You have forty-eight hours to do this, already her time runs out. You will hear more.' The phone went dead.

40

The Dragon looked out from the wheelhouse of the fishing boat. He had just spoken to the man who paid him and he was not happy. He had been ordered to release the girl, but what about Abdic? Their paths had crossed by chance; would anyone have cared apart from him?

The girl was locked in a cabin below. She had sobbed and pleaded with him, but any remorse, any finer feelings that might once have lurked in his breast, had long disappeared. In a life filled with death and destruction, there was only one constant: Abdic.

He saw again the battered figure, barely alive, trussed and bleeding on the Chechen street. He'd cut those bonds, tried to revive the man who had once saved his life. He saw the marks left by cigarettes, the burns left by electrodes taped to his genitals, the dry blood slathered down his left ear where his head had been forced against a loudspeaker and the volume turned to maximum. He pictured Abdic's tormentors laughing as the man struggled with the unbearable pain as the music burst his eardrum and penetrated his skull.

He could not abandon him now.

He had told the girl she would soon be free, only to dash those hopes when Abdic had been stupid enough to get caught. She was his only real leverage, the one chance he had of saving his friend's life.

He lifted the glass to his mouth and examined its contents, clear like water. In the morning he would have a sore head, a cloying fear in the pit of his stomach, but with alcohol, the pain lessened for a while, allowing him to breathe. Is this what their lives had become? Death and vodka.

At first, the faces of those he had stared at through the sights of his weapon haunted his dreams. Soon, though, as Abdic had said they would, he ceased to think of them at all.

He remembered Visonovich's words: 'Killing is no more important than taking a shit.'

But he had just spoken to this man again, and it seemed that some lives did matter to him. Some lives were so important that they must be taken. He must roar again.

The Dragon looked at an image on the screen of his smartphone. He remembered the big policeman who had stood on the beach in Kinloch such a short time ago, sniffing the air, sensing his presence.

He had to complete this final task, then he would save his friend, no matter what anyone wanted, said, or ordered.

He stared at the silver case. He was the taker of lives, he was the bringer of death, he was the Dragon.

Scott was used to taking his wife out for a meal occasionally, but usually that entailed sitting in a dining room filled with strangers, each table interested only in their own company. Young couples would whisper to each other conspiratorially, while their older counterparts seemed less likely to enter into conversation, often staring around the room as though anxious to get the ritual of dining out of the way and return to less inclusive pursuits such as watching TV or having a pint in the pub – well, in his experience anyway.

In Kinloch, however, things were different. In this Chinese restaurant, it was as though all present in the establishment were dining together. Nods, winks and ribald comments had been exchanged as they walked in and were seated. Once the novelty of that had passed, he sat and listened to conversations between tables when Annie left to 'powder her nose'.

'An' I jeest looked at him, Jessie, an' jeest says, no. It's no' going tae happen, no' until you dae something aboot that snoring,' remarked a large lady to her friend across the room. She spoke as though they were alone, not speaking over the heads of other diners, including Scott himself, whose table lay directly between theirs.

'An' whoot did he think o' that?' Scott turned his head as Jessie replied. 'From whoot you telt me aboot his habits, he widna like that one wee bit.'

'Aye, you're right. Sometimes I jeest wonder if I would be better on my ain. The weans are a' away an' me and him jeest sit aboot. If we speak mair than four sentences tae each other in a night, we're doing well.'

'Och, at the end o' the day, Senga, they're a' the same. Mine's mair interested in the new seat for his bike than taking a ride on the auld banger that shares the hoose wae him.'

Scott felt like a spectator at a tennis match as, despite himself, he turned his head back and forth in time with this very public conversation.

Then a head poked forward from beside Senga, and a man with an ample double chin spoke. 'Ur yous forgetting that me and Donald are here?'

Scott was relieved when Annie rounded the corner and smiled at him, a bottle of wine and two glasses in her hands.

Jessie and Senga, eyebrows raised, exchanged knowing looks.

'I've got a wee surprise for you when we get back tae the hotel, Brian,' she said in a stage whisper.

'Oh, eh, have you noo,' said Scott, beginning to wish he was enjoying a quiet pint in the bar at the County.

'Aye, I dae. And see you, Senga, you can stick that smile o' yours where your mother never kissed you. Noo, whoot will we order, Brian?'

'I know, Liz, of course I want that,' said Daley wearily into the screen of his computer. Liz liked to Skype, so now he had to like it, too. 'It's just there's so much going on at the moment. Couldn't you wait until it was all over?'

'No, darling, it has to be this way. Can't you see? The longer we leave things the way they are, the more chance there is that we'll never do this at all. I'm coming down at the weekend. You, me and James are going to be a family, a proper family.' She moved nearer to the screen, her face almost filling it. 'I love you, Jim Daley. Now get some sleep, you look knackered,' she said, dismissing him in the way he had become accustomed to over the years.

He hesitated. 'I love you, too.'

She blew him a kiss and ended the call.

He looked around his dining room. It was almost ten o'clock, but he hadn't yet bothered to turn on any of the lights. The shadows cast by the setting sun complemented the dark recesses of his mind.

Alice Taylor was clever, full of promise and hope for the

future, but she was in the hands of a man who cared nothing of life and death. Was she even still alive? Daley's heart was gripped by a cold hand, a familiar feeling that was tightening its grip as the years went by.

Another young woman's features filled his mind, her pale blue eyes filled with sadness and hurt. He felt his heart lurch at the thought of Mary Dunn.

He heard a buzz coming from the pocket of his jacket. He reached behind and pulled the smartphone from the inside pocket.

It was John Donald. Daley wavered, then answered the call. 'Good evening, sir. I'm not sure that you and I should be having any kind of conversation, given the way things are.'

'Listen, Jim, forget that shit,' said Donald, his voice thick on the other end of the phone; he had obviously been drinking, and the hard edge of Springburn was back in his accent. 'I need to meet you. I have information about the Taylor girl.'

'If you have information you can give me it now. This isn't a game, John. Regardless of what you've done, surely you have the decency to save that girl's life?'

'I can't tell you now. You have no idea the kind of scrutiny I'm under,' said Donald, sounding desperate. 'I only have a short time. I'll send you a text of the location – don't worry, it'll be near Kinloch. You won't recognise the number, but if you truly value Alice Taylor's life, you'll be there. This goes no further than you and I; any deviation and the girl will die, trust me.'

'Trust you! You fucking–' Daley didn't get to finish the sentence before Donald hung up. He flung the phone on the table in front of him, and looked out across the loch and the darkening sky.

41

The restaurant was in a fashionable part of Edinburgh; tucked up a cobbled lane, quiet and discreet. She had been going there for a number of years, and knew the owner well; in return for having a member of the government dining regularly in his establishment, he always made sure she had a table away from prying eyes, and that the rest of his customers on the night were not members of the fourth estate.

Her dining companion walked into the room a minute before he was due, and she was glad she had arrived early. He smiled at her; he was tall, dark-haired, clean shaven and wearing a grey suit, casual, but well cut. He leaned forward and brushed his lips against her cheek.

'Elise, you look ravishing as always.' His Home Counties was accent clipped and authoritative.

'Thank you, Jonathan. I do my best to look good for our little dates.'

'I do love my trips up north, you know, especially now you've managed to sort the food out. One can dine as well in Edinburgh as in just about any other European capital, these days.'

'We'll turn you into a flag-waving Scotsman yet,' she said, grinning.

'Let's not go too far, Elise. Lovely to get a break from the Big Smoke, but live here? Bugger off!'

'I had hoped that with me helping you, you would consider it polite to be nice about my home.'

'Your home – yes,' said Jonathan. 'Not fucking mine.'

Elise was amused by the way he even swore in an upper-class accent. 'Let's order, shall we?' she said, straightening her back and looking down at the menu.

Brian Scott had never been so happy to leave a restaurant in his life. Throughout their meal he and Annie had been watched by everyone. Annie had remained calm and cheerful, and, apart from a few brief words with Senga and Jessie, had remained pleasant company. Scott had the distinct impression that she was more than happy to be seen with him, and relished the fact that their Chinese meal would be the hot topic amongst Kinloch's battalion of gossips.

'Well, did you enjoy yoursel', Brian?' asked Annie, linking her arm through his as they walked towards Main Street.

'Aye, though I must admit I felt a wee bit awkward. You know, as though every eye was on us?'

'Och, jeest you keep your hand on your ha'penny. This is Kinloch, it's a wee bit like being famous. You can be sure that by the time we get back, they'll have me an' you re-enacting the scene wae the butter – you know, fae that film wae Marlon Brando.'

'Butter?' asked Scott, confused. 'I liked him in *The Godfather* an' *Apocalypse Now*, but I cannae say I ever had him doon as the culinary kinda fella.'

'No,' said Annie. 'You cannae have seen the film I'm on aboot.' She smiled and tugged his arm. 'Come on, me and you'll get back tae the hotel, an' I can gie you that surprise I was tellin' you about.'

'Oh . . . Aye, right,' said Scott, as they turned the corner onto Main Street and headed up the hill towards the County Hotel.

They were just about to order when Jonathan changed his mind, picking up the menu she had left on top of his in the middle of the table.

He was good, she thought. She hadn't noticed him remove the small flash drive she'd tucked into the menu; in fact, for a moment, she worried that he'd missed it altogether. Then he smiled at her, and held his hand up to summon a waiter.

'Sorry, I thought I'd missed something, Elise. I've got it now.'

'I'm glad to hear it,' she said.

They had a good meal, both starting with a delicious salmon terrine, followed by rack of lamb with crushed potatoes for her, and the venison served with a dark chocolate sauce for him. After lingering over the excellent Rioja, they had a glass of port each, coffee and shortbread.

Throughout the meal they had spoken about every subject bar politics. As he drained the last drops of coffee from his cup he yawned and looked at his watch.

'You'll forgive me if I retire. Off back to London early tomorrow.'

He asked for the bill and paid in cash. They exchanged a few pleasantries, then he stood, kissed her on the cheek, and left, shooting his cuffs as he did so and not turning back to wave.

As she sipped the last of her port, Elise Fordham let out a long sigh.

Her cab arrived quickly, taking her along quiet suburban streets to her Georgian villa on the outskirts of Morningside. As the cab pulled up, she was surprised to see a familiar car parked outside her front gate. She paid the taxi driver then walked over and leaned into the open window.

'Gary, what the fuck are you doing here?' she asked, concerned that this master of spin looked pale and worried.

'Jump in, Elise, something big's going down. I had to come and get you myself. This is too sensitive even for the mobile phones.'

'Fuck!' She rushed around the front of the car and jumped into the passenger seat. 'Right, give it to me as we go. I take it we're heading into the office?'

Wilson turned towards her. 'No CCTV in this neck of the woods, eh, Elise?'

'No, Gary, and even if there was, I doubt they'd be able to lip read what we're saying. Now, get on with it, what's going on?'

Without warning, Wilson pulled back his arm, and before she could take in what was happening, hit her square on the side of the head.

'Maybe it's time you got it installed,' he said, as he buckled his seat belt, started the car and gunned it down the street.

Brian Scott noticed how quiet the bar at the County Hotel was when he and Annie walked in. In fact, only two women were to be found, sitting at a table in the corner. The older of the two, probably in her late forties, stood and smiled, embracing Annie. Scott immediately noticed how alike they looked.

'This is my sister, Sissy,' said Annie.

'How you, Brian,' she said, 'I've heard a lot aboot you.' She winked at Annie.

'Aye, well. How are you doin'?' replied Scott, feeling uncomfortable at being introduced to Annie's family. 'Sissy, that's an unusual name. What's it short for?'

'Sister,' said Annie.

'Aye, since she's the auldest, she got her ain name, an' I got Sissy, you understan'.'

'Oh right, quite unusual, is it no'?' said Scott, struggling for something to say.

The two women looked at each other with puzzled expressions. 'No' really,' they replied in unison.

'Hey,' said the younger woman, still sitting at the table. 'I'm here tae.'

'Aye, an' you're lucky you're no' in the jail efter whoot you've been up tae,' said Sissy.

'An' if that wisna bad enough, you chose tae dae it in my hotel!' shouted Annie, who for a moment looked as she was ready to take a step forward and strike the young woman.

'Noo, ladies, what's this a' aboot?'

'You don't know this lassie's face,' said Annie, 'but you know her name: Tracy Black.'

Scott looked at the young woman. She was probably in her early twenties, but the bloom of youth had been removed by hard living, and most likely drink and drugs.

'I'm really sorry, Mr Scott,' said Tracy. 'I was jeest tryin' tae make a wee bit o' extra money. That weirdo promised me sixty quid if I said you tried tae sell me drugs, then tried it on wae me.'

'I should skelp your arse, Tracy.' Annie sat down, a look of disgust on her face. 'You widna believe it, Brian, but this is oor young niece.'

'Aye, takin' after her faither, unfortunately,' added Sissy.

'Oor brother has always been a dead loss, Brian,' said Annie. 'Mair at hame in the pub than by his ain fireside. Nancy, oor sister-in-law, has had a hell o' a time wae him.'

'Aye, an' jeest when she thought it couldna get worse, up pops this article; jeest a chip off the auld block,' said Sissy.

'I'm sorry, Mr Scott! I'll say anythin' you want tae put it right . . . Honest.' Tracy was almost in tears.

'Aye, well, what's done is done,' said Scott, tired yet relieved. 'I'll need you tae come up tae the office tomorrow and make a statement tae one o' my colleagues.'

'Does that mean I'll get the jail? You telt me I'd be all right, Auntie Sissy.'

'I said nothin' o' the kind. Whoot I said was: before you get yoursel' intae mair bother, put a stop tae it noo.'

'Listen,' said Scott. 'I cannae make any promises, but I'll dae what I can for you. You cannae go around lying aboot police officers though. I hope we've got that straight?'

After much contrition and assurances of good behaviour, Tracy and Sissy took their leave. On her way out, Sissy gave her sister a wink and a knowing smile.

'What can I say, Annie?' said Scott, glad that the shadow placed over him by Wiley had now been removed.

'Aye, well, a wee thank you widna go amiss.'

'That's a given. Come on an' I'll buy me an' you a wee nightcap.'

'Aye, jeest the one, mind you. I've got work the morrow, an' so have you come tae that.' She moved closer to Scott. 'I'm night duty manager the night, so I'm sleeping in the hotel, Brian.'

'Aye, well,' spluttered Scott. 'You're maybe right aboot the drink. I'm still feeling a wee bit groggy after that thump I took on the heid today. I think I'll just head off for a kip.'

'Oh, right you are, Brian. I'll need tae get tilled up here, anyhow. Jeest you get some sleep. It wisna fair o' me keeping you up so late, no' after the day you've had.' She moved to the till, opened it to a noisy chink of coins held within, then started counting bank notes.

'Aye, well, no bother. I fair enjoyed oor wee night oot, Annie,' said Scott, shuffling from foot to foot.

'Aye, me tae, Brian.' She kept her head down. 'Goodnight.'

As Scott left the bar and headed up the sweeping staircase, his feet felt heavy on the faded carpet. I wish tae fuck I'd had that nightcap, he thought to himself.

42

Daley arrived at Kinloch Police Office early the next day. He'd been unable to sleep; his worries ranging from Liz, Mary Dunn and John Donald, to the wellbeing of Alice Taylor. As he pulled into the car park behind the office, he hoped he'd discover Alice had been released or found safe and well. Sadly, after a quick word with the nightshift it was clear that, as far as the abduction was concerned, nothing had changed.

He could already feel the familiar pressure behind his eyes that presaged a blinding headache. It was almost half past eight; he decided to get a coffee then make a call he'd been dreading.

Daley knew Assistant Chief Constable Willie Manion was a notorious early riser, driving colleagues mad over the years with sudden appearances in the middle of the night, newspaper under one arm, a pack of sandwiches in the other, ready to face a full day's work which could begin as early as three in the morning. But even Kinloch's DCI was surprised when, after a gentle knock on the door of his glass box, the ACC popped his head around the door.

'Now, Jim, how are we today? Thought it was high time I took a wander down tae the far-flung parts o' the empire. I want tae take charge o' getting this bastard Abdic back up the road, tae.'

'Good to see you, sir,' said Daley, getting out of his chair to welcome his visitor with a firm handshake. 'Please, take a seat.'

Manion was adorned with the braid and extravagant epaulettes that befitted his rank, but somehow looked out of place with the zip-necked T-shirt that was now regulation uniform for the Chief Constable down.

'No word on the wee lassie yet?'

'No, sir. We've got just about everything out on this.'

'Aye, but what's your instinct, Jim?'

Daley thought for a few moments. 'Well, with his friend here, and given that he seems to have been very active in the area, I just sense that the Dragon, and the girl, aren't far away. According to Interpol, he and Abdic always work as a team, so unless he's managed to get help elsewhere, he's operating alone.'

'Aye, my thoughts precisely. That's why I've decided tae keep Abdic here for the time being. I know there's trouble communicating wae the bugger but you needn't worry aboot that. I've got an expert in such individuals on his way down. We'll get something out o' him.'

'He's asleep now, but the nightshift tell me he was awake until about four this morning, laughing fit to burst.' Daley sighed. 'I hope it's not too early to have a quick chat about something?'

'No, Jim, not at all. You know me, none o' this buttoned-up carry-on. Up and at 'em, that's what I say. What is it?'

Daley marvelled at the way Manion sounded and behaved like Scott, yet had risen to the top of the tree. They had the same disregard for political correctness and perceived etiquette, even accepted codes of practice. But Manion and Scott had been friends for a long time; Daley knew he could trust the man.

'John Donald contacted me last night, sir.'

'I've got tae say,' said Manion, 'in all my years in the job, I've never come across a mair slippery bastard than oor friend Donald. I'm tellin' you, if the shit hits the fan wae him the way I think it might, there's goin' tae be a few red faces up the road. What did he have tae say? Nae doubt he was lobbying you for support.'

'No, sir. He wants to meet me. He says he has information as to the whereabouts of Alice Taylor.'

'Does he now? Where an' when?'

'He's going to text me the location and time today, sir. What do you want me to do?'

Manion sighed, and rubbed his chin. 'Dae you think you'll be at risk, Jim?'

'Not really. I mean, he says he'll meet me here in Kinloch, so as far as risk is concerned, it's minimal stuff.'

'I'm pleased you talked tae me aboot this, Jim. We a' know the bastard is as bent as fuck, but he'll slide oot o' the net if we're no' careful. If we use obs or surveillance on him, he'll clock us straight away; and then there's the issue o' entrapment tae consider. I've been worrying aboot this for ages. You'll know that we had tae move against him earlier than we wanted tae.'

'Yes, sir, I gathered that from Inspector Layton.'

'Aye, Layton. As far as he's concerned, best no' tae mention what's been happening. Seconded fae Special Branch – no bastard has a clue aboot him, or which way he'd fall if we have some difficult housekeeping tae do, if you get my drift. But we may have won a watch here, what wae big John bein' stupid enough tae want tae meet you on the fly. You'll have tae wear a wire.'

'Really?'

'Aye, we want tae nail him good an' proper, Jim. Tell me, does oor Brian know aboot any o' this?' asked Manion, sounding hesitant.

'No, I haven't seen him since Donald called me last night.'

'Aye, well, oor auld buddy isn't exactly firing on all cylinders. We'll keep this between you and I. Tae be honest, Jim, I don't know how far this all goes.' Manion looked suddenly careworn. 'Me an' you'll nip it in the bud, old style, eh?'

When Manion left his office, Daley wished he had told him about the letter from Sarah MacDougall, but somehow the time hadn't seemed right.

Now he was to spy on his old boss. Was this the right time to bring the man down? Daley wondered.

Elise Fordham woke on a sofa, in a strange room. There were no pictures on the walls and what furniture there was looked old and cheap. Her head felt heavy, as though she had been drinking heavily.

She heard the door creak and someone enter the room.

'Not feeling as chipper as you were last night, I see?'

She squinted, trying see the man talking to her. The voice was familiar; she tried to focus through the fug that was clouding her brain.

'I'm afraid we needed more time, so I had to keep you quiet for a while.' The voice was coming from somewhere behind her, and she didn't have the energy to sit up and look over the back of the couch.

'Here, take this,' said the man, moving forward to stand over her with a glass of water in one hand and two white tablets in the other. 'Take these and you'll feel much better soon. Then we can have a wee chat.'

She squinted at the man's face in the dimly lit room.

'Gary! Gary, what's going on? What are you doing?' She made to get up, but couldn't.

'Take the pills and rest. You and me have a lot to talk about.' He thrust a tablet between her lips and held the glass to her mouth. Obediently, she sipped, but even this seemed exhausting, so she let her head flop back onto the couch.

'Get some rest,' she heard Wilson say as she drifted off to sleep.

Daley was about to draw a recording device from the stores in anticipation of his meeting with John Donald when Sergeant Shaw rushed up to him, shouting, 'News of the girl, sir!'

'What?'

'Come with me, sir. It'll be easier to show you.'

Daley followed the man into the AV room. Sitting at a desk behind a computer was DC Dunn, who smiled weakly when she saw him. Despite her presence, Daley's eyes were immediately drawn to the large screen on the wall that showed Alice Taylor bound and gagged. Her head lolled forward, moving from side to side even though she looked unconscious. In the corner of the screen a timer was running down; when Daley looked, it was at 23:16:52.

'What's strapped to her chest?' asked Daley. Alice was

wearing a dark gilet, strapped on to which was a dark box with a flashing red light. 'Please tell me that's not what I think it is.'

'I've got the audio, sir. Give me a second,' Dunn said, punching several buttons on the keyboard in front of her.

'This is Alice Taylor.' The disembodied voice echoed around the room via the sound system. 'Her time is running out. The Semtex attached to her will detonate when the clock runs down. This video you are seeing is in real time. It is also being streamed to her father. Release Abdic and the girl will live.' The man gave a mobile number, then all was silent.

'What the fuck is this?' The door burst open to reveal DS Scott, looking open-mouthed at the screen in front of him.

'This is our worst fucking nightmare,' replied Daley. No sooner had he spoken than the disembodied, echoing voice began again with exactly the same message.

'It's some kind of loop, sir,' shouted Dunn. 'I can't pinpoint where it's coming from. Somehow he's managed to tap into our internal communication system.'

'Find out what they can do at HQ,' replied Daley.

'Poor lassie,' said Scott, shaking his head. Just as he did so, from the crack in the door to the AV room, crazed laughter echoed around Kinloch Police Office.

43

Fordham forced her heavy body from the couch, and on her hands and knees made for the door of the room. She reached up to grab the handle, and with all of her might pulled it, but predictably the door was locked.

'Let me fucking out of here,' she called weakly, banging her fists on the varnished wood. She heard footsteps, slow and measured, growing louder until they stopped at the other side of the door. A key turned, and there, towering over her, was Gary Wilson.

'Gary, what is happening . . . just tell me.'

'Certainly not looking like a First Ministerial candidate now, Elise. Get up.' He grabbed her roughly by the arm.

'I'm going to be sick.'

He pulled her along a polished floor and kicked open the door to a small toilet. She managed to crawl towards the bowl then vomit into it.

'No, not First Ministerial at all,' Wilson sneered behind her.

When she had retched up the last of the sour, stinging bile, she paused, propping herself up against the toilet bowl.

'What have you done to me, you bastard,' she said, her eyes heavy with tears. Somehow, through her aching head and muddled thoughts, she knew she must remain strong. She willed herself not to cry.

'You come with me.' Wilson pulled her back across the polished floor and into the spartan room. 'Time for a little lesson in the realities of life, Elise.'

Scott and Daley were examining the video feed of Alice Taylor, this time on a laptop in Daley's glass box. It appeared as if the girl was beginning to rouse into consciousness, raising her head lazily for a few moments, before letting it flop back forward, her chin against her chest.

The image was at an odd angle, and was not stable, swaying slightly as the detectives looked on. Alice was slumped in a corner, and at her side, just in shot, the corner of something was visible, possibly a table or chair.

'She's on a boat, Jim,' said Scott. 'An' that bastard's going to blow her sky high if he doesnae get that giggling halfwit back.'

'How are we going to find her?'

'We better get somebody who knows aboot boats tae have a look, pronto.'

'Go and find Hamish. He'll either be on the pier or down at his cottage. Do you know where it is?'

'Dae you think that'll help?'

'Well, it might be a start.'

Scott pulled on his jacket and left the room, cursing as he tried to find his car keys.

Daley looked back at the screen just as Alice Taylor briefly raised her head again. Whatever drug she had been given to pacify her was wearing off. Soon she would be conscious and the full horror of her situation would dawn on her. Daley felt a wave of despair at the thought. How could they save her?

He knew that while the powers that be might try and negotiate, they would be unlikely to release Abdic. They had twenty-two hours and forty-six minutes to save Alice.

The chime from the phone in his pocket dragged Daley's attention from the screen. The text message was short: *Meet me on the last bench on the promenade at midday.*

Daley lifted the phone on his desk. 'Sir, Donald's been in touch.'

Elise Fordham was propped up on the couch, her arms folded across her chest. Wilson smiled at her. He was holding a large envelope.

'Now, let's have a look at what you get up to of an evening, Elise.'

'You know that half the Edinburgh Police will be looking for me now?'

'No, they're not. As far as anyone at parliament is concerned, you and I are holed up together, working through this Cudihey crisis. Sorry, Elise, another hope dashed, my dear. You have more pressing things to think about. Have a look.' He held out the envelope; after a slight pause she grabbed it with both hands.

She removed four large photographs from within and stared at the images in disbelief. In the first, she was in a park talking to a tall, good-looking man. In the next, she was sitting on a park bench with the same man, handing him something. As she flicked to the third image, she recognised the restaurant from last night. There were more images, one after the other picturing her with the same man in different locations, mostly in and around Edinburgh, but some taken in London, and even one from a recent trip to Brussels.

'You bastard, Gary. You fucking bastard!'

'Now, now, I think you've got off lightly, Elise. Just desserts for a traitor,' he said, looking at her malevolently.

'What do you mean?'

'Just what I say: you're a traitor. I know all about your little meetings and what you pass on to MI5. Very cleverly done: secret liaisons with your handler, and if anyone sees you, all they think is that pretty wee Elise has someone in her life at last; nothing over the internet that can be traced, hand-to-hand stuff. Classic little spy, aren't you?'

'You don't understand, Gary.'

'Oh, I understand very well. Your party is pushing for an independent Scotland, yet I have photos of you working secretly alongside the British security services. What exactly is it that you're giving to them, Elise?'

'It's not like that.'

'But that's how it looks. If I release these pictures, your career is over.'

'What? But why would you do that?'

'I know that you are familiar with Mr Visonovich. You met him a long time ago, during the Chechen war, when you were still a mere journalist.'

'Aye, and he's a ruthless bastard.'

Wilson took a packet of cigarettes from his pocket and offered her one which, despite her nausea and aching throat, she accepted with a shaking hand. 'When pathetic Walter Cudihey smelled a rat and did some digging, he told you what he had found. You recognised Mr Visonovich's name on the list of non-exec directors of NKV Dynamics.'

'Very good, Gary.'

'But I can't let you jeopardise his position with NKV.'

'What are you talking about? Tell me you're not the one responsible for that maniac getting a foothold in our country. Do you have any idea what you've done?'

'I know exactly what I've done. I'm making enough money to see me through a splendid retirement, one I'll spend happily by the sea somewhere, the sun beating down on me, as far away from this miserable little country as possible.'

'But why? How did you even get to know someone like that?'

'You, like many of your fellow politicos, firmly believe that life begins and ends with your little capers; that nobody else could possibly manage to do anything you can't second guess. You weren't the only journalist who spent time abroad, you know. I was the correspondent for our little rag in Germany when they still had a big wall and two football teams. News from the east was always welcome, and I met a very helpful young KGB agent.' Wilson smiled, showing his tobacco stained teeth.

'So you're working with Visonovich?'

'He pays me to gather information that might be useful to him, to whisper a few well-chosen words in the right ears. I take care of problems for him. Problems like you.'

'This guy will flood our country with drugs. They want to use us as a base to spy on NATO. Fuck me, Gary, they'll turn us into a satellite state. Is that really what you want?'

'Oh, not just me, Elise, though I suppose someone as clever as you has already worked that out. I'm merely doing the same job I've been doing for most of my life: I fix things, I get things done, things that others baulk at.'

'And so you kidnapped and drugged me, you bastard.'

Wilson blew a perfect smoke ring into the air, watching as it rose and dissipated. 'Nothing worse than a traitor, Elise.

We have lots of other stuff. Video, recorded conversations from phone taps – the works. All of them telling the same story: how Elise Fordham, the darling of the party, sold her country down the river for English gold.'

'I'm not. What I'm doing is for the good of the country.'

'And do you think the public will believe that?'

'All you care about is yourself. What about Cudihey and Lang? Did you have them killed?'

'No, in fact. We got lucky there. Poor old Walter had the hots for sexy wee Kirsteen – quite an obsession, in fact. A bit of pressure in the right place and up he goes like a bonfire Guy.'

'And Lang?'

'Pure luck.' Wilson smiled again. 'We would have had to do something about her. Though fuck knows the little bitch was ambitious enough to keep quiet, despite what lovesick Wattie had shown her.'

'So you're telling me it was just an accident?'

'Yes, a tragic accident. Sad, isn't it.'

'Why, Gary? Why would you do this?'

'We live in a changing world, Elise. You know that as well as anyone. A wee country like ours, we need friends. The special relationship is between Washington and London, not Edinburgh.'

Fordham stubbed out her cigarette. Her worst fears had been realised, and she could do nothing about it. All she had worked for, believed in, would be thrown to the four winds unless she could do something.

'And who are "we", Gary?'

'Just a happy little band of people in the know. We make things happen, influence events. You know what I mean.'

'You'll turn us into a failed state, corrupt and under the

influence of the Bear. Fucking brilliant! Scotlandistan. Visonovich has already tapped into the intranet cable that carries NATO traffic between North America and Europe. Did you know that, Gary?'

'You politicians, always the drama. It's time for new alliances, Elise. Anyway, we've been a launch pad for nukes for too long. I believe it was your own party who railed against the conditions of membership of that little club. It's time the tables were turned.'

'Great. I suppose you've addressed the currency question, too. Rouble, is it?'

'This coming from the party of no solutions.'

She was about to reply when Wilson held one finger up against his lips to silence her. 'This little episode needn't stand in your way, Elise. Everyone is due a lapse of judgement sometimes,' he said, gesturing towards the envelope. 'Here's what we'll do.'

Elise Fordham had overcome poverty, broken through the glass ceiling and worked until her whole body ached with fatigue, day after day, month after month, to get to where she was. Now she was trapped in this depressing little room with her erstwhile colleague, her career in tatters and her country – all she had ever really cared about – in peril.

'I did what I did for my country, Gary. No "English gold" changed hands.'

'Oh, not true,' said Wilson. 'While you were sleeping, my associates have been busy with your plastic, my dear. That's why we needed to pacify you for a wee while. I wish I had a leaf out of your bank book. So rich, despite your socialist principles, eh?' The smile faded from his face. 'Now, it's time we had a serious chat about how things are going to be from now on. This isn't the end for you, Elise, it's just the beginning.'

44

The little speedboat was sleek and fast. Green hills rolled above the breaking sea; short stretches of beach, dotted along the coast, shone like tiny white jewels, magnificent under a flawless blue sky. His thoughts were less idyllic, however. He thought about the girl – felt a twinge of pity for her, even – but she was a means to an end. He had to free his friend. He would free his friend – at any cost.

The man who was currently paying him was pragmatic. He adapted to suit events and opportunities. The Dragon knew this man was capable of rising to the top, but still, he worked with him – not for him. Circumstances had changed for them both; and so their plan would change too.

He gunned the throttle of the speedboat, raising its trim and the roar of its powerful engines. Soon, the Dragon would roar again.

'Brian, I want you and Rainsford to work this problem. I've got to go out, I shouldn't be too long.'

'Off on another secret meeting, Jim? Fuck me, anyone would think you're havin' an affair . . . Oh, eh, sorry,' said Scott, suddenly realising the unintended accuracy of what he'd said.

'Where's Hamish?'

'On his way. I eventually tracked him doon tae the doctors. He'll be here any time.'

'The coastguard and the Royal Navy are searching around Firdale where you nabbed that halfwit, so here's hoping they come up with something.'

'Aye, all very well, but they don't even know what they're looking for, dae they?'

'That's our job, Brian.' Daley rose from his desk, picking up his jacket from the back of his chair. 'The *Semper Vigilo* should be here soon. If we can't do anything else, at least we can start looking.'

'Another bloody boat,' said Scott, referring to the police launch, on its way to Kinloch.

'Afraid so, Bri. Right, I'll be back in less than an hour. Keep at it. I might have a lead, but keep going. We've got to save Alice Taylor.'

Scott nodded as Daley walked out of the CID Suite. Along the corridor, Daley turned into what had been MacLeod's, then Donald's and was now Manion's office. The Assistant Chief Constable greeted him warmly, then produced a tiny recording device from his desk, which Daley fixed behind the lapel of his jacket.

'Good luck, Jim,' he said. 'I hope we can save this poor lassie, an' nail that bastard Donald at the same time. Please don't gie him my regards.'

'Remind me to talk to you about a letter when I get back, sir.'

'A letter, who from?'

'Sarah MacDougall, sir. I should have told you earlier, but I wasn't sure what to do. I don't think John Donald is alone in all of this, boss.'

'And there's information contained in this letter?'

'I think so, sir. I would have used the normal procedure, but, well, these days . . .'

'Och, I'm sure you're right. We can speak aboot it when you get back. Who knows, your man Donald might just blow the whole thing sky high. This letter, gie me it now an' I'll take a look while you're away. It'll save time, an' that's no' a commodity we have a lot of right noo.'

'Here,' replied Daley, fishing into his pocket and handing a small key to Manion. 'Top drawer of my desk, tucked at the back.' He looked at his watch. 'I better go, sir. I hope Donald can give us something about the girl.'

Daley shut the door firmly behind him as he left, leaving Manion eyeing the little key. 'Aye, good luck, son,' he whispered under his breath, with a shake of his head.

Daley pushed open the heavy security door that led to the car park, almost knocking over the young woman standing on the other side.

'Sorry, I . . .' Daley stopped. Before him, stood DC Dunn, the pallor of her face exaggerated by her auburn hair and dark trouser suit.

'Mary, I have to dash now, but can I talk to you? Soon?' Lightly, he pressed his hand to her arm.

'Is your wife coming back?'

'Yes, but . . .'

'Then there's nothing to talk about. Would you excuse me, sir, I need to get back to my desk.' She looked at him with cold eyes, then slid gracefully into Kinloch Police Office without a backward glance. As he jumped into his car he felt a deep sadness at the pit of his stomach, and his head started to spin.

Seeing her walk away from him was like saying goodbye. It affected him in a way he hadn't expected.

He took a deep breath and forced his thoughts to Alice Taylor, a girl with only hours to live unless he could do something about it. He wondered how long it would take her to regain consciousness and finally realise how close to death she was. Death. There it was again; its cloying presence was never far. A trip to the seaside with his mother flashed into his mind. Her hand wiping the rain from his face. The memory disappeared as quickly as it had come.

The Dragon cut the engine of the speedboat, slowly bringing it to a halt. The loch was calm, glinting under the midday sun. He scanned the seafront; near the town, he could see children in a play park, their screams and laughter echoing out across the water. Two women, one pushing a pram, were walking into the town; thin ribbons of blue cigarette smoke rose over them. Beyond the park, some young men were playing football; he saw arms raised to heads and groans of disappointment as the ball shot between the two piles of bags stacked up as impromptu goalposts. An old man looked on, no doubt remembering his own days of laughter and fun.

In this country, you don't know how lucky you are, he thought. His own childhood had been a brutal fight for survival, not games of football in the sunshine.

He looked towards the end of the promenade. On a bench, the last one before the paved walkway gave way to the rocky shore beyond, sat a man who appeared to be staring straight at him. Undeterred, he lifted the slim metal case from the floor of the boat, opened it, blinking as the bright sun glinted from the gun sight. Methodically, he began to assemble the weapon.

Daley parked his car on the pavement opposite the promenade. He had no time to concern himself with parking etiquette; every minute wasted saw Alice Taylor's chances diminish.

As he pulled himself stiffly out of the car, he noted that to the east, beyond the island at the head of the loch, dark clouds were amassing. He looked across the promenade to the solitary figure sitting stiffly on the last bench.

John Donald heard Daley's footsteps as he stared out across the loch to the small white boat. He could see the figure aboard leaning on the gunwale, for all the world soaking up the blazing sun. He drew in a deep breath just before his view was obscured by the bulky figure of the man he'd known for so long towering over him.

'Good afternoon, sir,' said Daley. 'I don't want any shit, nor have I time for a lecture – or excuses, come to that. You told me you had information about the girl. I need it now.'

Donald coughed nervously. 'Jim, I need a few moments. I mean, I have to say something to you, before . . .'

'Fuck you! I don't have time for this. If you have any decency left, tell me where Alice Taylor is.'

Donald remained still for a moment, then rose from his seat, backing slowly away from Daley. 'I'm sorry, Jim, I really am. This is the last thing I wanted, please believe me.' Donald's voice wavered as he backed further away. He stopped, glanced across the loch for a moment, and with a gesture that Daley had seen a thousand times, raised his hand and swept it over his slicked-back hair.

Before Daley could ask what was happening, there was a brief, high-pitched whine, followed by a sickening thud.

Donald's eyes were wide and staring as he looked at his former DCI.

45

Hamish looked at the pathetic figure of Alice Taylor in the lopsided cabin, eyes now half open. He puffed at his unlit pipe, Scott and Rainsford watching him hopefully.

'Aye, it's a long time since I saw that cabin,' said Hamish. 'Well, the inside o' it, anyhow.'

'What do you mean?' asked Scott, puzzled by the certainty in the old man's voice. 'Hope you've not been oot on the bevy again. This is serious. That poor lassie will die if we cannae find her.'

'Yes, Hamish. No time for mucking about, here,' added Rainsford.

Hamish took the pipe from his mouth. 'Aye, thanks very much. If you remember, it's yous who are the polis, an' I'm here giein' you a hand. If I didna know whoot boat that was, I widna say I did. It's auld Joe Gilchrist's fishing boat, I'd lay my life on it.'

The two detectives looked at each other.

'How can you be so sure?' asked Rainsford.

'Och, it's no' that hard. It was the last o' its kind left fae the auld design made at the shipyard here. Can ye no' see the corner o' that table, an' the linoleum on the walls and floor, tae. It's the way they made them in the sixties. He nursed it through the years, kept it going after he retired, as a hobby, you understand. *The Girl Maggie*, aye, that's the name o' her.'

'So, what happened to the boat when Mr Gilchrist died?' asked Rainsford.

'Och, his family selt it tae some private collector who goes around the country buying auld fishing vessels, all sorts. Some folk have so much money they don't know whoot tae dae with it, except throw it doon the drain. Aye, I wish they would throw some o' it my way.'

Rainsford wrote a description of the vessel, then rushed off to alert the various agencies searching for Alice Taylor.

'You've come up trumps this time, auld fella,' said Scott. 'We might know what boat she's in, but bugger me, I wish I knew where it was.'

'When I last saw the vessel, she was . . . Noo, let me think.'

Scott was barely listening. The old man's help had been invaluable, but he didn't have time for one of his forays into nostalgia.

'Aye, she was anchored jeest off the second waters. Still looked good, though the red paint looked a wee bit faded.'

'An' I'll bet the Beatles were number one an' I was in nappies, tae. What year was this, Hamish?'

'Aboot two days ago.'

'What! Did you say two days ago, or two decades?'

'Two days. Jeest off the Second Waters, like I said. I hadna seen her for a long time . . .'

Before Hamish could finish, a police-car siren sounded and Rainsford swung the door open.

'Quick, Brian, there's been a shooting on the promenade. The gaffer's involved,' he shouted, then turned on his heel and ran back out of the office.

Years of training had left their mark on Brian Scott: whatever the news, good or bad, he reacted instantly. But this time, for a few seconds, he froze.

The eyes were dull and blood was trickling out of the mouth of the man lying on the paved promenade beside the last bench.

Out on the loch, a white speedboat turned in a wide arc, adjusted its trim as it sped up, and roared away. Gulls screamed as dark clouds from the east obscured the sun and darkened the day.

Sirens wailed as three police cars and a van screeched to a halt on the roadway and men in dark suits ducked across the grass towards the bench.

'Stay where you are!' shouted Scott, as he dived out of the car DC Dunn was driving. She paid no attention to him, climbing out of the driver's side and dashing across the road, neither shutting the door, nor looking for traffic. As she ran, Scott could hear her sobs.

The dark pool of blood around the dead man's body had spread across the promenade, and was dripping over the edge and down into the loch.

Scott's vision swam as he took in the scene. Faces, people, shouts, screams: all seemed distant as he stared at the dead body of the man he knew so well, the man he had worked with for so many years.

'Jim, fuck me, Jim!'

Daley was sitting on the grass, his knees raised to his chin. Mary Dunn fussed over him through her tears, kissing his cheek, all pretence gone.

'Come on, big guy,' Scott said, pulling at Daley's shoulder. 'Time to get you out of here. Are you OK? You're no' hurt?'

'No, I'm not. But I'm not sure I shouldn't be dead.'

Scott watched the ambulance skid to a halt on the road. Paramedics rushed across the grass towards the body, but already a policeman was shaking his head. One of the policemen, a fresh-faced young constable, turned away and retched over the grass.

John Donald – ambitious, perfidious, charismatic John Donald – was dead.

Rainsford shouted orders to the assembled police officers, and they started down the promenade to disperse the small crowd that was beginning to gather.

'Where will it end, Brian?' Daley looked up at his friend. 'Death everywhere. Archie, Frank, Sarah, nearly you. One of us lying in a pool of his own blood.'

Scott looked down at his DCI. 'Come on, big man. Remember, we've got tae save Alice Taylor. Aye, an' we've got a lead, tae.'

This news seemed to jolt Daley back to life, expelling some of the shock he was feeling.

'What? Do you know where she is?'

'Well, no' exactly, but we know what she's in. Noo, up an' at 'em.' He reached out a hand to help Daley up off the grass. 'We need tae get going!'

Daley stood for a heartbeat, looking at the paramedics surrounding Donald. It was clear by the way they handled him that any chance of saving his life had gone.

Daley leaned down and kissed Dunn on the head. 'I'm OK,' he told her. 'I have to get moving, we have a wee girl to save. You know how it is.'

'I know how it is, Jim,' she said, smiling up at him, large tears trickling down her face.

Manion was walking across the grass towards them as they made for their cars.

'Jim, what the hell's happened?' He looked both angry and bewildered.

'You tell me, sir.'

'We need tae get going, Willie,' said Scott. 'We've got a lead on the Taylor lassie. Will you handle this?'

Manion hesitated for a moment. He looked towards the body on the seafront, already covered by a green sheet.

'Aye, off you go. I'll do the necessary here.' He looked directly at Scott. 'And, Brian, be careful.'

As Scott jumped into the car, Daley was already on his phone. 'It's a white speed boat with a blue canopy. It's just passed into the sound now.' He ended the call. 'That wasn't murder, Brian. That was an assassination.'

Scott revved the engine, and they left the knot of policemen and paramedics behind.

Alice Taylor was becoming more aware of her surroundings. She shook her head to try and clear it. She remembered being thirsty, and gulping down a drink. After that, her memory was hazy. Where was she? The movement of the room made her nauseous and she gulped back a wave of sickness.

She couldn't move; her hands were bound behind her to her ankles. As the drug wore off, she began to feel agonising spasms of cramp in her back and legs. She sobbed quietly.

She became aware that she was wearing something unusual, something heavy. She looked down; a red light blinked at her. She was wearing a dark waistcoat, with wires sprouting from something bulky strapped to the centre of it.

She could make out what looked like the face of a digital watch. As she tried to make sense of this, she realised that the numbers were counting down.

As realisation dawned, she screamed and screamed.

46

The Dragon knew that time was precious and that, for him, the sea was no longer a haven. Finding Alice Taylor would be their priority. But he knew that despite the prospect of the girl being blown to pieces, they would never give in and release Abdic.

He passed the island and veered left, guiding the speed-boat towards a rocky shore. He had reconnoitred the coast well and, as he rounded the familiar headland, a small bay opened up on front of him. It had a narrow neck and was tricky to navigate, but he knew the entrance so well he could have sailed in blindfolded. He pointed the craft towards the far side of the inlet, tucked out of sight under the looming rocks above. This place had once been used by smugglers; it was almost impossible to detect the presence of any kind of vessel there from the open sea. His research, as always, had been meticulous.

He drifted towards an ancient stone jetty. As the boat bumped into it, he jumped onto the quayside, secured it to a rusted mooring ring and thudded back aboard. After retrieving the long silver case and other items from the craft, he made his way across the sand and rough machair grass, through some bushes, then over a fence into a small lay-by, where sat a battered old Peugeot.

He placed the metal case carefully in the back, sat in the driver's seat and, with the rumble and clunk of an aged diesel engine, pulled onto the road.

Soon Abdic, the man who had saved him, trained him, been like a father to him, the man who made him who he was, would be free. The police and all the other agencies would be searching for him and Alice Taylor at sea. On land, those guarding Abdic would be thin on the ground.

Daley paced around his glass box, his mobile phone pressed to his ear. The Royal Navy and the coastguard were looking for the white speedboat.

'How long will you be?' asked Daley. He was on the phone to the commander of the police launch, en route to Kinloch.

He slammed the phone back onto its cradle in frustration. 'He'll be at least another half an hour, and then they have to refuel. It'll be an hour at least before we can get out there and look for Alice.'

'OK, Jim, calm doon. We've got everyone out there looking. Even the beat cops are driving around the coast tae try an' find her. We've still got time.'

'Yes, you're right. But time is moving on.' He looked at the blank computer screen in front of him; Alice Taylor had started to scream just after they'd arrived back in the office, and she hadn't stopped. He couldn't bear it, so had turned the sound off. He hadn't forgotten that, as far as her life was concerned, every second counted.

'Listen, Jim, I'll nip doon and get some scran. You need somethin' in your stomach before we head oot tae sea . . . again.'

'Have a quick one for me, too,' he said to his DS, who didn't even attempt to deny that he was going to sneak in a quick dram before another dreaded sea voyage. 'Half an hour max, Brian, OK?'

'Aye, gaffer, nae bother.' Scott shut the door quietly behind him, leaving Daley alone with his thoughts. Seconds later, Abdic's laughter echoed around the office.

Manion sat in the office from where John Donald had once ruled over Kinloch. Though he had never cared for the man, he couldn't help but feel sympathy for him. Colleagues had already made their way to Donald's home to give his widow the news every police officer's significant other dreaded. The press had been immediately briefed by the force's PR team. As the killer was still at large, the story had to be managed.

He looked at his watch, then walked to the CID suite where he found Daley studying a map on the wall.

'I've just taken a conference call with the boss. With all that's happened, I had tae get him up to speed. I'm going for a wee walk to clear my heid.'

'Yes, sir. I'll keep at this. I'm sure the girl is nearby – we just have to find her.'

'Good man. I'll be as quick as I can,' said Manion. 'Listen, Jim, if you feel you cannae take it, just let me know. Fuck knows, you've been through enough today.'

'I'm fine, sir.' Daley turned back to the map.

'Aye, well, as you wish.'

The bell at the front desk of Kinloch Police Office rang through the station corridors. With most of Kinloch's police officers still tied up at the scene of Donald's murder, DC Dunn, standing forlornly at a coffee machine in the corridor, sighed and went to investigate.

'Hello, sir. Can I help you?' A tall man in a baseball cap stood at the other side of the counter. He was looking down at his phone, but in one smooth movement he reached into his jacket and produced a pistol, pointing it at Dunn.

'You have access to the cells, yes?'

'No,' said Dunn, desperately trying to stay calm. She realised she was now staring at one of the world's most wanted killers, but tried to remember her training: think, assess, address. 'I need to ask a senior officer.'

'Open this.' The Dragon gestured at the hinged part of the desk. Dunn's hand was shaking as she drew back the small bolt that kept it secure.

He stepped through the gap, never taking his eyes from her, the gun still pointed at her face. 'Walk slowly to where we can find Pavel.'

She turned, her legs trembling, but before she could take a step she was grabbed roughly from behind, the barrel of the gun thrust painfully into her temple.

'Do what I say, or I will kill you.'

She knew she should have raised the alarm, pressed the panic button – done something. But everything had happened so fast. She did as she was told.

Daley turned around when he heard Dunn enter the room. His smile turned to a look of horror when he saw the swarthy man holding her by the neck with one hand, the other pressing a gun to her head.

The high cheekbones, the scar on his face. Daley knew he was face to face with the Dragon.

47

Brian Scott sucked an extra-strong mint as he strolled back up Main Street towards Kinloch Police Office. He held a bag containing a few filled rolls he'd purchased at the County Hotel to feed himself and Daley; while there, he'd also enjoyed a couple of large vodkas, and was feeling more sanguine about recent events, as well as those yet to come. Thankfully, the bar had been empty, save for one old man often seen muttering to himself behind his whisky. With Annie absent, the young girl behind the bar had seen fit not to ask any awkward questions about earlier events on the promenade. But he had the feeling of being watched from cars and windows as he progressed up the hill.

Scott looked at his watch; his half hour was nearly up, so he hastened his pace. The skies, which had been a clear blue for so long now, had darkened. He felt a spit of rain on his face, and as he neared the front door of the office, shivered at a distant growl of thunder.

'Fuckin' typical. Aye, a policeman's lot is not a happy one, right enough,' he muttered as he opened the door, expecting to see the familiar face of Sergeant Shaw behind the reception desk. But all was quiet, and without anyone there to buzz the controlled door into the office, Scott walked through the hatch on the counter, which he was surprised to see raised and open.

Daley and the Dragon were almost the same height, though the latter was considerably leaner. In the images Daley had seen of him he had looked older; now, as he held the gun to Dunn's temple, despite the premature lines and livid scar, Daley could see that he was only in his thirties. His blank eyes spoke of a life that had left him hard and deadly.

'You can have Pavel,' said Daley quietly. 'But I want you to guarantee the safety of my officer.'

'You don't tell me what to do. I am the one who makes demands. If he isn't released now, this woman will die, then you will die. One way or the other, my friend will be free.' As he finished speaking, the roar of Abdic's laughter grew louder, as though he had somehow realised that help was at hand.

The door to the CID Suite swung open and through it came Brian Scott, swinging a white plastic bag of filled rolls.

'Where is every—What the fuck!'

The Dragon swung around, dragging Dunn with him. Daley, seeing the assassin off balance, launched himself across a chair and collided with Dunn and her captor. Dunn felt the Dragon's grip on her relax, and jabbed her elbow into his solar plexus before stumbling away from the two men, now locked in a struggle on the floor.

'Get a gun!' Scott shouted to Dunn, who scrambled out of the room, her face grey with fear. Scott tried to aim a kick at the intruder's head, but caught Daley on the arm instead; he cried out in pain and lost his grip.

Scott stood back, unable to intervene in case he hampered

Daley's efforts to disarm the Dragon. Using his weight advantage, Daley managed to swing his body half over the other man's and aimed a punch at the Dragon's side, feeling him flinch as he repeated the action. But he fell back, wheezing, as the Dragon landed a side swipe to his throat. Desperately, he tried not to black out.

Scott, his baton drawn, awaited an opportunity. Just as he was about to risk taking a swing at the Dragon, Daley managed to grab his fist and push the pistol away. The pair struggled, the gun now obscured by their writhing bodies as Scott looked helplessly on.

Then, without warning, there was a flash followed by the sharp report of a firearm, deafening in the confined space.

Behind him, Scott heard DC Dunn let out a choked sob as he wiped a splatter of blood from his eyes.

'There we have it, Elise. You carry out these little tasks for me, and life goes on as normal – well, as normal as it can.' Wilson held out some documents for her to sign.

'Do you know I have a speech at the Edinburgh Chamber of Commerce tonight?' she asked, looking up at Wilson, who towered over her as she sat at her desk in the Scottish Parliament.

'And?'

'I take it that you'll tell me what I have to say.'

'You're a big girl now, Elise,' said Wilson, pushing his face into hers. She could see a single thick black hair protruding from his nose that made her feel suddenly sick. 'Play the game, and in no time at all, you'll be First Minister. Don't play along, and you'll be . . . Well, you'll be fucked.'

48

'Where is she, you bastard?' shouted Daley, his hands around the throat of the man on the floor, whose blood was pumping from the red gore of his stomach. When the man spluttered, he tightened his grip. 'Tell me before she dies and you go to hell.'

'What time is it?' wheezed the Dragon, blood trickling from the corner of his mouth.

'Forget the time! Tell me where she is!' Daley lifted the dying man's head and smashed it back into the floor.

'Steady on, Jim!' yelled Scott. 'You'll get fuck all out of him like that.'

The Dragon opened his eyes and smiled, squeezing more blood from between his lips. A siren sounded outside as an ambulance turned into the yard.

'I know I am going to hell, why should I care? I have lived in it all my life. The time is important.' The Dragon smiled again, then his eyes glazed over. '*Baka,*' he whispered, then his body went limp. As Daley swore, a blood-curdling scream came from the cells at Kinloch Police Office.

'Sir!' shouted Dunn, staring at her computer screen. 'The time's changed on the screen – jumped forward somehow.'

Daley rushed to her side. The numbers in the corner of the

screen had indeed changed. Alice had little more than four hours to live.

'Quick, Brian, we have to get down to the pier. The launch must be there by now. There's still time.' Daley rushed from the blood-spattered office, DS Scott at his heels.

The pair jumped into Scott's car and sped to the pier where, sure enough, a vessel with a blue hull and white super-structure was being refuelled.

'We need to leave – right now!'

'Impossible,' replied a man in a life jacket that bore the insignia of an inspector. 'We've only managed to take on half of our fuel allocation.'

Not without difficulty, Daley clambered down a ladder slick with slime. 'We have to go now. The time frame has changed. The girl has less than four hours. We have to try.'

The Inspector thought for a moment, then gave the order to stop refuelling and put out to sea to join the search for Alice Taylor.

As Daley was being squeezed into a life jacket, and Scott was making his way down the treacherous ladder, a head appeared over the side of the quay.

'A wee word, Mr Daley,' said Hamish, envelope in blue pipe smoke.

'Not now, Hamish. We've no time, we need to find the girl now.'

'No success at the place I telt you aboot?'

'No, nothing. We need to go.'

'Well, I've got an idea – aboot where she is, I mean.'

'What?'

'Well, since I saw her the other day, I've asked a' the fisher-man if they spotted her. Given she's moved, an' you canna find her, despite whoot you've got oot there, I can only make one suggestion.'

'Well, hurry up and tell me.'

'The north-east side o' Ailsa Craig. Maist shipping passes to the south o' the island. No' the easiest place tae navigate, but if I was trying tae hide in the sound, that's where I'd go.'

Five minutes later, the police launch *Semper Vigilo* was speeding out into the loch and beyond, as dark clouds gathered over the sea.

ACC Willie Manion slumped in his chair at Kinloch Police Office. He had just spoken to the Minister for Justice, and the phone call had been a difficult one. Yes, two of the most wanted men on the planet had been taken out – one dead, one in custody – but a senior police officer lay dead, and the security of the Kinloch office had been breached in a spectacular way.

The press, held at bay by Alice Taylor's desperate plight, were straining at the leash. When they broke free, it would be his job to deal with them; the Chief Constable had made that eminently clear.

He sighed and looked at the framed black-and-white picture of the large poodle now sitting on his desk. 'Ah, Jinky. A right mess, an' no mistake.'

He had two files on his desk. The faces of Jim Daley and Brian Scott stared out from the official photographs appended to each. Between his fat fingers, Manion held Sarah MacDougall's letter. He sighed again.

He had a police radio on his desk so that he could follow the progress of *Semper Vigilo*. He picked it up.

'ACC Manion to *Semper Vigilo*, come in, over.' He waited only seconds for the crackly reply.

'Inspector Mason, sir, go ahead.'

'Sit rep, please, Mason.'

'We're just off Paterson's point, sir. Eh . . .'

'Whitever you have tae say, spit it out, son.'

'Nothing really, sir. Just that we seem . . . That is, DCI Daley seems happy to allow an old fisherman to dictate where we're to go.'

'Oh aye, an' where's that?'

'Ailsa Craig, sir. For some reason, the old man thinks that the vessel we're looking for may be there.'

'Oh aye, well, good luck. Let me know when you're approaching, I want tae save this lassie, an' I don't care if it's the Pope aboard tellin' you what tae dae. Out.'

He opened his briefcase and tucked Sarah's letter into one of its compartments, then removed a mobile phone and keyed in a few numbers.

There had been so much death already today.

49

The sea was heavy. Dark waves pounded the police vessel as it made its way towards Ailsa Craig, which was moving in and out of view as they were tossed up and down on the fury of the waves.

Scott, who had already been sick, was now huddled on a bench at the back of the cabin, his face a light shade of green.

Daley stood at the helm with Inspector Mason, who stared through the rain-lashed window, a look of deep concern on his face.

'If this gets any worse, we'll have to turn back,' he shouted to Daley, struggling to be heard against the roar of the engines, the howl of the wind and the battering of the sea on the side of *Semper Vigilo*.

'We have to see if Hamish is right,' shouted Daley. 'He knows these waters – it must be worth the risk. Carry on.'

'This may blow out soon, sir. Couldn't we sit off for a while, and wait until the helicopters can go back up and have a look?'

'There's no time. We're the only vessel in the area. At least if we know where she is, it's a start.'

Mason drew himself up, then steered the vessel on through the maelstrom.

*

Elise Fordham looked at the pages in front of her. She often wrote her own speeches, her time in the popular press giving her an insight into what caught the attention of the man in the street; an advantage she had over other politicians.

This speech was different though. She had never dreamed she would find herself in such a position. She heard the voice in her head telling her to be pragmatic, but there was simply no going back. The words before her would change her life forever.

She read the speech through again, took a deep breath, then, with her security detail, took a car to her home in the suburbs.

'Robert,' she said to the burly protection officer as she was leaving the car. 'Do me a favour while I'm getting ready. Get a hold of your boss and tell him I want security cameras installed on this street.'

Fordham walked into her home to get ready for the speech of her life.

Daley struggled to keep his balance as the vessel rocked from side to side. He could hear Scott throwing up again. Through the rain-splattered window, against a grey sky, he saw a flash of red.

'That's it, that's the fishing boat!' shouted Daley to Mason who, having spotted the boat himself, was now steering towards it, four or five hundred yards off the rocky shore of Ailsa Craig.

Mason picked up the radio mic. '*Semper Vigilo* to ACC Manion and all stations. *The Girl Maggie* has been spotted, anchored under the eastern lea of Ailsa Craig, over.'

'How soon will it take you tae get alongside?' asked Manion, the first to reply.

'In this, sir, better give me twenty minutes or so. I don't even know how alongside we're going to get, over.'

DC Dunn stared grimly at the screen of her computer. Alice Taylor was silent now, crouched on the floor, worn out by her own despair. She had one hour and forty-five minutes to live.

Out there, trying desperately to save the life of this girl, was the man she loved, adored with all of her heart. She had seen two men die today.

'Save her, Jim,' she whispered. 'Dear God, bring him back. She can have him, but just bring him back safely.' She prayed for the man whom she realised, one way or the other, was already lost to her.

Mason took his time and sailed *Semper Vigilo* as near to the old fishing vessel as he could. Even Scott had managed to drag himself from the bench in order to see the boat on which Alice Taylor was captive.

'Aye, the auld fella was right all the time, thank fuck!'

'Mason to ACC Manion and all stations. Alongside now, though how we're going to get aboard is anyone's guess.' The boats were about a hundred feet apart, as near as Mason dared go, given the gigantic swell. One minute *The Girl Maggie* appeared above them, then she would plunge out of sight as both craft were tossed by the huge waves.

'What do you suggest?' shouted Daley. Beside him DS Scott, an even deeper shade of green, struggled to hear the reply, terrified at what it might be.

*

Dunn heard the radio traffic and scrutinised the screen. She imagined what the conditions at sea were, able to hear the battering they were taking when Mason's voice issued from the radio. For a moment she wondered why these wild conditions were not reflected by the images of Alice Taylor, who was still gently bobbing up and down in the boat in the same way she had been since they had first discovered the sickening video feed.

Rapid movement of numbers on the screen caught her eye. The time was scrolling backwards, fast. She reached for the radio on her desk. 'DC Dunn to *Semper Vigilo*.' Before she could get the rest of the words out, the screen flashed and went black. 'DC Dunn to *Semper Vigilo*, come in, please.'

A sudden gust of wind sent a flurry of rain against the windows of Kinloch Police Office, as a rumble of thunder rolled across the hills above the town.

Daley was flung forward, his head colliding with a chair in front of him. Shards of glass from a shattered window stung his face. He could hear someone calling out, but the voice was muffled. It was as though he was underwater, such was the stunned silence that enveloped him. For a second, he started to panic, fearing he was sinking into the sea and his bludgeoned senses hadn't quite managed to communicate the fact to him. He was reassured when he felt a hand on his shoulder.

'Jim, are you OK?' Daley could see Scott's mouth move, but could barely hear him.

'I'm fine. What about everyone else?' The words were no sooner out of his mouth than a huge weight deposited itself on his shoulders. They had failed; Alice Taylor had been blown to pieces. The pain of this realisation pushed him back to the floor of the cabin, now swilling with seawater.

'Quickly!' shouted Mason. 'We're compromised. We need to get into the life raft, now!'

Daley hauled himself to his feet with Scott's assistance. The sea heaved, and the noise of wind and waves in the cabin managed to penetrate even Daley's temporary deafness. The men stumbled along the deck, slipping and sliding in the heavy swell.

'Stay there and hang on. If anyone goes over the side here, they've had it!' shouted Mason, making his way down the rolling deck. Whether it was the icy wind or the salt spray, Daley's head was beginning to clear. He looked back to see Scott and three other men huddled in a corner, clinging to various parts of the cabin. Daley lurched towards them just as a massive wave hit the side of the boat.

DC Dunn sat back in her chair. She'd heard a mayday call from *Semper Vigilo* and the response from the coastguard and other vessels nearby. Her heart was pounding; the memory of almost being dragged into the maelstrom that was Corryvreckan fresh in her mind. She thought only of Jim Daley now. The girl was dead.

The thunder was growing louder; lightning flashed, causing the office lights to flicker. Kinloch's Main Street had been turned into a river; the sudden deluge of rain had already overwhelmed the town's storm drains. Street lights popped into life as though under a night sky, not that of a summer's afternoon.

As a coastguard message about the horrendous conditions at sea burst forth from the radio feed she was monitoring, she pictured the wretched figure of Alice Taylor, slumped with exhaustion in a corner of the fishing boat set to become her tomb. Again, something about the gentle way the image had swayed didn't ring true.

She was jolted from these thoughts by Mason's voice, crackling over the radio feed. 'All crew and passengers of *Semper Vigilo* now in life raft awaiting rescue near last known coordinates, over.'

Dunn breathed a sigh of relief, then looked down at her computer. She knew they were still in danger, so to take her mind off their plight, she rewound the image of the girl trussed up on the boat, stopping at a random point just over three hours ago. The picture swayed gently; she had been told this was because of an unsteady camera aboard the boat. She sent the footage spinning forward again until just before the screens had gone blank. There was Alice Taylor, her head bent forward on her chest, the room gently swaying.

50

There was silence aboard the lifeboat, save for the rain, wind and waves battering the sides of the vessel, and quiet commands from Coxswain John Campbell, the large man sitting at the helm, far from his usual ebullient self.

They had spent more than an hour in the freezing life raft, and Daley was only now beginning to stop shivering. As he looked across at Scott, it was clear he was still suffering. They had changed out of their soaking clothes and been given warm survival suits. Apart from minor cuts and bruises and mild hypothermia, they had survived the explosion of *The Girl Maggie* miraculously well.

Their deliverance was down to the fact that when the fishing boat had exploded, it had been on the crest of a high wave on the swell, and their vessel in a deep trough. Had *Semper Vigilo* not been cushioned by a wall of seawater, the sheer compression of the blast would have been enough to kill them.

But Daley could feel no joy at his escape from death.

'We did all we could, big man,' said Scott, his teeth chattering. 'Everybody's feeling it, Jim.'

He looked around the cabin at the cold, tired, miserable faces. Here he was again, lamenting the loss of another young life; another to add to the long litany of lives he had touched, now all gone.

The thought had been in Daley's mind for a very long time; now he was sure. He'd had enough of dealing with the worst that society could offer, the detritus washed up for him to remove. Aboard Kinloch's lifeboat, as it ploughed on through heavy seas to harbour and home, Daley decided to leave his job. He no longer wanted to be a policeman. He wondered if he ever really had.

Elise Fordham stood before the crowd in the upmarket Edinburgh hotel. The lights on her were bright and warm, yet she shivered as she looked down at the lectern and her speech. To either side of the plinth, two screens stood ready to scroll her words down as she read them, making it appear that she was talking without notes.

At the front of the audience sat Gary Wilson, his face impassive, save for the hint of a sneer that she wasn't sure was real or imagined.

'Ladies and gentlemen, thank you so much for your kind reception,' she began. 'I hope you'll feel it was merited after I've bored you to tears for the next few minutes.' There was laughter at this, the exaggerated kind from people who had been drinking and were out to encourage the woman who stood before them. Fordham took a sip of water from the glass in front of her and started to speak. Her cheek was still sore from the blow from Wilson, but the bruise was artfully concealed with make-up. 'Everyone in this room, regardless of politics, is a proud Scot . . .' The screens scrolled, and she waited until the roar of approval died down. She was doing what she had for years, but this time the circumstances were very different. She glanced briefly at Wilson, then carried on – bright, confident, amusing, and glad to be back in control. Words spilled forward on the screen in front of her.

Daley climbed into the police car with Scott. They had been taken to Kinloch's cottage hospital after landing on the pier. Daley's cut face had been attended to, swabbed lest any of the glass from the shattered window of *Semper Vigilo* had embedded itself. Both he and Scott were still wearing the orange survival suits they had been given aboard the lifeboat.

'You coming in for a dram, big man?' asked Scott as the car, driven by a young cop, pulled up outside the County Hotel.

'No, thanks, Brian. I just want some time to myself.'

'Aye, well. Remember, you're no' tae blame. We did a' we could. Aye, an' nearly got drooned for oor pains.' Scott patted him on the shoulder, then left the car and walked towards the hotel, his survival suit bright in the gloom.

As he was driven past the loch, Daley noticed a patch of livid sky above the island, beyond which lay the open sea. Though the torrential rain had stopped, the wind was still strong, whipping up crested waves that lashed against the sea wall. All of a sudden they had been transported from July to January, or so it seemed. Winter had arrived in his soul, of that there was no doubt.

As they drove up the steep lane that led to Daley's home he was surprised to see a light in the window. A grey 4x4 stood outside.

He left the car, thanking the driver and, realising he didn't have his key, knocked at the door. He was bathed in warmth and light as the door opened. Framed in the doorway was Liz, holding their child. Though there were dark shadows under her eyes, she looked beautiful.

'Hello, darling,' she said, kissing his forehead. 'I know what's happened. They told me when I arrived.' She hesitated. 'We can talk about it if you like. Remember, I know you and I'm here now. So, come in, there's something in the oven for you.'

As he walked in, she handed him the child, his son. The baby squinted at him, then just as he thought the little face was going to crumple in tears, a huge smile beamed, transforming his features, and the boy gurgled happily.

She'd been away for months, but here she was, here *they* were. Jim Daley had a family again.

'To conclude, I would like to say something – something very important.' The words on the screen stopped; the operator had noticed that what Elise Fordham was saying didn't match the script. 'I love my country. My whole life, not just my political one, has been devoted to our nation, please believe me.' She looked straight at her audience, all except for Wilson, who was squirming in his seat, trying to catch her eye. 'Some time ago, it came to my attention that all was not well, that there were those at the very heart of our government, our civil service, even our police force, who were hell-bent on taking this nation in a direction that, should they succeed, would prove ruinous.' The audience gasped, and Wilson froze, held down by Fordham's protection officers, who pinned him to his chair.

'In the next few days and weeks, you will hear a great deal about me.' Fordham stared down at Wilson. 'The things that are true, I did for the best, for my country. I did them to stop this nation and her people from becoming pawns in a deadly game between good and evil.' The audience were uneasy, looking at each other in silent astonishment.

'Today, I spoke with our Justice Secretary, a man I trust, and who you will remember was almost forced from his position earlier this year, over accusations contrived by those who sought to bring him down and replace him with their own man,' she said, noting the flashing light on top of a TV camera. 'As of now, he has, as is his right under our constitution, suspended all operations in our parliament, and has asked the Commissioner of London's Metropolitan Police Service to investigate members of Police Scotland, our civil service, and, I am so sad to say, colleagues of mine, friends and fellow statesmen I thought I could trust. We must – we simply must – cut out this cancer!'

No sooner had these words left her mouth than all hell broke loose.

'Lies, all lies, I can prove it!' shouted Wilson as he was bundled away. Dragged past tables of astonished diners, he spat and kicked, his eyes bulging in fury. Journalists and photographers mobbed the podium. Cameras flashed and questions were shouted.

Fordham stood back from the lectern and took a deep, shuddering breath. It was done. The last thing in the world she had wanted to say, but the most important.

When Mary Dunn's mobile rang she rushed across to where it sat on the kitchen counter in her little cottage. She had hoped it was Jim Daley; it wasn't. A young doctor she had met at a party nearly a year before was calling. He'd asked her out a couple of times since, but she'd always been busy.

The voice at the other end of the phone was hesitant. 'I've been invited to a wedding, and the reception is tomorrow night.' He laughed nervously. 'I was hoping you might do me the great honour of accompanying me.'

She smiled at his formal manner, and the nervousness in his voice. She was about to say that she was working, too busy, but then thought, why not. She couldn't waste her time waiting for something that was never going to happen.

She thought of Daley, sitting beside the body of Superintendent Donald, stunned and bewildered. Her heart lurched in her chest and she gulped her tears away. The man she loved, so much that it ached in her chest, had been saved then lost – to her, at least – on the same day.

He was at home now with his wife and son. Life had to go on.

51

Daley was woken in the early hours of the morning by the cries of his son. From what Liz had told him, it seemed that Jim Daley Junior was as restless as his father.

Daley picked up the little bundle, cradling him over his shoulder, and took him into the kitchen to prepare a bottle, the way Liz had shown him. It was almost quarter to four, and already a pale light spilled through the windows. The storm had blown over, and all was quiet. Summer had returned to Kinloch, but Daley's heart still felt cold.

When Brian Scott awoke, he did so feeling thirsty, disorientated and with a thumping head. He had become used to the after-effects of alcohol, and on the very rare occasion that he didn't wake up with a hangover, felt as though something was wrong. He dragged himself out of bed and padded through to the bathroom.

The more drunk he had become the previous evening, the more he had thought of John Donald. The man who had tormented him for so long was gone. But had the bullet that killed him really been meant for Jim Daley? They had been dealing with one of the most ruthless and efficient assassins in the world. Did these people make mistakes? Did they ever hit the wrong target?

He stared at his lined face and bleary eyes in the mirror. Alcohol's effects were pernicious; he felt depressed, anxious, at odds with the world. The only cure was more booze, and the cycle would start again.

'I will be needin' a fucking scarf soon,' he said to his reflection, as he lifted the razor to his face with a trembling hand.

Daley made his way through the scrum of reporters already gathered outside Kinloch Police Office. He brushed aside their shouted questions, turning to face one insistent hack with a glare. He'd heard about Fordham's extraordinary statement on the radio news. He wondered how the scandal would affect the new Police Scotland; what was clear, as Sarah MacDougall had said in her letter, was that Donald had most certainly not been working alone. He would have questions to answer about John Donald, and about Sarah's letter. If it helped rid the police of the people who sought to undermine it from within, so be it.

He had just sat down at his desk when the large figure of ACC Willie Manion appeared in the doorway.

'Aye, good, Jim. Back in the harness already. We'll no' have many days as bad as that again, I hope.'

'No,' said Daley. 'I sincerely hope not.'

'Do you know about this bloody scandal, this Fordham woman?

'Yes, sir. I do. If you got the chance to read Sarah MacDougall's letter, you'll see that it hasn't exactly come as a surprise.'

'Aye, right enough. That's what I want tae say. We need tae get this bugger Abdic up tae Glasgow. An' I'll tell you, Jim, though I'm ashamed tae say it, I don't know who we can trust. I want me and you tae do the job.'

'Yes, sir,' said Daley, somewhat taken aback by Manion's proposal. 'Do you really think things are that bad?'

'Fuck knows, that's just the thing. I want Abdic safely under lock and key in Glasgow, then I can try and find oot how rotten oor job has become. Lucky me, I'm the one they've chosen tae open this Pandora's box.'

'Well, I did think it was no coincidence that you were having so much to do with the Donald situation, sir.'

'Aye, when a' the smart arses wae the degrees an' the contacts cannae be trusted, send for the old boys, eh? Anyhow, until we know just how hellish things are, we'll take it on ourselves tae get that bastard somewhere secure.'

'I suppose that makes sense.'

'I'm sorry aboot the lassie, an' John Donald, tae. He was a corrupt bastard, but naebody deserves tae die like that. The official line is that he was killed in the line o' duty.'

While Daley tried to absorb this, Manion made to leave. 'Tell me, does oor Brian know about this MacDougall lassie's letter?'

'Yes, he does, sir.'

'Aye, well, good,' said Manion. 'Good that ye had someone tae kick it aboot wae, Jim. I'm telling you, you did the right thing keeping it quiet. It's in my hands noo. We'll get tae the bottom o' these bent bastards.' He opened the door to leave and then turned around. 'Och, why don't we take Brian up the road with us. If nothing else, it'll keep him oot the pub.'

DC Dunn watched as Daley and Scott prepared to escort Pavel Abdic to Glasgow. The prisoner was manacled hand

and foot, then placed in a secure transport van, held in what was effectively a cage within the vehicle.

Scott winked at her as he got into the front of the van. After smelling his breath, Manion had decided that he and his old friend would be passengers, leaving the driving to Daley. Dunn stared at the man who had become so important to her. The previous day's events had proved to her that she loved him completely, with everything she had; but on the same day, she had lost him forever. Purposefully, she thought, he didn't catch her eye.

'Aye, she's bonnie, right enough, Jim,' remarked Manion as they drove out of Kinloch Police Station's yard.

Daley drove through the knot of reporters and said nothing.

Rainsford and Dunn looked at the recorded footage of Alice Taylor on *The Girl Maggie*. She pointed out to the DS that in the minutes before the explosion, despite the heavy seas, the slight roll and sway of the image remained steady.

'Could have had the camera mounted on some kind of stabilising frame,' said Rainsford.

'Then surely that would mean it would keep still and not move at all.'

'Yes, I see your point.' The DS rewound the last few moments of Alice Taylor's life.

There was a knock on the door of the CID Suite and Sergeant Shaw appeared.

'I've got a Mr Ronald at the front desk. He wants to speak to whoever's in charge. You're it, Sergeant.'

'What does he want? I'm quite busy.'

'He has a farm down at the Mull, middle of bloody nowhere. I think you'll want to hear what he has to say.'

52

Daley was fascinated by the easy relationship between Scott and Manion. The former was clearly worse for wear after yet another big night on the booze, but Manion joked and bantered with him as though the stench of stale alcohol didn't exist.

The weather had returned to its former glory. They drove along the winding road from Kinloch to Glasgow under blue skies, looking out across a calm ocean, its vista punctuated by purple islands in the haze. Through the open window drifted the tang of the sea, cut grass and the earthy, fresh smell always prevalent after a thunder storm.

They had nearly reached the end of the peninsula, and were about to swing inland, when Abdic, who up until now had been abnormally quiet, started to yell, as though in pain. Manion called out gruffly, but the wailing continued, much to Scott's irritation, as he was only now beginning to feel his hangover proper.

'Pull up o'er there, Jim,' said Manion. 'I cannae listen tae that racket any longer.' Daley slowed the vehicle and pulled into the roadside. 'I'll go and take a look,' Manion continued. 'Gie me the keys, Jim.'

Daley and Scott heard Manion unlock the back door of the vehicle and, thankfully, the wailing stopped.

'You OK, Willie?' shouted Scott a few minutes later. He was looking in the rear-view mirror, but could see nothing.

'This bugger's been sick, lads. Could you gie me a hand?'

'Fuck, this is the last bloody thing I need wae a heid like this,' groaned Scott, getting out of the van.

It took Daley a few heartbeats to process what he was looking at once he and Scott reached the back of the vehicle. But soon, it made horrible sense. Abdic was standing, free of his bonds, a smile spread across his huge, ugly face, while beside him stood Manion, a pistol in his hand pointing directly at them.

'Right, lads, no heroics or this big bastard will take your heids off. Just walk down the path there.' Manion waved his gun in the direction of a beaten-earth route through a pine forest.

'Willie, no. No' you, big fella, please, no' you.'

'Aye, me, Brian. Just get movin' and get your hands behind your heids, the pair o' you.'

They trudged down the pathway, the sun blocked out by the thick canopy of trees. Daley, at the head of the little procession, was trying frantically to devise a means of escape, all the time knowing that Manion's gun was pointed at his back.

'Jim, I can see that grey matter o' yours working overtime fae here. Just keep trottin' along,' said Manion.

The path led into a clearing, an amphitheatre amidst the tall trees. 'Right, stop here. Turn around, boys, but keep your hands where they are.'

'You fucking bastard,' said Scott. 'Fuck, I've known you a' these years, an' I never once saw this.'

'Shut up, Brian. I'll suffer none o' your sentiment. Maybe

if you'd no' pickled yourself a' this time, you might've been a wee bit sharper.'

There was a silence – a pause where nothing was said, the forest soundproofing the four men from the outside world. Without warning, Manion lifted the gun and fired two shots in quick succession.

'Mr Ronald, how can I help you?' asked Rainsford.

The old farmer, dressed in filthy bib and braces, looked back at him with watery eyes. 'Aye, well, it's maybe mair whoot I can dae for you, officer. I've got somethin' for the lost an' found.'

'Really, sir, you must understand, we're very busy at the moment. Please go with Sergeant Shaw here, and he'll take a note of what you've found.' Rainsford turned around to admonish Shaw, who to his surprise was not alone. He was standing beside a pretty teenager.

'Aye,' said the farmer. 'I found her wandering along the beach, miles fae anywhere.'

She looked tired, dirty and tearful, but she was alive. Alice Taylor was alive. She handed him a letter with shaking hands.

'He gave me this before he left me on the beach,' she stammered.

This is my tribute to life and to Baka. We live the lives that have been given to us. Destiny is all, there is no choice. I take lives, but most of those I kill are evil men. As my life was returned to me, I return yours to you. The debt is paid.

Manion kicked the body in front of him with the toe of his boot. 'Aye, deid as the proverbial dodo,' he said, smiling.

Daley looked on in horror. 'Why? Why would you do

this? You've got a good job, reputation. You'll have a great pension. Why would you sink to this – just for money?'

'Money, aye. But no' just that. You must know what it's like, watchin' a' these young pricks getting on. Look at oor Chief Constable, for fuck's sake; he's nearly young enough tae be my ain boy. That job should have been mine. Aye, an' it's no' just that. We can still make a difference, Scotland can go doon a different route. No need tae bow and scrape tae they bastards in London. Wae the right friends, we can make a clean break, no' the half-arsed compromise that's on the cards. A new, better country.'

'By inviting in Russian gangsters?'

'Och, just a means tae an end, Jim. I thought you'd be smart enough to realise that. Gie a little, get a lot. Fuck's sake, it's no' as if we've no' got plenty scum o' oor ain. At least these boys made a good job o' it. We'd soon have got rid o' them once we'd got what we wanted.' Manion looked down at the Abdic, his blood staining the earth.

'Aye, so what noo?' said Scott. 'You'll concoct a story aboot the Michelin Man here, an' you managing tae escape the hero, am I right?'

'No' as puggled as I thought, Brian, but a wee bit mair sophisticated than that.' Manion looked at Daley. 'Everybody knows fine that me and Brian here are best buddies. You, Jim, like your auld boss John, were part and parcel o' this corruption. You sprung Mr Abdic here, but me an' Brian managed tae fight you off. You killed him in a struggle for the weapon, which I managed tae get, then I killed you and Abdic in self-defence. Aye, I'll likely get the police medal, tae. Noo, best no' prolong the agony.'

'Stupid bastard!' shouted Scott.

There was a click and movement from behind the men that made Manion turn.

'Put the gun down, sir,' said Inspector Layton. He too was armed, standing on the edge of the clearing with three other men.

'Chief Daley and Deputy Scott,' said Michael Callaghan. 'The places I bump into you guys.' He smiled. 'Now, do what the Inspector says, Mr Manion. Personally, I'd like to put a bullet through your skull, but that's not how you do things in this country, is it?'

Manion threw the pistol to the ground. 'Aye, smart, boys, very smart. You'll need tae do a bit more tae change things than this, though. I'm just a cog.'

'A pure bastard would be mair apt,' spat Scott.

53

The service was tasteful and well attended. John Donald was laid to rest in a coffin wrapped in a union flag adorned with the gold-braided cap of a chief superintendent. Rows of uniformed police officers filled the large church in Glasgow, while quiet hymns echoed around its vaulted ceiling: dark suits and sad songs.

As the eulogy was read and fulsome praise heaped upon the dead police officer, it was all Daley could do not to be sick. He had been ordered to attend; an order which Brian Scott had refused to obey, regardless of the consequences. At the end of the service, Daley offered his condolences to Donald's widow and left the church as quickly as he could.

As he drove the long road home to Kinloch, he turned the music up loud to block the thoughts that plagued him. The whole episode had tainted even further his regard for the job he had been trapped in for so long.

The scandal was tearing its way through the echelons of Scottish society, but much of it, like John Donald's misdemeanours, was being covered up, silently swept under the carpet. The bile in Daley's throat began to rise again.

His resignation letter was written, tucked in the drawer of

his desk where Sarah MacDougall's missive had once been hidden.

The day had been difficult, so instead of driving around the loch and up the hill to his home, Liz and the baby, he parked in Main Street and went to the County Hotel. It was a Friday evening, the bar was busy and the locals greeted him with smiles. Annie, as companionable as ever, served him his drink and asked how the service had been.

'Aye, such a nice man,' she said, bringing to mind her memories of John Donald. For her, like the wider public, the dead policeman was a hero, mown down doing his duty. Daley gave her a watery smile. 'An' whoot aboot oor Brian, was he there?' she asked.

'No, he couldn't make it. Laid low with the flu.'

'Mair likely a hangover,' she said. 'We've one o' your colleagues in, at the back there.' She gestured to the rear of the busy room in a furtive manner.

Through the crowd, Daley spotted her as, almost at the same moment, she looked up and straight into his face. Mary Dunn was sitting with the young doctor. When she saw Daley, her broad smile faded, and for a second, she looked at him wistfully. For Daley the music stopped. The many voices in the room were silenced; he could only take in her beautiful blue eyes.

She returned his wave shyly and turned her attention back to her companion, who had carried on talking, oblivious to the moment that had passed between the two police officers.

He drained his glass of whisky and walked out of the bar. A song from the past that spoke of love, loss and a place where lights shone and everything would be all right drifted mournfully from the jukebox.

*

Moonlight bathed the room in a pale glow. The black-and-white framed prints and the straw hat with the red ribbon adorned the walls. He almost called out her name, but the distant cry of an infant pulled him into wakefulness. This room, the one he was really in, was dark, stark and minimalist, decorated to the tastes of his wife, who turned her head in her sleep, spreading her auburn hair across the white pillow.

He padded to the cot at the end of the room and picked up his son, taking him into the lounge where they sat together in the darkness, the tiny child suckling contentedly at his bottle of milk while his father looked out at the stars, bright in the velvet sky.

Callaghan had paid him a visit, just days after he'd saved his life. Daley had passed him the details of all the strange sights in the sky: the dates, times and locations. Callaghan hadn't seemed particularly surprised to report that on the night Brian, Hamish and the fishermen had been buzzed in the boat, Aurora had been safe in its hangar on the air base near Machrie.

'Lights in the sky, son. Lights in the sky,' he whispered, a tear meandering down his cheek.

A Note from the Author

Dragon Alley

The popular conviction that Europe left behind its taste for blood, brutality and genocide at the end of World War II is sadly mistaken. For those of us around at the time of the Bosnian conflict in the former Yugoslavia, the unfolding horror in a country that many had visited as a beautiful and historic holiday destination was almost unbelievable. Not only was this on our doorstep, it was playing out in full colour on our television screens every evening.

There is not nearly enough space here to dwell on the political, religious and sectarian dynamics at the heart of this tragedy, but it is sobering to recall just a few of the dreadful statistics that emerged from only one city caught up in the war. Bosnian Serb forces besieged Sarajevo, an historic town in the newly formed state of Bosnia Herzegovina, intent on forcing the creation of Republika Srpska. Lasting from April 1992 until February 1996, the siege lasted for 1,425 days, three times longer than that of its infamous counterpart in Stalingrad, and, although accounts vary, it is generally acknowledged that almost 14,000 people lost their lives at this time, more than a third of them civilians.

Ulica Zmaja od Bosne, or Dragon of Bosnia Street, the

main boulevard in the city, became a shooting range for Bosnian Serb snipers preying upon the local populace, who were trying desperately to feed themselves and survive. Signs bearing the words 'Pazi Snajper' ('Watch out – sniper') became common. Assailants in the surrounding hills and tall buildings within the city murdered over 600 people, nearly half of them children, at random, using high-powered rifles, on that thoroughfare alone.

Many of us, to this day, find it hard to remove the image from our minds of emaciated men being carted off in trucks to dig their own graves, before being shot through the head. It saddens the heart to realise that at the very moment I write these words and when you read them, similar atrocities are being perpetrated against humanity and the creatures with whom we share this planet.

The Phoenicians

Many years ago, during a boozy Hogmanay in Campbeltown, Gordon Campbell, a well-known local chemist (now sadly missed), foraged about in an oak bureau in his lounge and produced an old tin cigar box. Within lay a coin, tarnished silver in colour, with irregular edges and rudimentary markings. He went on to tell me the tale of how he had dug it up in the late 1960s in his garden in Tarbert, the beautiful fishing village at the very north of Kintyre. Recognising the find as something special, Gordon contacted the British Museum, to be told that the artefact was a Phoenician coin, dating back almost 3,000 years.

The Phoenicians, the world's first serious mariners, ruled the Mediterranean Sea, long before the rise of the Greeks and the Romans, from their base in what is now modern Lebanon.

Their great trading cities such as Tyre and Carthage have gone down in history as the first flashes of the modern world we now inhabit. However, due to the lack of written records, relatively little is known of them as a civilisation. For many years, scholars believed that their movements were restricted to the relatively calm waters of the Mediterranean. More recently, however, archaeological evidence points to the fact that they may well have traded with ports on the west coast of France, and possibly as far as the island of Ireland.

Famous not just for their trading empire and seamanship, but for the boats they built, they pioneered the use of the conical hull, a projection below the waterline that saw their vessels slip through the waves with more speed and grace than any of their contemporaries could muster. These sleek ships had something else in common; they had at their prow a carved horse's head, an echo of the symbol used by the Vikings with their dragon longships. The name Kintyre is commonly thought to mean 'the land of the horse people', though there is little evidence to suggest that the ancient population of the peninsula used horses in any significant numbers. In fact, Kintyre is more likely to translate to 'the land of the people of the horse totem'.

It is tempting to think that these first sailors made their way out of the middle sea and, hugging the coast where they could, navigated their way to the shores of ancient Kintyre. Frequently, they made their trading bases on promontories or peninsulas. In addition, on the shore at Kilkerran, just outside Campbeltown, can be found a geometric stone carving. I remember being taken there as a schoolboy. Looking a bit like a stylised flower, it was used as a logo by a local bakery in Campbeltown for many years. And, no doubt, readers of the *Courier* will remember it on the masthead of the paper. This very same symbol is now thought to be connected with Phoenician navigation, and could well be some kind of venerable seafaring signpost. For further reading on the subject, dig out a copy of Dr L.A. Waddell's *The Phoenician Origins of Britons, Scots and Anglo-Saxons*, most recently published by The White Press in 2014.

My old mentor Angus MacVicar had a 'bee in his bonnet' about it too; yet more inspiration from the great man. While linguistic link between the Phoenician city of Tyre and our Kintyre may well be tenuous, somehow I don't think Hamish would need much convincing.

Lights in the Sky

The large runway at Machrihanish, originally constructed during World War II for the Fleet Air Arm, then later transferred to the RAF, has long been connected with rumours of strange lights in the sky.

Recently, after many years of speculation, the US military confirmed that they had tested the revolutionary Stealth aircraft there during its development in the 1980s. Indeed, a large force of American servicemen were based at RAF Machrihanish from the late 1970s through to the early 1990s. It is said that at any one time a third of America's elite Special Forces unit, the Navy Seals, was stationed at the base. The question has long been: why?

I'm happy to say that such were the good relations between the visiting Americans and the Campbeltown locals, some of those reading this book will be doing so in the USA, happily married to people they met back then, and now far from home in the 'Wee Toon'.

It is interesting to note that the base at Machrihanish, mothballed since the mid-1990s, is on the shortlist to provide the spaceport for Virgin Galactic's proposed passenger service project. Looking at a map today, it is strange to think that Kintyre's location, which made it so attractive to seafarers dating back possibly as far as the Phoenicians, may yet prove attractive to those who are pioneering a paradigm shift in the way we travel in the future. As Hamlet said to Horatio, 'There are more things in heaven and earth, Horatio, than are dreamt of in your philosophy . . .'

Acknowledgements

As always, I would like to thank my lovely family, Fiona, Rachel and Sian, for their continued help and support, and for keeping me sane and relatively grounded (not an easy task). Thanks too, to all the team at Polygon, especially Hugh Andrew, and my talented editors, Alison Rae and Julie Fergusson, with whom I've had many an interesting debate over the last few months. You deserve much wine!

I owe a great and ongoing debt of gratitude to my fantastic agent Anne Williams of the Kate Hordern Literary Agency, who guides me through this strange world with seamless ease. Many thanks are due also to Kate herself.

I always remember my late parents, Alan and Elspeth Meyrick. I hope you aren't too annoyed by the swearing, Mum. God bless you both. To the people back home, I thank you all from the very bottom of my heart. It's been great to be back down in Campbeltown over the last few months and spend time with so many old friends.

The next time you're looking for somewhere to go on holiday, do not hesitate to take the long and winding road to

Kintyre. Certainly, as I reach a milestone in my own life, my thoughts are always to be there. Finally, thanks too, for the answer to a desperate prayer, when such shining uplands seemed so very far away.

D.A.M.
Gartocharn
April 2015

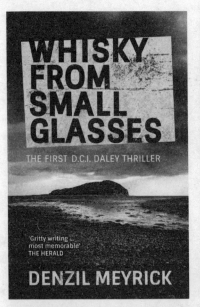

WHISKY FROM SMALL GLASSES

THE FIRST D.C.I. DALEY THRILLER

'Gritty writing ...
most memorable'
THE HERALD

DENZIL MEYRICK

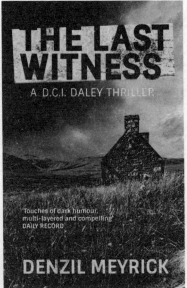

THE LAST WITNESS

A D.C.I. DALEY THRILLER

'Touches of dark humour,
multi-layered and compelling'
DAILY RECORD

DENZIL MEYRICK

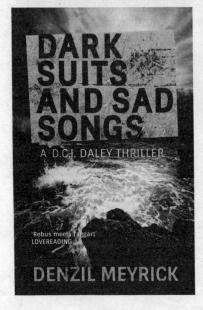

DARK SUITS AND SAD SONGS

A D.C.I. DALEY THRILLER

'Rebus meets Taggart'
LOVEREADING

DENZIL MEYRICK

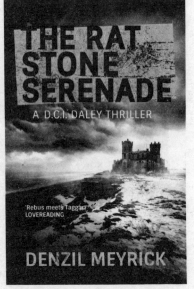

THE RAT STONE SERENADE

A D.C.I. DALEY THRILLER

'Rebus meets Taggart'
LOVEREADING

DENZIL MEYRICK

The D.C.I. Daley Thriller series

Book 1: *Whisky from Small Glasses*
ISBN 978 1 84697 321 5

When the body of a young woman is washed up on an idyllic beach on the west coast of Scotland, D.C.I. Jim Daley is despatched from Glasgow to lead the investigation. Far from home, and his troubled marriage, it seems that Daley's biggest obstacle will be managing the difficult local police chief; but when the prime suspect is gruesomely murdered, the inquiry begins to stall.

As the body count rises, Daley uncovers a network of secrets and corruption in the close-knit community of Kinloch, thrusting him and his loved ones into the centre of a case more deadly than he had ever imagined.

Book 2: *The Last Witness*
ISBN 978 1 84697 288 1

James Machie was a man with a genius for violence, his criminal empire spreading beyond Glasgow into the UK and mainland Europe. Fortunately, James Machie is dead, murdered in the back of a prison ambulance following his trial and conviction. But now, five years later, he is apparently back from the grave, set on avenging himself on those who brought him down. Top of his list is his previous associate, Frank MacDougall, who unbeknownst to D.C.I. Jim Daley, is living under protection on his lochside patch, the small Scottish town of Kinloch. Daley knows that, having been the key to Machie's conviction, his old friend and colleague D.S. Scott is almost as big a target. And nothing, not even death, has ever stood in James Machie's way . . .

Book 3: *Dark Suits and Sad Songs*
ISBN 978 1 84697 315 4

After a senior Edinburgh civil servant spectacularly takes his own life in Kinloch harbour, D.C.I. Jim Daley comes face to face with the murky world of politics. To add to his woes, two local drug dealers lie dead, ritually assassinated. It's clear that dark forces are at work in the town, and with his marriage hanging on by a thread, and his sidekick D.S. Scott wrestling with his own demons, Daley's world is in meltdown.

When strange lights appear in the sky over Kinloch, it becomes clear that the townsfolk are not the only people at risk. The fate of nations is at stake.

Book 4: *The Rat Stone Serenade*
ISBN 978 1 84697 340 6

It's December, and the Shannon family are returning home to their clifftop mansion near Kinloch for their annual AGM. Shannon International is one of the world's biggest private companies, with tendrils reaching around the globe in computing, banking and mineral resourcing, and it has brought untold wealth and privilege to the family. However, a century ago Archibald Shannon stole the land upon which he built their home – and his descendants have been cursed ever since.

When heavy snow cuts off Kintyre, D.C.I. Jim Daley and D.S. Brian Scott are assigned to protect their illustrious visitors. As an ancient society emerges from the blizzards, and its creation, the Rat Stone, reveals grisly secrets, ghosts of the past begin to haunt the Shannons. As the curse decrees, death is coming – but for whom and from what?

Book 5: *Well of the Winds*
ISBN 978 1 84697 368 0

Malcolm McCauley is the only postman on the island of Barsay, just off the coast of Kintyre, part of D.C.I. Jim Daley's rural patch. When he tries to deliver a parcel to the Bremners' farm he finds no one at home. A kettle is whistling on the stove, breakfast is on the table, but of the Bremners – three generations of them – there is no sign.

While investigating the family's disappearance, D.C.I. Daley uncovers links to Kintyre's wartime past and secrets so astonishing they have profound implications for present-day Europe. But people in very high places are determined that these secrets stay in the shadows for ever – at any cost.

Denzil Meyrick eBooks

All of the D.C.I. Daley thrillers are available as eBook editions, along with an eBook-only novella and the two short stories below.

Dalintober Moon: A D.C.I. Daley Story
When a body is found in a whisky barrel buried on Dalintober beach, it appears that a notorious local crime, committed over a century ago, has finally been solved. D.C.I. Daley discovers that, despite the passage of time, the legacy of murder still resonates within the community, and as he tries to make sense of the case, the tortured screams of a man who died long ago echo across Kinloch.

Two One Three: A Constable Jim Daley Short Story (Prequel)
Glasgow, 1986. Only a few months into his new job, Constable Jim Daley is walking the beat. When he is called to investigate a break-in, he finds a young woman lying dead in her squalid flat. But how and why did she die?
In a race against time, Daley is seconded to the CID to help catch a possible serial killer, under the guidance of his new friend, D.C. Brian Scott. But the police are not the only ones searching for the killer . . . Jim Daley tackles his first

serious crime on the mean streets of Glasgow, in an investigation that will change his life for ever.

Empty Nets and Promises: A Kinloch Novella
It's July 1968, and redoubtable fishing-boat skipper Sandy Hoynes has his daughter's wedding to pay for – but where are all the fish? He and the crew of the *Girl Maggie* come to the conclusion that a new-fangled supersonic jet which is being tested in the skies over Kinloch is scaring off the herring.

First mate Hamish, who we first met in the D.C.I. Daley novels, comes up with a cunning plan to bring the laws of nature back into balance. But as the wily crew go about their work, little do they know that they face the forces of law and order in the shape of a vindictive Fishery Officer, an Exciseman who suspects Hoynes of smuggling illicit whisky, and the local police sergeant who is about to become Hoynes' son-in-law.

Meyrick takes us back to the halcyon days of light-hearted Scottish fiction, following in the footsteps of Compton Mackenzie and Neil Munro, with hilarious encounters involving ghostly pipers, the US Navy and even some Russian trawlermen.

Here is a taster from the fourth book in the series, *The Rat Stone Serenade*.

The beach at Blaan, near Kinloch

He loved this beach, even though it was always winter, always cold, when he was here. He watched a gull riding the wind above the green storm-tossed sea – as though dangling from a string like the model planes on the ceiling of his bedroom in London.

Sometimes he could see ships on the horizon, but not today. The sky was slate-grey. At the far end of the stretch of fine yellow sand, the promontory thrust out into the sea like a rocky finger. He always imagined it had the head of a lion, big and bold. His father had told him stories of the castle that had once sat on the clifftop, facing the cold depths fearlessly from its tall perch. The boy was bewitched by thoughts of the olden days; to think that his ancestors had once lived there, on the high rock, in a time when men had swords and fought battles. Now, there were only a few stones left, an earthly reminder of times past.

When he had asked how many men their ancestor had in his castle – conjuring up in his mind the kings and princes he had read about in books and seen on trips to the big cinema in Kensington – his father had smiled indulgently.

'We weren't rich then, Archie. We fought for the clan chief, but we were strong and fierce.'

When Archie looked towards the other end of the beach, up to the high cliff on which the great house stood solid and indomitable, he couldn't imagine his family having ever been anything else but rich. He'd seen some children begging in the streets near home, just before Christmas. His mother told him they were poor. He'd studied one miserable little boy with a dripping nose and in ragged clothes and decided that he never wanted to be poor.

Up at the big house, he could see his mother on the terrace from time to time; no doubt checking that he hadn't strayed too near the sea. Like him, she was wrapped up against the cold.

He wanted to play a trick on her. He looked around. There, between two dunes, a small burn trickled over soft sand. As he followed its course backwards, away from the sea, he could no longer see the cliff, the house, or his mother.

His young mother shivered as she looked out from the terrace and to the beach below. She breathed deeply. The cool moist air was so fresh, so different from London. Glancing at her watch and deciding it was time that both she and the boy were out of the cold, she looked for her son.

She had seen Archie what seemed only moments before as he skipped and played on the sand, but she was dismayed to note that, so engrossed had she been in her novel, more than twenty minutes had now elapsed since she had last checked on him. Now, there was no sign.

She rushed to the balcony railing, a slight dizziness making her aware of the sheer drop on the other side. Leaning out as far as she dared, she could see nothing of her son on the beach, or the steep path that snaked up the cliff towards the mansion that loomed behind her.

'Archie! Archie!' she called, her heart pounding, face stinging against the cold. Some primeval instinct was pricking her. She craned her neck out further, terrified that she would see her son struggling in the crashing surf. But there was no one there and the cold green sea went about its relentless business.

The boy stopped in his tracks. When he looked back, he could still see the beach between the cleft of the large dunes, but as he made his way along the burn, the grey light seemed to darken and the sound of the waves grew muffled, as though he had his woollen bobble hat pulled over his ears. The smells were different, too; the salty tang of the sea gave way to something earthier, a rotting smell, like on his father's compost heap. He wrinkled his nose. This was the stench of something old, something decaying.

Startled by a faint rustling noise, he looked ahead.

'Hello?' he called, his voice dampened by the rough clumps of machair that clung to the sides of the dunes. 'Oh!'

There, only a few feet in front of him, stood a figure, still and silent, dressed like the monks he had seen on holiday in Italy. The hood of the man's dirty white cloak covered his bowed head.

'Hello. I'm Archie Shannon,' the boy said, accustomed to meeting strangers and raised to be polite. He turned around, wishing he could see the cliff, the big house and, most of all, his mother. Was this one of the boys from the village he'd played with on holidays? It was too big. But there was something intriguing about the hooded figure, something that compelled him to take a few steps closer . . .

And here is a taster from the fifth book in the series, *Well of the Winds.*

Kinloch, 1945

The spring evening had given way to a night illuminated by a full moon, intermittently obscured by dark scudding clouds. Elsewhere, a bright night like this was dreaded: cities, towns and villages picked out in the moonlight, prey to waves of enemy bombers, or worse still, the terrifying whine of the new super weapon: the doodlebug. Not so here on Scotland's distant west coast – here, there was a safe haven.

Out on the loch, the man could see a dozen grey warships looming, framed by the roofs and spires of Kinloch and the hills beyond that cocooned the town. Crouched behind a boulder down on the causeway, he watched the breeze tugging at the rough grass that gave way to the rocky shoreline and the sea hissing and sighing.

In the distance he heard the stuttering engine of a car making its way along the narrow coast road from Kinloch which skirted the lochside before disappearing into the hills. The headlights cast a weak golden beam, sweeping across the field behind him. The engine stopped with a shudder and the lights flickered out as the vehicle came to a halt in the little lay-by beside the gate to the causeway. The man held his breath as the car door opened and then slammed shut.

It was time.

He'd always known this moment would come, but a sudden chill in his bones compelled him to draw tighter the scarf around his neck. He reached into the deep pocket of his gabardine raincoat, feeling the reassuring heft of the knife. He closed his fist over the wooden handle and waited, heart pounding.

He saw the beam of a torch flash across the waves and gasped as a creature – most likely a rat – scurried away from the light. He breathed in the cool air, tainted by the stench of rotting seaweed. The footsteps were getting closer now, scuffing across the rocks in his direction. He heard a man clear his throat.

'Hello . . . are you there?' The voice was deep and resonant with no hint of trepidation. For a heartbeat, he wondered how the end of existence could creep up so suddenly – unbidden and unannounced. Was there no primeval instinct at work, protecting flesh, bone and breath? How could the path of one's life come to a sudden dead end without even the tiniest hint?

He stepped out from behind the boulder, shielding his eyes from the glare of the torch now directed straight into his face.

'What in hell's name are you doing here?' Though the question was brusque, the voice was calm, almost uninterested. He watched as the man turned the beam of the torch back along the way he'd come and firmly pulled down his trilby when a gust of wind threatened to send it spinning into the waves.

Ignoring the remark, he rushed him from behind. He hooked his left arm around the man's stout neck and snaked his right arm across the man's waist. Up and twist, right under the ribcage, as he'd been taught – plunged into him again and again. There was only fleeting resistance as the long sharp blade did its job. The man had been completely unprepared for the attack – just as they'd said he would be. His victim tensed, then went limp. A gurgle – almost a plea – came from the depth of his throat, as his life drained away. Aided by his assailant, who took his weight, the dying man sank to the ground.

He dragged the body behind the boulder that had been his hiding place, almost losing his balance when a deep sigh – the last sign of life – issued from the victim's gaping mouth. Leaving the corpse propped up behind the boulder, he stood up straight and took deep gulping breaths.

He waited, with only the thud of his heart in his ears and the restless surf for company.

It had been as easy as they'd predicted.

In what must only have been minutes, but seemed like hours, he heard another car making its way slowly along the narrow road towards him.

His job was done. The greater good had prevailed – the greater good must always prevail.